Poetry

Slammed

BAY BROWNING MYSTERY SERIES

The Medusa Murders
BOOK 1

Shake-speared in the Park
BOOK 2

Poetry Slammed
BOOK 3

DEEP LAKES COZY MYSTERY SERIES

Deep Dark Secrets
BOOK 1

Deep Bitter Roots
BOOK 2

Deep Green Envy
BOOK 3

Deep Dire Harvest
BOOK 4

Deep Wedded Blues
BOOK 5

Deep Flakes Christmas, A Nisse Visit
PREQUEL

 Follow Joy on Substack

joyribar.substack.com/about

 *Joy Ann Ribar Wisconsin Author*

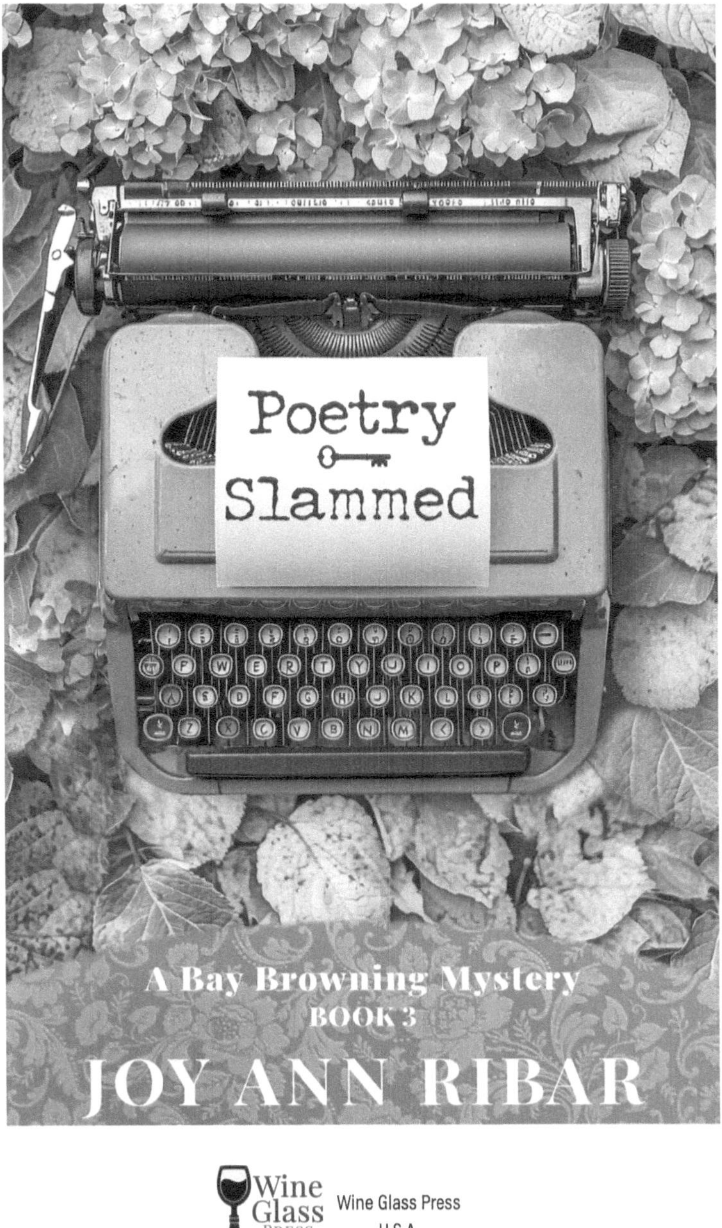

Poetry Slammed

A Bay Browning Mystery
BOOK 3

JOY ANN RIBAR

Wine Glass Press
U.S.A.

Wine Glass Press, U.S.A.

Poetry Slammed: A Bay Browning Mystery, Book Three

© 2026 by Joy Ann Ribar

All rights reserved.

Published in the United States by Wine Glass Press.

GENRES: Mystery, Amateur Sleuth, Women's Fiction.

There Came a Wind Like a Bugle (ca. 1883) reprinted from yourdailypoem.com This poem is in the public domain but did appear in *Great American Poets: Emily Dickinson* (Clarkson N. Potter Publishers, 1986).

There Came a Wind Like a Bugle is a poem by Emily Dickinson (1830–1886) and is in the public domain because the author died in 1886 and the poem was published posthumously before 1923.

ISBN: (paperback) 978-1-959078-36-4

ISBN: (ebook) 978-1-959078-35-7

EDITED BY: Kay Rettenmund

COVER AND INTERIOR: Terry Rydberg at Fine Print Design

FIRST EDITION: 2026

PRAISE FOR
Poetry
Slammed

BAY BROWNING MYSTERY SERIES • BOOK 3

A propulsive, galloping ride filled with surprises!

~ **Christine DeSmet**
Author of the Fudge Shop Mystery Series and
Mischief in Moonstone mystery-romance novellas

Featuring not one but two mysteries, plenty
of literary references for book lovers, a touch
of romance, and the type of suspense that
keeps you turning the pages to the very end.

~ **Kelly Young**
Author of the Travel Writer Mysteries

Joy Ribar is razor-sharp at crafting a
tense atmosphere, layering it with rich
imagery and the ever-present sense that
time is running out and the other shoe is
about to drop. But no matter where you
look, you won't see it coming—and that,
dear reader, is what kept me riveted.

~ **Laurie Buchanan,**
Author of the Sean McPherson crime series

Poetry Slammed

Cast of Characters

WITH BRIEF DESCRIPTIONS

Bay Browning: Literature Professor at Flourish College, a private college specializing in fine arts, located in Prairie Ridge, Wisconsin.

Casandra Browning: Bay's older sister. An ex-con, reformed grifter with paranormal powers. Cass specializes in the field of apothecary.

Diana Poulin: Bay's and Cass's half-sister. Works at the reference desk at Flourish College Library.

Aunt Venus: The aunt who helped care for Cass and Bay after their mother, Penelope, died.

Jen Yoo: Bay's colleague and friend. Professor of Art History at Flourish.

Stasia Andino: Associate Dean. Bay's immediate boss. Stasia is caught up in helping extended family by insisting Flourish employees patronize their businesses.

Bryce Downing: Prairie Ridge police detective. He and Bay are dating.

Nolan Harris: Detective Downing's partner.

Marilyn Smart: Interim police chief after Chief Sessions retired. She pairs up with her ex-partner in this book.

Vivian Rossi: Bay's colleague who hosts the poetry slam and is part of a foundation called Project Square One to help foreign students and refugees.

Valeria: Vivian's sister who is an authentication expert on historical documents.

Miriam Greggs: Semi-retired office manager and secret keeper for the Lange Group.

Marcel Domingas: A friend of Posey's and member of Project Square One foundation.

Gabriel McNelly: Religious Studies Professor at Flourish and a thorn in Bay's side. Ex-priest who seems to know many secrets about the community.

Angelica Trevino: a new hire at Flourish College in the theater department.

Bluff Birds: members of the wealthy crowd and founding families who live on Angel-Bird Bluff

Posey Hollingsworth: Owner of Spirit Gardens estate. Cassandra was her personal assistant until her death. Her secret past is one major subplot in this story.

Malcolm Hunt: Wealthy heir to the Hunt fortune. He and Posey were fond of one another.

Abigail Adams: Mistress of Bluebird Hill across the road from Spirit Gardens. She is the oldest living Bluff Bird.

The Ex-Ladies Lange: Attorney Monroe Lange's ex-wives in order: Suzanne, Gretchen and Heather. Each has a daughter with Monroe. Now they make him miserable. Gretchen is the estate attorney for Spirit Gardens. Suzanne is a frequent customer at Spirit Gardens for tinctures and tea remedies.

Marva: Marva is Posey Hollingsworth's housekeeper. She is working with Cass to inventory the estate for probate.

Fanta: Marva's sister who is the housekeeper at the Hunt estate.

Arlyss Mills: The retired housekeeper for the Hunt family before Malcolm took over the estate.

Janet Mills: Arlyss's niece who is a home health nurse for Abigail Adams.

Olga: The former beloved housekeeper for Ramona Hollingsworth who was replaced by Monica Frazer.

Monica Frazer: The former housekeeper for Ramona Hollingsworth when Posey was a teenager.

Joyce Strost: Posey's friend, not part of the in-crowd on the bluff. President of the Literary Society.

Linda Trevino: Angelica's mother and former member of the Literary Society when Ramona was in charge.

Joanna Stengel: Posey's estranged cousin with a criminal history.

Anthony McGann: He was Posey's personal attorney and is romantically involved with Cass.

Aria: Dean Stasia's niece who work at the family dry cleaning company.

Sister Philomena: a nun connected to Posey's past.

Cliff Marsden: A private pilot with a shady reputation.

Daniela: a student from Colombia sponsored by Project Square One.

Aneka: a student sponsored by Project Square One.

Joaquín: Vivian's neighbor who cares for her cats when she's away. Also a police asset.

Inside every one of us,

little poetry eggs are waiting to hatch. Incubate them!

With gratitude to Emily Dickinson, a perpetual mystery

and staggering wordsmith. And for Louisa May Alcott, who

believed the power of the pen also belonged to women,

but more importantly, who promoted human equality

for all Americans.

chapter 1

Follow the Butterflies

Forget the proverbial butterflies in the stomach: Cassandra Browning has butterflies in her head. A soft flutter initiated her sixth sense—she could see the intruder in her mind's eye. On high alert, the butterflies opened their wings, beat out a rhythmic cadence, line dancing through her brain.

Cass slipped from the coverlet in the bed where Posey Hollingsworth once lay her head, and descended the grand stairway barefoot. At the bottom, she stopped to sniff the air, raised her head, turning it left to right, ears pricked, wondering if she was prey or predator.

The butterflies tilted toward the left, Posey's study. In the hallway, Cass grabbed the bronze sculpture of Don Quixote, a gift to Posey's ophthalmologist father from a grateful patient in Mexico. She hurried on, ready to wield the Spanish hero at the intruder. Cass turned the doorknob in silence, holding her breath. She threw it open with force and saw the desk lamp aglow where a figure rummaged through drawers.

"Fanta Sweet? What in the name of Zeus are you doing here?" Cass lowered Don Quixote but kept her hand grasped around his middle.

Fanta blew out a breath ending in a raspberry before flouncing onto a nearby settee.

"I suppose I'm searching for the same thing you are, Ms. Browning. Posey's treasure. You ain't found it yet, right?" Fanta appeared unruffled at being discovered.

Cass hovered closer, holding Don Quixote in front of her like an Oscar. "What gives you the right to break into this house and look for a treasure meant for me to find?" Her voice was soft, even, and cool.

Fanta cocked her head and sat up taller. "I suspect I might know what you're going to find, and I intend to protect me and mine. That's why."

"What do you mean, Fanta? Speak plainly." Cassandra's alarm levels dropped to normal, but the whiff of something fishy remained.

Fanta, riled now, displayed her full height of five feet, with her head jutting about like a pecking hen. "If Posey's so-called treasure reveals anything damning about Mr. Hunt, it could ruin the family. I like Mr. Malcolm and Edison, so there. And I like my position in their home."

Fanta, one of the three Sweet Sisters, was the housekeeper for Malcolm and Corrine Hunt at Fox Hollow, an old-money home the founding families built on Angel Bird Bluff, overlooking Prairie Ridge. Edison was the eldest Hunt son.

Cass set Don Quixote on a lamp table and perched on the edge of Posey's desk. She stared at Fanta, considering her next move.

"I hope you didn't break any windows or door frames busting into Posey's house."

Fanta offered a pleasing smile and dangled Marva's key under Cass's nose. Marva was the long-time housekeeper at Spirit Gardens House, continuing after Posey's murder until the estate could be settled.

"Bet she didn't give that key to you," Cass said. She trusted Marva's loyalty, even to a dead mistress.

Fanta yanked it away and shoved it in her pocket. "She doesn't know I'm here. I pilfered it." She sounded pleased with herself, and Cass could relate to the adrenaline rush of pulling off a heist, no matter how small.

Following a prison stint for larceny, Cass moved to Prairie Ridge where her sister, Bay, teaches English at Flourish College. After almost a year of keeping a clean slate, Cass hoped for an early release from parole.

Memories of her past along with Posey's murder clouded Cass's mood. It was time to get tough with Fanta. "I don't care if Marva is your sister, not only will I tell her about your exploit, but I'll call the police to arrest you for B and E. Tell me what you think you'll find in here."

Fanta recoiled and lost herself in the settee cushions. "Miriam Greggs."

Cass knew the trick to listening to a Sweet Sister was patience. They often spoke in the middle of a story as if one was there from the start or already privy to the meat of the conversation. "Who?"

"The office manager for the Lange Group. Just retired. You can bet she's got the poop on every family in Prairie Ridge, 'specially the Bluff Birds."

The Bluff Birds was the common term used by the locals in reference to the wealthy families living on Angel Bird Bluff, past and present. The moniker bounced around during gossip sessions, and the bluff families knew it.

In eighteen thirty-seven, President Martin Van Buren sent a commission from Milwaukee to survey the land for locating Wisconsin's capital. When the party discovered the bluff, with its picturesque view of Spindrift Lake, many of the founding families settled there, although the city of Prairie Ridge sprouted on the flatter fields below the bluff. Augustus Bird and Colonel Angell were among the original founders, hence the bluff's name.

Cass asked, "What did Miriam Greggs tell you?"

"We both helped with the library's book sale, chatting it up. Miriam's not exactly a fan of the Hollingsworths, you know. We talked about Posey's murder and Joanna Stengel. Anyway, it came out there's a nun who knows all about a secret adoption. Of course, she wasn't about to give away a name or anything."

Even Cassandra's psychic gifts failed to connect the dots within Fanta's rambling. "How does that information bring you into Posey's house?"

Fanta narrowed her eyes and looked off into the distance. "Oh, don't you see? It's the way she said it, the look on her face. Something's off about Posey's mother and Joanna Stengel. There must be a connection."

Cass tucked aside the information for later. She knew Posey grew up the only child of Ramona and Lionel Hollingsworth and that her relationship with her mother was fraught with struggles. Mother and daughter didn't see eye to eye on almost anything, while Posey and her father had a tight bond.

Joanna Stengel murdered Posey after blackmailing her to get pieces of Spirit Gardens estate. Federal agents controlled the case data, and revealed the bare minimum, leaving empty spaces to fill. Cass wouldn't be satisfied until she discovered Joanna Stengel's motive.

"Let's say we agree on your point, Fanta. If you're looking for adoption papers here, you're not going to find any." Cass waved one hand toward the filing cabinet. "I've been through Posey's files. Anything top secret, well, those files are missing if they exist at all." Cass knew two people who whisked files out from under her nose: Federal Agent Madrid and Attorney Anthony McGann. The latter was, dare she say it, Cassandra's boyfriend.

Hands on hips, Fanta tucked a lock of burnt orange hair behind her ear. Each gray-haired sister selected a few locks to dye from the rainbow palette. Fanta's choices reflected the autumn season.

"I might have known you'd been through her study. Seemed like a sensible place to start."

Cass wanted to be angry about Fanta's audacity but found herself giggling like a child.

"You're something else, Fanta."

"What's that supposed to mean?" Fanta's cheeks flushed red.

"Caught in the act somewhere you don't belong and you're not a smidge contrite. Instead, you act as if you have the authority to snoop around." Cass stood toe-to-toe and stared into Fanta's face.

Fanta swallowed hard and took a step backward, colliding with the antique floor lamp. One ornate bronze phoenix wing clung to Fanta's sleeve as both the lamp and the woman toppled over.

Cass grabbed Fanta's arm, which managed to raise the woman and the lamp at once. She righted the lamp and helped untangle Fanta's coat sleeve from the wing.

"Ouch! Watch it would ya." Fanta gazed at a scrape on her wrist where a welt began forming.

A gratifying smile bloomed on Cass's face. "You're welcome. I probably saved you from a worse injury if the lamp landed on you. And that concludes tonight's escapades. Go home, Fanta."

Cass began nudging Fanta toward the door, but the woman spun around to face her.

"I'm curious. When did you start sleeping here? Have a falling out with that professor sister of yours?"

Cass and Bay, despite a turbulent history, were getting along well, but Cass found herself spending more time at Spirit Gardens, pulled in by Posey's murder and the puzzling letter she left behind. After the July funeral, Cass's sleep was disrupted by twisted dreams, leaving her awake and ruminating over the letter. Rather than drive up to the bluff estate in the dark, she began sleeping in Posey's room a few weeks ago, free to explore the house at will.

"That's none of your business. For what it's worth, my sister and I are quite fine." Cass nudged the woman forward.

"Wait. Don't you think we could work together to find answers? Two heads are better than one." Fanta struck a blow. "You've been at it—what, three months? Thought by now someone with your abilities…"

Cass's glare transformed into a vacant stare. The truth was, she spent most of the three months distracted by grief.

Early on, disbelief captured her mind while Cass wandered the estate, expecting to find Posey in the greenhouse or the Firehouse, conjuring tinctures.

Sorrow kept her company, too, shaking her to the core, first robbing her appetite, then snatching her sleep and replacing it with torment. Cass reeled backwards into prison nightmares, a plummet she could ill afford. Those nights, she revisited her worst inmate encounters. The vilest of the incarcerated wanted to befriend the pretty, slight, blond Cass for the price of her soul in exchange for protection.

Finally, Cass made the terrifying choice to reveal her abilities and take charge of her own protection. It was an infernal deal she couldn't take back—ensuring her personal safety at the expense of others. She chose her victims with care, the vermin with dreadful secrets. After the revealing the dark secrets of a third inmate, her safety was bought and paid for, allowing her a little sleep, a little ease. More than earning respect, Cass was feared. Nobody wanted to touch her, on purpose or by accident.

Starting a couple weeks ago, she began waking up drenched in cold sweat, distracted by a new companion: Anger. Cass would pace outdoors in her pajamas and shake her fist at the sky for allowing the worst slime to breathe air, while Posey, a woman with a generous heart and valuable purpose, lay silent and still in the cold ground.

Anthony McGann may be the best or most impossible distraction yet. His gentle ways and loving heart permeated through her thin skin. Once he whispered "Cassie" while kissing her ear, and she almost allowed it. But her killer expression made him shrink in fear. *He doesn't know the truth about me and when he finds out, he won't allow himself to love me.*

Cass snapped out of it, cutting into Fanta. "Be quiet. My abilities are not magic, Fanta. No, I don't need your help. And you don't belong here." The nudge became a shove.

Fanta sputtered and muttered her way out the front door. Cass leaned against the closed entrance and breathed in the cool September night air, reclaiming her calm. Maybe Fanta was right. Maybe she needed help. But from whom?

She padded up the grand stairway, Posey's memorized letter floating ahead of her like an apparition:

You and I are sisters of the sacred earth, daughters of the midday sun and the full moon, and I am grateful for the time we were planted together in the same soil. Please take my book of remedies from the summer kitchen and keep my spirit alive by remembering me when you craft them. This will be justice. As a witness to my indiscretions, I beg you not to judge me too harshly. None of us want to be in calm waters all our lives. Your friendship is assuredly the finest balm for the pangs of disappointed love. But do not miss your chance at happiness. You are the bravest person I know—not since my father have I known someone so brave. You asked me often about the past. The answers are here, in the treasure I left for you. The key will unlock it. Seldom, very seldom, does complete truth belong to any human disclosure; seldom can it happen that something is not a little disguised or a little mistaken. —Posey. ■

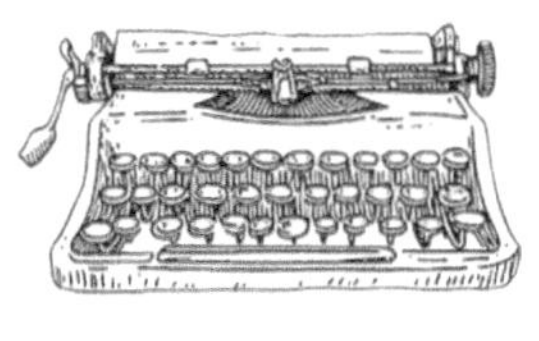

chapter 2

Vivian Alert

A quiet tap on Bay Browning's office door preceded Professor Vivian Rossi's breezy arrival.

"Good morning, Bay. I brought you some scones from Sweet Cheeks as a gracious thank you for helping me finalize Friday's lineup." With the finesse of a magician, she produced the signature pink bag from her usual cargo, waving it in the air before setting it on Bay's desk.

After two years, Bay was comfortable around Vivian's idiosyncrasies, including her manner of carrying around possibly half of what she owned in the world. To be honest, Bay had never seen Vivian's house; but she thought perhaps the English professor was a hoarder.

Bay looked up from the personal essays she was reading, an assignment designed to know her students better.

"Thank you, Vivian. That wasn't necessary, though. I was happy to help." She opened the pink bag where the inviting scent of lemon, chives, and herbs brightened her day. "Nice choices. Sweet Cheeks is the best bakery in town."

Vivian nodded and leaned against an office chair to rebalance her load. Bay could see a colorful bouquet of mums peeking out of one wide canvas bag decorated with bright stripes. An oversized umbrella stood tall in another bag.

"Would you like to sit down? Or could I help you carry things to your office?" Bay could go either way but was curious why Vivian hesitated.

The woman sat, leaned the two oversized bags against Bay's desk and crawled out from the paisley quilted pack slung around both shoulders. The backpack landed with a heavy thud by her feet.

"Is something wrong?"

Vivian's pale eyes widened, and her mouth dropped open. She snapped it shut and began shaking her head as if to loosen something while waves of black and silver hair moved like a flock of birds in formation.

"Just nerves, I believe. I'm reciting the Dickinson poem Friday night." Vivian's eyes darted around the office as if the specter of Emily Dickinson herself might materialize.

Bay couldn't believe the seasoned professor, who hosted poetry readings every fall and spring, and was, in fact, a poet in her own right, would suffer a case of the jitters. No, Vivian Rossi, for all her oddities, was acting stranger than usual lately.

Bay reached across the desk to quiet the woman's fluttering hands. "You're a pro, Vivian. I'm certain your recitation will do Dickinson justice."

Vivian's eccentric ways escalated after she discovered a previously unknown Dickinson poem last winter. An antique silver music box, a gift from Vivian's mother, had stopped working, so Vivian took it to a local antique expert who said she could repair it. Both the expert and Vivian were astounded to find a folded paper in a secret compartment underneath the music mechanism.

Bay recalled a bubbly Vivian sitting in her office regaling the tale and showing off the poem displayed under archival glass before it went to auction. Bay enjoyed poems about natural phenomena and appreciated that, unlike much of Dickinson's poetry, this poem was accessible to everyone.

Entitled, *There Came a Wind Like a Bugle*, the seventeen-line poem describes a sudden storm ushered in by wind and how it affects an individual. There is fear and beauty, destruction and resilience. Nothing is ever straightforward with Dickinson, who often examined how nature and humans could be at odds or in harmony, often both. Vivian reveled in the found treasure for a time, but something shifted.

After the poem sold at auction, Vivian grew paranoid and nervous, suffering panic attacks in crowds. She fainted at the spring commencement ceremony despite the comfortable weather, and since she was on stage assisting the dean in presenting diplomas, the incident became a memorable spectacle.

Bay's helpful comment brought Vivian back from unknown parts. Her eyes flashed and her smile was serene.

"Thank you, Bay. I've been practicing three or four versions of the thing. You know, a multitude of variations exist. Should the speaker be resolute or frightened, fragile or flippant?" Vivian turned her head to consult her inner self.

"You are coming, correct? You know many of the performers, of course." Vivian rose and began gathering her merchandise, hoisting the backpack around her shoulders. Her slight frame was stooped under the pack's weight.

"Yes, I'm coming. Here. Let me carry your bags to your office. You've got enough on your shoulders." Bay dashed around the desk to grab the bags before Vivian could argue. "You know, carrying around excess weight is hard on your back and shoulders. What's in there anyway?"

A huff escaped from Vivian when she adjusted the pack, wincing. "Oh, you know. I have Dickinson's biographies and poetry collections. I've been studying. I'll be teaching an extended unit about her, and I'm scheduled to present a symposium in Amherst next semester." The revelation lifted Vivian's posture, like a rigid marble statue.

Bay warmed at the idea. "One belle presenting about another belle and on Dickinson's home turf. You should be honored." She walked behind her to her office down the parallel hallway, settled the bags inside, and offered final reassurance.

Minutes later Bay saw Cassandra waiting at her office door with a box in one hand, coffee cups in the other.

"There you are. I brought breakfast on the off chance you were hungry." Cass followed Bay inside and set the items on her desk.

"Ha, you always seem to know." Bay's hand traveled over the box cover. "Let me guess. You brought an avocado spinach scramble on a croissant and an oat milk latte with cinnamon."

Cass unzipped her fleece jacket and laid it over the back of the chair. "Wait, are you psychic, and holding out on me?"

Bay pursed her lips. "You'd be the second to know if I were, wouldn't you? I guess you conjured up what I was craving.

Thank you." She slid the cardboard container from the box, opened it, and savored the fragrance of cheese, herbs, and bread. She passed a croissant to her sister.

Bay studied Cassandra for a few moments while chewing her first bite. She knew by instinct and their close bond that something was amiss. "What's happened?"

Cass paused midsip, considering whether to tell Bay that her powers of observation were as much a gift as Cassandra's own psychic abilities.

"Posey's house had an unwanted visitor in the middle of the night." Cass waited a beat. "Fanta Sweet. I found her rummaging through Posey's study."

"What? Why in the world…"

"I'm thinking about that, too. Fanta said she's concerned about Posey's secret treasure, that it may bring ruin to the Hunt family, and indirectly, to her, too."

Bay frowned. "I imagine Fanta knew about the letter ever since the funeral, so why go hunting now?"

"She mentioned someone named Miriam Greggs. Ring any bells?"

Bay considered the name. "I don't think so. Who is she?"

"The office manager at the Lange Group. At least she used to be. Apparently, she told Fanta something about an adoption and a nun she should look up. Nothing Fanta said made sense."

"That's nothing new. Those sisters have their own coded language." Bay snorted. "Changing the subject, maybe you shouldn't be staying at Spirit Gardens alone. It's such a huge property."

Cass shrugged. "You may be right. I might hire security. If Fanta is willing to dig around, someone else could be lurking with worse intentions."

"You might ask Anthony to stay with you." Bay set the bait. Cass and Anthony McGann, Posey's personal attorney, were an item.

Cass took an oversized bite of her sandwich, avoiding the suggestion. She liked Anthony more than she should, especially since she believed he was keeping secrets from her about why Posey was being blackmailed by Joanna Stengel, the woman who killed her. Anthony admitted to handling the blackmail payments to Joanna, the mysterious JS, but claimed no knowledge of the story behind the demands. Cass didn't buy it.

"Perhaps Marva would like to move in, at least temporarily," Cass said.

"Marva! I can see the two of you fighting off intruders. Marva's what? Five feet nothing."

"Don't underestimate the woman. She's compact but packs a potent punch. And you know I can take care of myself just fine, Lulu." Cass's pet name for her sister slipped out when Cass was affectionate or like now, parental.

Cass drained the coffee and threw the cup in the trash along with her sandwich wrapper.

"At any rate, I'm heading to the house to speak with Marva about her sister. Wish me luck." Cass donned the fleece and shivered, anticipating the walk to the parking lot. "It sure feels like fall today. There's a certain Halloween sting in the air."

Bay's entire face lit up at the mention of fall. "I know. I love this time of year. Many people see autumn ushering in the year's end, but when you're a teacher, fall is a new year with fresh beginnings."

Cass produced a grudging grin. "I do enjoy the changing colors, but cold, gray days, are not my cup of tea."

"You get used to it, knowing spring will come again. Will I see you Friday night?"

Cass turned around, her eyebrows two question marks.

Bay folded her arms. "You and Anthony are meeting us at Beans and Scenes at six-thirty. The open mic poetry night?"

Cassandra's blank look set off a tiny tempest inside Bay. "Cassandra Phoebe Browning, you promised. You and Anthony joining us is the only way I could convince Downing to come."

Cass's lips parted into a wide grin. "Do you think I'd let down my sister and the good detective? We'll be there." ▪

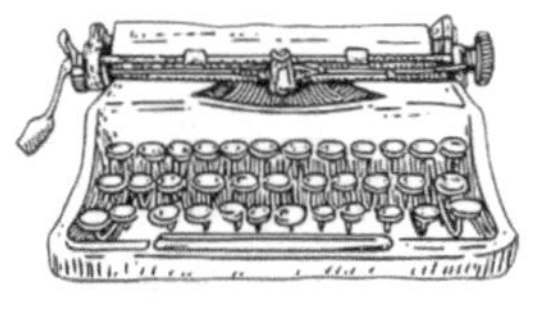

chapter 3

Horse of a Different Color

Cassandra encountered Marva reading a fall cooking magazine, a look of yearning on her face. When Posey was alive, Spirit Gardens bustled with monthly parties, teas, dinners, and group luncheons. Cass shuddered, thinking the last social event in the house was the Shakespeare Midsummer party three months ago, the party where Posey lost her life.

"Good morning, Marva. You must be bored with no social functions on the calendar."

Marva propped her chin in her hands as she leaned over the magazine on the counter. "You got that right. I've cleaned the whole kitchen and lost count of the trips I made to the local food pantry."

Since Posey's death, Marva kept busy cleaning the kitchen—her domain—and assisted Cass in other rooms of the house, including Posey's pride and joy—the greenhouse. Neither woman knew with certainty which items to keep when it came to the estate's belongings. Taxed with taking inventory of every room for the estate attorney, they were permitted to donate sundry items, so some things were delivered to the thrift store, while anything of value occupied its original space.

"What are we working on today, Cassandra?" Marva turned down a page corner showing a recipe for stuffed butternut squash and closed the magazine with a smack.

"Before we start, we need to talk. Did you know Fanta was here in the middle of the night, going through Posey's study?"

A storm cloud crossed Marva's face, and she sucked in air before answering. "Fanta told me this morning. Said you'd be talking to me, so she'd better come clean. It won't happen again."

"I appreciate that. I have questions, though. First, we could use extra security at the house. Everyone knows Posey's gone and this place could be a target for thieves and treasure hunters, if you get my meaning." Cass helped herself to coffee, adding the oat milk Marva kept on hand because Cass liked it that way.

"It's a smart idea. I can't say I like you here alone, especially since you're often sleeping here." Marva's accent was tough to pin down, a mixture of New England meets the Midwest.

"Agreed. I'll talk to Gretchen Lange." Gretchen was the attorney for Posey's estate. "Item two. Why did the manager for the Lange Group tell Fanta about an adoption and a nun?"

Marva cut two slices from a cinnamon streusel loaf and passed one to Cass on a floral dessert plate. "You speakin' about Miriam Greggs?"

Cass nodded.

"Fanta knows something about that woman, and that

woman doesn't want it out. I suppose they made a trade. Before you ask, I don't know what Fanta knows."

"And the secret adoption?" Cass spread butter on the loaf.

Marva half-closed her blue eyes, thinking. "Posey's mum, Ramona, used to help orphans get jobs around the bluff. Helping with housework, sewing, the gardens, and stables. Sometimes she found them permanent work on farms around the area." Marva slurped her coffee.

"Did you work for Ramona?" Cass tried to piece together a timeline.

"Not me. Miss Posey hired me here after her mother passed. Plenty of folks around here knew about Ramona and her doings."

"Did Posey say anything about Ramona's orphan work?" Cass knew Posey wasn't close to Ramona. She also knew Posey was part of a foundation supporting orphans in Central and South America, making sure they were educated and sheltered.

Marva rolled her head around in exaggerated fashion. "Oh, Miss Posey hated it when someone brought up her mum's charity work. Called it ex-ploi-ta-tion. She said the charity group shoulda found good homes for the orphans, not jobs." Marva thumped one foot on the tile floor for emphasis.

Cass stifled her laugh. "That's what I suspected." A sudden idea blossomed. "Marva, do you think Ramona considered adoption since she couldn't have children?" *What else could Miriam Greggs have meant?*

Marva helped herself to a second slice from the loaf. "Naw, Miss Posey never said a thing about being adopted. Don't you think someone would know that? You can't keep secrets forever on the bluff. You might want to check with the last housekeeper." Marva puffed out her chest and looked sideways at Cass.

"Where can I find her?" Cass let Marva enjoy her gotcha moment.

"I don't know, but Malcolm Hunt does. I happen to know that Mrs. Hunt is away on business." Marva took a dainty bite of cake and dabbed her mouth with a napkin.

Cass flew upstairs to the rose bedroom, the main guest bedroom in Spirit Gardens. The second story bedrooms were christened with a name befitting the décor. Posey told Cass the rose bedroom belonged to her mother. The room boasted a three-wall walk-in closet that housed the costumes Posey loaned out for her famous themed parties. Posey's equestrian garb also hung there, although Posey didn't ride following her multiple sclerosis diagnosis. She insisted Cass enjoy wearing them and ride Posey's horses stabled at the Hunt estate.

She pulled on a simple pair of full-seat breeches and a long-sleeved polo shirt and headed down the road to Fox Hollow without calling. When Cass knocked on the back door, Fanta thought she was in trouble.

"Ah, you're wanting to ride? Mr. Malcolm is off to the stables, so you can meet him there." Fanta fanned her face with a potholder.

What luck. Cass found the debonair Malcolm talking with the stable groom, looking regal as ever in jeans and a pale denim shirt. Cass liked Malcolm better each time they met, and she understood why Posey had been smitten with the man. The feeling was mutual, at least from what Cass witnessed whenever the two were together. Cass wondered why the two didn't marry—part of the mystery Cass intended to solve.

Malcolm raised his eyes in greeting; a contagious smile played on his face. "Ms. Browning, to what do I owe this visit?" He registered her outfit. "Ah, you're here for a ride. Spencer, would you please saddle up Fauna?"

"I'm afraid Flora is a bit under the weather, but she's on the mend. I'm going out myself. Care to join me?" Flora and Fauna once belonged to Posey, but Malcolm homed them at his stable after Posey stopped riding.

Cass nodded. "I apologize for not calling. This was a lark, and I guess I lucked out."

Wooded acres surrounded the bluff properties. Decades ago, the estate owners agreed to carve out trails crisscrossing the entire bluff, so everyone with horses could enjoy riding there.

The nip in the air carried a whiff of autumn as leaves were just beginning to give up their green garb. The maples were dotted in flames of orange and red, and the oaks showed off dapples of gold.

After Malcolm and Cass walked the horses to the wooded trails, they urged them to a canter until both horses and riders were satiated from the run.

Malcolm trotted up the trail to ride beside Cass.

"The cool air feels refreshing now, don't you agree? Something's on your mind, Ms. Browning. Coming over here on a lark—what prompted that?" Malcolm searched her face for clues.

Cass swallowed a lump wondering why she found it difficult to trick or trap Malcolm Hunt. She was a professional con artist, after all.

"I'll get to the point. Did Ramona and Lionel Hollingsworth

adopt Posey?" Cass looked down to avoid the sunshine streaming through the trees, a move she saw as a disadvantage because she couldn't gauge Malcolm's reaction.

Malcolm halted his horse. "Where did that come from? Not that I know of."

Cass couldn't tell him about Miriam Greggs or Fanta, his own housekeeper. "Is there someone who would know for certain? It might be important."

"Ah. You're still searching for whatever secret Posey left behind. You think she might be adopted? If she was, she didn't know it. Posey and I didn't keep secrets from each other." Malcolm's focus drifted inward.

"Can you tell me anything about the Hollingsworths' housekeeper? Before Marva."

Malcolm produced a boyish grin. "Olga was delightful. She made special treats for Posey and her friends. She would entertain us in the kitchen with songs and stories. I remember she made a fun hideout behind the garden where we had tea parties."

"She sounds wonderful. Is Olga still alive?"

"Well, I'm not sure. She left Spirit Gardens when I was in high school. I came home from a summer trip and Olga was gone. After that, Ramona hired a new housekeeper. Let me think." Malcolm stared into the trees.

"Mrs. Frazer. I can imagine Posey holding her nose every time she said her name. Nobody could replace Olga." Malcolm set the horse into a trot, not a useful gait for conversation.

Cass followed. "Did you like Mrs. Frazer?"

He shrugged. "I never got to know the woman. My parents kept me busy with French lessons, polo, golf, tennis, and social engagements." His voice faltered. "I didn't spend time with Posey after that summer."

"Do you know what happened to Mrs. Frazer?" Cass wouldn't settle for a dead end.

"I'm afraid I don't, but our former housekeeper may. I keep in touch with her. I'll give you her contact information."

Back at Spirit Gardens, Cass changed into her regular clothes and offered Marva two options.

"Feel free to take the rest of the day off, Marva, unless you want to start doing inventory in the lemon drop bedroom."

"Exactly what put the bee in your undies, Miss Cassandra?" In the greenhouse, Marva set the hose nozzle to a light spray as she padded up the rows of perennials she and Cass brought in from the outdoor beds.

"I'm on a mission to see Malcolm Hunt's former housekeeper. She lives in Cottage Grove, just eight miles from here."

"I'll finish up watering and probably go home. I have some shopping to do." Marva yawned. Lack of a normal routine made her sluggish. She wheeled around to face Cass.

"Ahem. One thing. Let's step up and finish this inventory for the lawyers, eh. I want to be a real housekeeper again—to someone."

Cass agreed, but inside her mind needled her. *You're avoiding the inevitable. Once the estate is settled, you'll need to find a new job.* "And maybe never see Spirit Gardens again," she mumbled.

Arlyss Mills lived in a condo complex on Grove Avenue

with her niece. Cass forgot to call ahead in her excitement to excavate information from the former Hunt housekeeper. After parking in the complex lot, she bounded up the steps and buzzed the first-floor unit.

A woman answered. She didn't sound elderly.

"Can I help you?"

"I'm here to see Arlyss Mills, please. Malcolm Hunt gave me this address."

A chime rang out and the electronic door lock blinked green. A middle-aged woman dressed in patterned scrubs and clogs stood in the hallway by the door to Arlyss's unit.

"Am I interrupting a medical visit? I'm Cassandra Browning. I work at an estate on the Prairie Ridge bluff." Cass thrust out her arm to shake the nurse's hand.

"I'm Janet, Arlyss's niece. We live together." Janet's strong handshake suggested she was used to heavy lifting. "My aunt is getting some fresh air on the patio. I'm off on a home visit. See you in an hour."

Cass smiled at Janet's smock depicting cartoon cats riding skateboards and bicycles. "Thanks, Janet. I'm sorry to drop by without calling."

Janet waved off the comment, car keys jangling in her hand. "No need. Aunt Arlyss likes company."

Janet left and Cass wondered about upsetting Arlyss by barging into her space.

She called from inside the patio door, waving. "Hello. Mrs. Mills?"

The old housekeeper looked up from a word puzzle, mouth set in a straight line. "Are ye a friend of Janet's?"

Cass reached for the woman with a gentle hand. "My name

is Cassandra Browning. Malcolm Hunt gave me your name and address. I'm hoping you can help me. Mind if I sit with you?"

Arlyss closed the puzzle book and set it on the metal table beside her. "How is Malcolm? He was my favorite of the family." Her beaming smile said it all.

Cass picked up on a British accent. "He's fine. I rode horses with him this morning. That's how I heard about you." Cass cut to the chase. "We were talking about Olga and Mrs. Frazer, two of the Hollingsworths' housekeepers."

Arlyss scrunched her face and leaned in to examine Cassandra from head to toe, as if selecting the perfect watermelon. "Are ye living on the bluff?" She arched one skeptical eyebrow.

Cass giggled at the shrewd woman. "No. I worked for Posey Hollingsworth until her sad departure. I'm working at the house until the estate is settled. Mr. Hunt is kind enough to let me ride his horses."

Arlyss sniffed. "Poor Master Malcolm. He's gone through enough. First his son, now Miss Posey. I'd say he lost the two people most dear to him."

Arlyss held her breath but swallowed her words. "How 'bout we put on the kettle and have a brew and a proper chat?"

When she rose from the chair, Cass noticed the tall woman walked like someone half her age, erect, with a spring in her step. Arlyss was thin, but not bony, and her creamy skin sported minimal wrinkles. She led Cass past the living area into a roomy kitchen and waved toward the tall chairs at the island for her to sit.

Arlyss added water to the kettle and brought a wooden

box with a variety of tea sachets to Cass. She selected a vanilla chamomile and handed it to Arlyss. Cass saw the woman place an Earl Grey teabag into her cup.

"Olga was a luv, she was. I learned lots from her and it's a shame she's gone." Arlyss turned around and began digging through cupboards for tea accompaniments.

"I'm sorry for your loss. I didn't know Olga passed on," Cass said.

Arlyss filled an embossed glass platter with packaged tea cookies and turned around, her eyes crinkled in glee. "Gads no. Olga's naught dead. She met a nice man and married him. They moved to Canada, somewhere in Ontario, aye."

Cass deflated. "What about Mrs. Frazer? Where can I find her?"

Shrouded in steam, Arlyss poured water into the delicate cups and placed lids on top to steep, then carried them over to the island. Like a server completing her routine, she spun around and collected the glass platter of cookies, sugar bowl, and cream pot. A scowl replaced her gleeful expression.

She sat beside Cass and settled two cookies on a plate for herself. "Help yourself, lass. Naught fancy but it's tea. If I knowed you were dropping by, I woulda made my ginger orange biscuits."

"Ah now, Monica Frazer. That one. Nothing friendly there." Arlyss looked to be conjuring the woman from memory. "Stiff as broom straw." A sudden smile erupted. "There's one time I saw her smile."

Cass interrupted to get back on track. "When was that?"

Arlyss blinked and dropped two sugar cubes into her cup. "There was a garden picnic party at the Hollingsworths'.

Monica Frazer nipped into the punch, if you get my meaning. O'course she had a thing for one of the staff, but he had eyes for someone else."

She poured a thin stream of cream into her cup and stirred, then passed the cream to Cass. "Sorry for prattling on. Monica Frazer is in Madison somewhere, living with her sister, is it?"

Cass relaxed and sipped the flavorful tea. "Thank you. I'll try to find her. What was it like, working for the Hunt family?"

Arlyss closed her eyes, thoughtful for a few moments. "It was another life. Mr. Emmett and Mrs. Claudia were formal. I was young and didn't know rubbish about working for folks like them. But I learned. Twenty-two years I was there, starting just before Master Malcom was born."

Cass envisioned the woman serving the Hunts into retirement. Arlyss seemed capable of running a large household, even now. "You must have still been young when you left."

Her lips were set in a firm line. "Forty-four."

"Why did you leave?" Cass preferred a direct approach.

"The time was right. The Hunts wanted to live abroad, but they wouldn't leave until their sons were settled. Once Mitchell won his House election, his parents were happy." Arlyss nabbed another cookie and dunked it in the tea.

Cass knew Mitchell currently served in the Senate, representing Michigan. "He was supposed to run Hunt Industries though, right?"

"Aye he was. When he decided to get into politics, it threw a clinker into the works. Master Malcolm was eight years his junior and didn't know enough about the business. Mrs. Hunt had bees in her knickers to go abroad, and she wouldn't be put off, but there was the matter of who would run the company." Arlyss passed Cass a knowing look like she might be in on the story.

Cass refilled the woman's empty cup. She hoped her encouraging expression would urge Arlyss to reveal more. "You were saying about Mrs. Hunt…"

"Mrs. Claudia handpicked Corrine for Master Malcolm. Their marriage solved two bouts of misery, it did." Arlyss checked the tea and fetched another sachet from the wooden box. "More tea?" She held the kettle aloft.

"Yes, please." Cass accepted another tea sachet. "So, Malcolm and Corrine are in an arranged marriage."

"Corrine was promised to Mitchell first, but when he pursued politics, the families renegotiated. Mrs. Claudia was hot about the botched-up affair and didn't want Corrine stirring up a mess for the family. It was Mrs. Claudia who worked it out. Master Malcolm needed an older woman with a firm hand."

"How much older?" Cass knew the delicacy of her question.

"Eleven years. She was older than Mitchell, too."

Cass stirred cream into her tea, trying to assemble a clear story line. "Did you work for Malcolm and Corrine?"

"Naw. The timing was right for me to leave. They married. The Hunt parents moved to France. I knew Corrine would have her own way of doing things, and I was set onto Mrs. Claudia's ways."

Cass did some quick math in her head. Malcolm must have been about twenty-one when he married Corrine. Untested, naive, and under the thumb of his parents. *How did Posey factor into this?*

Cass tossed her fishing line into a new stream. "Did you know the Hollingsworth family? I worked for Posey such a short time, I don't know much about her parents."

"I should say so. Mrs. was a hard woman. Dr. Lionel was kind. He didn't look down his nose at the help. Miss Posey and Master Malcolm were bosom friends until…well."

Cass held her breath. *Don't stop now, until when or what?* "Until?"

Arlyss began playing with the hem of the floral placemat under the serving platter. Cass saw the woman's hesitation in her shaking fingers. "I believe Miss Posey's heart broke after Master Malcolm's engagement."

Cass believed the story had missing details. The timeline cracked somewhere before the engagement, she was certain. "Olga, the Hollingsworths' housekeeper. Why did she leave? Posey was what—seventeen?"

Arlyss shrugged and turned toward the wall clock. "It's getting late, dear. Promise to come and see me again? I'll bake biscuits."

Damn. I've lost her and the story. "Of course. I appreciate your time and the tea." Cass picked up the serving tray and set it near the sink. Arlyss walked Cass to the door and clasped her hand, covering it with the other. Cass, gifted with the ability to read others through the sense of touch, received sincerity mixed with sorrow from the woman.

She met Janet in the parking lot unloading bags from her minivan.

"Ms. Browning, I hope Aunt Arlyss didn't talk your ear off. She likes a captive audience."

"Not at all. I enjoyed hearing her stories," Cass said.

"Right. Take it all with a grain of salt. Aunt Arlyss is in and out of reality these past couple years. Poor lamb."

Cass tried to conceal her astonishment at the housekeeper's mental state. Arlyss seemed lucid as far as Cass could tell. "Oh, that's a shame. She made perfect sense to me, though. We talked about her time working for the Hunt family."

Janet shut the van's hatch and settled the bags on the pavement. "Hmm. If you want to know about the history on the bluff, you should talk to Mrs. Adams. She's my main client." Janet explained she was a home health nurse. "I spend five mornings a week with Mrs. Adams at Bluebird Hill."

Cass gasped. "Bluebird Hill? The pink house where the tiny white-haired woman sits in the front window most of the day?"

Janet nodded. "Mrs. Adams is ninety-nine. The oldest one left of the founding families, and not a cobweb in her head either."

Cass climbed into the Subaru and slumped over the steering wheel. "I'm not sure I got the information I came for. In fact, I gained a whole lot more than a horse of a different color. I think I found a stable full." ■

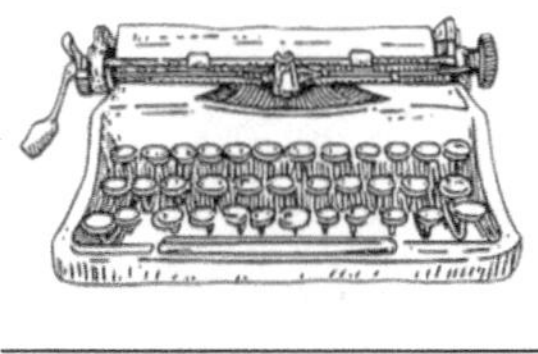

Slams, Snaps, and Grabs

Beans and Scenes coffeehouse brimmed with people. Tables and chairs held fussy drinks along with college students and staff, plus the artsy folks from the community.

Bay and Downing arrived early to nab a table against the back wall, something the detective always insisted upon. "I want to be able to observe the whole place," he said.

He slugged his iced tea and took Bay's hand. "Remind me what to expect from a poetry slam." He made a sour face when he said the two words, followed by a sheepish grin.

Bay chuckled; happy he agreed to come. "You're going to hear poems performed. Not exactly acted out, but the performers will be in costume and will offer a dramatic recitation." She leaned her head in. "Most people will snap their fingers as a form of applause."

Downing rolled his eyes.

"You'll be fine. Just watch everyone else and follow along." Bay checked her phone a third time. "Cass and Anthony better not ditch us. It's almost show time."

Downing snorted. "They probably had to park in Timbuktu."

As Bay watched, the door opened to admit her colleague and friend, Jen Yoo, and Andrew Peng, Jen's date. They made a beeline for Bay's table.

"Thanks for getting here early enough to get seats," Jen said.

"Nope. These are for Cass and Anthony. If you'd told me you were coming, I would have grabbed a larger table."

Jen stuck out her tongue and stood behind Downing and leaned against the wall. "If they don't show, I get first dibs."

Downing jerked around to face Jen. "I don't think I can let you stand there. Can you move over about a foot that way." He jerked his thumb toward Bay's seat.

"I guess so." Jen sidestepped, shrugging her shoulders.

"It's the detective in him. Everything has to be within his line of sight. You know, just in case," Bay explained.

"In case of what? A mass riot of poetry readers?" Jen laughed.

Vivian Rossi, the woman of the hour, drifted past the audience toward Bay. She wore an alabaster peasant dress, reminiscent of Emily Dickinson, and laced up white boots, looking ready to host a séance or even a pagan fire dance.

Bay couldn't help but smile seeing the glow radiating from Vivian. "Amazing dress, Vivian, and I like your hair." Vivan wore a flower wreath with ribbons braided around her thick curls.

"Thank you for coming, Bay. You too, Jen. The stars portend a successful evening." Vivian swept her arms above her in reference to the sky and floated behind the coffee bar, where a hallway led to the stage.

Cass and Anthony, each holding a beverage, scooted to Bay's side and sat down.

"Where did you two come from? I've been watching the door." Bay sniffed.

Before they could answer, Downing indicated the side entrance. "Over there. I'm guessing you had to park on Westport."

Cass jutted out her hip and folded her arms. "Guessed, huh?" She turned toward her sister. "Once a cop, always a cop."

"Seriously though, I didn't know a shindig like this would be so popular. Glad you saved us a spot."

Cass turned around to wave hello to Jen and Andrew and perused the room. "I thought Diana was coming."

Bay pointed to the table at the corner near the stage. Diana sat with Dean Stasia Andino, Bay's boss, and four student performers.

Cass's mouth dropped open. "Diana's reading?"

"No, she's introducing Vivian tonight. Excellent, right?" Their half sister was notoriously shy.

As if on cue, Diana took the stage to welcome guests and introduce Vivian.

"Flourish College is proud of its community of artists, many of whom are successfully published writers. We are excited to celebrate our fifth year of poetry performances, thanks to this delightful venue, Beans and Scenes. Most of all, tonight would not be possible without the dedication and talent of Professor Vivian Rossi."

Bay leaned in to whisper. "Diana's doing well."

Cass agreed, but her eyes darted around the room as people

applauded for Vivian. Three things caught her attention. A white-haired woman bounced in her chair with unbridled enthusiasm. Two students studied the audience. One, a woman who dressed in a silvery-green loose tunic and trousers and wore a matching hajib oozed fear, while the young man in jeans and a dark hooded sweatshirt showed disdain. The third thing, though, bothered Cass the most. Wafting around the coffeehouse was the scent of deception.

Anthony and Bay watched Cass, each waiting for her forecast. To Bay's dismay, she turned toward Anthony.

"Anthony, who is that?" Cass knew he had the answer. She tipped her finger toward the excited white-haired woman.

"That woman? Why, that's Miriam Greggs. The office manager for the Lange Group." Anthony crinkled his brows at Cass.

Cass sighed in satisfaction at the helpful revelation. Miriam Greggs was on her radar, and she'd be watching the woman. "Why is she here?"

"Supports the arts." Anthony's whisper lingered in Cass's ear, unnerving her.

On stage, Vivian announced the opening performer, a student dressed in a black ensemble with skeleton bones, his face a mask of black and white makeup. With the voice of a mysterious angel, he performed Sylvia Plath's *Danse Macabre*, a tale of skeletons rising from the dead to dance again on Halloween.

A chorus of hoots and howls followed the poet, who presented the next performer, none other than Cher DeVane, a student who created substantial drama during the college's summer theater production and in Bay's classroom. But that was all in the past as far as Bay was concerned. The circumstances of last summer made the college junior grow up.

A poised Cher occupied center stage dressed in a crimson silk cape over a gauzy ebony gown. The cape's red hood framed her golden hair that hung in two long braids down her chest. Reciting Anne Sexton's *Little Red Riding Hood*, her voice confessed and accused while her eyes challenged every person in the audience.

> *Many are the deceivers:*
> *The suburban matron,*
> *proper in the supermarket…*

Hearing the opening lines, Cass sucked in her breath and inhaled another waft of deception. *Is it Miriam Greggs or the woman in the head scarf? Who is it?*

The Sexton poem, bleak, gory, and sad, begged attention and received it from the audience, who gaped and gasped until Cher broke the spell by walking offstage. Booming foot stomps and howls proclaimed her powerful performance.

Macabre poems ruled the night, and no wonder, with shorter days and autumn chills, the season of death descended upon the coffeehouse. Two students performed selections by Poe, necessary and expected.

Bay noticed Stasia's niece, Aria, fully vibrating in time with a handsome student's rendition of Robert Frost's *Ghost House*. The poem surprised some listeners, including Bay, who only knew Frost's gentle poems of birches, mending walls, apple picking, and snowy evenings in the woods.

The two sisters turned in surprise when Diana was called to the microphone a second time. Wearing a tailored utility suit of royal blue wool, Diana emerged as if from a World War

Two advertisement. Her blond victory rolls bounced in time with her tapping patent leather pumps when she walked to center stage and began reciting the French poem, *Chanson d'automne* (*Autumn Song*) by Paul Verlaine, but in English.

Written in eighteen sixty-six, the poem depicts the woes of aging, using musical phrases and sad tonal words, which were later transformed into a popular song. More importantly, the poem served the French forces during World War Two when the Special Operations Executive broadcasted secret plans for the Battle of Normandy using lines of the Verlaine poem on two different dates. "The long sobs of autumn's violins" meant the operation would start in two weeks. The phrase, "wound my heart with a monotonous languor", signaled the French to begin sabotage of the railroad system forty-eight hours ahead of the battle.

After sharing the story behind the poem, Diana repeated her melancholy delivery in French. The melodic repetition of soft French vowels mesmerized the audience as the phrases floated about the room like falling leaves from Diana's red painted lips.

Bay and Cass clasped hands until Diana's final word, *morte* (died), descended onto the crowd. The sisters' breaths came in quick wisps while their hearts thudded in their ears. They dropped hands and joined in the enthusiastic finger-snapping, raising their hands in the air for Diana to see their pride.

Finally, Vivian took the stage to regale the story of finding Emily Dickinson's unknown poem, *There Came a Wind Like a Bugle*, the painstaking authentication process, and the triumph of deeming the poem an original.

Vivian recited the poem, invoking the wind as a tormenting,

forceful, uninvited guest. To illustrate Dickinson's complicated voice, Vivian varied her tone from wary to mystical, and her pacing changed, too. The first two stanzas suggest the practicality of humans to shut out the storm, while the second half builds with intensity at the wind's power. Vivian's voice became a whirlwind of highs and lows matching a cadence that sometimes rushed, sometimes lagged.

There came a wind like a bugle;
It quivered through the grass,
And a green chill upon the heat
So ominous did pass
We barred the windows and the doors
As from an emerald ghost;
The doom's electric moccasin
That very instant passed.
On a strange mob of panting trees,
And fences fled away,
And rivers where the houses ran
The living looked that day.
The bell within the steeple wild
The flying tidings whirled.
How much can come
And much can go,
And yet abide the world!

Rewarded with reverent snaps from the audience, Vivian dropped a bombshell.

"But Emily's poem kept company in that antique music box. A letter to the 'Master.'" Vivian paused to gauge the response. Most gasped. Some frowned. Some were flummoxed.

Vivian schooled the audience on Emily Dickinson's strange

collection of letters written to a mysterious "Master." Her voice held passion and intimacy, and the audience hung on every word.

"Emily Dickinson wrote three letters between eighteen fifty-eight and sixty-two to someone known only as 'Master'. Historians and biographers speculate about who 'Master' is or I should say, was. Some argue it is one of the men Dickinson herself referred to as her masters. There was Leonard Humphrey, the principal of Amherst Academy, where she attended school. She wrote passionate letters to Samuel Bowles, editor of the *Springfield Republican*, who printed seven of her poems. Perhaps Thomas Wentworth Higginson, a journalist for the *Atlantic Monthly*, was the mysterious 'Master.' After all, Emily sought his approval of her poetic form and content, and Higginson proved a difficult man to please. Ah well, aren't all critics?"

The audience laughed. Vivian's delivery resembled a conversation over tea with friends. She moved about the stage with ease and grace.

"Some believe she is writing to a spiritual master: God or the Muse." Vivian spun in a circle and her alabaster ruffled dress whirled, Marilyn Monroe-like. She offered her subjects a saucy smile.

"Of course, no puzzle is worth pursuing without juicy bits of tittle-tattle. You see, my friends, these letters are ripe with desire, yearning, and passion. Dickinson expresses devotion and sacrifice, while she searches for—well, something that cannot be named. Consider that 'Master' may be her bosom friend and sister-in-law, Susan Gilbert, a woman she wrote to for years, a woman who read the majority of Emily's poems.

Perhaps 'Master' is Charles Wadsworth, a Philadelphia minister she met while staying with friends. Most of her correspondence to the reverend is passed through her friend, Mary Holland, suggesting Emily and Wadsworth conducted a secret affair." Vivian spoke the last sentence in a stage whisper.

Vivian leaned in, conveyed the litany of possible "Masters" with conviction, without suggesting her opinion on the matter.

"I know what you're thinking. After all this time, we must have the answer to this puzzle. Surely after experts studied Dickinson's letters, poems, and life, and interviewed surviving relatives…surely, someone made revelations. Someone turned speculation into fact."

The audience was ready to hear the mystery's resolution. Vivian held them captive, hanging by invisible threads she wove into story.

"I'm sorry to disappoint you. All we have are partial answers and suppositions. Some pieces fit while others occupy lonely margins. We believe what we want to believe. So do they—the scholars, I mean. Dickinson cannot be contained. There's the rub."

Vivian stepped back, disconnecting herself from the audience, prepared to read the found letter, undated, like the others. "Time will tell where it fits into sequence of the other three. Knowing the contents of those three, I suspect the letter follows the second of the series. In that letter, our Daisy, as Dickinson refers to herself, entertains suffering as part of longing for something. Could it be the love of another, someone unattainable? She specifically asks the recipient to come to her in Amherst, suggesting that she (Daisy) would not disappoint them. Could it be answers she seeks about the meaning of life and death and the afterlife? She struggled to make sense of these throughout her life—in her poems and letters to others. In the letter, she speaks of Heaven as a place too full of others and says she has asked for redemption but did not receive it."

Vivian captivated the audience, regaling them with juicy bits of Dickinson's oddities and paradoxes, swooning over some of the poet's profound lyrics, like *if you saw a bullet hit a Bird—and he told you he wasn't shot—you might weep at his courtesy, but you would certainly doubt his word. One drop more from the gash that stains your Daisy's bosom—then would you believe?*

Vivian's delivery was a transformation; she appeared to become the poet herself, pulling the audience into the tapestry as she wove it, making one and all complicit in overhearing Dickinson's confessions.

Vivian pressed the newfound letter to her breast and spun in a slow circle as the light changed to a radiant beam, a ghostly specter materializing from elsewhere. The contrast of the dazzling figure against the black stage caused the audience to lower their eyes. In a different tone and timbre, the figure recited the letter:

Master, your Daisy is restless now, a fly buzzing about the cerebellum. There is no comfort in not belonging, would you agree? One's inner self a cushion yet no resting place, a pickled puzzle—perfidy, yes, perdition—even. Too much to know to indulge in idle frivolities—and, faith, too. Daisy waited—she said she would wait—in white, too. And still she waits—a butterfly in cocoon—a flower in the bud. Will you come now—to witness the metamorphosis? What may a bee accomplish in dancing alone on a blossom? To the hive it must submit its treasures for honey. Master, set Daisy free—if by fire, if by ice—both defer the darkness.

Nobody moved, let alone breathed, until a collective exhale filled the space, where most stood in awe and applauded.

Diana took the stage to acknowledge the appreciative audience and bid them good night, while pointing out refreshments along the side wall where a reception was about to begin.

Cass surveyed the room and saw the young guy in the hoodie speaking to a well-muscled man who looked like an Eastern European. The guy removed his hoodie, emptied his pockets like someone being screened by security, and showed the muscle man a card or perhaps a photo. Studying the scene, Cass noticed he sported an arm tattoo depicting a thick broken chain with a fist in the middle.

Some people left, including the female dressed in forest-green wearing a head scarf. Disappointed, Cass had hoped to engage the woman in small talk and "accidentally" brush against her to gauge her intentions. Instead, she made a beeline for Miriam Greggs, who was talking to Vivian, their heads bent in private conversation.

Cass marched up to the pair with no propriety for the moment. "Dr. Rossi, that was breathtaking!" She shook Vivian's hand while Vivian searched her memory files.

"I'm Cassandra Browning, Bay's sister. Well, Diana's too, for that matter."

"Yes. Forgive me. I thought you might be one of my students

for a moment. I'm pleased you came."

Vivian looked to finish her conversation with Miriam, but her attention turned elsewhere.

Cassandra swayed sideways and stepped on Miriam's foot.

"Excuse me. I'm terribly sorry. I was distracted." Cass's voice and pose faked contrition.

"Never mind," Miriam Greggs said. Her pursed lips and knitted brow suggested disgust at Cass's double impertinence.

"We may have met before but I'm not certain. I'm Cassandra Browning. I was Posey Hollingsworth's personal assistant." Cass, now perfectly poised, offered her hand in greeting, and Miriam accepted.

"I cannot recall you, but I know or knew Ms. Hollingsworth. Miriam Greggs. I managed the offices of the Lange Group." Miriam's silky response suggested pride and importance, but Cass detected a stockpile of secrets in their brief encounter.

"Oh, I see. So, you no longer work for the Langes?"

"I am retired but called upon on occasion to perform tasks for the company." Miriam was wound tighter than a mummy. "And what are you doing now that Ms. Hollingsworth is no longer with us?"

Cass shivered in the wake of Miriam's cold delivery. "I'm managing the estate while it goes through probate. I miss Posey dearly. We'd become close, and I wish I knew more details about her life." The bait was set, waiting for Miriam to nibble.

"I'm sorry for your loss, Ms. Browning. I knew Posey's parents, of course."

"Did you? I thought perhaps you were too young for that."

Miriam thawed a bit. "Ha, you are a flatterer. I'm old enough to be Posey's mother." Her mouth snapped shut like a trap, cutting off whatever else she intended to say. "It was lovely to meet you, Cassandra. Please excuse me." Miriam sauntered off, looking about the shop, perhaps for Vivian.

Cass surveyed the room. Bay chatted in a cluster with her friend, Jen Yoo, Diana, and Dean Stasia Andino while Detective Downing held up the wall behind them. Anthony knew everyone and navigated the room.

She recognized Aria, Stasia's niece, holding captive an attractive male performer who appeared to have a queue of eligible ladies waiting to speak to him. I remember those days, Cass thought, a wistful smile in place. Disappointed that the woman in the head scarf, Miriam Greggs, and Vivian had vanished, she made her way toward her sisters.

The chitchat continued with praise for the poets and opinions about the pieces and the performances. The Beans and Scenes servers buzzed about the café, clearing dishes and dismantling the reception tables, signaling their desire to close up and go home.

Anthony scuttled beside Cass and tucked his hand in hers while bending to whisper in her ear. "I saw you talking to Miriam Greggs. Did you catch any fish there?" He grinned.

Cass couldn't outwit Anthony, something she found admirable yet annoying. "I did not, if you must know. Let's say the ice is cracking, but there's still a lot beneath the surface."

Cass turned to Bay and Downing. "We're heading out. I'm glad you talked me into coming tonight. What a spectacle!"

"We're leaving, too, and so are Jen and Andrew. Let's walk out together," Bay said.

The café server locked the door behind the six, who walked in twos down the sidewalk toward the parking garage past the coffee shop. Off the main drag, the streets were darker than usual with the cloudy sky obscuring the waning moon and stars. Bay and Downing reached their vehicle, which was parked on the street nearby.

As the group said their final farewells, strange noises and movements coming from behind the coffee shop building drew their attention. Someone called out while footsteps thudded on pavement. Breaking glass and clinking metal echoed into the street. Downing began to run sideways toward the noise, the others hot on his heels. He held up his finger against his lips, his other hand rested on his service revolver.

"Stop! No, stop! Here, take my purse!" A voice cried in despair.

Bay held her breath. That voice belonged to Vivian Rossi. Bay sprang from the shadows, ready for action, but Downing's arm pushed her backward against the side of the restaurant by the alley behind the coffee shop. Cass huddled with her sister, grabbing her hand to keep her steady.

More noises and shouts ensued, then Vivian's scream was muffled by something. Downing peered into the alley, gun raised. A black van, nose facing the exit, blocked his view. The rear doors slammed and someone shouted, "Go, go, go!"

An automatic rifle fired a couple shots from the front passenger window as the van exited the alley. Downing returned fire, aiming for the tires, but the van accelerated, rocking a little, tires squealing. It disappeared around the corner onto a narrow one-way street.

"Call it in, Bay. I'm going after the van. All of you—wait here." Downing vaulted to his unmarked car and peeled out to follow.

Bay didn't have the chance to tell the detective she'd called it in the minute she heard Vivian's cries.

Anthony and Andrew continued to the parking garage to pick up their cars, telling the women to stay on the sidewalk under the streetlight by the restaurant. The three women nodded at the men and made a beeline to the scene, cell phone flashlights on. Bay's beam followed a trail of broken glass where the remains of an Italian syrup bottle lay beside the dumpster. Evidence.

She hoped Vivian had cracked one of her kidnappers over the head with it. The dumpster lids were open, exuding a foul smell, and Bay crept closer to peer inside when someone darted from their hiding place by the dumpster and ramrodded Bay, knocking her off her feet.

Cass chased after the figure and managed to catch a glimpse of them before they jumped into a car parked at the corner. *The guy sitting beside the woman with the head scarf.* She noticed part of the broken chain tattoo visible on his left wrist. She couldn't see the driver through the tinted windows.

Back at the scene, Jen and Bay sat on the steps behind the coffee shop, waiting for the police.

"Any luck?" Bay asked.

"No, and yes. I pegged the guy, recognized him from the poetry slam. He took off in a waiting car. Are you okay?"

"Yes. Just humiliated. The cops are going to yell at us for contaminating the scene."

"No, no," Jen protested, "We didn't touch anything."

Anthony and Andrew pulled up opposite the alley as a squad arrived. Bay recognized Detective Harris jumping from the passenger side but didn't know the uniformed officer driving the squad.

Harris was first to greet the three women. "Everyone okay?" The three nodded. "Okay, let's move you away from the scene," Harris said.

Officer Clark rapped on the rear door where lights were visible, shouted "police, open up," and two café workers stuck out their heads, gaping like deer in the headlights. The oblivious workers took out their earbuds and ushered the three women and Harris into the café. So much for the workers' account of the incident.

Harris interviewed Bay, while Clark took Cassandra's statement, and Jen waited, texting Andrew about the situation.

Harris's poker face failed to conceal his worry.

"What's the news from Downing?" Bay worried, too.

"He had to give up. He's on his way here." Nolan Harris and Downing partnered for less than a year, but they made a balanced team. Downing's rough and ready style to Harris's folksy, small-town demeanor, combined to crack suspects.

Harris took notes from Bay's description of what she heard and saw, including the figure who knocked her over. She thought she heard two voices besides Vivian's but couldn't be sure if a third perp was the driver.

"I don't know why anyone would want to kidnap Vivian. Honestly, she's eccentric but sincere and honest." Bay was embarrassed to confess that she knew nothing about her personal life.

When Cassandra's turn came, she told a similar story as Bay's but figured it would take two people to tackle the fighting Vivian and toss her in the back of the van. "My opinion, I'm thinking there are four perps. Two in the van, two in the second car. They're meeting somewhere to join forces."

Officer Clark curled his lips into an amused sneer. "Oh, you do. And how did you come to this conclusion, Ms. Browning?"

Cass stared down Clark. "I've worked several heists. That's all in the past, but I know the drill, Officer."

Clark's sneer vanished. He took Cass by the arm and guided her out of earshot. "I'm listening. What else did you notice?"

Cass was pleased to be taken seriously. "The guy hiding behind the dumpster had a tattoo. I can draw it for you. I noticed him inside the café, talking with a bulky man, who looked like a foreigner. The inked guy sat with a young woman wearing a green head scarf."

"Can you come down to the station tomorrow and describe these people to a police artist? Look at some photos of people in the system?" Clark snapped his notebook closed.

"Of course. But wouldn't the wheels turn faster if I did that now?" Cass saw the need for speed. Poor Vivian Rossi. ■

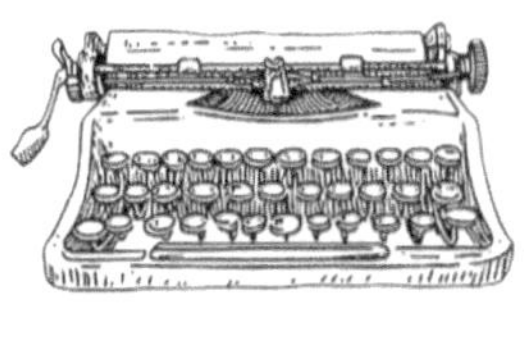

Vivian's House of Curiosities

Downing met Bay and Cassandra at Vivian Rossi's home on Lilac Lane before dawn. The women parked on a nearby street, as instructed, and wore dark clothes and caps, Downing's second request.

Downing moved from the shadows when he saw Bay and Cass skirt the hedges along one side of Vivian's statuesque Victorian; its towering turret stared down, foreboding.

"I scoped things out. We're going to use the side entrance." Downing indicated the hedges which blocked the view of the neighbors.

They climbed the steps and crossed the wraparound porch with Downing shining a penlight over the door and landing the beam on the keyhole.

Bay slid the old-fashioned heavy key into the lock, and the door gave way. Three mewling cats greeted the trespassers with one insistent yowler leading the pack. Cass bent down and gathered up the milky white cat whose ears curled backward.

She looked at the cat's engraved collar.

"Hello there, Amherst. It's okay. We're not going to hurt you." Cass whispered into the cat's ear while stroking her with a gentle hand, and Amherst began to purr as she curled closer to Cass. The other two cats quieted, too, but wove a path between Bay's and Downing's legs.

"We got lucky with the key," Bay said. "First try."

Bay and the detective met at Vivian's Flourish College office around midnight after the kidnapping. As department chair, Bay held keys for all of the English offices, and since neither of them could sleep, the office visit was a must. Bay found the antique key in Vivian's desk drawer.

The office looked undisturbed. Unlike Vivian's habit of carrying around clutter, the organized office was shipshape.

"Maybe we got lucky, maybe not. Most old houses like this have one key that opens every door. At least the key opened Vivian's house." Downing began throwing the flashlight beam around the room, which appeared to be a study. He saw an antique desk covered with stuff and turned on the floor lamp for a better look.

Opened leather bound books lay this way and that, crisscrossed over one another, some weighted down with paperweights. A speckled glass one here, a carved marble one there. A vintage Corona typewriter squatted in the middle, owning its spot on the blotter based on the faded outline around it.

Downing handed nitrile gloves to the two and directed them to go through the drawers on either side. "I'll go look around."

The drawers were stuffed. One held newspaper clippings and photographs from various decades. Two were piled with old bills and receipts held down by an ancient tape dispenser in one drawer, a vintage candy tin filled with paper clips and safety pins in the other.

"Bay, look at this." Cass pulled a trail of scarves, one after another, from a drawer, like a magician's trick. "Why in the world would she use her desk drawer for scarves?"

Bay shook her head while investigating a drawer filled with glass bottles. "I've got perfume, essential oils, mineral drops, and who knows what else over here."

Another drawer held stamps and ink pads, sealing wax, candle stubs, matches, calligraphy pens, and a wooden box of brass seals, all settled on top of a child's coloring book of woodland critters. The contents charmed Bay.

"Wait a minute. What?" Cass called out, staring into the bottom drawer, which was deep and empty.

Bay came to look as Cass ran a finger down one interior edge. "Rose petals. Something's been taken out of here recently. See, you can smell roses and see the rectangular imprint."

Downing returned. "Find anything remarkable? Get any vibes?" The second question was meant for Cass. After her involvement in two separate investigations, even Downing was half-convinced Cassandra's extrasensory powers were real.

"There's something in the house, but this desk is a dead zone, except for the vacant drawer here. I think something was removed recently."

Bay added, "Vivian's silver music box. It's where she discovered the Emily Dickinson poem and letter."

Cass brightened. "Yes. People often put flowers to dry in decorative boxes."

Downing scratched his chin. "Would Vivian be careless

enough to have the box and letter sitting around unlocked?"

"No. She mentioned the contents were out for authentication. I can't believe anyone would kidnap her for an antique music box. They'd just take the box, right?"

Downing pitched forward, snapping his fingers. "They stole the box, discovered the contents were missing, and kidnapped Vivian to get the letter. It must be valuable, right?"

Cass agreed while Bay shook her head. "Remember, the real letter is being authenticated. Vivian has a copy."

"Did you find anything?" Bay asked.

"It's hard to tell. The woman collects any weird thing you can think of. She has mannequins upstairs wearing hats, feather boas, and belts. Odd woman."

"Mind if I do a walk-through?" Cass asked.

"That's exactly why I asked you to be here." Downing gestured down the hall.

While Cass toured Vivian's house, Bay found the kitchen and searched for kitty food. She found dry food in the pantry and noticed three empty bowls near the sink. The clatter of kibble against porcelain summoned the cats, who paraded in, purring.

Downing proved helpful by filling water dishes and settling them on the throw rug.

"Look at that." He gestured toward the shelf above the stove that held all manner of egg timers: a menagerie of critters including an owl, a bat, a bunny, a cat, and a penguin kept company with fruits, vegetables, and famous cartoon cavemen. "Who needs that many timers?"

Bay giggled. "Some people collect salt and pepper shakers, others..."

Downing held up one finger. "Did you notice that every room has a clock? Including the bathrooms."

"Vivian frequently loses track of time. That's probably all there is to it." Bay defended her colleague.

"What made you abandon the chase last night?" One thing Bay knew for certain: the detective would not retreat from a hot pursuit.

"The van. High speed and erratic driving on the highway. I had to think of everyone's safety." Downing stopped, sucked in a heavy breath, and set his jaw.

"There's more. You followed them?"

"Yes, up to an airfield surrounded by security fencing. By the time I got there, they were boarding a small plane. I called Madison PD for help. The plane took off before Madison arrived."

"And?" Bay pushed on.

"Waiting for a warrant before I'm off to the airfield to get some answers."

Cass wandered into the kitchen, her eyes barely slits as she took in the room in swaths, her breath a rhythmic pattern. She stopped short of stepping on the three cats perched near empty food dishes. She surveyed the room without seeing Bay or Downing: She was in the zone.

"There's a lot of mixed energy bouncing around this house," she said. "It's hard to pinpoint anything specific, but there's a hot current running through Vivian's bedroom."

Downing blinked. "The bedroom. Fantastic. You think she has a wild sex life to go with all this?" He swept his arms in a wide circle.

Cass folded her arms and scoffed. "There's a safe in the wall behind the painting of the satyr picnic."

"You mean that monstrosity hanging above the head of the bed?"

"Precisely. I can hear it breathing back there." Cass's eyes twinkled.

Downing pulled out his work phone, scrolled for messages, and frowned. "I'd like to give you a crack at the safe, Cass, but I need to press Judge Holtan for a warrant."

"Don't you have someone else who can supervise me?" Cass was about to burst.

"How about me?" Bay volunteered.

Downing clenched his fist and bit into the knuckles. "Look. You two are here unofficially, so no way. Go home. We'll have to come back tonight."

"Harris?" Bay took a chance. After all, she had worked with Harris before in an official capacity.

Downing took Bay by the arm and began ushering her toward the door while motioning for Cass to follow.

"Sorry you two. I can't put Harris in that position."

"I'll ride to the station with you. Officer Clark asked me to look through some photos for possible suspects," Cass said.

"Uh, no." Downing's voice held exasperation. "I don't want anyone to know you were here. Got it?"

Cass stood ramrod straight and saluted. "Aye, aye, Captain.

The sisters regrouped at their Windflower Gardens apartment where Bay showered and dressed to participate in theater professor interviews at Flourish. Bay's colleague, Desmond, left the area to join his partner Claire in Ohio, leaving an unfilled vacancy for the fall semester, which was currently filled by a temp. The interview panel included professors from the theater, music, and English departments, since they often collaborated.

Meanwhile, Cass cleaned up and drove to the police station to meet with Officer Clark.

After an hour, Cass exhausted the collected photos. "I'm sorry I can't be helpful."

"No. Thanks for trying. It's not a surprise, really. This happens a lot." Clark walked Cass to the lobby.

"Hold up. I see the sketch artist Madison PD said they'd send over." Clark greeted Tricia Frye. "Hey, great timing. Meet our witness. She just went through photos in the system with no match. Cassandra Browning, this is Tricia Frye. She works for Dane County."

Tricia held up her electronic tablet. "Hello, Cassandra. Let's hammer this out."

Cass followed Tricia and Clark into a conference room where the artist connected to the internet and patted the chair beside hers.

"You're not going to draw freehand?" Cass asked.

Tricia held up a digital pen. "Sort of. I partner with this software that turns the sketch into a digital drawing that can be sent out anywhere in the world. My sketch will talk to the database of people in the system and look for matches. Pretty slick, huh."

"Yes, I'd say so." But inside, Cass thought, *if this app was around when I was on the run, I probably would have gone to prison sooner.*

The whole process took less than fifteen minutes thanks to Cass's excellent descriptors, at least that's what Tricia said.

"Okay, we'll let the database do its thing and if something comes up, we'll give you a call. Thanks for coming forward. See you, Clark."

Cass passed Downing's office and noticed it was dark. "Darn. I was hoping to check in with the detective." Cass pegged Clark for a boy scout and hoped to transmit innocent disappointment.

"What's the problem? Maybe I can help." Clark offered.

Eyes cast downward, she fumbled for an explanation. "It's just that I'm supposed to be helping with something at the kidnapped woman's house. There's a wall safe and I have, well, I can, that is, I may be able to open it."

Clark's jaw dropped. "How do you know there's a safe?"

"My sister works with Vivian Rossi. They're both English professors at Flourish College." Cass hoped the lie would serve.

"Oh, I see. You're telling me you have professional skills at safe cracking, Ms. Browning? What else are you an expert at?"

Cass faltered, giving the officer time to continue.

"Let me speak to the chief. I could accompany you to Doctor Rossi's house. The chief considers this case high priority."

Clark returned minutes later, grinning, car keys in hand. "Follow me to the house."

The adrenaline rush filled Cass like a reunion with an old friend. She scolded herself for the way she hustled the police officer, but after three months of failing at Posey's house, she needed a win.

Cass followed Clark to the entrance, strutting past the monitoring cameras flashing a thumbs up. Clark unlocked the padlock chained to the door, a sign the police wanted to keep a low profile. No police tape was visible, and the cameras were secured to trees on the property. Cass knew most people would miss these details, but she wasn't most people.

Inside, Cass pretended to look for Vivian's bedroom on the ground floor before proceeding up the stairway, Clark on her heels.

The massive painting concealing the wall safe leaned against the closet doors. Clark did a double take at the bawdy scene of drunken satyrs dancing with or chasing after half-naked women and nymphs.

In no time, Cass found the switch that tripped an opening in the wall, revealing a metal door with an electronic keypad. She was disappointed, hoping for an old school combination. She could hack an electronic lock, but not without hacking tools. In her former life, an expert hacker taught her the basics for breaking into an electronic lock with two simple tools. Her favorite was a digital device that short circuits the password system, allowing a new passcode to be set up in less than a minute.

She scrutinized the safe, checking to see if it was locked and armed. It was. She stalled for a few minutes to think of options. Announcing her need to use the facilities, Cass walked into Vivian's bathroom. She shut the door to peruse the room. She picked up Vivian's hairbrush from the vanity. A mean humming began in her ears. Eyes closed, she tucked one hand into the pocket of Vivian's bathrobe. The humming intensified.

When she opened her eyes, she noticed Amherst, Vivian's cat with the curled ears, monitoring every move Cass made. Amherst crept forward to place her front paws over Cass's feet and purr in time with the hum in Cass's ears.

It became clear to Cass that she and the cat had a connection. She crouched down and chucked the cat under her chin. "What is it you want to tell me, Amherst?" Bay told Cass about Vivian's eccentric ways, including her famous absentmindedness.

"If I were your mistress, how would I remember my passcode? I wouldn't, would I? No, I'd have to keep it somewhere secure, where I wouldn't forget." Amherst jumped onto Cass's knees, and she almost fell over.

The fluffy white cat lifted one paw to scratch under her collar. Cass noticed the monogrammed charm circled in tiny pearls dangling from Amherst's velvet collar.

"You are certainly the belle of the house, aren't you, Amherst." Cass stroked under the collar to extra purring. Instinctively, Cass turned over the collar charm. The numbers engraved on it were likely Amherst's registered ID, but did they serve a dual purpose?

Cass emerged from the bathroom, Amherst in her arms, greeted by a quizzical look from Clark.

"I can't crack an electronic safe. I was hoping for a combination lock." Cass shrugged. "But I'd like to try the numbers I found on the cat's collar."

Clark raised an eyebrow. "I guess. What's the worst that can happen?"

"An alarm triggers a call to the police."

"Oh, yeah. Go for it. Ah, I'm going to use the bathroom."

With Clark temporarily out from under her, Cass relaxed. She held Amherst and entered the seven numbers, careful not to fumble. The screen turned green, made a happy sound, and the safe clicked. Cass pumped her fist and set down the cat after bussing its ear.

A voice told her to wait for Clark, but she ignored it and opened the door. Inside, lay an accordion file labeled "Project Square One." Cass opened it and found several documents marked by name and background information. Each document included a photograph. She awakened her phone to take snapshots of the top pages, when a photograph fell out and landed on Vivian's bed. Cass began to shiver, seeing the faces of Vivian, Posey, Posey's two friends from Guatemala, and a Latina-looking woman, around twenty years old.

Without thinking, she stuffed the group photo into her handbag, then snapped three photos before Clark pushed open the bathroom door.

"That worked? The cat collar?"

"Yes. I'm surprised, too. I'll set the contents here." She hoped her secretarial actions would suit Clark. She set the accordion file on the bed and removed the remaining stack of file folders from the inside.

"Wait, wait a minute. Don't touch anything else. I'm calling this in. We need some evidence collection bags out here." Clark stepped up to the wall to block Cass, who obediently stepped aside.

She could see the safe was empty now. No music box. What was in those file folders was anyone's guess. At least she had the photograph, the name of some project, and three pictures from the front pages. Why in the world did Vivian have this information locked away at home, and what did Cass's former boss, Posey Hollingsworth, have to do with it? ■

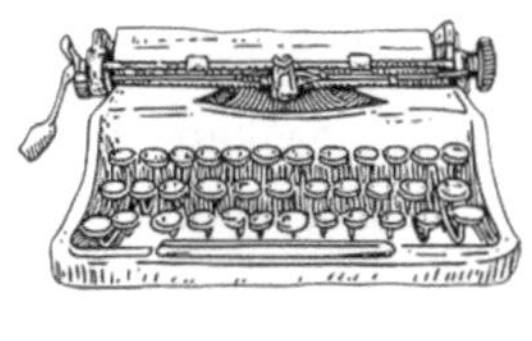

chapter 6

Business as Usual

Cass waited outside the police station for Downing to return. Her constant struggle to stay on the straight and narrow won her over, and she'd come clean about breaking into the safe before the detective heard about it from Clark.

Streaks of sunlight warmed Cass's spot on a bench across the street at Liberty Park, a tidy greenspace with picnic tables, a unisex restroom, and tiny pavilion. She sipped herbal tea and munched a spinach, tomato, and feta wrap from the café on Windsor while she waited.

Downing nodded her direction when he pulled into the police lot, the Charger dimmed the surrounding fall foliage with its garish orange paint. He was alone and made quick steps toward Cass, notepad at the ready.

"You waiting to see me?" Downing positioned a pen over a blank page.

Cass laughed. "Deductive reasoning wins the day. You should know I convinced Officer Clark to let me have a crack at Vivian Rossi's safe this morning. The contents are waiting for you in the evidence room, I imagine."

Downing pushed his sunglasses over his nose. "I guess you were successful."

Cass glanced downward. "More like lucky. Vivian's cat led me to the password."

"You conned the new guy." Downing nodded. "I'll go easy on him. Thanks for being honest." He turned to go but pivoted for a parting shot. "I already knew. Harris called to say he received the contents."

Cass's sly grin conveyed that she'd already figured that out.

The fifth-floor reception area in the Gray Lady, the Flourish Humanities Building's nickname, buzzed with conversation.

Dean Stasia Andino settled the theater interview candidates into the faculty lounge and directed the panel members to the smaller of the two conference rooms down the hall.

Bay carried extra beverage cups and styrofoam plates to the lounge while Stasia arranged muffins and Danishes on a tray next to a bowl of apples and bananas.

"Thank you for pinch-hitting on these interviews." Stasia's quiet voice barely carried to Bay, who was almost a foot taller, but the dean wanted everything to seem normal and held her breath that Vivian's kidnapping wasn't common knowledge.

"Of course, Stasia. We're all putting on our best faces today."

Bay studied the candidates. Three would be interviewed today with two more tomorrow. The panel narrowed the field from a dozen to five finalists. Vivian was part of the original panel, and Bay studied her notes and comments a few hours earlier to get up to speed.

Bay passed Vivian's office on her way to the conference room, a sick feeling gnawing at her insides. *How was Vivian being treated by her captors? What did they want from her?* Bay paused stock-still to fill her lungs with air, replacing the fear she felt for her colleague. She had to keep her feelings under wraps until the interviews were finished.

After the interviews ended, Bay made a beeline for her office and shut the door, leaving the lights off. She closed her eyes to process the three candidates and their conversations with the panel.

She marveled at Stasia's newfound manner she'd adopted the past several months. The abrasive, demanding assistant dean conducted herself with precision and compassion. She continued to promote her family's businesses around Prairie Ridge but didn't browbeat the faculty to patronize them. Stasia extended respect toward her charges, who were learning to trust her in return.

Today was a case in point. The old Stasia would wring her hands and worry out loud about Vivian's kidnapping and how it would affect the college. Every candidate on the interview slate would think that the college's reputation took precedence over its missing professor, and Stasia wouldn't comprehend her inappropriate behavior.

Instead, the interviews were a successful exercise in diplomacy. Stasia set the tone by introducing the panel and explaining Bay's presence, a substitute for the esteemed Vivian, who was absent from campus.

Bay prayed Vivian's ordeal would end before news broke about the kidnapping. The candidates might be furious at the deception. The best ones might reject employment at Flourish.

Bay's eyes flashed open when someone rapped on her door and opened it without waiting for a response, letting light filter into the room from the hallway.

"Hello Doctor Obasi. Please switch on the light." Bay pointed at the wall by the door.

"Sorry to disturb, Doctor Browning. Do you have a headache?" The Nigerian professor sat down without flipping on the lights but left the door ajar.

"No. I'm enjoying the quiet after a couple of long days. How can I help you?"

Bay remembered the African professor's zeal at the prospect of directing productions at Flourish. Ziki Obasi, a guest professor at a large university in Louisiana, complained he couldn't do any hands-on theater work there. At a college the size of Flourish, the man could assist and even direct productions. His enthusiasm at the prospect filled the interview room.

"I hoped you could tell me when Doctor Rossi would return. I must speak with her." Ziki Obasi leaned his large frame over Bay's desk to emphasize his urgency.

Bay's stomach knotted. She opened her desk drawer, searching for papers that didn't exist. "I'm sorry, I don't have her contact information handy. Perhaps I can help you."

Doctor Obasi settled into his seat and blew out a breath. "It is no matter. You see, I must find my niece, Aneka. She is a student at university in Madison. I have news about her mother that is important."

"And Doctor Rossi knows where she is?" A variety of scenarios ran through Bay's mind, most of which led her to one central thought: she didn't really know Vivian.

Doctor Obasi's head danced between a vigorous yes and no, causing his woven fila to slip off his head. One massive hand grabbed it midair and set it aright again. "Doctor Rossi helped Aneka when she came to study here. I have not spoken to her in a year or longer, and I do not know how to find her."

"I see. I'm sorry that I can't help you at the moment, but I will see what I can find out about your niece. Will you write her name down for me, please?" Bay passed a slip of paper and a pen to the doctor, who jotted down her name and her major, the things he knew for sure.

Obasi clasped both of Bay's hands inside his massive warm ones and thanked her. "Please tell Doctor Rossi I called on her and hope to hear from her."

Obasi shut the door behind him and Bay whispered, "I hope to hear from her, too."

A tinny chime drew Bay out of a sleepy stupor. She eyed her blinking phone and noticed less than thirty minutes had passed since the interviews concluded. She must have dropped off soon after Obasi left, yet her brain fogged like a nightmare hangover.

The tinny whimper summoned her again. Why did it sound like it traveled through jello? She checked the side buttons and remembered. She'd silenced it for the poetry event and never changed the settings again.

Bay reached over the desk to flip on the lights, an attempt to recharge her brain. Scrolling through her phone, she found three missed calls, one from an unknown number, one from Cass, and one from Jen Yoo.

Jen's message filled her ear like a chittering squirrel. "Any news about Vivian? Are you working on the case with Downing? Is there anything I can help with? Oh dang, I forgot you're doing interviews at work. Let me know how it goes. Bye-ey."

Cass's voice message held intrigue. "I opened the safe. Call me when you can."

Bay hesitated. Should she bother with the unknown call, probably a message from a textbook company. Oh bother. First things first: listen to the message.

The agitated voice spoke in a staccato whisper, raising the hairs on the back of Bay's neck. It was Vivian.

"I don't know what may happen, but I know I can trust you to be determined and true. That's why I left you what I did. In your office. Please help."

"What did Vivian mean? She left something in my office?" Bay squinted at the phone screen, hoping it would reveal details.

She clicked on the unknown number then smacked the end call with her finger. "What am I thinking? That could connect to the kidnappers, or who knows." She needed to contact Downing. She looked at the date and time of the call. It was left the night of the poetry slam, before Vivian took the stage.

She had to think this through. She texted Downing to buy herself some time: *I have information about Vivian that might help.*

Bay pictured their meeting days earlier. Vivian, loaded down with totes and whatnot. She did seem twitchier than her normal scattered self. Anxious perhaps. But that was about the Dickinson poem, wasn't it?

'That's why I left you what I did.' The bag of treats from Sweet Cheeks bakery? That bag went promptly to the trash after Bay devoured its contents. She'd even checked for missed crumbs at the bottom of the bag.

Bay knelt on the floor to search under her desk and the visitor chairs on the opposite side. Nothing. Her pulse ramped up while her eyes scanned the room, looking for anything unusual.

Wait—the shelf on the wall by the door. Where did that candle come from? An ordinary ivory pillar on a wooden base taunted her memory. If Vivian put it there, Bay credited her uncanny stealthiness.

She strode around the desk to retrieve the candle. It resembled wax in texture, but the base had a switch which she turned on to reveal a realistic flicker. Hmm. She examined the base and exterior. A seam near the bottom of the candle revealed a tiny nub that looked like wax. Bay slid her fingernail around it and the candle snapped open. The inside was partially hollow, a hiding place. Bay pried her finger into the hollow and pulled out a rolled-up scroll. She unrolled it and squinted at the tiny, typed message and reached into her desk for her lighted magnifying glass, a necessary tool for grading poor handwriting.

If you're reading this, the worst has happened. In trying to make a difference, I believe I've mucked it all up. The poem. The letter. I should never have. I am a sponsor for her and others. Please find Daniela and protect her. If they found me, they will find her. She's too important. Call her. The last line was a phone number.

Bay assumed the number would connect her with the

Daniela in the note, but she was mistaken.

"Hello, is this Daniela? I'm calling on behalf of Vivian."

"Doctor Browning?"

"Yes."

"Oh God, so it's true? Someone has taken my sister," the voice rose on the other end.

"Vivian's your sister?"

"Yes. We shouldn't speak on the phone. Mine may be monitored for all I know. We need to meet."

Bay faltered. "Yes. Where? How can we make that happen?"

"I'll call you from another line." The connection cut out.

Within a couple of minutes, Bay picked up an unknown call.

"Hello?"

"Doctor Browning. This is Valeria Kibben, Vivian's sister. This line is secure. I'm using my husband's cell. I only use it for business calls. It helps me screen callers, for starters. A male voice greeting helps, you know. I'm sorry. Joel died months ago, but I kept his cell activated."

Bay followed along as best she could. "I'm sorry to hear about your husband."

"Indeed, it was a blessing. He'd been suffering with kidney disease for two long years. But thank you."

Silence. Should Bay wait for Vivian's sister or start asking questions?

"On to the matter at hand. My poor sister. Vivian's gotten herself into a tangle. She feared she may be in danger and told me if anything happened, I would hear from you." Valeria seemed to occupy the same worldly space as Vivian, not quite in step with the mainstream.

"Didn't the police call you?" Bay assumed the police would contact Vivian's family in a situation like this.

Valeria gasped. "Why yes, of course they did, but I hung up. It could be the real police or some thugs. But I was told I could trust you, Doctor."

"Bay, please. Call me Bay." Her forehead crinkled, trying to decide if this woman was savvy or scatterbrained. "But what if the kidnappers want a ransom? Wouldn't they call you?"

Valeria nodded without thinking. "I imagine so. Except that my stubborn sister wouldn't put me in danger, so she'd pretend there was nobody to call."

"I'm afraid I don't understand. What do the kidnappers want, if not money? They should have worked that out before they took her." Bay bit her tongue.

Valeria began muttering accompanied by mousey squeaks. "They're after a bigger prize. They want the location of a refugee Vivian brought to America."

"And who would know that information? Do you know?" Bay figured this could be the Daniela mentioned in the scroll.

"Not me. This is all quite overwhelming."

"Why did Vivian leave your number?" Bay's frustration sounded through the question.

"Please bear with me, Bay. We must puzzle this out. Vivian trusts us, and perhaps we are the only people in the world she trusts. I'm in Boston, but I can meet you in person soon. I must finish up a task my sister left for me. I'll call you again with the details." Before Bay could respond, Valeria was gone.

Bay swiped Downing's number immediately.

"Hey, I didn't expect to hear from you so soon. What's going on?" Downing's voice was strained, his usual tone when he was harried about a case.

"Plenty, I'm afraid. Vivian left a voicemail for me the night of the poetry slam. I think she knew someone was after her. There's more. She hid a note in my office with information about someone named Daniela. Vivian's sister said Daniela is a refugee Vivian sponsored and she's here somewhere."

"Whoa, slow down. I can't keep up. Can we meet at The Pig Squeal, go over this with dinner?"

"Honestly, I think I should come to the station and give you what I have, Downing." Bay's stomach knotted with worry, and eating wasn't a priority, despite the cop hangout's tempting dishes.

Vivian Rossi did not know where she was being kept. She remembered flying or was that her body, coming and going from consciousness? Her head hurt like mad, and her bound hands made sleep impossible. Time meant nothing. If she had paper and pen, she would write down things her captors said, that is, if her hands were not tied. Instead, she constructed letters in her mind.

Dear Miss Dickinson,

Pardon the intrusion, but I cannot lie here in the darkness as insomnia infiltrates my body and soul. You see, my worst fears are realized. I've been kidnapped by rebels, all because I used your poem to buy freedom for a young woman in danger. Ever since I found your lost poem, I've had no rest, as if your words about a coming storm unearthed some deep personal foreboding.

Now that I'm in captivity, I'm almost relieved. At least that part is over. Most of my treasured belongings are sitting at the coffee shop and I feel ill at ease without them. Time is my enemy now because I cannot imagine what comes next.

If Bay succeeds. If Valeria can assist. If Daniela remains safe. Has your life turned on the actions of others, too? And what if I escape? Perhaps that is the best course. Until next time. —Vivian ■

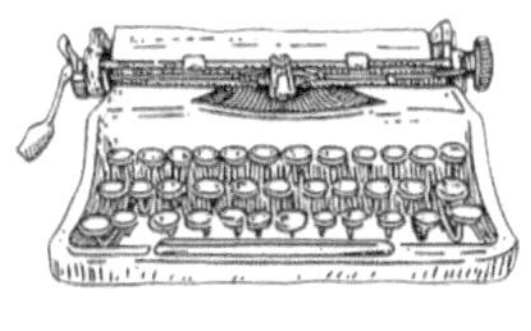

chapter 7

Inside the Totes

The September sky dimmed to a slate gray with sunset approaching when Bay entered the police station, which was empty except for the second shifters. She knew many of the officers after helping with two murder cases, besides casually dating the detective.

Downing stood at the end of the security desk, anticipating her arrival, and waved her into his office.

He closed the door, lowered the blinds, and gave Bay a fast kiss.

Bay dismissed the goose bumps. Every minute of delay meant more trauma for Vivian.

"Here's the voice message. When you finish listening, here's the note Vivian left for me." Bay set the note on Downing's desk and pressed play on the message.

Downing listened to it twice before he sent the recording to his office phone. After he read the note through a few times, he held his hands open, ready for Bay's revelations.

"I called the number Vivian left and reached her sister in Boston, Valeria. Last name Kibben. She's a widow. I wrote down the conversation. Here you go." Bay passed the note to Downing.

"From this note, I'd say Valeria seems a little strange, like Vivian. I'll call her." Downing added it to his list, which grew longer by the hour.

"Do you have any insights you want to share?" In the past, Downing would be entertained chatting about case clues with Bay, but not today. This case wasn't about a dead person, but someone alive, and he wanted it to stay that way.

"I wish I'd spent more time getting to know Vivian better. The fact she sponsored a refugee here? I wonder why and how that came about." Bay paused a moment.

"There's something off with the sister. Almost as if Valeria knew Vivian was kidnapped. It's possible the kidnappers already contacted her. I think she's hiding something." She pointed her finger to a spot on the note she transcribed. "See. She said she hung up on the police. Why would she do that?"

Downing ran a hand through his hair and tapped a cadence with one foot. The case was wearing him out already and it wasn't yet twenty-four hours old. When he spun his office chair around to face Bay, his expression was thoughtful.

"Bay, it seems the department needs your help again, if you agree to give it."

Bay fixed her gaze on the detective. She'd known the man less than a year, yet her services were requested on three police matters. *What kind of relationship was this?*

Bay shoved aside the anxiety of her fall semester workload

and thought of Vivian. "Devil's horns and hedgepigs! All right; I'll help." She enjoyed invoking her own brand of swear words.

Downing laughed and clasped her hands in his across the desk. "It's not dangerous, just tedious. We don't have the manpower here to give this case the attention it deserves. The interim police chief gave permission for you to go through Vivian's tote bags. I sold her on the idea because you're the most likely one to recognize if something's related to the kidnapping or not."

Bay was relieved. "I'm your glorified sorter and sifter. Lead the way, but you owe me dinner."

Downing walked Bay to the evidence room and signed out two large, covered boxes marked with Vivian's case information. "Thanks, Keene."

The officer in charge initialed the clipboard. "It has to be returned before my shift ends, Detective."

Downing set up Bay in his partner's office at a long table facing the window. He handed her a pair of gloves. "Set aside anything notable. Put the rest back in the bag you took it from, and keep the piles sorted per individual bag. I have to log the relevant items myself. I'll be next door."

"Where's Harris?" Bay suspected the two detectives had to divide the case load leads.

"He's chasing down possible witnesses and persons of interest in attendance last night. That's going to take a ton of time. I'm searching for Daniela and any connections to Vivian." The detective reviewed his checklist. "The getaway van, and the car Cass reported. Both are still MIA."

Bay arched an eyebrow and frowned. "You were chasing the van almost all the way to the airport. Where could it be?

Besides that, you don't seem surprised about Vivian being a sponsor for foreign students. What's up?"

Downing picked up both of her hands in his. "Off the record."

"Two things," he continued. "Your sister cracked the vic's safe. No music box, poems, or secret Emily Dickinson letters, but we found files of refugees being sponsored under Project Square One. Harris and I are reviewing them, trying to determine where these people are now." He kept his voice low and cocked one ear toward the hallway.

Bay smiled. "Cass told me we needed to talk. Her skills continue to surprise me."

"Two. I went out to the airstrip near Truax field. Jeff Johnson's got a plane there. He's been a pilot thirty years and is unofficially the hangar manager. With a warrant, we looked through the flight logs. A plane went out Friday night with four passengers and landed somewhere in Maine. Jeff said the handwriting belongs to a sleazeball named Cliff Marsden. Apparently, Marsden will fly anyone with enough cash anywhere, no questions asked. That's why the log didn't have names or an exact locale."

"Maine," Bay repeated. "Did you talk to Marsden?"

"Nope. His plane isn't there, so he's laying low or flying another customer. The log doesn't show him returning. Jeff is going to look at the traffic control report. Said he can get that faster than I can."

"Is that it?" Bay deflated in her seat. The information wasn't a lot to go on.

"Now you know why we need all the help we can get." Downing winked at her and shut Harris's office door.

Vivian's tote bags were easy to recognize. Bay saw her

schlepping them around multiple times. She started with the nautical print canvas bag, remembering it was left behind at the coffeehouse the night before. Bay noticed it tucked under the table near the stage when Harris interviewed her.

Bay pulled items out one at a time: a folder of notes about Emily Dickinson, including Vivian's script for the performance; Dickinson's biography with dog-eared pages; a wire-bound notebook with a pen clipped inside the spiral; a folded white button-down sweater; a partially filled box of hard candies; a medium-sized flashlight; a clear box holding an assortment of safety pins, push pins, paper clips, and rubber bands; a stick of deodorant; and a cell phone.

"Cell phone!" Bay cried out, bringing Downing to her door.

"What's going on? Found something?"

Bay held the cell phone aloft like a trophy. "Vivian's cell. She didn't have it in her purse."

Downing put on one glove and took it from Bay.

"Why do you look dismayed?" Bay considered the cell phone a big score.

"Look at this thing. It's ancient." Downing slid the cover aside to reveal an old-school keyboard." "I don't think it has internet." He pressed the buttons and scrutinized the screen. "Anyway, it's locked."

"I don't suppose you have an expert password hacker at your disposal." Bay doubted it.

"Right, fat chance. We use different technology to break into phones these days, Professor. Problem is, it won't work on this antique." Downing leaned over the table to log the cell phone and slid it into an evidence bag.

"As long as you're here, I don't see anything alarming. Can I put the rest of this stuff away?"

"We'll bag the sweater for DNA. The pen, too. You can return the rest." He held open a large zip lock bag for Bay to slide the sweater into since she wore two gloves. The pen went into a smaller bag. "Good work. Soldier on."

Three more tote bags to go. The satiny cat print bag contained a mixture of kitty treats and human snacks, along with jingling kitty balls and a catnip stuffed mouse, fish, and canary. Bay made a face. She didn't have an aversion to cats but believed in snack segregation.

A jumble of hard cover and paperback books occupied another canvas bag advertising the local library. The tote would humble most weight lifters and was probably kept in Vivian's car. Bay couldn't remember seeing the professor carrying it last time they met. Some of the books held bookmarks or pieces of scrap paper, and Bay spent the better part of an hour checking the marked pages for anything relevant to the case. Unless there was a cryptic code in the texts, she dismissed the idea, stood up, and stretched.

The woven fall-themed bag was a catch-all of lunch preparation items and personal care sundries. Old-fashioned embroidered handkerchiefs neatly folded inside plastic zip bags, hair gel, barrettes, and a curling brush were separated by a large daily planner, a divider of sorts. On the other side, restaurant sauce packets, salad dressing pouches, artificial sugar packs, and seasonings occupied a lidded container, and she discovered another timer—this one a whimsical mushroom with a cute face. Underneath, Bay pulled out a large, quilted potholder mitt with curiosity. Inside, she found three pairs of reading glasses in bright designs. She held up the colorful parrot ones and peered through to check the strength.

"Does this bag even have a bottom?" Bay asked aloud, pulling out the twin to the first potholder mitt. This mitt held a stack of ticket stubs looped with a rubber band and a brown bottle of medication. "How is Vivian managing without her medication?" Bay removed it to give to Downing.

She guzzled a long cool drink of water from her portable bottle, took a deep breath, and dove into the final bag, a souvenir tote from a national park. Bay paused to consider Vivian's life and psyche while viewing items best described as treasures a child might carry. A stuffed snowy owl, one eye hanging on by a thread, and a dolly wearing gingham pajamas with frayed ribbons testified in silence. A drawstring bag held crackle glass marbles in every color. A tin box decorated with painted fairies held crayons and an old maid card game. Two children's coloring books sat on the bottom. Bay fanned the pages of each in case something fell out. Empty. A plaid wool golf cap snuggled underneath the color books, exuding a grassy scent. Bay pulled it up by its bill to reshape it when out fell an aftershave bottle with a few drops inside. *That's where the earthy scent came from.* She tipped the bag upside down. A plastic circlet with a metal clip landed in front of her. The faded ink on the hospital bracelet read, Danielle Rossi.

Bay's emotions ran wild. Fishing through Vivian's bags was a personal intrusion. Once more, Bay opened the coloring book of circus delights, paging through it with dogged determination. There, tucked between the carousel horse and trapeze artist: a polaroid photo of a young woman holding a cherub-faced giggly child. She held the photo to the light. It must be an earlier version of Vivian. Vivian, who never spoke about a husband or a child, seemed to be missing both.

Bay wiped at tears she couldn't control and knocked on Downing's door.

"I'm all finished. I found a prescription that Vivian must need. And, come look at the contents of the last bag."

A shadow fell across his face. "Sure. Are you okay?" He followed Bay out the door.

Downing registered the child's toys with uncertainty. Bay handed him the polaroid. He studied it and took silent inventory of the toys again. Downing picked up the plastic bracelet and joined the two ends to reveal a tiny circle. He swallowed a lump of stomach acid. "Poor kid. Poor woman."

He shook his head and began placing the items with care into the tote bag. Bay helped him, tears escaping down her cheeks.

Downing closed the box after placing the evidence bags on top and gathered Bay into his arms. "Do you know if Vivian had a child?"

"No idea. But someone named Danielle meant a lot to her. And now she's protecting someone named Daniela. It's a lot to contemplate." Bay could have stayed that way longer, enclosed in Downing's arms, but there was too much to do.

He cleared his throat. "I'm going to walk this to Evidence. I'll put the bags we logged into a separate box and mark this one with a note that it was sorted. Thanks for doing this, Bay."

"Are we done for today?" Bay asked.

"For now. Let's grab dinner, Professor. We could both use some brain fuel and comfort food."

Bay agreed.

———————————

Dear Miss Dickinson,

Saturday is about over. Nothing happened all day, but it is important for me to keep track of the calendar. When nothing happens, time is an anchor, my head swims, and thoughts are swirling saucers on poles. The rebels speak Spanish, and my limited knowledge of French and Italian allow me to imagine I understand fragments. My head and body hurt from knocking around the van they tossed me in. I struggle to remember how far we traveled. I know we flew in a small plane, but I was blindfolded. Did you know that absence of one sense throws off all the others? I always heard losing one sense sharpens the rest, but that didn't happen to me. Maybe the bump on my head.

There are four of them. The one I beaned in the back of the head with an Italian syrup bottle is called Cerdo. He is at the bottom of the pecking order, and I almost feel sorry for him because he is often bullied. They do not speak to me except to threaten they will find Daniela and take her home. They enjoy arguing, and the noise hurts my noggin. I know why you sought seclusion—to think, because I cannot think all day long.

They offer water, which I drink each time because instinct wills it, almost as if that's all there is to hope—human instinct, I mean. It forces hope. You wrote a poem about hope, saying it perches in the soul and never stops at all. I say those words in my head sometimes when I think I may die, Miss Dickinson.

The men do not ask me where to find Daniela. I cannot comprehend why they took me, because to find her is all they want. And they must not, or I will have failed again. My own Danielle, my daughter. I was supposed to walk her to school that day. Not Joe. Both are gone. I vowed to be a better protector for Daniela. Until next time. —Vivian ∎

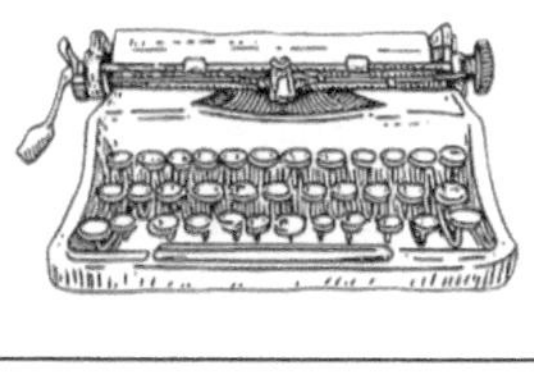

chapter 8

Bluebird and Breakfast

Cass returned to Spirit Gardens and brewed a tonic to reassemble herself. Between Vivian Rossi's kidnapping and muddling over Posey's riddle letter, Cass's mind could best be described as battered.

The house was empty, but Marva left a note saying she was taking tomorrow off and would be ready to roll up her sleeves Monday to get work done. Cass could hear Marva's scolding voice. The woman did not like unfinished business. Cass knew sooner or later she must complete the estate inventory for probate.

Now, however, she trotted to the Firehouse, Posey's name for her screened-in summer kitchen overlooking the greenhouse on one side and gardens on the other. Cass and Posey spent hours there drying herbs and flowers for teas and tinctures. Cass opened the floor-to-ceiling rustic cabinet where rows of wide-mouthed jars sat like an army of nurses ready to deliver medicinal magic.

Labeled alphabetically by their prime ingredients, Cass found the tincture to help restore harmony bearing the label: Rhodiola rosea, the root of a plant from the stonecrop family commonly found in succulent gardens. The jar she grabbed included valerian, a sleep aid. She poured six ounces into a pot and heated it on the propane burner, transferred it to a coffee mug, and carried it to the veranda.

She closed her eyes and rubbed a trigger point on her neck and breathed deeply until her breath sounded like the whooshing sea. She thought about the pilfered photo from Vivian's safe. She remembered meeting Marcel and Lisa Domingas when they visited Posey's greenhouse, and again, at her farewell service. Friends from Guatemala. Posey said her father knew Marcel's family, and Cass knew Lisa was pregnant after shaking her hand. How were they connected to Vivian, and what was Project Square One?

Cass opened her eyes, sipped the warm tincture, and reminded herself it was medicine and wasn't supposed to be tasty. She absorbed the view of the hydrangea bushes surrounding the perimeter of the Firehouse. Their serene blue blossoms were Posey's favorites, but in autumn, the lilac-blue clusters transformed to silvery-green, forecasting the season ahead. She sipped again, gazing further afield, past the trees lining the drive where she could see a light.

She knew the location might be Bluebird Hill and she wondered if Mrs. Adams was awake and alone. On impulse, Cass drained the tincture, made a sour face, and promenaded down the drive at a steady clip.

The nipping wind made her wrap the fisherman knit sweater tighter around her middle. She crossed the road in darkness and poked along the driveway to Bluebird Hill. The front of the house, bright pink by daylight, was a foreign fuchsia ombré, but one constant remained. Mrs. Adams sat reading in an oversized rocking chair silhouetted by the lamplight emanating through the picture window.

Cass stalled at the entrance, afraid to knock on the door. The tincture strengthened her resolve to lift the carved iron bluebird and let it fall against the door, producing a thunderous bang.

Cass saw Mrs. Adams jolt, then push aside the lace curtains to peer into the driveway. Cass let the bluebird knocker fall again, controlling the noise level. Mrs. Adams rose with the help of two canes, arriving at the door faster than Cass expected. She could see the woman trying to peer through the prism panels.

"Hello, Mrs. Adams," Cass called through the door to introduce herself. "I'm sorry to call without notice, but I saw your light on. I was Posey Hollingsworth's assistant, and I've been doing inventory at her home."

The carved door opened wide, revealing a sturdy round woman wearing a bright purple dressing gown, wielding the cane in her hand as if brandishing a sword. When she saw Cass in the entry light, she settled the cane by her side.

"You don't have to shout, you know. My ears work. See, I'm still using the original models." Mrs. Adams tucked her long hair back to reveal two petite ears without hearing aids.

Cass giggled, liking the woman straightaway. "Your canes suit you, or I should say, suit your house." Cass admired the carved bird handles atop each ornate cane, painted to resemble bluebirds.

Mrs. Adams chortled. "A birthday gift a few years ago from a dear friend."

"How nice to have such a thoughtful friend. I'm Cassandra Browning by the way."

Mrs. Adams shimmied a half turn to the inside. "Ah, she's dead though, poor dear." The abrupt proclamation jarred Cass. She hoped Mrs. Adams wasn't making a prediction.

"Are you coming in or what? We can't have tea unless you're going to make it." Mrs. Adams pointed with her cane. "Down the hall to the left. I assume you know how to find things in a kitchen."

Cass followed the brawny sprite inside, closed the door, and found the kitchen, decked out in candy pink appliances from the fifties. The black and white ceramic tile gleamed, and the bluebird accents brought memories of Mary Poppins.

The tea kettle was at home on the stove, so she added water and settled it to heat while she browsed the cupboards for tea. Mrs. Adams clearly imbibed, indicated by the cabinet above the stove holding sugar and honey along with an antique tea chest, adorned with hand-painted pink roses and violets. A second shelf offered assorted bone china cups, while two silver tea trays lay on the third shelf.

Mrs. Adams hollered from her chair in an unladylike fashion. "Are you finding everything?"

Cass stuck her head around the kitchen archway. "Yes. All good."

"There's cake in the icebox and cookies in the cupboard next to the tea."

Shortbreads in every flavor made up the inventory, but when Cass's hand hovered over the chocolate ones, the choice was made. Soon, Cass carried the tea service into the cozy parlor where Mrs. Adams sat, and returned to the kitchen for the tea chest.

"Oh yes. You brought the chocolate biscuits. They're the best. I'll have Lady Grey." She reached into the chest without difficulty. "And for you, the Dragon Oolong." Her bright eyes challenged Cass as she handed her the sachet.

Touché, Cass thought. There was more to Mrs. Adams than a lonely old lady.

"Now, suppose you tell me the reason for your visit. You've been working on the bluff for months and this is the first time we've met, yes?" Mrs. Adams perched the canes between her chair and the lamp table and leaned closer to study Cass.

"To be honest, I thought you were a recluse, a bit odd, always watching the world from a distance." Something about Mrs. Adams compelled Cass to be forthright.

"Ha!" The woman tilted her head to laugh, revealing straight pearly teeth amid gold-capped ones. Lovely plums for cheeks sprouted when she laughed. "I'll have you know I'm ninety-nine, Cassandra. Did you expect me to dance a jig up and down the road?"

Cass felt relaxed enough to smile. "I suppose not. My apologies. I heard about you from Janet when I visited her aunt Arlyss recently." Cass left out Janet's nursing position, a salute to Mrs. Adams's dignity. "Janet says you're a walking, talking history book where the bluff is concerned."

Mrs. Adams plucked two cookies from the tray, popped one in her mouth and seconds later, the second one. She held her hand under her lips to catch the fallout and raised her cup of tea.

"And what is it you'd like to know?" The bright eyes were warm and welcoming.

Where to begin, Cass thought. "Did you know the Hollingsworth housekeepers? Olga and Mrs. Frazer?"

"Context, my dear. Could you place them in a time period for me? I've been on this bluff most of my life." Mrs. Adams tucked into a third cookie.

Cass rewound pieces of her recent conversation with Malcolm Hunt and his former housekeeper, Arlyss, and found reference points to the summer Posey and Malcolm were seventeen; the summer Olga left, and Mrs. Frazer came.

Mrs. Adams reached under the writing table sitting beside her chair. Her fingers touched the spines of office binders while she squinted to read their labels. She drew out the correct one and opened it. "Nineteen ninety-one, I believe you said. Yes, well here I am with Mr. Adams. We were in our prime, see." She tossed her head back with a laugh. "Almost."

Cass saw photos of Mr. and Mrs. Adams at a garden party, a pool party, and a summer picnic. She recognized the picnic location.

"This picnic was at Spirit Gardens. I see Lionel and Ramona Hollingsworth in the group photo. I don't see Posey, though." Cass scrutinized the photos on the page.

"Hmm. The estate was called Bellflower Meadow in those days. Miss Posey and Mr. Hollingsworth changed the name, despite the seething objections of Mrs. H. I can't recall if Posey attended the picnic, but see, here is Mrs. Frazer with the other staff."

"It must be late in the season. Olga left mid-August." Cass recalled.

"Ah, the last party of summer, no doubt." Mrs. Adams appeared to absently turn pages in the binder and closed it with a snap. "That was a most topsy-turvy year. You see, Malcolm Hunt's parents did not attend the picnic, either."

"Is that unusual?" Cass asked.

"Everyone on the bluff socialized in kind. Unless someone was traveling or ill, that is. Mr. and Mrs. Hunt snubbed the Hollingsworths that summer. It was the talk of the bluff."

Cass warmed to the bluff history, anxious to learn. "What did people say?"

"Plenty, I imagine. It was all quite odd because everyone in our circle expected Malcolm and Posey would marry once they completed college. After the winter socials here, nobody saw the two of them together again. That autumn, Malcolm attended a private school near Chicago for his senior year."

Mrs. Adams looked wrung out from the conversation and collapsed into the chair cushion. "I believe I need a nap, Miss Cassandra. Do come visit again."

The next morning, Bay pulled her Land Rover into the porte-cochère and rapped on the front door at Spirit Gardens, breakfast in hand.

Cass answered, carrying a coffee mug and still wearing yesterday's clothes. "Hey Sister. What ya got there?" She eyed the large paper bag.

"A peace offering. I'm sorry I didn't get back to you last night, but I'll fill you in over breakfast from Morning Glory's." She twirled the bag around to show it off. Morning Glory's, a breakfast bistro on Windsor Street, offered upscale food and an atmosphere meant to impress.

Cass pointed down the expansive hall. "Let's eat in the kitchen nook. I'll make coffee."

Bay assessed her sister's appearance. Something kept her up all night. Cass wore an eager expression mixed with preoccupation. She needed to unload.

Cass turned from Bay's scrutiny to prepare a fresh pot of coffee while Bay drew out a broccoli quiche and apple Dutch baby from the bistro bag. "Any maple syrup around?"

Cass directed her gaze to the French door refrigerator. "In there, bottom shelf. Bring out the cream and butter, too."

The sisters tucked into food with satisfied sighs. Bay decided it was fair for Cass to go first. After all, she'd left Bay the message asking to talk.

"Tell me how you cracked Vivian's safe."

Cass added cream to her coffee and tapped the spoon against the rim. "Oh, I wish I could dazzle you with my skills, but it had an electronic lock, and I didn't have any gear with me." She stirred, took a sip, added another splash of cream, and sipped with approval.

"Luckily, I can read cats. Amherst. You know the green-eyed white kitty with curled ears? She wound herself around me in Vivian's bathroom. I couldn't ignore the fact she wanted to tell me something. The fancy charm on her collar is engraved with seven numbers, and that was the combination."

Bay clapped twice, eyes twinkling. "And you say you didn't use your skills? Nobody else would have figured that out. Downing told me about the files, and something called Project Square One, a group that helps refugees come to the U.S."

"Right. But look at this." Cass opened a folder she'd carried into the kitchen and slid the photograph across the table.

Bay examined the photo, recognized Vivian and Posey. Questions ran through her mind. "Did you find this in the safe?" Her brow darkened. "Cassandra, do the police know about this?"

"Relax a minute. I'll turn it over. I needed time to study it." Her finger moved over the faces in the photo. "These two are married. Marcel and Lisa Domingas. I met them last summer here. Posey's father and Marcel's father knew each other in Guatemala, and Posey recommended Marcel for a post at UW-Madison."

"So, you'll reach out to them. What about this woman?"

"She might be one of the refugees Square One sponsored to America. And yes, I'm dropping by Marcel's office tomorrow."

"Good plan. My turn." Bay cleaned the remnants of syrup from her plate with one final sweep of her fork. "Maple syrup is the best."

Cass vibrated in her chair. "I knew you were holding onto something major when you walked in the door, so out with it."

Bay told the tale of Vivian's voicemail followed by finding the candle in her office with the rolled-up message. "I called the number, but it led to Vivian's sister in Boston, not to Daniela."

"Daniela might be this woman in the photo." Cass allowed her fingers to rest on the woman's face. "There is something familiar about her, as if she's near but out of reach."

"What's your take on the sister?" Cass asked.

"Odd. But knowing Vivian—it could be a family trait."

Cass reached across the table to play at slapping Bay's arm. "You mean like us, huh?"

"Us, odd? I have no idea what you could mean by that." Bay

smiled and perused the photo a second time. "I think we're missing something important, Cass. Who took this photo? If we could find that out, it might help in finding Daniela and Vivian."

Cass agreed. "I hope Marcel Domingas can answer that tomorrow. Meanwhile, are you up for another expedition on Lilac Lane?" Cass held up an antique key that matched the one Bay used to open Vivian's door.

Bay frowned at the sparkle in her sister's eyes. Did she need to worry that Cass was returning to her old ways?

"Don't look at me like that. I found it in Vivian's bedroom drawer while I was there. Right under Officer Clark's nose."

Bay parked the Land Rover on Dogwood Court, a quiet side street near Vivian's home. The sisters donned black clothes they found in Posey's closet and tucked their hair into baseball caps with the bills pulled low over their foreheads.

They skipped the front porch where the police padlocked the door and skirted around the side, avoiding the security camera, to the rear door. Rounding the south corner, Cass glimpsed a young man walking down the steps.

"Hey!" Cass shouted, running at the figure.

Meanwhile, Bay ran around the house in time to collide head-on with the guy and knock him off his feet.

The winded man squinted into the sunshine as he looked up at the women from the grass. "Why did you do that?" He spoke with an accent.

Cass shushed Bay to protect her identity in case the intruder was a Flourish student. "What are you doing here?" Cass used her authoritative voice.

"I'm sorry. See." The man held up a key that appeared to match Vivian's keys. "I feed her cats when she's gone."

Cass folded her arms, unconvinced, while Bay gave the man a hand to pull him up.

"Wait. You performed at the poetry slam Friday night." Bay recognized the handsome young man that made Aria's heart race.

"The Robert Frost poem," Cass said, remembering him, too.

"Yes, that's me. Joaquín. And you ladies are?" The charming man bowed, a coy look on his face.

Bay straightened her shoulders and held a defensive stance. "No, you first, young man. How do you know Professor Rossi?"

Joaquín relaxed and brushed off his backside. "I live just there." He pointed to a large house across the street. Bay knew it was one of the three-story monsters converted into student flats years ago.

"I see. How do you know Professor Rossi?" Bay repeated.

"She helps people like me. Here from other countries. I cut her lawn, shovel snow, and keep an eye on her house. I see her car is gone, and I hear the cats mewing, so I come to feed them."

The sisters exchanged looks. Perhaps Joaquín knows something helpful.

"And you don't know where the professor is? Did she contact you?" Bay continued the interrogation.

He shrugged. "No, but that's not unusual. She tells me to keep watching her place at the poetry slam Friday."

"Did you see anything suspicious Friday night?"

"No, but I don't look for anything. What is going on? Why are police hanging around?" Joaquín's concern seemed genuine.

Again, the sisters exchanged looks. What should they tell him?

Bay lay her hand on Cassandra's arm, stopping her from saying whatever she planned to share. "We're not sure what's going on, but we're worried about the professor. That's why we came here. To look around. Do you know anyone named Daniela?"

Joaquín's sharp intake of breath and tormented expression indicated he did, yet he shook his head with fervor.

Cass stepped forward and pushed on. "We know she's a refugee, but we're worried she's in danger. We want to protect her. Please help us."

But Joaquín's fear took center stage. He wiped sweat from his forehead with his palm, composed himself, and pasted on a false smile. "No, I cannot help. I don't know her." ■

chapter 9

Stirring Up Spirits

After the dustup in Vivian's yard, Bay and Cass parted ways.

"Sorry, I need to change for interviews at Flourish. If the panel agrees, the college should be able to hire someone soon to take the theater position." Bay cast a longing look at Vivian's house, anxious about what else the sisters might discover.

"I suppose I shouldn't go in alone," Cass groaned.

"Nope, definitely not," Bay answered before Cass could argue.

"When are you talking to Aria about Joaquín?" A sly smile played on Cass's face.

"Mind reader," Bay mumbled. "Tomorrow. The dry cleaner is closed today."

A restless Cassandra busied herself in Posey's herb garden. The first frost of autumn would claim the greens soon, so Cass harvested what she could in small baskets, loaded them into the garden wagon, and wheeled them to the summer kitchen.

Her mind wandered as she pulled apart thyme branches

and laid them on trays to dry. The savory fragrance reminded her of crafting tinctures with Posey, and she wished she could conjure her presence to work beside her.

A single tear dripped down Cass's cheek. The next best thing would be making some tinctures with the herbs the two dried after the early summer pickings. Many of Posey's customers asked about mixtures for allergies, especially with autumn molds, mildews, and late-blooming ragweed giving them grief.

From memory, Cass gathered gill-over-the-ground, peppermint, elderflower, goldenrod, violet, and nettle. Although gill-over-the-ground, commonly known as creeping Charlie, was a pain in the rear for gardeners, the ivy plant offered relief for sinus headaches.

Cass opened the bottom cabinet where she kept Posey's recipe book and began turning pages to the allergy section. When she landed on the Autumn Ease recipe, wispy rays of sunlight began dancing around the page like fireflies. Cass blinked, certain the light played tricks on her.

She took a breath, her eyes trained on the beads of light flitting about the page. Maybe the light would land on words meant for Cass. Her gaze grew intense. In a sudden sizzle of light, a sharp breeze lifted several pages of the recipe book, and a note card fluttered to the tiles near Cass's feet.

She scooped up the card and settled it on the counter. The words summoned her attention.

Persuade Emma to ride the gray ghost on the wind to the Abbey. Meet her under the giving tree where the mangoes grew before cholera. The Three Sisters follow the owls where the moon wanes to find the victor of pain and valor.

Cass read the card over and over until the riddle melded into a nursery rhyme. Then the verse tilted and seemed to break apart while the cadence shifted and each word floated around her brain, elusive gnats she couldn't corral.

She forced her eyes away from the card and grew dizzy in the sunlight, the squiggling glowworms followed her to the tiles where she landed on her bottom. The card sailed into her lap to mock her.

Cass studied the bottom border following the script. The hand drawn scrollwork in ink featured evergreen boughs, pine cones, and a raven with a coin in its beak. The raven captivated Cass from its gleaming eye to its leathery claws gripping an arrow pointing downward.

Cass jolted from sleep, sat up, and rubbed her temples. The afternoon sun was still bright; its beams bounced around the Firehouse as if no time had passed. Note card in hand, Cass stood up, feeling refreshed. The time on her phone showed she'd taken herbs from the cabinet only minutes ago.

She wasn't about to fall under the spell of the card again, so she stuffed it in her apron pocket and turned to the tincture recipe for something useful to focus upon. She measured spring water kept in the refrigerator into a row of opaque amber bottles, filling them partway to anchor the herbs she would add next.

As she finished topping the herbs off with a high-proof alcohol, her cell phone rang. Gretchen Lange was working on a Sunday.

"Cassandra. I got your message about inventory taking longer than expected. The court intends to schedule the estate hearing in December. Let's see, I'll need to file the inventory no later than November fifteenth." The attorney's crisp voice was all business.

"Thanks for letting me know. I work better with a deadline."

"Your message said you had additional questions?" Gretchen was drumming her fingers, or a pen perhaps, on a desk.

Cass paused to consider. Gretchen had caught her off guard. "Yes. You know Posey was famous for her social gatherings. I wonder if I could host one here in October."

"What exactly is the occasion?" Gretchen asked.

"A one-hundredth birthday party for Abigail Adams." Cass smiled to herself, thinking about her conversation with Mrs. Adams of Bluebird Hill.

"That old bird across the way is going to be one hundred?" She hesitated. "I don't see why not. The estate left funds to continue operating. I guess a birthday party fits the definition of normal expenses. Knock yourself out—within reason."

"Of course. Marva will be thrilled. She's been bored to tears. Thank you," Cass said.

"You mentioned security. I don't care if you're staying on the property, Cassandra. In fact, it's not a bad idea. I've authorized a security company to work nights starting Monday." Gretchen signed off.

The call with Gretchen whisked away the remainder of the headache caused by the animated note card and short blackout. Cass whistled a tune, set new herbs to dry on trays, and made another batch of allergy tincture. She made the executive decision to email Posey's customer list to tell them the apothecary was back in business. Inside the apron pocket, the note card radiated heat.

At Flourish College, Bay thumbed through the theater candidates' curriculum vitaes to prepare for round two of interviews. Occupied with Vivian's predicament, Bay wanted to get the interviews wrapped and hoped the committee could agree on which candidate to hire.

A short knock on the door and Stasia, the assistant dean, entered with a whoosh and collapsed into the chair by Bay's desk.

"What's wrong, Stasia?" Bay steeled herself for bad news.

"You mean besides needing to hire a theater professor while we're short one English professor? Isn't that enough?" Stasia removed her eyeglasses and wiped them with the sleeve of her dress, a classy cranberry, white, and black patterned V-neck wrap that made the short woman look taller.

"Has Vivian's kidnapping gone public?" Bay knew that would turn Stasia's crank another notch.

"Ach, no. Don't say it!" Stasia spit into the air, a habit she practiced to prevent bad luck.

"It's only a matter of time, Stasia." Bay hid her repulsion at the flying spit. "The most pressing matter is Thursday." Flourish was on a fall conference break for three days.

"What should we do about Vivian's classes? I'm happy to fill in where it fits my schedule, and I can talk to my department staff, with your permission."

Stasia reached over to pat Bay's hand and clicked her tongue in a soothing manner. "Nothing to worry about. I called the university, and they have a list of adjuncts who can help us out. I already lined up two. They're coming in Monday. I'd like you to be here to meet them."

Bay might have known Stasia would be successful lining up

teachers. Her connections went beyond Prairie Ridge. She was the central figure of a huge Greek family that sprouted new members on the daily. Relatives of both the immediate and shirttail variety constantly relocated to the area, where Stasia helped them settle and succeed. Of course, their success relied on Stasia's urging the Flourish staff patronize their businesses.

Furthermore, Stasia spent the past thirty years in Madison and Prairie Ridge, so she logged plenty of encounters thanks to her expressive nature and, of course, all her relatives.

"Just say when. I'll be here." Bay noticed the time. "We should head to the conference room."

Following the interviews, the panel decided to meet the next afternoon to discuss their choices. Bay slid the candidate folders into her brief bag. Besides reviewing them, she wanted to share their photos with Cassandra. She knew her sister would sniff out any trouble and give her clarity to make a sound choice.

Professor Obasi's folder glared at Bay. Fiddlesticks, she was supposed to talk to Downing about Obasi's niece. She dropped the folder and rang the detective.

"How's my favorite professor today?" Downing seemed cheerful.

"Finishing theater professor interviews. I need a favor." Bay bit her bottom lip, realizing how abrupt her greeting sounded. "I'm sorry, Bryce. There's a lot to sort out here with Vivian's disappearance. Any news?"

Downing exhaled. "Only that I can't reach Vivian's sister, Valeria. We've got Boston's finest looking for her." He didn't try to hide his frustration. "What's the favor?"

Bay hesitated. Now wasn't a good time. "I interviewed a

Doctor Obasi from Loyola, via Nigeria. He's looking for his niece, Aneka. She's a student at UW-Madison, but he doesn't have her contact info. He hoped to speak to Vivian because she supposedly helped Aneka come to the U.S. from Nigeria."

"What? I'm glad you told me. If we can find the niece, she may shed some light on Vivian's activities. It could help the case." Downing perked up. "And yeah, I can share her address with this Obasi guy if the niece consents."

"Thank you, Detective." Her voice warmed. "Let's carve out some time for each other soon."

"I'd like that, Professor. My boat's itching to get into the water before she goes into winter storage. I've got a spot with your name on it."

Cassandra was waiting at the entrance when Bay rolled up to Spirit Gardens, brief bag in hand. She hadn't thought about dinner, but her rumbling stomach reminded her the berries and yogurt she had before the interview had no staying power.

Cass squeezed her around the neck. "I hope you're hungry. Marva was bored."

That could mean only one thing—Marva had cooked up something delicious.

"You're singing my song. I'm starving." Bay trotted beside her sister to the atrium, a garden dining room near the kitchen.

The table was set with purple asters and golden mums, a beautiful contrast to Posey's sable enamel plates. Cass must be ready for Halloween early. The tureen in the center resembled a cauldron, but its steamy scent smelled homey.

"Marva made pork stew and garlic knots." Cass ladled the savory stew with chunks of carrots, potatoes, and cabbage into pottery crocks and slid garlic knots onto their plates.

Bay inhaled the steam rising from the crock, catching a whiff of thyme and autumn savory. She eyed the ceramic salad bowl filled with leafy greens, roasted squash slices, and goat cheese, dressed with a cider vinaigrette, and helped herself.

"Delicious," she murmured between bites.

"Save room for apple cranberry cobbler. Warm from the oven. Marva keeps her weekly shopping routine at the farmer's market in Madison, as if she's still cooking for Posey and her guests." Cass wished she could return to summer before everything changed, too. She loved sharing a meal with Bay and missed their normal dinner routine. Cass's preoccupation with Posey's secrets took a toll. She needed sleep for starters, and living between Bay's apartment and Spirit Gardens left her unsettled.

"I miss our dinners together," Bay broke into her thoughts.

"And you doubt your skills. I was just thinking that very thing." Cass winked.

"I wasn't reading your mind, Cass." Bay admonished her. She knew they both had their talents, but the Charming gift of extra sensory perception that carried over to both Cass and their half sister, Diana, skipped over Bay. Their mother, Penelope Charming, and her sister, Venus, practiced their special skills without apology. At least, that's how Bay remembered the short time she had with her mother, who died when Bay was a child.

Cass grabbed Bay's hand, startling her to the present. "I didn't mean anything bad by it, but you're not aware of how in tune you are sometimes. Plus, your photographic memory is a gift all its own." She nodded toward the brief bag. "Did you bring something to show me?"

Bay stood up and raised the brief bag with the interview folders inside. "I did. I'd like to pick your brain. But let's clean this up and go somewhere else where we can spread out papers."

The sisters wheeled the serving cart of leftovers and dirty dishes to the kitchen, loaded the fancy dishwasher, and placed food containers in the gleaming commercial refrigerator.

Bay patted the fridge door like a trusted friend. "It's sad to see this well-equipped kitchen not being used for meetings and parties. No wonder Marva's bored."

Cass gasped in excitement. "I didn't tell you, but I talked to Gretchen Lange, and she said Spirit Gardens could continue to operate as normal. She approved us to host a birthday party for Abigail Adams." Cass clapped, but the news was lost on Bay.

"Abigail Adams?"

"She's an elderly woman who lives at Bluebird Hill, the estate across the way. She's turning one hundred in October."

Bay's puzzled expression remained.

"I made friends with her recently. She's a hoot, a historian about the Bluff Birds, and sharp as an ice pick. Everyone knows her and she deserves a party. It's a worthwhile endeavor. Posey would have wanted it, and Marva needs it." Cass finished without offering specifics, but Bay noticed her mysterious expression.

"There's more to it. Did Abigail Adams tell you things about Posey?"

"She did, and the next time I visit with her, I'll dig deeper. Of course, she knew Posey's parents. She gushed about Lionel, and I could tell she respected the man. Apparently, he offered free services to anyone who couldn't afford an eye doctor, and I suppose that's why he took all those mission trips to Central America."

"What did she have to say about Posey's mother?"

Cass furrowed her brow and frowned. "Every time I learn something new about Ramona Hollingsworth, it troubles me. I know she and Posey had a complicated relationship, but I don't know why. Abigail Adams called Ramona a cobra."

"How charming."

"I talked to Malcolm Hunt's childhood housekeeper, Arlyss."

Bay's brows shot upward like spikes, interrupting Cass, who waved a hand dismissively.

"Long story," Cass continued, "but Arlyss told me Ramona was a hard woman. And Marva said Ramona used to help orphans find work on the bluff. You know, manual labor jobs, and sometimes field work on the area farms, too. She said Posey didn't approve, considered it exploiting the misfortune of the orphans."

"How is any of this helping you find whatever it is Posey is hiding in this house?"

Cass shrugged, deflated. "It's a feeling I have. Everything's connected." She shared a tidbit of what she'd learned from Abigail Adams and Arlyss the housekeeper, but the time wasn't right to add more.

"Changing the subject: what's the news on Vivian?"

Bay's brooding continued. "More to worry about, I'd say. Vivian's sister is missing, and the Boston police are looking for her. Nobody has heard about a ransom, so what do the kidnappers want with Vivian?" Bay worried about Vivian's life and strength. She wasn't exactly fragile, but Bay couldn't imagine the thinner older woman would hold up for long in the hands of the thugs who took her. The memory of the automatic rifles shooting from the van windows haunted her.

"Maybe the reason is connected to her sister. There are a lot of unanswered questions." Cass suggested, turning from Bay's scrutiny.

"Cass, the detectives need that photo. It might be important."

Cass pouted. "I know. I promise I'll give it to the cops after I talk to Marcel Domingas tomorrow."

"Let's go to Posey's study. Show me what you brought."

Posey's antique rosewood desk gleamed in the study, a room with floor to ceiling windows offering views of the rose garden and glorious sunsets.

Bay laid out the photos of the theater candidates like a police lineup. She tucked the closed folders with their information behind the photos so Cass could only get impressions from their appearance.

Cass pulled the drapes to darken the room, shutting out the remnants of sunlight before it painted the sky. She held her hands above each photo, closed her eyes, and practiced yoga breathing. She opened her eyes, closed them again, and made another pass over each photo.

She turned on the floor lamp, shining bright light onto the desktop, and opened the drapes to reveal a sky awash in orange, yellow, and red.

"Is it my imagination, or do the Bluff Birds get better sunsets than the simple folks?" Bay laughed.

"Any words of wisdom about them?" Bay pointed to the spread on the desk.

Cass pointed to Ziki Obasi. "This man is brilliant, but ambitious. He might want more than he deserves. I would question his motives for coming to Flourish."

Bay was anxious to hear more.

"I'm not getting much from these three, just average, run-of-the-mill vibes. That could mean they're solid candidates and honest ones, too," Cass said.

"And number five?" Bay held her breath in anticipation of Cass's verdict.

Cass swallowed. "There is strong energy coming from this one."

"Positive or negative?"

"Positive, vibrant. But there's something strange. Something is familiar about her. I can't explain it. Is she local?"

Bay grinned. "Almost. Her name is Angelica Trevino. Her father was a history professor here before she was born. He moved years ago, and he's passed away since, but Angelica says she was drawn to the position when she saw it listed."

"Interesting. And what do you think of her?"

"She's my number one choice. Her answers to our questions fit the college's vibe and mission. She has a lot of fresh techniques to offer, and she's qualified. She's been teaching at a college in rural Iowa and wants to move closer to her mother, who returned to the area after her father died."

"You have my blessing if it carries any weight. Now you need to convince the interview panel."

"I don't think I can sway them if she's not the top pick. I wasn't supposed to be on the panel, and the theater profs will have the most say." Bay swept the photos back into their folders, thinking about tomorrow's meeting. "Thank you for confirming my impressions though."

Cass nudged her sister. "Let me show you what I've been working on today." The two headed, hand in hand, to the

Firehouse where Cass showed off several rows of clear and colored glass bottles, ripening tinctures inside.

"It's great to see you concocting in the kitchen again, Cassandra." Bay hugged her and Cass laid her head on Bay's shoulder, happy for the comfort.

Dear Miss Dickinson,

I have company now. One of my captors left last night and brought my sister Valeria here. My tears came fast when I saw her. She was one of the "ifs" I hoped for, except she's caught, too, and we cannot speak to each other.

Two men leave to look for Daniela. Two men stay to guard us. They are getting bored already. That is good.

We are being kept in a room where supplies are stored. The scent of pine and sawed lumber is pleasant at least. But you know what I wish for? I would like to take a bath. And I miss my cats. My American Curl is a pure white kitty named Amherst. I thought you'd like that, although you consider cats scroungy vermin.

I know why they have my sister. The men sat Valeria at a table with her laptop, its screen locked onto an official government site. Valeria is a document expert who can create new identities for the men. The man called Ruiz trained his gun on both of us and said she must do this, or they will kill me. Now I know why I was taken.

Have you ever felt useless, Miss Emily? Some of your writing suggests you have. You wonder at your purpose and conventions that dictate you should marry to be useful. You wonder about the afterlife. Now, I do, too.

Until next time. —Vivian ▪

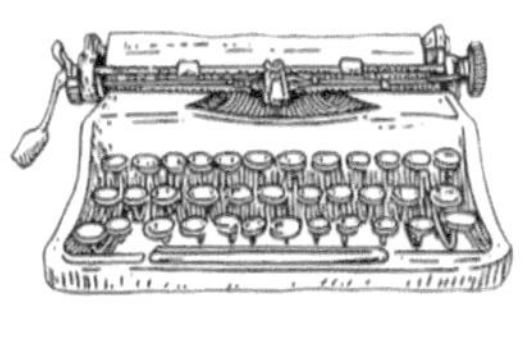

chapter 10

Manic Monday

A cold rain shower slashed through Cassandra's overcoat as she dodged puddles making her way to the double doors of Moore Hall on the UW-Madison campus. The ivy covering the brick façade splatted raindrops atop Cass's hood while she shook out her umbrella before entering the hallway.

Her shoes and bottom of her jeans were dripping after the mile-long hike from the Johnson ramp to Linden Drive, but since Marcel Domingas sounded pleased to hear from her, she hoped the trip was worth the soaking.

Cass stopped in the restroom, removed her raincoat, and dried her face with a paper towel. She ran a comb through her damp hair and unstrapped the satchel she'd hung inside her coat. It remained blessedly dry, and she patted it, thinking about its contents from Vivian Rossi's safe.

She rode the elevator to Marcel's fourth floor office and found the tiny alcove, its door opened in greeting. Marcel rose to say hello, clasping Cass's hands in his and indicating a cushioned chair by his desk.

"Nice to see you, Cassandra. The last time was a sad occasion," Marcel said, remembering Posey's memorial service.

"Yes, it certainly was. I miss Posey." Cass conveyed her sorrow in a few words.

Marcel sat hunched over in his office chair, elbows propped on his legs, hands folded. "You said you wanted to show me something."

Cass opened the satchel and pulled out the manilla file containing the photo and snapshots of the front-page documents from Vivian's stack in the Project Square One folder. She handed the photo to Marcel, who straightened in his seat.

"Where did you get this?" Marcel's tone was a gruff whisper.

"From Vivian Rossi. What is Project Square One?"

Marcel stood up and closed the office door. "Cassandra, forgive me. You must be cold from the rain. Let me get you some tea." Marcel removed a glass carafe from a hot plate beside the window and grabbed a mug from the shelf below.

He opened a desk drawer and pulled out a container. "English breakfast, hibiscus, or yerba mate?"

"English breakfast, please." Cass thanked Marcel when he handed over the hot mug, which felt good on her cold fingers. She waited for him to speak.

"Square One is a branch of Posey's orphan foundation operations in Central and South America. Except that Square One helps refugees who seek an education in the U.S. Most come from Central and South America, but some are from Africa, too." Marcel allowed his tea bag to drain over his mug before he squeezed it between his fingers.

"The refugees are here legally?" Cass asked.

"Yes. They must have government forms and approval to come, but they need sponsors here to help them find lodging and give financial support. Didn't Vivian tell you all this?"

Cass faltered and decided to move on without answering. "Is this woman on the end one of your refugees?" Cass indicated the brunette on the end who dressed like any American college student might.

Marcel sipped tea with shaking hands. "She is, yes. But why didn't you ask Vivian this? Vivian is Daniela's sponsor."

Ah, the mysterious Daniela. Here we go. Cass chose her words carefully. "Vivian's out of town, and we need to find Daniela."

Marcel puckered his lips and blew. "She's under protection. I can't tell you where." He stared into the steaming mug, his face a mixture of brooding, uncertainty, and fear.

"Why is Daniela being protected?" Cass took the direct route, hoping for the best.

Marcel was smart. It wouldn't take long for him to realize things didn't add up. He massaged his temple with his fingers in response.

Cass figured she might have another chance. "Marcel, who took this photo?"

He looked up from the mug, bewildered. "What? It is a woman named…" He rubbed his knuckles against his chin. "Marian, I think. She files the legal paperwork for the foundation."

Cass practically launched from her chair scattering the file's contents across the floor. "Miriam Greggs from the Lange Corporation?"

"Yes. Miriam, not Marian." Marcel's relief turned to worry. "If Vivian is out of town, why do you have her papers? Those papers." He stared at the documents scattered on the floor. Based on the mug shot type photos on the front pages, Cass guessed they were refugees sponsored by Square One.

She swallowed hard and tried to conjure a story. "No, I misspoke. These are from Posey's file cabinet, but she can't shed any light and neither can Vivian, so I came to you for some answers. Marcel, I'm working for Posey's estate under the instruction of Attorney Gretchen Lange. It's important for me to sort out her foundation documents before probate court finalizes the estate. So, can you tell me if these three refugees are in the U.S. and who is sponsoring them?"

Marcel was perplexed trying to follow the story line and details. He picked up the three documents, looked at the faces, and read their identifying background. "This is Aaron from Colombia. Posey sponsored him and he's been here about a year. After Posey passed, Lisa and I took over his sponsorship. He's a Madison College student and we're keeping tabs on him."

Although Cass reviewed the photos before meeting Marcel, she studied the photo again, but she didn't recall seeing Aaron at the poetry slam Friday night.

"This is Nacio from Guatemala City. Lisa and I sponsored him first. He's finishing his nursing degree at Edgewood with help from Saint Raphael's congregation. We're quite proud of Nacio."

Cass didn't recognize Nacio either. She was impressed with the Domingases' dedication and compassion. "It must be expensive to sponsor two refugees, especially with your growing family." Lisa was expecting their first child.

Marcel's glowing smile said it all. "Lisa and I are excited to welcome our baby, but Square One matters to us, too. With Posey gone, there are fewer of us sponsoring students. Do you think the court will allow the estate to keep funding the foundation?"

Cass hoped so, but she didn't know anything about estate finances or what was included in Posey's will. "Knowing Posey, I can't imagine she would leave the foundation without a means to continue."

Cass looked at the headshot on the third document that Marcel absently returned to her without comment. "What do you know about this person?" She wished it was Daniela because she'd at least have some background about the mystery woman under Vivian's protection.

"I don't know her. Perhaps she came here before Lisa and I were part of Square One. You could ask Miriam or wait for Vivian to return."

Cass pressed on. "Besides you two, Posey, and Vivian, who else volunteered for Square One?" She reasoned others were part of the group.

"A big man. I'm bad with names. That's why I work with plants." Marcel looked sheepish. "If I think of it, I'll call you. Lisa may remember. We just met one time."

Cass thanked Marcel. "The tea was what the doctor ordered, and I appreciate you telling me what you could. Please call if you think of anything, and I'll ask the attorney about the foundation's finances. I know the foundation was Posey's pride and joy." She clasped Marcel's hand with conviction.

Cass returned to the parking ramp umbrella free, but the heavy air wrapped the area like a thick wet blanket. She anticipated turning in the photo to Downing and spent a few minutes plotting her speech about holding onto it.

First, however, Cass would keep another appointment downtown where she must concentrate on her acting and pickpocketing skills to succeed. Telling herself the deed was on Posey's behalf, she entered the IRS office and changed clothes in the lobby restroom.

Cass emerged dressed in a business jacket, skirt, and pumps wearing bright red plastic eyeglasses and a platinum blond wig styled in a sleek chignon. She introduced herself to IRS agent Wilson as a social worker assisting Monica Frazer with her tax mess.

"I appreciate you meeting with me, Agent Wilson. Ms. Frazer is anxious to settle her accounts before, well you know…" Cass trailed off on purpose.

Wilson's desk was a haphazard mess of piled folders crisscrossed every which way, three squatting coffee mugs, each partially filled with brew, and a framed photo of a toy poodle. Cass's job was going to be easy.

She learned enough about the Hollingsworths' former housekeeper, Monica, to con Wilson into disclosing additional details.

Wilson looked at Cass over the top of his reading glasses. "Settle her accounts? Ms. Frazer's case is currently under review since she provided the documentation we asked for. You know, a list of assets and bank statements."

Cass flashed a business smile. "Yes, of course. I'm here to collect copies of her documents. I faxed you Ms. Frazer's authorization." Cass indicated the humming dinosaur on the table in the adjoining room, visible thanks to the glass walls between cubicles.

Wilson reddened as he searched the stacks on his desk. "It's here somewhere Ms. Garbo. Ha. Garbo, like the silent film star?"

"Naturally. No relation. My father liked the name Greta." Cass remained cool.

"Let me print Ms. Frazer's statement, inventory, and financials." Wilson sent the documents to the mammoth printer towering over the fax machine.

"Let me see here. Oh yes, Ms. Frazer agreed to make payments after our initial assessment. We didn't proceed with a payment plan, however, since we placed her file into further review. Honestly, between you and me, Ms. Garbo, it'll be another two to three years before we get to the filling in this cake." Wilson chuckled as if the IRS's lack of speed was a joke.

"I see. As I said, she's most anxious to finalize any business she has left while she's able. I appreciate your cooperation in providing the documents in light of my client's condition."

Wilson's head snapped up from the computer screen. "Oh, I see. Excuse me while I collect them."

Cass watched Wilson through the glass window. He retrieved the papers and disappeared down the hallway.

Memories flashed in Cass's head while her blood pressure pounded in her ears, making her a bit dizzy. Was she about to get caught? She considered fleeing before Wilson returned with management or security. Instead, she closed her eyes, counted five breaths, then stood up to smooth her skirt.

Wilson turned the door handle. He was alone.

"Oh, I'm sorry. Did you need to use the restroom?" He noticed she was standing.

"I have another appointment, Agent Wilson. I was organizing my things."

Wilson handed her the printouts. "To be clear, Ms. Frazer's income reporting errors amount to her owing the government less than three thousand dollars, which would not pass on to her heirs, unless she's married." Wilson's face held a catlike smile. The man was pleased with himself for sharing information that would save Ms. Frazer from ever paying her debt.

"How noble of you to tell me that. You're giving the blood thirsty IRS a bad name." Cass snapped the papers against her leg and hurried out the door. She patted her skirt pocket where she tucked Agent Wilson's badge. It had been easy, since he'd left it unattended on his desk.

Cass reviewed Monica Frazer's information, including two prior and one current address, assets which were suitable for a rummage sale, and bank statements showing minimal income from sporadic part-time jobs paying minimum wage.

"Let's see. Posey fired Monica twenty years ago, making her fifty-seven. No spouse listed on her statements, so how is she able to afford to live in Madison?" Cass intended to find out soon.

After stashing her wig, red glasses, and business outfit, Greta Garbo was once again Cassandra Browning, driving down East Washington Avenue, the granite dome of the Capitol with its gilded statue atop, gleaming in her rear-view mirror.

She sighed in exhaustion from the morning of playing questioner with Marcel Domingas and conning the IRS agent. Once she sat in Detective Downing's office, she was too tired to make up any stories.

"Hi, Detective. I stopped by to give you this." She passed him the photo from Vivian's safe.

"What's this?" Downing squinted at the faces in the photo. "I see Vivian Rossi and Posey, but what am I looking at?"

Cass took a turn around the office and stared at Downing's framed credentials. "I took it from Vivian's house. It slipped out of the Square One folder when I pulled it out." She turned around and moved closer to him.

"This person on the end there—that's Daniela. Before you ask, all I know is that she is living under someone's protection."

A tick pulsed in Downing's jaw. "And you know this because…"

Cass pointed to Marcel in the photo. "He's a friend of Posey's. I went to see him this morning to ask about the woman. He told me her name and that she's under protection. He wouldn't say why."

"Let me see if I got this right. You kept the photo, which is evidence in a kidnapping, so you could do my job."

"No. Because I knew Marcel Domingas, and I thought it was likely he'd answer my questions."

"Cass, please say you didn't tell him about Vivian's disappearance." Downing spoke through clenched teeth.

"Give me a little credit. Of course I didn't tell him. I said I came to him with questions because Vivian is out of town and we need to find Daniela." Cass gasped. "Oh, I forgot to tell you that Vivian is Daniela's sponsor. I gather you already know Daniela is a refugee here."

Downing nodded. "You know I'll interview this Marcel anyway and probably this woman, too."

"Lisa Domingas. Marcel's wife. Together they sponsor two refugees that Square One brought here. I'm glad you're going to speak with them. You'll probably get farther, being a cop and all. Where they come from, most cops are the bad guys, so be nice if you can." Cass knew better but blurted out the insult because Downing made her feel like a child.

"Come on, Cassandra." Downing softened his voice and gave her some space.

"Do you want to know what I think?" Cass asked.

"Go ahead."

"There was something off about at least three people at the poetry slam Friday. First, the guy in the dark hoodie with the tattoo and second, the woman in the green tunic and headscarf. Third, Miriam Greggs. Not to mention Vivian's cryptic message to Bay."

"Cass, we have your statement and we're looking for the guy. The same guy hiding behind the coffee shop dumpster you chased after, and the other man you saw him talking with at the event. We're looking for the woman, too. What about Miriam Greggs? I don't remember."

Cass hesitated. She already divulged enough for the detective to interfere with her plans. "I can't spell it out for you. It's just a feeling I have."

"If your feeling turns into something concrete, promise to let me know." ∎

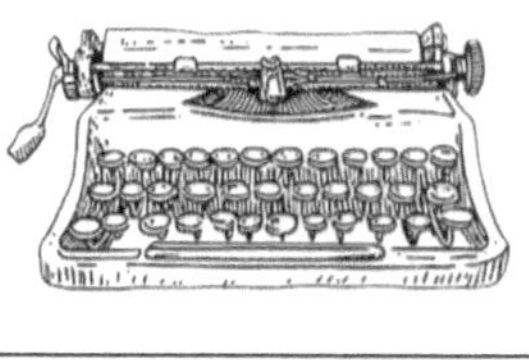

chapter 11

Motivation Monday

Enroute to the humanities building offices, Bay stopped at Giorgio's Tender Touch, the dry cleaning service Stasia Andino's nephew owned. Giorgio considered himself an Adonis, but his cleaning services were impeccable, so Bay put up with him. Most of the time he wasn't there, leaving the business in the capable hands of his relatives, including his niece, Aria.

"Good morning, Aria. I'm glad you're here. I was hoping to talk with you." Bay noticed Aria's troubled expression.

"Are you dropping off or picking up, Professor Browning?" she asked while scrolling through customers on the computer screen.

"Neither. I wanted to ask you about one of the performers from the poetry slam Friday. Handsome, dark-haired guy who recited a Robert Frost poem."

Aria turned crimson. "I don't remember that one." She turned to the computer.

Bay pressed. "Oh, I believe he's memorable. Joaquín something."

Bay received a black look in return.

"If you already knew, why are you asking me?" Aria snapped.

"I wasn't trying to trick you. I wondered what you know about him. I bumped into him yesterday at Professor Rossi's house when she wasn't home." Bay tried to convey her concern about the young man without divulging information about Vivian.

"Oh, I see. Well, there's no way Joaquín would do anything wrong. He's a really great guy." Aria's eyes brightened and her breath quickened.

"I see. Are you two friends?"

"Not exactly. He's always nice, really polite, too. He's a student at Madison College, but he's from Nicaragua on a student visa. He organizes food drives and helps at the student food pantry at the college." Aria's face glowed.

"How do you know this?"

"He stops by every month to collect unclaimed items with Giorgio's permission. Joaquín distributes them to students who need clothes."

Bay was impressed by Joaquín's compassion. No wonder Aria liked him. Bay wondered if Daniela was a recipient of the repurposed clothing, and if she was, it would prove Joaquín knew her, including where to find her.

On the fifth floor of the humanities building, or The Gray Lady, as the staff called it, Bay rapped on Stasia's office door. Stasia was supposed to arrange a meeting between Bay and the two adjunct UW-Madison professors contracted to replace Vivian.

"Hello, Bay. Vivian's temp replacements are in the break room waiting to meet you. Do you have what they need to get started?" Something preoccupied the assistant dean this morning. Stasia barely glanced at Bay while she read something on her computer screen.

"Yes, I'll bring them to my office. See you in an hour."

Stasia waved her out the door. "An hour? Oh, yes, yes."

Sybil Noonan and Edie Rainey left retired life to help Flourish College with their English department predicament. Both appeared capable and excited to work with students, although Sybil possessed an airy quality, and Bay pondered if that was a prerequisite character trait of poetry instructors.

She handed the women syllabuses for the poetry sections and multicultural literature sections. Bay would take Vivian's Shakespeare section herself, since she already taught the course.

Sybil flipped through the pages with excitement. "This is just wonderful. I love Transcendentalist poets. Social expectations, nature, the Divine, individualism… Such great topics for discussion." Sybil bubbled over.

"Vivian will applaud your enthusiasm. Transcendentalism is her specialty, and she wrote her dissertation on Dickinson." Bay felt sorry to say it, almost as if she betrayed her colleague by praising Sybil. Besides, wasn't Emily Dickinson responsible for Vivian's kidnapping, in a roundabout way?

"I'm pleased to be able to offer my help," Sybil said. "Doctor Rossi's discovery of a new Dickinson poem is the talk of the university." Sybil's gushing fanfare was excessive.

"Really? Did you attend the reading Friday night?" Bay asked.

"No. I didn't hear about it in time. I hope I'm able to meet her when she returns, though."

"I hope to meet her, too." Edie's breathless echo showed fervor for Vivian. Edie salivated over the multicultural course materials. "I'm glad I've read these books. Students respond well to *The Kite Runner*, and though *Things Fall Apart* is harder for them to connect with, it's such an important book for discussion on colonialism."

Bay rose to shake the women's hands. "I'm sorry I have another meeting to get to, but I believe Vivian's students will be in capable hands. Please come to me with any questions. I'll introduce you to Trevor, our office assistant. He will help you set up a password and show you how to use the attendance and grading programs."

Bay was last to arrive in the conference room to discuss the theater professor post.

"Sorry to keep you waiting. I was meeting with new temporary staff." Bay cut herself off and caught her breath. "Oh fie."

Stasia rescued her. "Don't bother, Bay. I briefed everyone here about Vivian's absence. They know she's ill and will be taking the rest of the semester off to recuperate." She gave Bay a pointed look.

"Oh, I see. We're hoping for nothing but the best for Vivian." Bay added a silent prayer to her statement.

"Let's get on with the matter at hand. We have four candidates to talk about. Let's begin with Professor Sturgis who is currently on staff at Coker College in South Carolina. The theater staff will speak first about each candidate, and we can weigh in afterwards."

Bay raised her hand to interrupt. "I'm sorry. Don't we have five candidates to discuss?"

Stasia answered. "Ah, yes we did. Professor Obasi withdrew his application."

Bay hid her astonishment but planned to ask Stasia about Obasi later.

After discussing the four candidates, each of the panel voted their choice on a slip of paper. Besides the three theater professors, Stasia, Bay, and Matt Quincy, the music professor most involved with theater productions, made up the voting. The panel agreed that the winning candidate needed four votes. Anything less and discussion would continue.

Stasia read the votes aloud, tallying one vote for Vasili Sturgis and five votes for Angelica Trevino. Inside Bay's stomach, a burst of joy flared that she couldn't explain. Everyone appeared to be drawn to Angelica, so Cassandra's vibe was accurate.

Matt Quincy raised one finger to speak. "I'd like to say my vote was for Vasili because he had extensive knowledge of music and has directed a variety of musicals. I also agree that Angelica will be a suitable choice."

The members voiced their relief at the consensus. Rob Shirley, the new theater department chair, said he would be on the call when Stasia made the formal offer.

"Angelica Trevino will balance out our department. I'm excited to work with her."

Stasia appeared positively blissful. "We will have a welcome party for Angelica before she begins teaching second semester. Can I count on the six of us to organize that?"

Again, everyone agreed to help.

"Thank you all. Bay, please invite your department professors to attend, and the new temps. It will be good for everyone to get to know each other. Matt, the music department should come, too. Well done, all of you. Dismissed."

Bay caught Stasia in the hallway.

"What happened with Professor Obasi?"

"His college threatened to send him back to Africa if he doesn't finish his sabbatical with them." Stasia's expression was blank, but she couldn't resist a jab. "Good riddance to bad rubbish."

Bay welcomed a quiet night of relaxed reading before her short break ended. Tomorrow, she would organize course materials for an upcoming unit, including Vivian's Shakespeare section, which would begin The Tempest on Thursday. Without Vivian. Bay couldn't shake how time slogged on, how every minute Vivian wasn't found seemed a minute closer to something terrible. She understood why Downing was driven to solve crimes.

Her cell sounded off and plans for a restful night faded.

"How's my favorite teacher?" Downing's voice held energy she wasn't feeling.

"Tired. Has it only been four days since Friday?" Bay refused to say Vivian's name or kidnapping, in case it jinxed the night.

"That's why I'm calling. I mean. Well, that didn't come out right. Can you meet me at The Pig Squeal? I want you to hear what my pilot buddy has to say."

Bay wanted to sink deeper into her comfy reading chair but

forced herself upright. "Are you there now?"

"Yep. Jeff's due in about fifteen minutes. What do you say? Corona and a lime wedge? Pork carnitas?"

"You sure know how to romance a woman. Okay, See you in fifteen."

Bay disconnected and shuffled to the bedroom. She donned jeans and a flowing print top. "I promise you'll see me sooner than later," she whispered to the warm pajamas she'd just shed.

The Pig Squeal vibed with energy and laughter, typical of the hangout's Monday night crowd—plenty of patrol cops who logged long weekend hours and needed somewhere to shake off the tension.

Bay didn't see Downing in the dim lighting of mismatched chairs and tables, but someone yanked on her arm with a smirk. Mandy Harris, a rookie and sister to Downing's partner, waited tables at The Pig Squeal as part of her initiation into the force. Mandy still sparred with Bay every other week. The recruit taught Bay self-defense tactics, skills she used to save her life less than a year ago.

"Hey there. If you're looking for Downing, he's out on the patio with some guy. By the looks of him, I imagine he's a boat captain, motorhead, or a snitch." Mandy was trained to observe and assess.

Bay admired the skill. Her photographic memory was her best asset. "He's a pilot. So, you were close."

"Snitch," Mandy said in Bay's ear to drown out the noise.

Bay slid the glass door to walk onto the patio, glad she brought her fleece jacket with her. The night air was brisk but silent. Downing pulled out the chair next to him for Bay, grinning.

"Thanks for coming on short notice."

"You made me an offer I couldn't refuse. Where's my Corona?" Bay deadpanned.

"On its way, along with carnitas nachos and a basket of deep-fried stuff."

Bay noticed the patio was empty despite the portable propane heaters near each table. She was happy to be far from the inside clatter.

"Bay Browning, please meet Jeff Johnson, professional pilot and owner of a Pilatus PC-24 private jet." Downing spoke with a reverence Bay had not witnessed before.

Jeff stood and held out his hand to meet Bay's. "Never mind him. I love his boat. He covets my plane." Jeff shrugged.

Bay gave him the once-over. The tan boater hat with sunglasses propped on the rim did scream "boat captain" while his greased stained running shoes suggested a car enthusiast. But a snitch? Maybe the ripped jeans.

"Professor, you're staring." Downing broke into her thoughts.

"I'm still processing the private jet thing. What is a Pilatus PC-24, pray tell?"

Jeff answered. "It's pretty posh, high tech, and can land in the bush or on a short runway. I fly fishing parties up to Canada and the business set to New York or LA."

"Versatility is the key to success. It does sound like the best of both worlds." Bay admitted. "On to the reason we're all gathered here."

Drinks arrived, beers all around, and Mandy brought a platter of deep-fried cheese curds, pickle spears, mushrooms, onion rings, and green beans—all the stuff anyone could hope for in bar food—with dipping sauces.

Downing and Jeff chatted about flying in bad weather, the right time to dry-dock the boat, and problem clients Jeff flew places. To his credit, he wouldn't name names. Bay was happy to munch and sip, contributing a quip now and then when the men looked her way.

Mandy delivered the nachos with two more beers for the men while Bay opted for water with a lime wedge. She was groggy already and the two talkers she was with were slow to get down to business.

Finally, Downing pulled his notepad out of his shirt pocket, the signal things were about to get official.

"Jeff, you brought copies of the flight reports from Dane County?"

"I did. Off the record, right? Because you'd have to subpoena these to make it official." Jeff was serious and he was right.

"Yes. As we agreed. You said you could get the information faster for me than a warrant and subpoena, so here we are. If this wasn't an urgent matter, I wouldn't ask." Downing eyed Jeff, straight-faced.

"You were asking about Cliff. I told you he logged four people for a flight to Maine Friday night. The thing is, he never flew to Maine. His plane landed a couple hours from Boston on a private airfield. Cliff didn't return until late last night, logging two passengers."

Downing and Bay exchanged worried glances.

"Have you seen Cliff?" Downing asked.

"No. But he's probably sleeping off the late-night flight. I checked his schedule. He's flying a fishing party to Alaska on Thursday." Jeff swigged his beer and stared at Bay.

"Mind if I ask why the professor is here? It's not any of my business, but my neck's on the line."

Downing squeezed Bay's knee, a sign he'd handle it. "She's been a consultant with the police on other murder cases. This time, she's a witness to a kidnapping. The missing woman is her colleague."

"Wow. That can't be good. You think Cliff is involved in this? I mean, the guy's a jerk, but I didn't think he'd stoop this low."

Downing nodded. "I know I saw a plane take off with four passengers, and Cliff was the only pilot out that night. Maybe he doesn't know what business he's mixed up in, maybe he does. If he shows up at the field, call me."

"I will, Bry."

Bay realized Mandy was right. Jeff might not be getting anything out of the deal, but he was willing to snitch on Cliff.

Jeff drained the rest of his beer and said good night.

Downing and Bay finished the nachos, listening to the sound of vehicles leaving the gravel parking lot.

"Must be about closing time."

Ten o'clock was late closing hour for a Monday night. Bay checked the time. Nine forty. So much for her promise of an early night.

"I have to tell you something before I go," Bay said. She wouldn't enjoy ruining their evening, but she wouldn't hide information from Downing.

"Go on, say it." Downing steeled himself.

"Cass and I went back to Vivian's house. We saw a young man walking through her yard, and we chased him down. His name is Joaquín, and he lives down the street. He says he looks after Vivian's cats when she's not home, so he came over to check on them because her car was gone. He performed at the poetry slam Friday night."

"Do you two believe him?" Downing asked.

"Yes, but I noticed Stasia's niece, Aria, giving him the eye on Friday. I talked to her this morning at the dry cleaner's. She said he's here on a student visa and organizes food drives for students in need. He comes to the dry cleaner's every month to pick up unclaimed clothes to give away." Bay bit her lip, ready for an earful from the detective.

"Okay." He sat up straight. "You and your sister are a lot of trouble. I didn't say you were in trouble, but man. You can't drop by Vivian's house whenever you get an itch. And you chased after someone without knowing anything about the guy—are you crazy?"

Bay sat stone-faced. "At least I wasn't alone. Aren't you going to scold me for talking to Aria?"

"Nope, fine work, Professor. I'll follow up." Downing stood up and stretched after a long stint of sitting. "I'll walk you to your car. Keep this information to yourself. Tonight's included. Our interim chief runs a tight ship. I can't afford to get under her skin."

"How exciting! You have to answer to a woman." Bay teased.

Downing groaned. "Not just any woman. Marilyn Smart is a highly decorated captain, former army. Some top brass coaxed her out of retirement to keep our station shipshape until a new chief is hired. She's fair but tough as rawhide. I don't plan to cross my eyes in her direction."

Bay reached for Downing's hand and kissed his palm before clasping it in hers. "Thanks for going easy on me, Officer."

He kissed her, encircled his arms around her waist, and studied her face. "Be careful. You're starting to make me look like a lightweight cop."

The two stood by Bay's Land Rover for a long time, keeping warm under the moonless sky.

Dear Miss Emily,

Were you there Friday, in spirit I mean, when I recited your poem and letter? I remain dressed like you, all in white, but the dirt will never come out, I'm afraid. The men removed my blindfold for good it seems. They've stopped caring if I see the path and the woods around me enroute to the portable potty by my cabin prison. My hands are bound with zip ties, so my hygiene is…I'm not going to say.

Valeria's hands are free and busy. She tells the men that creating authentic documents takes time, especially for four people. They believe her, thank the heavens.

Today is Monday. I know Valeria is plotting for both of us. She cannot speak to me except with her eyes and gestures because the men always watch, take turns sleeping, watching, speaking so seldom their words hurt our ears, which are unaccustomed to human sounds.

Valeria found a pen light and kicked it across the floorboards toward me. All day long, I sit on the cot that is my bed, thinking about Valeria's plan or thinking about what I will write to you in the darkness.

Until next time. —Vivian ∎

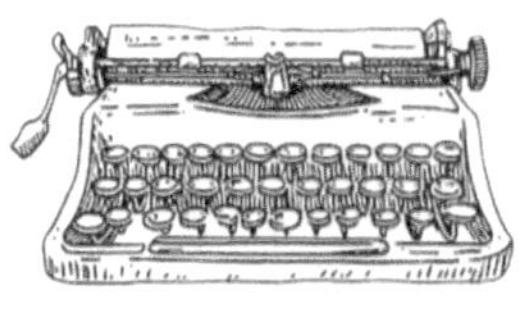

chapter 12

Old Tricks

Cass spent a sleepless Monday night concocting tinctures in the Firehouse, her mind abuzz with plans for visiting Monica Frazer. Working with herbs, inhaling their pungent or sweet aromas while she cooked, provided a balm for her brain.

Her caring fingers traced the recipes in Posey's bound book and lingered on the illustrations Posey had sketched in colored pencil. The delicate blossoms Posey preserved between some pages begged to be sniffed. The multi-sensory experience brought relief to Cass's troubled mind.

Cass checked on the progress of herbs she began drying throughout the summer months. Many were ready, and she lined up clear green bottles for the anti-nausea tincture offered to pregnant and non-pregnant people alike. Made from dandelion, ginger root, milky oat seeds, burdock, and skullcap, Cass poured apple cider vinegar over the plants instead of alcohol, changing the flavor but enhancing the health benefits for the user. The added benefit of skullcap and oats aided in a restful night's sleep.

Cass yawned, thinking she might make a milky oat, valerian tea for herself before bed.

She enjoyed using the colored bottles as an identification system of sorts. Anything in a green bottle was safe for children, pregnant, and nursing women, for instance.

She corked the bottles and carted them to the dark closet Posey referred to as the root cellar, although it wasn't underground. Cass stowed the anti-nausea bottles on a shelf, turned the cart around, and stopped by the storage area to gather a set of translucent amber bottles for a new recipe.

She spoke to Gretchen Lange that afternoon, sharing Marcel's concerns about funding the foundation and Square One from Posey's estate. Gretchen was vague in answering but assured Cass the foundation would continue.

"While I have you on the phone, Cassandra. My sister-in-law Suzanne wonders if Posey's tinctures are available. She's suffering with full throttle headaches several times a week."

"I resumed drying herbs and crafting tinctures from Posey's recipes. I'll see if we have the headache remedy ready and text you."

Gretchen cleared her throat. "Cassandra, are you making liver detox potions?"

Cass understood. Suzanne imbibed frequently, sometimes starting with breakfast. The Ladies Lange, as the three sisters-in-law were called, looked after each other's best interests.

"We don't call them potions, Gretchen. There's nothing magic about them—simple herbs and roots. I'll make some liver tincture this week, but it needs to sit for a month before it's strong enough to be effective."

The liver support tincture, simple to concoct, required milk thistle, a purple flower on a tall thorny stem, often considered invasive. Many tinctures called for milk thistle in its entirety: blossoms, leaves, stems, and roots, so that was good news for the farmers who wanted to get rid of the aggressive plant.

Cass remembered harvesting milk thistle in a nearby field on the bluff. Heavy leather work gloves kept the nasty spikes from penetrating her hands, but it was sweaty work during hot August days with extensive prairie plants and weeds to gather. She imagined doing this with Posey, another sting at her spirit as she endured harvesting alone.

Although the tincture suggested the use of quality vodka for the liver tonic, Cass used glycerol. No sense taxing the liver with any alcohol when glycerol sweetened the tincture with its mild taste while it preserved the herbs.

Cass brewed some sleep-aid tea and admired the Firehouse while the tea steeped. She untied the apron and felt the stiff card in the pocket that she'd placed there after it tumbled from the recipe book. Somehow, she'd forgotten about the cryptic instructions and wondered if Posey intended for her to ignore the card while looking after matters.

Cass rocked in an antique rocking chair in the Firehouse, sipping tea and listening to the familiar creak and rhythm of the curved oak bands against the tiles. She fell asleep there, empty mug in her lap, her body tucked into an oversized cardigan. The mysterious note card drifted to the floor to hide under the Firehouse hutch.

Hours later, Cass awoke stiff, her arms numb and immovable. She cradled the mug in her lap to keep it from crashing onto the tiles while she shook out both arms and stamped her feet against the floor.

Once blood circulated through her limbs, she rose with the mug in hand and walked to the kitchen. Four in the morning. She could sleep a couple of hours before dawn then prepare for another performance, this time for the housekeeper Posey fired. Without any evidence, Cass passed judgment against the woman.

Cass hummed along with Fleetwood Mac, chiming in when Stevie Nicks sang "tell me lies, tell me sweet little lies." She stood at the full-length mirror in Posey's costume closet, admiring her vintage pantsuit with a giggle. The wool blend was sure to get itchy, so Cass wore lightweight tights underneath the plum, yellow, and black plaid bell bottoms, their crisply pressed seams indicated the wearer was all business. Underneath the matching jacket with its feminine rounded bottom, Cass wore a ribbed turtleneck. She fastened the bulky plum buttons up to the lapels and turned to the side for another view. The black platform shoes were a shout-out to nineteen-seventy, so clunky she had to practice walking to and fro a few times.

She was ready to test her first mark. Marva was puttering around the kitchen looking at ideas for Abigail Adams's one-hundredth birthday party.

Cass stood in the doorway until Marva noticed her. The housekeeper picked up the heavy skillet from the range's burner and held it aloft.

"Who are you and how did you get in here?" Marva examined the elderly woman, deciding if she was a real threat.

Cass chose the gravelly voice of a smoker. "I'm looking for Cassandra Browning. She promised to make me something to help me get rid of this cold."

Marva lowered the skillet and squinted at the woman. Something was off. The curly gray hair was stylish with a side sweep and mess of loose tendrils. Wrinkles rested around her mouth and eyes, but her makeup may have concealed more. Then she saw it—the bright blue eyes hidden under the wide rhinestone cat glasses.

"Cassandra Browning indeed! Well, I never." Marva set the skillet on the burner and tsked at Cass, waving one finger. "What's all this about?"

"I'm on a mission this morning and wanted to try out the look and voice on someone first. What do you think?"

"The look is fine. Are you a teacher, or somebody who's been locked up in moth balls for years—ah, a funeral director." Marva smacked her lips.

"Gee thanks. I'm supposed to be dressed for business, but yeah, old-fashioned."

"Unless you're showing up reeking of cigarette smoke, you might ditch the rasp. How old are you supposed to be anyhow?" Leave it to Marva to level with a person.

"Well past the age of retirement. Experienced. I want to sound harsh, no-nonsense." Cass snapped her fingers in the air for show. "I've got it. I'll talk like you, Marva." She spun around to dart from the kitchen.

Marva called after her. "Guess you don't want a chocolate cranberry scone."

"I can't get crumbs on my pantsuit. Bye, Marva."

Cass followed the GPS to a tiny house on Madison's north

side. The neighborhood had more concrete than grass and the road noise was enough to keep people inside with the windows shut tight.

She pulled into the short cement driveway next to an older model midsize sedan and took in the surroundings. The meager brown house squatted like a square box on patchy crabgrass. The low roof sloped over an open porch that sat almost flush with the ground and sagged a little.

A chain-link fence bordered the driveway, leaving a footpath around the house where Cass spied a child's bicycle with dirty pink ribbons dangling from the handlebars. A narrow piece of grass on the side matched the front grass in length and width.

It's possible she miscalculated Monica Frazer's worth. This was no lap of luxury. A middle-aged woman poked her head out the screen door.

"Can I help you?" She wore jeans and a sweatshirt, and her long hair was pulled back from her face.

"Yes, I believe you can. I have business with Monica Frazer. Is she at home?" Cass spoke in a nasally tone, her head cocked in a superior fashion.

The woman evaluated Cassandra's appearance and determined the curious creature might be a weirdo, but harmless.

"I'm Monica Frazer's niece, Dorie." Dorie expected Cass to respond in kind.

Cass peered around Dorie at the girl peeking out from a filled clothesline hanging on the porch. "And who might you be?"

Dorie jolted and turned around. "Emmy, go inside."

"But I want to meet the old lady," Emmy whined.

"Finish getting ready for school. The bus will be here soon."

The girl was about nine or ten and looked cute with her toasted blond curls and school outfit.

"Monica Frazer?" Cass repeated, her haughty voice raised a notch. She tapped her foot and looked at her wristwatch, another relic from Posey's costume collection. The watch didn't work, but Dorie didn't know that.

"Do you have an appointment with her?" Dorie huffed, frustrated at the morning interruption.

"Yes."

Dorie was flustered by Cassandra's terse answers and her need to get Emmy off to school. "Really? I'm surprised she didn't give you her correct address."

Aha, Dorie is getting cagey. Cass changed tactics, softening her tone. "This is the address the jackpot crew has on file. Monica Frazer is a Red, White and Blue Lotto winner." Cass's voice dripped with honey.

Dorie steadied herself against the porch column. "Holy guacamole. That woman has all the luck. I'll write down her address and bring it out."

Dorie returned with Emmy, who toted a glittery backpack and purple lunch bag. She waved at Cass and took a spot near the curb to wait for the school bus.

Dorie handed Cass a grocery receipt with Monica's address scrawled on the flip side. "I don't imagine you can tell me what she won, huh?" Dorie's hungry eyes bore into Cass's.

"I'm sorry, no. Thank you for the address." Cass clunked past the sedan in her platform shoes, dust covering the shiny patent leather.

She checked the grocery receipt against the two addresses she had listed for Monica and grinned. Cass reclaimed her former opinion of Monica, while she plugged in the Lake Mendota address in Windwood Hills.

"This is exactly what I expected, Monica," Cass said when she pulled up to the house, avoiding the driveway in case she wanted a quick getaway.

The modern cocoa-colored house had a vertical tower in the center while its horizontal sprawl nestled into landscaped rocks and flowers on one side and lovely woods on the other. The lot was spacious with no visible neighbors on either side.

The two-car garage was closed and the driveway sat empty, so Cass crossed her fingers and rang the doorbell, after clipping on her IRS badge atop the breast pocket of her plaid blazer.

A large woman swung open the door, out of breath from the effort perhaps. She brushed something from her fancy zebra-print kaftan and glared at Cass, her bloodshot watery eyes blinking as if taking in the sight of Cass was too much to bear.

"Monica Frazer?" Cass held a laptop case in one hand, a modern accessory that didn't match her persona.

"Yes." Monica elongated the word, uncertain.

"Grizelda Chartreuse. May I come in please?" The words flew from Cass's mouth in a flurry, and she pushed the door open wider when she said them.

Monica sputtered. "Charlotte who? Well, I suppose." She moved aside.

Cass ushered herself into the room closest to the door, a living room of sorts, where a big screen television was blaring a game show. Cass helped herself to a seat on the baroque-style sofa and opened the laptop case on the matching glass-topped coffee table.

Monica returned to an oversized cushy chair where a side table revealed her breakfast plate: a stack of toaster waffles swimming in syrup and a bright orange can of Touchdown, an energy drink made from rocket fuel.

To Monica's credit, she ignored her plate, clicked the remote to mute the game show, and turned her attention on Cass.

Cass opened her computer to a fake IRS website she'd discovered yesterday and took out the printed statements and financials from Agent Wilson.

"I have a number of questions about your inventory and financial statement, Ms. Frazer." Cass began paging through the papers.

Monica bolted from the chair in a hobble, her kaftan shimmering in the sunlight that streaked through the bamboo blinds.

"What's going on here?" She headed toward Cass to sit beside her, but Cass raised her hand, palm out.

"No, Ms. Frazer. Step back. Sit over there." Cass pointed to a companion baroque chair nearby, out of Monica's line of sight.

"In reviewing your tax returns from the past fifteen years, we found a number of discrepancies, you see. The agency sent me to interview you in person."

"How long were you employed at the Hollingsworth residence?" Cass began typing.

Monica leaned forward, alarmed. "But I thought you were from the Lotto. Didn't I win a jackpot?" Monica began to perspire.

"You were misinformed." Cass suspected Dorie would call her aunt with the news. "How many years were you employed, and what was your position?"

Monica gripped the arms of the chair and closed her eyes. "Look, Mrs., Ms., I've already settled with the IRS. I completed the forms, and they placed my file in review."

"Yes, Ms. Frazer, and I'm the agent in charge of your review. Let's continue. Answer my question, please."

"Thirteen years. I was their housekeeper." Monica watched Cass click the keys.

"Can you explain your long lapse without income? You say you were self-employed, but for the past twenty years, your taxes are a net zero. And, let me see, you are fifty-seven years old?" Cass hoped to confuse the woman.

"I did housework and odd jobs for people, but like you said, I made little money. Not enough to owe any taxes." Monica puffed out her chest in defiance.

Cass continued typing. "I see. On your statement you list this house as a previous address and your niece's house as your current address. The public records show this house and your niece's house are both in your name. How were you able to purchase two houses, Ms. Frazer, with so little income?"

Monica's chest deflated and she puffed out her cheeks instead, trying to produce words. "I had a pension from Mrs. Hollingsworth." She finally muttered.

"A pension? I don't see any record of that. How long did you receive pension payments?" Cass kept her voice robotic.

Monica fidgeted in her chair and snatched a tissue from an ornate box to wipe her upper lip and forehead. "Pensions are not taxable, Mrs., Ms." Monica blew a raspberry in frustration.

"Chartreuse, Ms. Frazer, and pensions are indeed taxable income in Wisconsin. How long did you receive payments?"

Cassandra's fake name rolled around Monica's brain, as she puzzled about whether it was a name or some technical IRS term. "Oh, I didn't know that. I always assumed…"

"You know what they say about assuming things. How long, Ms. Frazer?" Cass almost felt guilty at the pleasure of her interrogation.

"Still," Monica mumbled.

"Still? You mean, you're currently receiving payments?"

Monica gulped and tipped her head once.

"Come, come now. Mrs. Hollingsworth's been dead twenty years." Cass screwed her face into a scowl.

"I said she was a generous employer." Monica choked out.

Cass continued typing, flipped a few pages ahead in the paperwork, and took a deep breath. "We'll come back to that. I wonder if you can help us out, Ms. Frazer. We're looking for an Olga Bergen."

Monica's eyes bugged out, but she relaxed a little, the pressure subsiding for the moment. "She was the housekeeper for the Hollingsworths before me. I don't know her."

Cass's tone was grave. "Surely you must know something more. She left in August of nineteen ninety-one, and you were hired less than a week later. That is quite odd."

"She and the Mrs. had a falling out. Everyone in the neighborhood knew it." Monica rose to grab the can of Touchdown and took a clumsy gulp, spilling some down her bosom.

Cass kept pressing, knowing she could get the answers she came for. "The IRS finds it remarkable that Olga Bergen received the same pension as you when she held the position for thirty years and you only worked thirteen."

Monica Frazer was close enough to the trap. She wouldn't be able to sidestep it much longer. "I was let go after the Mrs. passed. I'm sure I would be working there now if she was alive. I'd have my thirty years in."

"That may be true, Ms. Frazer. Why didn't the new owner want to keep you on?"

Monica wrinkled her nose as if a dog did its duty on the lush Turkish antique rug under their feet. "We didn't see eye to eye. She was nothing but a spoiled heiress." Monica spat the words out.

Cass almost lost her cool; the anger roiled her insides. *Calm down*, she told herself. *You're getting somewhere.*

She mumbled. "Hmmm. And how did you learn of the housekeeper vacancy? It would be helpful for you to have a character reference on file, Ms. Frazer."

"But that was over thirty years ago." She protested.

Cass held the woman's gaze.

"Oh, all right. Rita Simpson was housekeeper for Mrs. Alcott, a neighbor to Mrs. Hollingsworth. Rita knew I was looking for a job and told me they'd lost their housekeeper. It was a perfect opportunity."

Cass logged the information. "How did you know Rita Simpson?"

Monica blushed. "I was dating her brother at the time."

Cass made a show of straightening the papers and shutting the laptop before offering Monica an icy dose of skepticism.

"Here's what I think, Ms. Frazer. Something happened in August of nineteen ninety-one. Something important enough that Mrs. Hollingsworth was willing to buy your cooperation—or silence."

Cass took off her glasses, folded them, and waved them around like a pointer presenting the facts. "Numbers don't lie. Numbers are factual and logical, and these don't add up. Thirty years and thirteen years. If Mrs. Hollingsworth had a falling out with Olga, why pay her a pension at all? And why did Mrs. Hollingsworth list you in her will months after hiring you? You're hiding more than a luxurious home decorated with antiques and paintings, Ms. Frazer."

Monica held her head in her hands and cried. "Am I going to prison?"

It took willpower for Cass not to shout at the woman. *Yes, you're going to prison, you, you, you...* Instead, she regained her poise.

"Now Ms. Frazer, about those pension payments. With Mrs. Hollingsworth dead, where are the payments coming from and how often?"

Monica sniffed and blew her nose like an air horn. "They come from someone at Lange Corporation. They must have handled Mrs. Hollingsworth's affairs. They send payments four times a year."

Cass already suspected the Lange Group handled the estate, just as Gretchen Lange handled Posey's. Gretchen, however, was not with the Lange Group but had her own practice. She must revisit that tidbit.

"It would be to your benefit to come clean, Ms. Frazer. You could save the IRS precious time by providing a payment stub of some kind." Cass remained icy.

"Of course. I have papers in my desk upstairs if you can

wait."

"I'll wait."

While Monica trudged upstairs, a long walk in a spacious house, Cass roamed freely, opening drawers and cupboards, and taking photos of valuables. Just in case.

When a breathless Monica returned, Cass met her in the hallway, handbag in tow.

"I helped myself to the use of your washroom," Cass said brightly.

Monica glowered at her. "Here are the receipts from last year, so your people can see the whole year. It should be all you need. What will happen next?" Monica leaned closer to read Cass's name tag and badge number.

Cass straightened the ID to inform Monica she knew what Monica was up to. "The IRS will determine if you've provided enough information, not you, Ms. Frazer. If I were you, I'd start applying for jobs. Maybe two. Today."

Cass picked up the laptop case and file, taking in the large living room. She made a point of counting the paintings and antique accessories as she walked in a circle. Cass knew the value of Monica's treasured antiques, paintings, and ornaments after participating in heists at the expense of the rich. Monica's were a mix of exquisite and mediocre. Cass wondered if the exquisite ones came from Spirit Gardens House.

"Perhaps you should sell some of these before your assets are frozen." She waved her arm around the room. "You're going to owe the government a lot of money, whether you're charged with fraud or not. Tax fraud carries a penalty of up to one hundred thousand dollars and five years in prison." Cass quoted the penalty with ease. She learned all about crime and punishment in prison.

Monica sank into the chair and sobbed.

"Tsk tsk, stiff upper lip. Your savings account and investments can be dissolved. Anyway, the matter is out of my hands. Your case will be passed up the chain of command. You'll be hearing from them within a week or two, up to nine months. I'll see myself out."

In the car, Cass glanced at the payment forms. The dollar amounts might be enough to support Monica's expensive home and the second house where Dorie lived. Her eyes scanned the document to the signature on the bottom. "Hmm. Of course. Miriam Greggs." She would be the pension manager.

Cass pulled away from the curb, thankful she'd stopped short of insinuating Dorie and Emmy had more to lose than Monica. None of this was their fault and Cass, despite years of burying her broken heart, was heartless no longer. ■

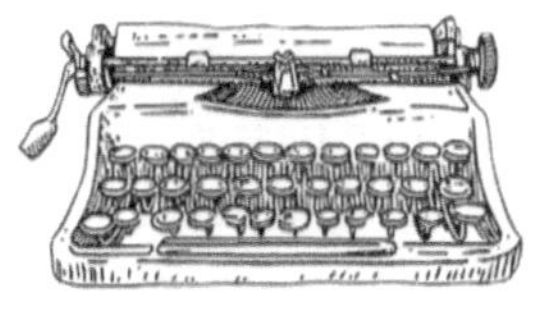

chapter 13

Filling in the Cracks

Marva ushered Suzanne Lange to the Firehouse where Cass was experimenting with ingredients to make skin cream. A double boiler simmered on the burner with a combination of sweet almond and coconut oil. Cass grated sticky beeswax to add to the concoction.

The summer kitchen smelled sweet, earthy, and citrusy from Cass's middle of the night crafting of teas and tinctures, but Cass craved a challenge, and she'd been planning to branch into skin creams and cleansers for months.

"Hello, Cassandra." Suzanne announced herself, ignoring Marva, although Marva stood in the tall woman's path.

Cass righted the grater that leaned over a shallow bowl of the honey-colored wax and raised her eyes, waiting for Marva out of sheer respect.

"Ms. Cassandra, Ms. Lange is here to purchase some remedies." Marva spoke with stinging sharpness.

"Thank you, Marva. Is there anything else?" Cass asked.

"Hmm. No, I'll be returning to inventory upstairs." The stinging voice took on a shrill tone Cass understood. Inventory. They were supposed to be sharing this burden.

Suzanne shuffled from one foot to the other and fake yawned. Marva stalked off.

"Good afternoon, Suzanne. How have you been feeling?" Cass intended to test the woman's patience.

Suzanne Lange was known as the First Lady in social and gossip circles. She'd married, then divorced, Monroe Lange, a wealthy lawyer in the area and one of two partners in the Lange Corporation. Suzanne was not a woman to crawl off in silence, and their contested divorce became the hot topic of the year. Suzanne scored in the end and relocated herself and her daughter to a posh condo on Lake Monona.

Monroe traded wives like baseball pitchers: each one several years younger than the last. Now three ex-Ladies Lange lived in the Lake Monona condo complex in style with their daughters, while Monroe's fourth wife would deliver their first child in October. Everyone held their breath to see if the child would be a boy, the successor.

"Come on, Cassandra. You know why I'm here. Gretchen gave you my order on the phone." Suzanne ducked when a honeybee from the garden skirted past her ear with a hum.

"Sorry. The bees come and go. They get confused this time of year, trying to find late blooms. Plus, I'm working with beeswax today making their sense of direction wonky." Cass wiped her waxy hands on her apron, where they stuck to the fabric.

"Excuse me while I wash my hands." The salt scrub by the faucet would do the trick, and Cass inhaled its minty lemon fragrance while she rubbed the wax off and rinsed it down the drain.

Suzanne continued her foot-hopping jig. Cass surveyed the woman's appearance. Dark sunglasses might be hiding more than crow's-feet, and the bronzer did little to conceal her sallow complexion. Cass was concerned, but she needed to balance her concern with the bargain she planned for their meeting.

"You seem out of sorts. Why don't you sit down while I brew you some tea?" Cass dried her hands on a towel and indicated the rattan seating area.

"Really Cassandra. I don't have the time. I'm not feeling well." The First Lady dropped her head toward her chest.

"Exactly. That's why you must sit down. Besides, I'd like to offer a trade." Cass measured her words and the tea leaves at the same instant.

An assortment of mugs and teacups were on standby, and the kettle was always filled and steaming, ready to accommodate visitors. Cass chose a mug painted with a scene of a storm at sea and poured the water over the tea ball.

Suzanne fidgeted with a fringed pillow like a petulant child, her legs splayed wide open, the pillow on her lap. "What do you want from me?"

The First Lady's reputation as a matriarch for single, wealthy, cast-aside women went to her head. Suzanne believed in her power and would not forfeit it.

Cass brought two mugs, spoons, honey, and cream to the rattan table and sat opposite Suzanne. "When the tea looks ready, you may add honey and cream if you wish." She was the epitome of gentility.

"I know how to fix tea, for God's sakes," Suzanne countered. "What do I have to do to get out of here with my remedies?" She rubbed her temples for emphasis.

"I prepared bergamot tea for you. Sip slowly. It will ease your headache." Cass sat in repose and lingered over the dainty taste of blueberry tea from her mug where she stirred in a touch of honey.

"My remedies?" Suzanne found it difficult to keep her head erect.

Cass set down her mug. "All right. Miriam Greggs."

Suzanne's lolling head popped upright. "What about her?" She wasn't about to play guessing games.

"I know she's the keeper of your ex-husband's corporate secrets. How did she get that kind of power?" Cass picked up the mug again and pretended to relax.

"Miriam Greggs is a creation of Jefferson Lange. He never saw Miriam coming." Suzanne poured a shot of honey into her tea and sipped, placed the pillow behind her head, and laid against it.

"Looks like we'll be here a while. Would you like cookies or a scone?" Cass concealed her irritation for the moment at Suzanne's lack of answer.

The idea of food made Suzanne queasy. "No, thank you." She leaned forward, cradled the mug between her hands, and closed her legs.

"Miriam's husband died in nineteen seventy-eight from an accident at the fertilizer plant where he worked. It was terrible. Made the TV news. Fertilizer chemicals are like a bomb, you see. The investigation found the factory was at fault for violating safety standards."

"Let me guess. Jefferson Lange was Miriam's attorney in the wrongful death of her husband?" Cass imagined the case settled for big money, not that money would compensate for Miriam's loss.

"Yes. He represented both wives who lost husbands in the explosion. Here's the thing. He missed the filing deadline, and the judge had no option but to dismiss the cases."

Cass didn't see this coming. "You're kidding. Why?" She pictured an incompetent Jefferson Lange overcome with a drinking problem or perhaps involved in a romantic affair.

"Jefferson accepted a bribe from the plant owner, a businessman with a lot of pull. Of course, that nugget didn't surface for months after the dismissal." Suzanne sipped more tea and took off her sunglasses. The headache subsided some.

Cass brought the kettle over and added water into Suzanne's mug. "You have a little color in your face at least." But Cass noticed Suzanne's weight loss and bony arms.

Suzanne stiffened. "Do you have anything stronger, Cassandra? Brandy?"

Cass ignored the request. "Back to Miriam. Jefferson screws up. What's Miriam's move?"

Suzanne smiled. "Miriam may be young at the time, but she's savvy. Jefferson doesn't count on that. The second widow moved away. He expected Miriam to roll over, too. Instead, she used her husband's life insurance payout to hire a high-powered attorney. Together, they threaten to go public with a smear campaign."

Suzanne stalled. "Brandy, please. I know where Posey used to keep it."

Cass stood up. "On one condition. You eat something, too."

Cass interpreted Suzanne's shrug to mean she'll eat if she must, and Cass trotted to the kitchen and returned with the bottle, a tumbler with ice, a cheese scone, and a cinnamon muffin.

"Eat something first, Suzanne." Cass dangled the tumbler in front of her like a chalice.

Suzanne nibbled the muffin, slurped the remaining tea, and ate a bit more. "There. I'll finish it. Give me time." She reached for the tumbler sitting on the rattan table and downed the brandy in a single draught. "Top me off and I'll tell you the rest."

Cass cringed inside but poured a shot into the tumbler and added another ice cube. "Sip this one."

"Jefferson offered Miriam a job in the secretary pool where she trained for the position of office manager. Within months, Jefferson promoted Miriam and offered her an extravagant salary for a manager, with stocks and fringe benefits to boot. People at the company talked, but it didn't change anything. Miriam was there to stay." Suzanne sipped the brandy and finished the muffin.

Cass twirled the honey spoon in her mug, thinking. "I don't get it. Why would Jefferson offer Miriam a management job? Wasn't it public knowledge he screwed up?"

"No, not at all. Jefferson paid Miriam for her silence. Nobody knew the real story until after Jefferson died, and it was made public by the retired lawyer who represented Miriam. She came out of that smelling like a rose."

Cass cleared her throat. "To be fair, she lost her husband. Not exactly a rosy deal."

"Pishposh. What's it to you, anyway?" Suzanne hiccupped

and shoved her glass toward Cass's face. "Please."

Cass held the tumbler but didn't move. "I'm trying to find out about a case handled by the Langes. This is about Posey." She closed her eyes and tamped down her emotions. On one hand, she hated disclosing anything personal to Suzanne. On the other hand, Suzanne was a well of knowledge.

"If anyone knows, it's Miriam. Could I have a tiny bit more?" Suzanne's eyes began to glaze over.

Cass set the tumbler down. "Finish your tea and we'll see." She picked up a printed paper bag with the headache remedy in it and carried it to Suzanne.

"Where might I find Miriam? I can't talk to her at the Lange offices, not that she's often there since she's retired." Cass handed the bag to Suzanne.

"Headache remedy. Follow the instructions as usual. The liver detox won't be ready for another four weeks. But I added some loose tea that should help in the meantime."

"Delightful. What do I owe you?" Suzanne fumbled through her handbag.

"Nothing this time. You answered my questions." Cass hoped for additional details.

"If you want to corner Miriam, she volunteers at Peace Lutheran every Wednesday. They have a secondhand store in the basement."

"Thanks, Suzanne. I appreciate it." Cass hesitated, steeling herself. "You may not want to hear this, but you need to lay off the booze. It's going to kill you eventually. The liver detox won't stand a chance if you keep flooding your organs."

"I didn't ask your opinion. Excuse me." Suzanne stormed off.

The reception area in The Gray Lady welcomed Bay like a friend as she selected a sitting spot near the giant arched windows where the morning light flooded the wing chairs with sunshine. When Bay needed a reprieve from the close quarters on the fifth floor, she picked up her laptop and a tote bag filled with office necessities to huddle into one of the cozy spaces the reception area provided.

Bay stared through the windows, enjoying the autumn display of changing colors. Abundant sunshine warmed temperatures while a slight breeze made a few leaves dance off the trees in a slow twirl to the ground.

Her intent was to focus on class preparation for Thursday, and included a study of Vivian's students by name, photograph, and major. Her laptop held dozens of mostly new faces; she taught some of them before but most were blank slates to her.

Visions of Vivian bound and blindfolded made Bay lose focus. Time was such a master, moving too fast and too slow at once. Vivian disappeared four days ago, but it seemed like weeks. How did Vivian measure the hours through her ordeal?

Someone familiar walked through the main entrance, another distraction. Bay allowed her eyes to trail the figure. Officer Mandy Harris, an unexpected interruption. Bay abandoned the laptop to flag her down.

"Hey, Bay. I was on my way to your office. Want to ride along?" Mandy's usual swishy ponytail was contained by pins under her uniform hat, so this must be official business.

Bay turned toward the wing chairs in the east corner. "I'm set up over there. Will that work?"

Mandy followed in response. "I want to speak to you about Aneka Umar. Downing passed on the request to find her, since he's tied up with the kidnapping." Mandy kept her volume low, then settled into the chair opposite Bay.

"I found Aneka yesterday once I received her class schedule from the registration office. I told Aneka she had a message from her uncle, Professor Obasi, which puzzled her. It was strange. She asked to see his photo, but I didn't have one. Aneka said she's kept in touch with her uncle since she arrived in Madison." Mandy pressed a loose hairpin into place.

Bay frowned, opened a new computer tab and searched the Loyola University staff pages. Her eyes widened and she turned the screen to show Mandy. "This man is not the Doctor Obasi who interviewed with us Saturday, nor is he the man who asked us to locate Aneka."

"Do you have a photo of the man claiming to be Obasi? Maybe in the interview documents?" Mandy asked.

"Yes. All the candidates submitted photos. I'll ask Stasia, the assistant dean. She has the files. Let's go." Bay gathered her bag and laptop.

The elevators opened onto the fifth-floor reception where they found Stasia instructing Trevor and Isabella, the new glorified gopher for the department.

Stasia's expression soured at seeing Officer Mandy. Police visits to their floor usually meant bad news, and since this cop was with Bay, the assistant dean wondered if the news concerned Vivian.

"Hello, Dean Andino, I'm Officer Harris. We need a moment." Mandy's smile alleviated the situation.

"Follow me." Stasia led the way to her office and ushered them inside, shutting the door behind them.

"I understand you have photos of the candidates you

interviewed Saturday. I need a copy of Doctor Obasi's photo and anything with his handwriting, if you have it."

Stasia glowered, looked from Mandy to Bay and back again. "What's going on?" She plunged ahead, opened a drawer, and pulled out the appropriate file.

"Doctor Obasi may have been an imposter," Bay said.

Stasia fluttered her fingers, casting a curse. "He rubbed me the wrong way. Perhaps now I know why." She opened the file where Obasi, wearing a confident smile, occupied the cover page.

"I'm not sure there's any reason for us to pursue this man, but I'd rather have his face on file." Mandy took the file, scanned the cover page, and browsed for the man's handwriting, which she found on the bottom of the application waiver page. She took a photo of the handwriting and the cover page with her police camera.

Nobody could prove Aneka was in danger unless this fake Obasi followed up with a call to check on her location. Bay recalled a weighty detail from the conversation.

"Wait. This man wanted more than Aneka's location. He asked about Vivian and said he hoped to see her at the interview. He said he knew Vivian helped Aneka get into the U.S., and he wanted to personally thank her." Bay wrung her hands. "This can't be a coincidence. People are looking for the refugees Vivian sponsored. At least two of them that we know about."

Stasia took the file folder from Mandy. "I'll make a copy of Obasi's application, signature page, and cover. You can take the originals, Officer. If you're trying to find this charlatan, you need a clear photo and original handwriting. Yes, yes."

Stasia handed over the originals to Mandy. "I hope this helps you find Vivian."

Bay was dizzy. The new information might mean Vivian had enemies on several fronts. Before she could speak, Mandy took the reins.

"Don't worry, Bay. I'll give Downing this information. And I'll stop at the university and tell Aneka to stay vigilant."

Bay worried that Aneka's vigilance wouldn't be enough. "Should Aneka hide or have police security?"

Mandy patted Bay's shoulder. "We don't have the manpower to provide police detail. I get the impression Aneka can take care of herself, but I will warn her to be on guard and make sure she's not walking alone."

After Mandy left, Bay turned to Stasia. "I wonder how many of Vivian's sponsored students are refugees. Aneka is from Nigeria. Daniela is either from Central or South America. It seems like two different criminals are in play here."

"Two that we know about. Can you find out anything about this Project Square One Vivian is part of?" Stasia's mysterious voice rang with uncertainty, rattling Bay.

"Stasia, I don't have any inroads this time. I don't know the members of Square One, and I don't have time to play sleuth with extra classes to teach." Bay's eyes pleaded with Stasia to let her off the hook, but Stasia pressed her lips together and waited.

"You heard Mandy Harris talk about being understaffed. We both know you want to help Vivian. You're skilled at this. I'm certain you can manage."

Bay groaned. Whether she could balance teaching with sleuthing or not, she was on the hook for both.

Bay walked down the hall to her office and bumped into Jen Yoo enroute.

"There you are. I just knocked on your door." Jen was breathless. "I haven't seen you since Friday night. What's the latest?" Jen shook a pink bag from their favorite bakery.

Bay waved her inside her office. "No need to bribe me with Sweet Cheeks fare. I'll fill you in."

Jen snorted. "It's not a bribe. It's our shared guilty pleasure. When there's dirt to dish, only Sweet Cheeks will do."

Bay shared everything she could remember from the past few days between bits of cinnamon orange and cranberry chocolate macarons, new autumn offerings.

"What can we do to help the detective, and Vivian, of course?" Jen salivated over the opportunity to play Jessica Fletcher.

"For starters, let's poke around online and find what we can about Valeria Kibben. And knowing Daniela's last name would help us find out more about why bad guys are looking for her." Bay gritted her teeth. Downing must know who Daniela is. It would be in Vivian's files.

Jen moved the office chair to the other side of Bay's desk. "Shove over, so I can see what you're doing."

Bay clicked on several dead-end sites before Jen elbowed her.

"You said Valeria seemed to know about the kidnapping, and she knew about the music box, the Dickinson poem, and the Dickinson 'Master' letter. Maybe Valeria works in the antique business." Jen's suggestion was worth a shot.

Bay used a variety of search terms for antique dealers in the Boston area but didn't find any linked to Valeria. She swiveled toward Jen. "Let's turn the search up a notch. Vivian is a scholar. Valeria might have a specialty, too."

"Antique dealer is plebeian work. We need to find a profession where the patricians rub elbows." Jen pinched her nose.

"Art curator?" Bay suggested. Bay tapped in the generic curator to yield maximum results along with Massachusetts, rather than the specific location of Boston. Several hits highlighted the name Valeria Grenelle. Bay's pulse intensified. Jen leaned in.

"Could that be her?" Jen pointed at an official photograph of Valeria Grenelle.

"The resemblance is definitely there." Bay squinted for a closer look at the brunette woman who shared a similar nose, eyes, and face shape as Vivian's.

Jen scrolled on her phone and smacked it with her index finger. "Ha. Look at this: Vivian's maiden name is Grenelle."

Bay acknowledged the findings with satisfaction. "Valeria works for the Kent Society in Boston. She authenticates historical documents." Bay could barely breathe.

"Such as newly found poems and letters?" Jen squealed. "The kidnappers wanted Valeria, too. Does that mean they want the Dickinson letter?"

Bay scrunched her eyes shut. "It doesn't add up yet. We need to figure out who Daniela is. And for that, I need my sister. She has a connection to Square One: Marcel and Lisa Domingas." ■

chapter 14

Truth or Consequences

The day had robbed Bay and Cass of routine and spiked their emotions on top of it. What the sisters needed was a night out. Diana decided the three should abandon their principals and go dancing at Isthmus, a hot spot on Atwood Avenue in Madison.

Cass agreed with the idea of an outing, after all, it was her goal to cement a bond among the three despite their initial awkward encounter months ago. When Diana announced she had passes to the popular nightclub, Cass grimaced, but she couldn't back out and had to convince Bay to go, too.

Bay's idea of a night out included early dinner and attending a play or perhaps a concert. A loud nightclub wouldn't make her top one hundred.

"Come on, it will be fun. The three sisters. In Madison. Where nobody knows us. It'll be a great change of pace." Cass browsed Bay's closet to find something suitable for her to wear.

Bay crossed her arms and squeezed them against her chest.

"A nightclub doesn't sound like a fun change of pace. Sounds noisy and…sweaty." She landed on the two best negatives she could conjure.

"Admit it. We all need to burn off some steam, Bay. Don't be a party pooper." Cass pulled out the two dresses Bay owned that qualified as club material, one red, one black.

Bay yanked the red dress out of Cass's hand and hung it back up. "Nope. Not the red one. I don't intend to stand out."

Cass clapped. "Hurray, you're going." She gave the black sheath a once-over. Off the shoulder rosette sleeves paired well against the shimmery bodice. The midi length ended in a slit. "Yes, you're going to look hot." She clapped her mouth shut too late.

"Ugh. Hot, like I said. A club is another term for a sweatshop." Bay spoke through gritted teeth but took the dress into the bathroom.

"What are you wearing?" Bay called out.

"I pulled something from Posey's closets before I came over. I'll change and show you. We need to get moving, though. Diana is meeting us downstairs in reception in fifteen."

The two sisters gasped when they glimpsed Diana primping before the mirror in the reception area. They'd only seen her in casual or professional attire, so the fringed miniskirt in cotton candy pink and sexy white on white blouse took them by surprise.

"Trés chic, Diana," Cass exclaimed, walking around her sister for a closer look.

Diana held her breath waiting for Bay's comments.

"You could take on Paris, Diana. I won't have to worry about anyone gawking at me at least." Bay smiled, hoping Diana would take the compliment and ignore the second half.

Diana pulled her sisters into a group hug. "Thank you. I've been wanting to go out, you know, in a big way. I feel safer with my two sisters." She gazed at their outfits, sporting her French-Canadian accent, "You both look fantastique."

Isthmus, as Bay suspected, rocked with loud techno-pop music, college and twenty-somethings gyrating, shouting, and laughing from every nook and cranny. Diana navigated them around a group of dancers to a black-tufted booth backlit in blue lights, perfect for three people.

A server in a skimpy uniform materialized immediately to take their drink order, which Diana handed to her on a slip of paper.

"Trust me," Diana said, her wide smile accented by candy pink lipstick.

"How did you get a booth here?" Cass's skepticism didn't match her sunny yellow jumpsuit embroidered with daisies.

Bay scooted into the recesses of the booth, trying to shutter a memory. Her one club experience happened the year she turned eighteen. After graduating from high school at sixteen, she was a college junior then but still as green as if she were a freshman.

Bay and five other initiates, escorted by sorority officers, found themselves at Club Y, after being blindfolded and forced to wear bright yellow jumpsuits—not pretty like Cass's, but garish. The initiates resembled utility workers. All they needed were hard hats.

Bay knew the name of the game was to drink in excess, and she wanted to get it over with. When the shots came in quick succession, she downed them without hesitation and lost her dinner after the sixth round.

Bay's hope for a quick exit was snatched away when Jess, the head sister, jammed a crown on her head and slung a red satin sash over her bearing the title PUKER in gold letters. To make matters worse, Jess handcuffed Bay to another initiate, so she couldn't leave.

After a long humiliating night, Bay decided she would never join that or any sorority. She showered, threw the jumpsuit and every article of clothing from that night into the trash, and walked to the sorority house in the early morning hours where she tied the sash to the door and trampled the crown into the doormat.

She faced harassment for about a month but stood her ground through all the torment and threats. Bay didn't realize it at the time, but now she wondered if she had channeled the Charming women's gift of assertion. She inspired another initiate to quit, and the two became friends and roommates.

Diana snapped her fingers before Bay's eyes. "Hey, you okay in there? Drinks are here."

Bay opened her eyes, expecting to see shot glasses with gold flakes in them, but a pretty martini glass with rose liquid greeted her.

"I know you like old-fashioneds, but you can't get that here. I took a chance. It's a cosmo."

Bay took a sip. "It's nice. A little on the boozy side."

The sisters drank a round, then a second one, elevating the mood by a mile.

Cass announced, "Let's play Truth or Consequences!" She eyed Bay. The game was one the two played as kids, their own version of truth or dare, mostly when they'd been hiding things from each other or when one of them was going through a rough patch.

Bay leaned in and spoke louder, loosened up from the drink. "I'll start. Cass: truth or consequences?"

"Consequences," Cass said.

Bay slapped the table. "Just like always." She looked around the club and dance floor. "Okay, see that guy over there. The shirtless one with the light-up bow tie. Go dance with him."

Cass wasted no time floating over to the attractive man, throwing her arms around his neck, pulling him to her, and whispering something in his ear. The man enjoyed the attention and circled his arms around Cass.

Diana's mouth dropped open. She wasn't acquainted with this side of her sisters.

Bay laughed. "Now I'll never get to ask my question. Darn Cassandra."

The sisters continued to watch Cass's performance when Bay noticed her attention drifted elsewhere, becoming hawk-like. She followed her eyeline toward a man with a military haircut, dressed all in black. His eyes darted around the club, the tension obvious as he jerked his neck right to left and stuck out his chest.

Cass gestured to Bay behind the back of her bare-chested dance partner, a camera clicking motion. Bay understood and took some discreet photos of the man in black. Something about him jarred both of their memories.

Bay wondered if she should call Downing but knew it would take a half hour to get to Isthmus, and the man might be long gone by that time.

Cass abandoned her dance partner and staggered over to

the corner of the bar where the man was leaning, alert and guarded. She ran into him and stepped on his foot.

"Whoops. Sorry about that. Come dance with me." Cass began swaying with her arms around the man's neck.

He growled and grabbed her wrist.

Bay whispered to Diana. "Here's my phone. Call Detective Downing and tell him to come. He's in my contacts."

Bay was at the bar in quick strides, glaring at the man. "What's going on here? Let her go, tough guy." Bay prepared to roundhouse the man if he didn't take his hand off Cassandra.

The man removed his hand, playing it cool. "There's no problem here. I think this woman is drunk, so you should probably take her home." He spoke with an accent.

Bay was close enough to peg him for the driver of the van that took Vivian. While she couldn't be sure, she couldn't shake her gut feeling either.

Cass sashayed backward, swaying her hips. "I hoped to dance with a handsome man." She sounded tipsy. "But I can see you're looking for someone. Just my luck you have a girlfriend. Who is she?

As Cass asked the question, she put the palm of her hand against the man's taut chest in a familiar way, hoping for an answer.

Daniela. And someone else.

Cass's hand recoiled as if on fire, and Bay looped her arm around her and drew her aside.

"I apologize for the trouble. She's going through a bad breakup," Bay said over her shoulder.

The man in black grunted and went upstairs to the second floor.

On the way to their booth, the shirtless man placed a gentle hand on Cass and asked to finish their dance. Cass winked at Bay, who didn't know what to make of it.

The server returned to the table with two plates: one bearing glazed chicken yakitori skewers; the second with savory wontons. Bay and Diana sighed in relief at the welcome sight of food to tame the alcohol.

"Another round of drinks, babes?" The server asked. She winked at the two after eyeing Cass on the dance floor.

"One more round." Diana decided even though Bay placed a hand on her arm to hold off.

"Did you call Downing?" Bay asked under her breath.

"I did, but it went to voicemail. What's going on anyway?"

Bay glowered at her sister, unwilling to explain.

"Excuse me. I'm going to go rescue that acrobatic wonder from Cass."

Bay reached the pair and twined her arm through Cassandra's. The shirtless man looked at Bay in surprise at first, but surprise turned to admiration.

"What do we have here. Come on in, Baby. I can tango with both of you." The man's smile was open and charismatic.

"You must be Penny's friend. She says you're out having a hen night. You Brits are a handful." The man spun Cass around with one hand while encircling his arm around Bay.

Bay recognized Cass's favorite alias, laughed, and made a trial run British accent. "Oh Penny. We can't leave our mate sitting alone. What kind of bridesmaids would do that, right?"

Bay disentangled herself, bowed to the handsome man, and pulled Cass out of the way, but not before the half-dressed man bit off one of the decorative daisies from Cass's outfit and tucked it into his belt.

"Time for you to put some food in there, Penny." Bay pointed at Cass's mouth and whispered, "Seriously, what was that about?"

Cass leaned in. "I'm trying to be stealthy. The Chippendale was watching the whole scene with the man in black. I think he's one of Vivian's abductors. The man in black, I mean."

Bay agreed. "I took photos. Hope they turn out. I asked Di to call Downing, but it went to voicemail. He'd recognize my number, so he must be working."

"Do you think we should follow him?" Cass sensed danger when she touched him, which both frightened her and attracted her at once.

"Are you nuts? No. And yes. But we can't do this alone. We need backup."

Bay's phone rang.

"I got a voicemail from Diana. What's going on? Where in hell are you?" Downing was wound up.

"We're at Isthmus, a night club on Atwood Avenue. There's a man here. He's poking around the place. Cass and I think he's one of the kidnappers."

"Don't go anywhere near him and don't leave. I'll meet you there. I'm sending a local." Downing was gone.

"Downing says we need to stay here and wait for him. We're not supposed to go near the man, so let's enjoy our food and try not to appear suspicious."

Cass scowled, disappointed she couldn't pursue the culprit.

Diana was taken aback first by the sisters' playacting, then by being informed about the potential kidnapper in their midst.

"I have a lot to learn about you two," she said.

Bay and Cass remembered the game was in progress and both turned to Diana.

"Truth or consequences? You're graduating in the spring, Di. What's next for you?"

"Wait a sec. I thought I had to choose between the two without knowing the question," Diana said.

"Oops," Cass said. "I guess the drinks made us forget." She was an expert at hiding her emotions and she switched to party mode, hoping Diana would relax.

Diana giggled, tipsy, too. "This isn't for publication, but I hope to begin getting librarian credentials." She paused to let that sink in.

"Wait a minute. Are you a candidate for the college librarian position?" Bay asked.

Diana nodded. "The board said they've received positive feedback about me and asked if I might become certified. Meanwhile, an interim librarian is coming out of retirement to train and mentor me."

Tears glistened in Diana's eyes. "I hope my sisters don't mind that I'm sticking around."

"Mind? We're thrilled." Cass chirped.

Bay added her approval, squeezing Diana's hand. Inside, the uncertainty about Diana bothered Bay. Only months ago, she heard the news that her mother had a child with another man while married to Bay's and Cass's father. She reminded herself it wasn't Diana's fault.

The teetering emotions of the night and the effects of the drinks made Cass scooch closer to her sisters. "I'll answer your question now, Bay."

"Uh, I didn't ask you a question." Bay reminded Cass, who shrugged.

"You want to know about Anthony. I have real feelings for him, but I think it's a hopeless endeavor."

"Why do you say that?"

"It's simple really. Anthony's a blue blood with a polished reputation. And you both know who I am." Cass lowered her eyes to stare at the tabletop. When she spoke again, the sisters strained to hear her. "And he doesn't."

The sisters each leaned on one of Cass's shoulders.

"Don't sell Anthony short. He's a gentleman, yes, who is wild about you," Bay said.

"You'll tell him when the time is right, Cassandra. And you'll know when that is." Diana spoke wisely for the youngest among them. Her attention turned toward Bay.

"And what of you and Detective Downing? Is it serious?" Diana asked.

Bay considered, although she expected the question. "Bryce and I are busy people, dedicated to our careers. Our relationship is clever and playful, and a wonderful tension tamer. We're far from serious though."

Saying it aloud to her sisters sounded true, but Bay knew it rang hollow inside her. The truth was, she had not spent time in deep introspection about her and Downing. She liked the fact their connection was simple, and she was content to keep it that way.

Cass and Diana didn't buy Bay's easy answer. Both could see below the surface to her emotional state, and they could sense the strong spark between them.

The three turned when an officer entered the club and

made a beeline for the bartender. He showed the bartender something on his phone, probably the photo Bay sent to Downing. The bartender nodded toward the second floor, and the officer took the stairs at a trot.

The sisters didn't see the man leave, but the officer was upstairs a short time before he was at the bar again. A few minutes later, Downing arrived and surveyed the room. He did a double take when he saw the three sisters, held up a hand signaling them to wait, and went to the bar to join the cop conversation.

The noise level dropped after the first officer arrived and numerous people, sensing trouble, vacated. The local officer left and soon after, Downing joined the three women.

"Wow, I feel out of my league, ladies." Downing was enchanted with one lady, though: Bay. He snapped back to reality in seconds. "Talk to me." He pulled out a notepad.

"Wait a minute. What happened to our mark?" Cass asked.

"He disappeared. Back stairs is my guess. The bartender said he asked about two women and showed their photos. The bartender said unless someone shows him a badge or warrant, he always says he's never seen them."

Cass sucked in a breath. "I knew it. When I placed my hand on his chest, I heard him thinking about Daniela and someone else, but I couldn't make out who it was."

Downing wrote that down. "At least we have a photo. A crisp, clear one, too. We should be able to run it through the state system. Probably federal, too. And Interpol."

Bay and Cass understood while Diana looked from one to the next, bewildered.

"If these guys are after Daniela, they're probably from

another country, too." Bay bit her lip as her insides churned, thinking of Aneka.

Downing finished taking notes and rose to leave. "It's going to be a long night. Talk to you soon."

When he smacked a kiss on Bay's cheek, she whispered her need to tell him about the search for Valeria and ask about Aneka. Downing said it would have to keep and dashed out the door.

The sisters, exhausted from the ups and downs of the evening, ended the night with sodas and a final round of Truth or Consequences aimed at Bay.

"Why is it my turn, again?" Bay complained. She didn't feel like dealing with any more truth tonight. "Okay, I won't spoil your fun. Consequences."

Cass clapped. "I need a favor, Bay. I need you to follow Miriam Greggs, take notes, and take photos."

"Sounds risky. You know I can't do anything to jeopardize my job, Cassandra." Bay twisted in her seat. The snug dress was becoming more uncomfortable by the minute.

"Of course not. You can pretend you're a private detective. I'll throw in the starting square on the game board, easy peasy." ◾

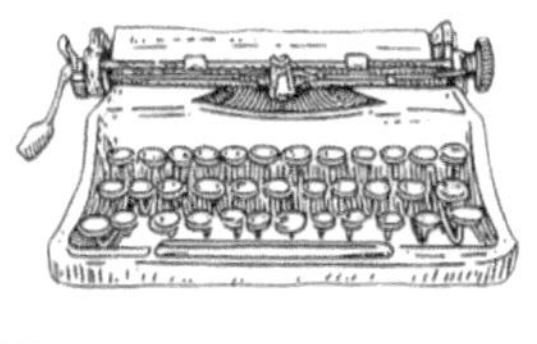

chapter 15

Natural Habitat

Bay rose before sunrise and took stock of the nightclub's toll on her body. The darkness meant the hour was early and her late-night escapades hadn't ruined her normal wake-up routine. Thank goodness, because it was Wednesday. Today would be her last chance to prepare for tomorrow's classes, including the addition of Vivian's sections.

Bay propelled herself up the stairs of The Gray Lady rather than take the elevator. Her body craved exercise, so she climbed several flights, given a day of sitting in the office.

Stasia's light shone beneath her door. Bay knocked. Might as well take care of business first.

"Bay. Good morning. Any news on that fake Obasi fellow?" Stasia's stack of files and mail testified to her early arrival.

"Nothing yet. We both have a busy day ahead. I need to ask a favor." Bay leaned her hands on the desk.

"I see. A trade. You help with Vivian's case, and what can I do for you?"

"Right. Does your nephew still work at Chez Martini?" Bay asked, remembering that Stasia often touted the food and ambience at the award-winning restaurant.

"Indeed. What do you need?" Stasia raised her brows.

After Bay shared a thin version of her plan, Stasia sweetened the deal. It seemed the matriarch of an expansive Greek family had connections to every useful business in town.

Outside Bay's office door her phone rang—Downing.

"Hey. I was about to call you," Bay admitted.

"It's been another late night, but I didn't forget you needed to talk about Valeria and Aneka. Mandy Harris shared the stuff about the fake Doctor Obasi and your concern. There are rebel forces in Nigeria. I turned Aneka's information over to the International Rescue Committee. They can find out if she's connected to any turmoil there."

Bay probed the detective. "Did you do the same with Daniela? Get the IRC involved?"

Downing was clever enough to skip over the bait. "You're asking if I know who Daniela is?"

"I imagine her file was in with Vivian's papers. So, you have her last name, home country, and..." Bay knew she walked a fine line. She didn't have any claim to this information.

"What we found wasn't much help. Not for Daniela or Vivian. I hoped to connect with Daniela on campus Monday, but her professors said she sent them an email stating she had a flu bug and would be absent all week."

"Smart woman. She must know she's a target. Could you contact her by email?" Bay asked.

"We can't risk it in case someone hacks her account. Besides, if she thought the police could protect her, she would have called us, right?" He shifted. "Now, what about Valeria?"

Bay sensed Downing's fatigue amid his frustration. "You might know this already, but Valeria is known professionally by the last name Grenelle. She works for the Kent Society as an authentication expert. She knows how to separate the originals from the fakes when it comes to historical documents."

Downing scratched the details on his notepad while Bay spoke. "This is new information, Bay. Glad you looked into her. Like I said, we don't have enough people working on this. Looks like Valeria could be an asset to the kidnappers."

Bay gasped. "Does that mean you know who the kidnappers are?"

"Off the record." He weighed each word. "We identified the man in black from the club last night. Turns out he's part of an underground rebel army from Colombia. Your sister's description of the fist and broken chain tattoo proved helpful. Every member of that army has that tattoo."

"Does that mean Daniela is Colombian and, and…" Bay tried to form a complete picture. *The army wants to recruit Daniela, or they already did but she changed her mind?*

"We can't jump to conclusions. Honestly, I don't know where she's from. We hit a dead end using the name and information on Vivian's forms. That's why the IRC is involved. You know how I enjoy sharing case info."

In general, the detective didn't play well with others, especially the feds. Bay knew that Downing had the fortitude of a dog searching for a buried bone, digging up the whole yard until he unearthed it. "Thanks for telling me what you could. I have to run—get my game face on for tomorrow."

Bay chewed on the remains of her lunch sandwich as she watched the white clapboard church on Bristol Street, waiting for Miriam Greggs to exit the building. Peace Lutheran was a charming structure, its brilliant exterior flanked by Gothic arched windows. In contrast, the bell tower wore an inky ruffled skirt at the roofline while its top resembled a pointy witch's hat. Inwardly, Bay giggled, thinking her description didn't complement the traditional religion.

Bay discarded the bread crusts and nibbled carrot sticks, swigging water in between. Cassandra told her Miriam worked at the church store on Wednesdays and drove a Lexus, the color of a black pearl. Bay knew what Miriam looked like, since Cass pointed her out at the poetry slam.

Bay's attention turned toward the front door where a man dressed in a dark shirt with a white collar carried in the sandwich board store sign and shut the door behind him. An identical sign stood on the sidewalk near the parking lot. Two ladies heaved the sign with purpose and dragged it in through the side entrance.

Soon, the helpers streamed out the side door to their vehicles, including Miriam, whom Bay spotted among two other white-haired women. Miriam's tall, willowy frame stood out like a pillar between two fence posts. Her hair resembled the brilliant clapboard in the afternoon sunshine, a polished do, traditional but updated.

Bay was ready when Miriam pulled into the street and followed, allowing a car to take space between them. Bay was three or four car lengths behind when the Lexus left the outskirts of Prairie Ridge and took the interstate on-ramp. Bay followed without fear of being suspected, since the interstate filled with commuters and shoppers alike bound for Madison.

As traffic increased, Bay needed to concentrate. It would be easy to lose Miriam in a sea of vehicles of matching hues. She sped up but hung back, watchful. Finally, Miriam signaled her exit onto Highway RM, and Bay did the same in a smooth maneuver.

The Lexus cruised along the winding county road with other traffic. Bay retreated, allowing a truck to pass her and slide in between the Land Rover and the Lexus to wait for the next passing zone. The drive, lined with wooded areas and occasional new houses among the older farms, was pleasant. Many of the hardwood trees showed off variants in oranges, reds, and yellows interspersed with the evergreens.

The Lexus didn't signal but made a sharp turn onto a road labeled "private drive" and Bay continued past for fear of being noticed. Bay turned left onto the nearest road, made a U-turn toward the private road, and turned in. The pavement was new blacktop and wide enough to accommodate two vehicles. It ended at a fork, one way through a stone gate requiring a code or down a gravel drive where a sign announced "deliveries."

Bay weighed the options. She could buzz the gatekeeper and wheedle her way in, if she had Cassandra's skills, or she could take the delivery drive and pretend she was lost if someone quizzed her.

The gravel road ended at another gate, this one guarded by security who asked for her paperwork.

"Paperwork? I think I must have the wrong address. I'm supposed to meet with Miriam Greggs." Bay made steady eye contact and controlled her breath, the way Cass taught her.

The guard looked amused but appeared to believe her story. He opened the gate and pointed to the black Lexus parked behind a sprawling stone building, resembling a resort. Miriam leaned against the Lexus, waiting.

Bay relaxed, happy the hard part was over. Tailing a car and inventing stories wasn't in her wheelhouse. As a teacher, negotiating was something she excelled at. It was time for the latter.

Bay parked a few spaces from the Lexus and opened the door in a rush. Miriam pushed her sunglasses to the top of her head and offered a hard stare in greeting.

"Do I know you?" Miriam asked.

"Professor Bay Browning, a colleague of Vivian Rossi's." Bay held out her hand, but Miriam declined it.

"Congratulations on tailing me here. I didn't catch on until right before my last turn. What do you want, Professor?"

"Information. May I?" Bay indicated her cell phone. When Miriam inclined her head, Bay pulled up the saved photo of Vivian, Posey, the Domingas couple, and Daniela.

"I understand you took this photo," Bay said.

"So what?" Miriam dismissed Bay and proceeded to the driver's side of the Lexus.

Bay took a deep breath. "I'm trying to find this woman. It's important for her safety." She pointed at Daniela, and Miriam flinched and turned around.

"How would I know? And why haven't you asked Vivian? She's your colleague." Miriam shoved her hands into her coat pockets and kicked up a little gravel, like a mustang eyeing its escape.

Bay pocketed the phone and fingered the envelope in

her purse. "You're a wanted woman around Prairie Ridge. Infamous, I understand." Bay viewed her surroundings. The grounds behind the facility were posh, despite the gravel delivery area. She shaded her eyes, catching a glimpse of groundskeepers pruning shrubs and tending flowers near a spectacular pool area. She caught a whiff of cedar and imagined a sauna might be the source. *An exclusive spa, perhaps? Maybe Miriam was the owner.*

Miriam snorted. "Wanted indeed? This isn't the first time someone's accused me of keeping secrets, Doctor Browning. That's been my job description for years. Please excuse me." Miriam crunched over the gravel with her fancy boots and walked around the Lexus.

Bay didn't move an inch. "I overestimated you. You're not a bit interested in a trade?"

Miriam made a quarter turn. "What could you possibly have that I would want?"Bay's laugh was a challenge. "Everyone wants something. I have dinner for six at Chez Martini." She patted her purse.

"Please." Miriam's voice was flat. "You don't think I can acquire those myself?"

Bay read the eagerness on her face, however. Perhaps Miriam could get reservations, but… "These are for the VIP Chef's table."

"I see. Chez Martini," Miriam said the name like it was a landfill. "You can't trade small potatoes for the information you want. Stop wasting my time."

"Very well." Bay dug in her bag for her car keys.

"Wait." Miriam faltered. "Ask for something I can give you."

"Valeria Grenelle. What's her role in Project Square One?"

Bay's pointed delivery drew Miriam's admiration.

"Valeria is Vivian's sister, but you know that. Let's say Valeria uses her particular skills to help with documents. You understand refugees cannot get into this country without legal documents." Miriam's voice was a lighthearted tinkle.

Bay caught Miriam's drift and reached into her purse. She drew the dinner passes from the envelope, walked around the Lexus, and held them out. Miriam met Bay, two adversaries squaring off.

"Anna Mylonas." Bay wasn't accustomed to speaking in choppy phrases, but she knew that less was best from watching Downing. She was right.

Miriam crinkled her brows for a microsecond before light dawned. Miriam had sought out the renowned masseuse a year ago, hoping to lure her as an employee. "I'm listening."

Bay made a mental note to thank Stasia for the tip. Anna and her soon-to-be ex-husband owned a lavish spa in Madison. "You were hoping to employ her. Let's make another trade?" Bay held up the envelope and waved it.

Miriam eyed the envelope. "What's your question?"

Bay asked and Miriam printed the answer on a piece of paper Bay provided. It was Bay's turn to make good on the trade.

She passed the envelope to Miriam. "I happen to know Anna is going through an ugly divorce and is anxious to secure employment elsewhere. Her personal cell number is in here, along with a note of introduction from her cousin, Stasia Andino." Bay hoped she wasn't throwing Anna Mylonas into a worse situation than sharing a workspace with an ex. She didn't trust the level of power Miriam possessed.

"I underestimated you. You're quite daring for an

English professor."

"Never pigeonhole a woman, Miriam. We all have our battles to fight. Who knows? I might want a membership in this hidden club out here." Bay played a hunch with nothing but a theory. She knew Miriam had a personal secret she wanted to keep.

Miriam's smug expression showed her advantage. "I doubt you'd fit in here, Professor. Nice doing business with you." She held the envelope between praying hands and touched it to her heart in a namaste gesture. "My guard will open the gate for you."

Bay tapped the steering wheel while she rolled through the security gate, half-satisfied. She wanted to snag a bigger payout from Miriam. Now she was out of cards to play and had to think. She tucked the paper scrap into her pants pocket for safekeeping, intent on stopping at Spirit Gardens to deliver it to Cass and watch her reaction.

At the end of the gravel driveway, Bay stared at the member entrance with its keypad, camera, and impressive stone pillars. No sign announced the name of the place, adding to its secrecy and exclusivity, she guessed.

Instead of turning toward Prairie Ridge, she drove the opposite direction and zipped into a wide spot near a historical marker. She parked and waited for sunset, watching traffic in the mirrors while she slunk down into the seat. Traffic was sparse, only six vehicles and none of them seemed interested in her Land Rover at the wayside.

As the sun waned, Bay settled into the back seat and changed into the cat burglar clothes stashed from her prowl with Cass at Vivian's house. She grabbed her field glasses equipped with night vision, which she used on occasional wildlife hikes. The fresh air felt cool through the long-sleeved black turtleneck, pulled up to her nose. She headed straight into the woods.

Bay estimated she was less than a half mile from the resort property and hoped it wasn't surrounded by razor-wire fencing and trail cameras. She relied on her internal compass, a natural tendency she honed during childhood on archaeology sites with her father and navigating Chicago while living with Aunt Venus.

Golden fingers of light barely penetrated the canopy, but she stayed the course. She raised the field glasses and thought she could see the rear corner of the stone building in the distance. She moved faster but stopped when she heard voices that seemed close by. She leaned against a tall hickory, arms stiff by her sides, and held her breath.

"Hey. Max, isn't it? You're the newbie." A man in uniform stood about three trees up from Bay's hiding spot.

"Yes. I'm Max. You have a good memory, uh…"

"Dave. How you liking this gig?" Dave chuckled, sharing a private joke.

"It's a chill gig." Max commented, realized he'd made an amusing quip, and laughed heartily.

Dave caught on. "Ha, high five. Yep, it's the easiest security job around. I mean, nobody can be caught with a concealed weapon."

The two laughed and slapped each other on the shoulder.

"Have a good night."

Dave's footfalls swished along the ground, and Bay thought she heard a metal clanking from a door or gate. She waited, unsure where Max was.

She relaxed when the footfalls moved in a different direction.

She peered around the tree and could see the guard walking along a perimeter fence. The fence was the chain-link variety, so Bay's vision wouldn't be blocked if she was lucky. "No Trespassing" signs were posted on the fence every ten feet or so.

With her field glasses, she saw Max enter an opening in the fence and climb steps to an elevated guard station. As she raised the binoculars, she saw a sign on the station: "Natural Habitat" painted in green letters on redwood.

"Toad warts," Bay said. "Well, the light's about gone, and I'll have to make nice with the forest floor." She duckwalked toward the entrance Dave used and took in the view.

A terraced pool and waterfall occupied her field of vision. It was a beautiful piece carved from nature. Lights illuminated the water from below and around the rock crevices. The pool was empty, but she could hear a woman's voice on the other side of it. The woman sounded like Miriam.

Bay felt a cramp in her calf and stood up to stretch where a tree blocked the guard's station. She did some hamstring and calf bends, then ducked around the tree to skirt the fence for a better look.

She refused to believe what she saw. She pulled the field glasses up, leaving off the night vision since the area behind the pool was lit with LED candles and fairy lights. Miriam led a relaxation class, including instructions for partner or group massage, and everyone in the class was stark naked.

Bay forced herself to look away. *So, this is Miriam's secret. A nudist colony.* If Bay had a hundred guesses, this would not have been one. She'd never heard any scuttlebutt about a nudist colony, resort, spa, whatever it was, in this slice of Wisconsin, a half hour from Prairie Ridge, in the boonies.

Soft chanting sounded from the class platform, accompanied by tinkling bells and the hum of a singing bowl. The music was familiar to Bay, who had taken yoga classes and visited an ashram with her family in Thailand during one of her father's anthropology sabbaticals.

The vibrations hypnotized, and she found herself swaying side to side for a few moments before snapping out of it. She raised the binoculars once more when movement drew her attention. The class members lay prone or in child's pose while Miriam sat in a lotus position, chanting. The movement came from three figures wearing loose clothing who placed steaming towels onto the foreheads of each participant.

Bay focused on each individual worker. One young woman, tall and brown-skinned, wore her hair in multiple braids bound with a tribal print wrap. The second woman was diminutive, older, her long silver braid intertwined with beads hung over her collarbone, and Bay noticed she was barefoot. Bay gulped when the third figure came into focus, another woman who matched the photo of Daniela. Her hair was pulled into a low ponytail sectioned off by colorful rag ties. The three were silent, floating among the nude bodies like feathers on the breeze.

Bay held up her cell phone to take a photo of Daniela, but the low lighting ruined her chance, and the camera produced a grainy image that could be anyone. She couldn't risk using the flash, not that it would make the photo clearer. The distance was too far. Besides, she'd overstayed her welcome.

She crept through the woods, a hike in near darkness, avoiding tree roots, creeping vines, and saplings. The night vision glasses couldn't help her navigate at a useful speed.

Once she couldn't see the Natural Habitat compound, she used her phone screen to guide her.

Bay enjoyed the victory: she knew Miriam's secret, which could be leveraged against Daniela's whereabouts. She needed to tell Downing, but how? Bay didn't want to be a snitch, not in a community the size of Prairie Ridge.

Something skittered across her path, shaking her to the present. She peered ahead, squinting in the direction she hoped would lead to her parked SUV. A spotlight flooded part of the woods behind her. She was being chased. She veered left, caught her foot on a tree root and almost tumbled to the ground. Momentum and adrenaline propelled her onward. The light bounced on her right and Bay crouched behind a tree, knowing the light would bounce left next. Her heart thudded hard enough she thought her ears might explode, and it seemed she crouched forever, when it was only a minute or two. The light turned around and began to disappear toward the resort property again. In minutes, she saw the road, wayside, and the dark hulk of the Land Rover.

Bay's adrenaline rush subsided by the time Prairie Ridge came into view, and she was anxious to deliver intel on Miriam Greggs to Cass. The moon was on the rise now, increasing to a full moon in a few days.

Cass waited by the entrance, wrapped in a woolen shawl, when Bay pulled into the circular drive.

"How long have you been standing out here?" Bay asked.

"Not long. Come in. I have a teapot waiting and a casserole Marva made." Cass held the door wide.

A homey scent teased Bay, setting her stomach growling. "Whatever it is, I want some."

The two sauntered to the kitchen and sat in Marva's favorite reading nook near the window overlooking the herb garden. Cass carried the casserole, a chicken potpie, to the booth and dished it up. She poured a hearty chocolate chai tea into their mugs, tantalizing for a brisk fall evening.

Bay began the tale of her escapade while they waited for their supper to cool, relishing her recital and her sister's reactions.

Cass, mesmerized by Bay's derring-do, crowed when Bay revealed Miriam's secret.

"A nudist colony! I have to admit that didn't cross my mind. I'm no prude, Lulu, but I'm guessing Miriam's position with the Lange Group and her church would be in jeopardy if word got out." Cass enjoyed a drink of tea and taste of the potpie.

Bay followed suit, exclaiming over Marva's cooking skills. "I admit, my curiosity won over my better judgment. I had to find out if there was more to Natural Habitat than a fancy spa resort. Besides, I'm not great at bargaining, Cass. I'm sure you would have finagled prime information out of Miriam."

Cass bore a pained smile. Intimidation may be her strong suit, but she wasn't always proud of it. She imagined Miriam would never willingly give up information without an arm twist. "I think you managed just fine."

Bay smiled over her tea mug. "I came away with something for you, too." She passed the scrap of paper from her pocket to Cass.

"Sister Philomena. Sisters of Saint Francis. Milwaukee." Cass read aloud. "What is this?"

"I hope a useful source of information about Posey. Miriam claims this nun can answer your questions." Inside, Bay hoped

Sister Philomena would bring Cass closure and help her move on from Posey's death.

"Thank you." Tears welled in her eyes. "Now, what are you going to do about Daniela?"

That was the million-dollar question.

Dear Miss Emily,

Today is Wednesday. My apologies for not writing yesterday. I slept. It seems the body knows more than the mind about what it needs. I guess that's why therapists and doctors say we should listen to our bodies. You and I are inclined to be mindful individuals, right? Your poems almost always challenge the mind, and many speak of the brain, the most powerful part of who we are.

Today is different. I am writing to you before sundown. One of the men comes and goes. I believe he is searching for Daniela. Often, he takes another man with him, leaving just two men to guard us. They grew weary and locked us inside the cabin to explore the property. We heard gunshots and waited. They are outside nearby, and a sickening smell rises in the air through the cabin walls. Valeria pushed the table to the single high window in this room. She stands on it and can barely see outside. She whispers they shot a deer and are skinning it, gutting it, and making a fire. Valeria cringes. I know what she's thinking. That could be me out there in place of the innocent deer.

Valeria tells me her plan, but I am not at liberty to speak of it, Miss Emily. I'm afraid these men will read my thoughts.

I miss my cats, and I hope that dear boy Joaquín is tending to them.

Until next time. —Vivian ∎

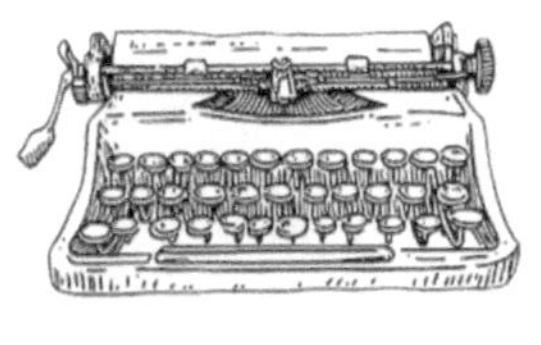

chapter 16

Sweeten the Deal

Marva tracked down Cassandra in her usual space of late. The Firehouse bustled with bubbling kettles of beeswax and coconut oil as Cass concentrated on perfecting her skin cream, which she soon hoped to add to Posey's traditional offerings. The skin cream offered a viable distraction for her grief, even a balm for her emotions.

"Smells altogether lovely in here, Miss Cassandra." Marva complimented Cass, despite their delay in completing the estate inventory.

"Here. Take this apple crumble pie over to Bluebird Hill." Marva set a tray on the stone table. The delicious scent of cinnamon, sugar, and cooked apples vied for attention with the lavender ylang-ylang body cream.

"Smells scrumptious. Did you make any for us?" Cass asked.

"As if I wouldn't," Marva said. "Miss Posey took apple crumble pie to Mrs. Adams every year, and I wouldn't want to disappoint her."

"How sweet of you to think of it, Marva. You're indispensable, you know. I don't tell you that enough." Cass stirred the kettles and turned off the burners.

Marva sputtered and waved off the comment. "Never mind that. The sooner you get this witchcraft done, the better. I don't care what that lawyer said, the inventory isn't going to finish itself. It's no use for either of us to dawdle about it."

Inwardly, Cass agreed. "Thanks for being patient with me. I need a little longer."

Marva wasn't buying the procrastination, and neither was Cass, but the housekeeper bobbed her head and left.

Cass poured the finished cream into jars to set and bagged herbs from the drying racks before she toted the pie across the road to Bluebird Hill.

Janet, Arlyss Mills's niece and personal nurse to Abigail Adams, answered the door and inhaled the incoming fragrance from the pie on the metal tray.

"Cassandra Browning, how nice to see you again. Come in. Mrs. Adams finished her bath and breakfast. Your visit and your pie will be welcome sights." Janet's positive attitude and bright uniform covered in pumpkins, autumn leaves, and apples, ushered Cass inside where Abigail perched in her chair by the bay window.

The aged woman's sour expression transformed when Cass breezed in to give her a gentle hug. "How are you today, besides squeaky clean?" Cass giggled.

"Hmph. I see you've talked to Janet. I told her I didn't need a bath, and I have a headache." Abigail pouted like a small child.

"Lucky for you, I brought a cure. Marva baked an apple crumble pie and Janet's in the kitchen plating it up this minute."

Cass sat in the chair opposite the robust woman.

Janet brought two dishes to the women, each with a towering piece of pie. The nurse had poured cream over Abigail's piece, her preferred way of indulging. Abigail closed her eyes, enjoying an exaggerated bite.

"Why the cream?" Cass asked.

"This is how my grandmother and mother served apple pie. They made this version with the crumble top and poured fresh cream over it instead of serving it a la mode. It takes me back to my happy childhood, Cassandra."

Janet passed tea to the two women, then held up a finger, remembering something.

"Cassandra, I was going to bring this over to you, but since you're here, you've saved me a trip." Janet handed an empty envelope to a perplexed Cass.

"What's this?" she asked, looking at the envelope addressed to the former Hunt housekeeper.

"Aunt Arlyss exchanges cards twice a year with Olga, the Hollingsworth housekeeper. She received a birthday card from Olga in August, and I found the empty envelope under her bed." Janet stabbed the corner. "See, here's the return address."

"Thank you for this." Cass beamed.

Abigail indulged in her pie while Janet and Cass chatted. "Do you plan to connect with Olga? Perhaps I can answer all your questions." Abigail puffed up like a peacock and turned to the nurse.

"Janet, my plate appears to be empty. Could you remedy that, please?"

Janet rolled her eyes and strutted out with the empty plate, shaking her head the whole way.

"Now, tell me what questions I can answer for you today." Abigail prodded, patting a few damp hairs back into her bun.

Cass admired the shrewd woman and tried to imagine how the Bluff Birds handled her during her heyday. "Hmm. Any chance you know a nun named Sister Philomena? She may have visited the Hollingsworth house."

Abigail thought about it. "Not anyone by that name, but Ramona Hollingsworth worked with the Catholic orphanage. The nuns ran the place, and Ramona was in the thick of it. She found all sorts of jobs on the bluff for those poor souls. The orphans, not the nuns."

Abigail's comment confirmed what Cass heard from others.

"Did Ramona employ any of the orphans? Someone named Joanna, for instance."

"Joanna. Perhaps. There was a girl that lived with them for a while, but Ramona kept her out of sight. Meaning, I never saw the girl at social outings." Abigail sipped a smoky liquid from a large mug, which Cass knew was chicory, something a Southern cousin introduced to Abigail when she was in her teens.

"Mind you, Ramona and I were not friends, Cassandra. Anyway, after Ramona had Posey, I never saw the girl again."

Abigail drifted off, added a spoonful of brown sugar to her mug, and stirred, deep in thought. "Is Browning your true name?"

Cass looked up in surprise. "It is."

"And are you related to the great poet, Robert Browning?"

"My father and grandparents always said he was somewhere in the tree."

Abigail patted Cass's knee. "Naturally, it must be true. Those gifts are passed on, Cassandra. Your sister's a prodigy scholar—literature runs through her veins. And you, you make poetry in your teas. Flowers and herbs are your words, and your tinctures are the verses."

Cass enjoyed Abigail's philosophical outlook. "What about you? It must be fate that you married a man named Adams. I think you'll be remembered for your namesake, even if she wasn't in your bloodline." Cass admired the historical Abigail Adams, a strong woman who ran the family farm and raised children alone because John Adams was away much of their married life.

"You know, I've been Abigail Adams for seventy-eight years. I wish I could have kept my family name. I'm the end of the McPhee line you know, an only child. Just like Ramona Weis."

"Who?"

"Oh dear. Ramona Hollingsworth, of course. She had a twin brother, Reuben. He drowned in the fishpond in their backyard. Crawled there when he was a year old, following his sister, who was already walking. Mr. Weis was never the same without a namesake. Or so people on the bluff said. Ramona's parents were ecstatic about marrying her off to Lionel, though. It seems her Madison prospects were dismal." Abigail tutted to herself, shaking her head. Perhaps she could muster empathy toward Ramona, after all.

Bay sat on the Natural Habitat bombshell until she finished teaching for the day. No matter how compelled she felt to involve Downing, she didn't want the police to bombard the colony and perhaps spook Daniela into deep cover. At least, that's what she told herself. Her final class ended at two o'clock, and she still didn't know how to approach the detective.

When she arrived in Downing's office, Bay squirmed in her seat.

"Spill it, whatever it is, Professor," Downing said. He had piles of information on his desk, and his disheveled exterior suggested he spent more time at the office than at home.

She couldn't waste his time. "Yesterday I followed Miriam Greggs after her volunteer job. The trail ended at a nudist colony, Downing!" Bay waited for his reaction.

"Just a minute." Downing rapped on the wall he shared with his partner, Harris.

Harris and Downing made a matching rumpled pair, a sorry indication of how Vivian's case was progressing. Harris sat and Downing instructed Bay to repeat the story.

"I saw Daniela working there. At least, I think it was her. It would be a decent place to hide." Bay added the new details.

Harris broke out in laughter. "Which one of us is going in undercover? Or should I say, uncovered?"

Downing echoed Harris's fit of laughter, uncharacteristic of the serious detective.

Bay looked from one to the other. "You two need to get some sleep."

"That's the naked truth, Professor." Harris roared and fist-bumped Downing.

Downing reined in his giggles when Bay glowered at him.

"You said you followed Miriam Greggs yesterday?" He took out his notepad.

"I did."

"Why didn't you call me last night or this morning?" Downing's eyes bored into hers.

Bay's dander rose. "Honestly, I don't think it's fair to expose

Miriam's secret. She's obviously working hard to keep it. I'm no snitch. If you two show up there, she's going to know I'm your source."

Harris suppressed a snort at the word "expose."

Downing ran his hand over his face. "The professor's right. Miriam will recognize me, so I can't go undercover. Does she know you, Harris?"

"She doesn't know me. I'm the new kid in town." Acting chief Marilyn Smart stood in the doorway, hands on hips. "I thought you two had gone off the deep end, cackling like apes. I came to find out."

"Begging your pardon, Ma'am, but do you intend to pose as a nudist?" Harris flushed red uttering the word in the presence of the chief.

Downing warmed to the idea. "It's a good plan, Chief. You can get a tour of the place and look for Daniela. Maybe ask about employment opportunities, you know, or like you're on the fence if you want to join the club."

Chief Smart held her palm forward like a stop sign. "I'm not going in as a prospective member. I'm going in as a state official making a surprise inspection. That should throw her off her game." The chief didn't smile but her eyes crinkled all the same.

"Professor Browning, get out. The detectives and I will handle this from here. If you don't want Miriam Greggs to know you tipped off the cops, try to lay low."

Bay was at a loss for words. Chief Smart was a force and Bay respected her. Without a backward glance at Downing, Bay gathered her things and exited. ∎

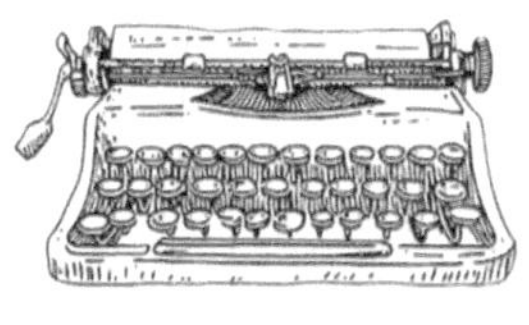

chapter 17

Undercover Operations

Chief Smart acquired a state car after calling in a favor from a colleague. She deputized her former partner, too, who agreed to accompany her in case of trouble. The chief couldn't afford to use Downing and Harris, whose time was valuable.

Downing liked the chief's chances with Miriam and wished he could witness the show. He knew the kind of power Miriam wielded in the small community. She'd be a tough nut to crack, but Chief Smart could be her undoing. Of course, finding Daniela was the prime objective.

In tandem with the chief's operation, Downing set a trap to catch the Colombian rebel looking for Daniela. Vivian's neighbor, Joaquín, agreed to help the detectives acting as a plant at the campus cafeteria, where the Colombian, Interpol identified as Ruiz, was seen showing around Daniela's photo.

Downing leveled with the student about the risk involved. "Joaquín, you should know this guy is a member of the ELN, the former National Liberation Army. He's dangerous, so if anything goes sideways, use the code word and we'll come to you."

Joaquín understood. "I want to help. I've met Daniela and some of the other refugees. They're here because they face danger in their home countries. But here they have hope."

Downing and Harris waited for Joaquín's signal behind the dormitory near the cafeteria, where Ruiz was seen hanging around the past two days. The detectives parked Harris's nondescript SUV in a tow-away zone.

Joaquín sat near the serving line, pretending to read a book and take notes. His cell screen opened on the photo of Ruiz that Bay took at the Isthmus Club, along with a description.

After a half hour, Joaquín started yawning and decided to order a coffee. When he joined the order line, he spotted Ruiz leaning against the wall peering around the cafeteria. Lunch was in full swing, the room was buzzing, and Joaquín knew it would take time for Ruiz to study everyone there.

Ruiz watched the line dwindle while students found seats, the moment Joaquín was waiting for. He approached a worker wiping down a table within hearing distance of Ruiz and struck up a conversation with him in Spanish.

Ruiz tuned in, especially when Joaquín mentioned Daniela's name in passing. When the worker shrugged, Joaquín picked up his belongings and left, Ruiz following behind him. Joaquín walked the opposite direction from the dormitory where the detectives waited, then paused pretending to check his cell phone. Ruiz grabbed his elbow.

"Hola, amigo. Sabes esta mujer?" Ruiz showed Joaquín the photograph of Daniela.

"I know her. Why?" Joaquín acted defensively and looked at

Ruiz with suspicion.

Ruiz relaxed his shoulders and flashed a friendly smile. "I'm Daniela's cousin from home. I'm here to surprise her." Ruiz leaned in to share a secret. "I tried to get the student office to give me her address, but you know how that works."

Joaquín nodded in agreement. "I know where she lives. Follow me."

Downing and Harris readied themselves to ambush Ruiz.

Joaquín lured the Colombian toward the dormitory building and skirted past the main doors.

Ruiz stopped in his tracks and grabbed Joaquín by his jacket. "Is this the building? Why aren't we going in those doors?" He scowled.

"It's shorter to go up the back stairs. Come on." Joaquín sidestepped the brute and picked up his pace. He hoped the Colombian wasn't on to him and would follow. Ruiz could be desperate enough to ignore the easy setup.

Joaquín rounded the building, then disappeared into a group of chatting students near the entrance. Ruiz took the corner, charging like a bull, his eyes darting around for Joaquín, which is why he failed to notice the detectives. Downing tripped the man, and Harris landed on top of him, pinning him to the ground and announcing the arrest. Downing cuffed a swearing Ruiz, who struggled all the way to the police SUV.

The two detectives enjoyed the small victory and hoped it would buy Vivian another three days of safety before they would have to charge Ruiz or release him.

On their way to the station, Downing's phone brought an unexpected lead from his pilot friend, Jeff Johnson.

"This is Downing." He saw the caller ID but wanted to protect Jeff with Ruiz in the back seat.

"Hey, Detective. I've got an interesting bit of information for you. Cliff Marsden's plane that landed in Massachusetts last week? Yeah, well he fueled it once, and that was on Saturday. I looked at the log dates again."

"What are you saying?" Downing pressed.

"Marsden didn't fly anywhere far on Friday night. He's got a parking place on his property. The official log shows him at an airfield in the Berkshires owned by one Robert Zabel, corporate bigwig, on Saturday, not Friday." Jeff waited for Downing to think it through.

A bubble of hope burst inside the detective's belly, but he couldn't say anything with Ruiz in the car. "Gotcha. Thanks for the information, Man. We'll talk soon." He hung up and glanced at Harris with an eager grin. Vivian and the kidnappers never left Wisconsin. In fact, he wagered they were nearby.

Miles away in the countryside, Chief Smart, dressed in a state uniform, buzzed the entrance to Natural Habitat. Her former partner, semi-retired officer Dotson, chomped at the bit to act out his part.

"I'm glad you called me, Marilyn. I've been doing desk work for seven months, and well you know me, my feet are itchy for some action."

The chief offered a lopsided smile to the partner she'd spent nineteen years beside. She trusted him more than her own family. "Take it easy, Maverick. You've got five months until full retirement. I won't be able to look Connie in the eye if something happens to you."

Dotson chuckled. "I can't die. That woman has oodles of projects waiting for me."

"What's your name and your appointment time, please?" A man's voice intoned.

"Inspectors Gray and Manning from the state." The chief added extra gravel to her voice.

The gate slid open, and the Ford truck drove up the immaculate tree-lined drive and parked in the visitor lot. A youthful man dressed in tan slacks and a navy-blue polo shirt bounded toward the two before they exited the truck.

"Hello. I'm Damien, the office manager. May I see your paperwork?" Damien picked an invisible lint from his shirt and examined his manicured nails, a bored expression on his face.

Chief Smart handed official-looking paperwork to the young man and flashed her badge.

"Hm. I see. I don't have an inspection on my calendar today." Damien, rather put out for the intrusion, blinked several times, lips puckered. "Could you reschedule?"

The chief and Dotson looked at each other and burst into simultaneous laughter, putting Damien at ease.

The laughter stopped abruptly, and their faces turned to stone. "Of course not. This is a surprise inspection." The chief scanned the paperwork. "Let's see. The proprietor listed here is Miriam Greggs. We'll get started outside, while you fetch Ms. Greggs. Tell her to bring a list of everyone employed here." The chief flicked her hands at Damien in dismissal, and the manager left in a huff.

Smart and Dotson divided the perimeter according to the posted signs.

"You can take the grounds that way, Maverick." She motioned toward the wooded walk, stone meditation circle, and artist workshop. "I'll take the sauna, pool, and outdoor exercise deck. Let's meet here afterwards and compare notes."

"Sounds good, Chief."

"And Maverick? Don't get unduly distracted." She chortled.

Smart was halfway to the pool area where she spotted several people lounging under cabanas. The heavy scent of coconut assaulted her nose, making her sneeze, attracting attention from some women.

"Damn." What was the proper protocol here? Should she wave or ignore them? She let the state uniform dictate her move. Official business. She'd ignore them. She kept walking, stopped to examine the pool house equipment, and counted life jackets. All the while, her eyes searched for workers.

Miriam hurried down the walkway and appeared at the nature pool where Smart was checking the water temperature.

"Excuse me, Inspector…" Miriam was the picture of calm, looking ready to board a sailboat in her pale blue seersucker pants and top.

"Gray. Are you Miriam Greggs?" The chief made certain to scan the document for her name, pretending she had a long list of names on today's agenda.

"Yes, Inspector. Damien says you asked for a record of employees." Miriam held out a folder to comply, but the chief waved it away.

"In due time. I'll finish my outside inspection first. Afterwards, you'll take me for a tour inside."

"I believe we passed our inspection last year with flying colors. I've no doubt you will find everything as it should be,

Inspector Gray." Miriam tilted her chin upward and sniffed the air, resembling a standard poodle, except her curls hung loose and carefree.

"Where's your assistant, Inspector? I'm afraid I cannot allow anyone to traverse the grounds unaccompanied." Miriam explained with a pretend apology.

"He's on the path to the woods and meditation circle." Smart's nonchalant manner made Miriam bristle, which the chief expected, and left Miriam with the conundrum of following the chief or chasing down Dotson.

The chief scrutinized the natural rock pool with interest. "Where's the motor for this pool? And what sort of chemicals do you use? I don't smell chlorine."

Miriam puffed up with pride. "It's a saltwater pool. The lap pool is too." She pointed toward the nude cabana loungers.

"I see." The chief was noncommittal about the benefit of saltwater versus chlorine, to Miriam's dismay.

Miriam tried to be helpful in hopes of expediting the process. "Here's where the equipment, temperature controls, and motors are." She led the chief behind the natural pool where a door was cleverly concealed among the rocks.

"Thank you. I'll check the report sheets." Smart whirled around to face Miriam. "You know, Ms. Greggs, you could have one of your employees show me around outside and save you the trouble."

Miriam smarted as if she'd been slapped. "No, I'm afraid not." She gazed toward the wooded path and meditation circle, as if she could materialize in both places.

"Feel free to check on Inspector Manning. I'll be checking the exercise equipment on the deck over there." Smart turned in that direction and saw a dark-haired woman wearing yoga pants and a wide crop top. Daniela. Smart was half certain.

Miriam followed the chief's eyeline and changed course. "Let me show you where to find the exercise gear."

The chief hustled toward the deck while Miriam struggled to keep pace in her fashion sandals. Smart greeted the woman, sure this was the refugee her detectives sought.

"Hello. I'm Inspector Gray. Do you work here?" she asked.

Daniela couldn't find her voice, wary of any strangers. She narrowed her eyes and made her own inspection of the inspector, who seemed to look the part. "Yes, I work here. Sometimes I teach yoga."

"Could you point me in the direction of the exercise equipment?"

Daniela waved the chief over to a tall rattan cabinet and opened the double doors revealing blocks, mats, hand weights, straps, and bolsters. The bottom shelf contained sanitizing cleaner and an inventory sheet.

Miriam joined the two women. "I've got this, Maria. You may continue what you were doing."

"No. I need her to stay." Smart fixed her eyes on Miriam, her tone stern. "Let's sit down somewhere private."

Miriam's confusion turned into anxiety. "We can enter my office from that walkway." Miriam led the chief, with Daniela in the middle, down a stone pathway surrounded by hydrangeas with fading cone-shaped blossoms. The chief was satisfied Miriam had no place to bolt to unless she jumped through the bushes, and Smart held the advantage, bringing up the rear.

Miriam pulled keys from her pocket and unlocked the

side entrance that led to offices and private guest rooms. She opened another door onto a spacious office decorated in muted green and lilac. Chief Smart caught a sharp lavender scent as she indicated both women should sit. The chief closed the door and pulled a chair to the side of Miriam's desk, between the two women.

"What's going on here?" Miriam folded her arms across her chest.

"You called this woman Maria, but that's not her name, is it, Ms. Greggs?" Chief said, evenly.

"I guess you're not a state inspector." Miriam tossed her head defiantly.

"No. Police Chief Smart from Prairie Ridge. We've been looking for Daniela Vargas in connection with a kidnapping. You both could help us by being honest." Marilyn Smart was a smooth operator who expected compliance.

Miriam relaxed a tad. "I've been trying to keep Daniela safe ever since Vivian Rossi disappeared. This was the most secure space I could think of for her."

The chief held Miriam's gaze until the woman shifted in discomfort.

"I appreciate your efforts, Ms. Greggs, but the police have a job to do." Chief Smart turned toward Daniela. "I'll be taking an official statement from you."

Daniela wiped perspiration from her upper lip while looking for direction from Miriam. "Right now?" she asked.

"Yes. Unless you wish to come to the station with me."

Daniela wilted in the chair.

"Ms. Greggs, could you bring us some water, please?"

Miriam returned bearing two fancy glasses of water with

slices of lemon and cucumber floating among the ice cubes and a pitcher filled with the same. To her consternation, she found the chief seated behind her desk, rifling through the drawers.

"Ah, perfect. Now I just need a writing tablet." The chief held her pen aloft.

Miriam's face clouded with annoyance. "Oh, let me." She opened the middle drawer, shoving it harder than necessary into Chief Smart's chest. "Use this." She pushed a yellow pad toward the chief.

"Thank you. If you could wait outside. I still need to speak with you, too." The chief was the picture of serenity.

Miriam stomped out the door and slammed it, then poked her head in a beat later. "What am I supposed to do with your assistant, officer? I imagine he's not doing an official inspection either." Her tone was haughty.

Marilyn Smart laughed. In her success at finding Daniela, she'd forgotten about poor Maverick. "Go find him, please. That will give you something productive to do while I take Daniela's statement. He would enjoy one of these." She pointed at the water.

Miriam shut the door a little less loudly but with a firm smack to make her point. Behind the door, the chief and Daniela heard her mutter. "What am I, a common serving wench?"

With gentle encouragement from Chief Smart, Daniela talked about the sponsorship by Project Square One.

"Vivian Rossi contacted me after hearing about my plight in Colombia. Although my country was recovering from drug cartels and violence, the ELN works in secret to gain members and rebuild its power. My father is an important politician in the government and the likely future candidate for the presidency." Her face filled with worry.

"Tell me more about how you came to the United States."

"The professor flew to Cartagena to meet with people who could help me escape. My stepmother is related to some of the head recruiters for the ELN army. I don't trust her. She knew I found out about her and threatened me. She's behind a plan to have me kidnapped by the ELN and force my father to leave his position." A sob caught in Daniela's throat, and she gulped some water.

Chief Smart reached for her hand and patted it. "How frightening for you and your family. Does your father know where you are?"

Tears dripped down Daniela's face as she shrugged. "I couldn't contact him until I was out of my country. I sent him a message and disabled my phone afterwards. He knows I'm in America, but he doesn't know where."

"You said Vivian Rossi met people in Cartagena. How did you escape?"

Daniela curbed her tears and drank more water. She smiled. "Vivian is a wonderful, brave woman. She brought legal documents to me in Colombia and flew with me here. Vivian and her foundation found us housing and helped us find part-time work and English tutors." The happy memory was short-lived, replaced by fear for Vivian and the danger of her current situation.

"The men who took Vivian are looking for me. I'm certain. I know a member of the ELN has been showing my photo around campus. I wore a disguise to the poetry slam, to avoid being recognized."

The chief caught on and considered Cassandra's description of suspicious people at the coffee shop. "Were you the woman in the green headscarf and long tunic?"

"Yes. I knew if I wore a Muslim outfit, I could be unrecognizable. I've been careful not to be found. That's why I emailed my professors that I'm ill and won't be in classes this week. Miriam gave me a room here for a hideout."

The chief frowned and began considering the need to bring in the feds. "You said Vivian brought legal documents. Were they from the government or United Nations?" There were missing connections in the case, including how the ELN knew about Vivian.

"I don't know. The documents changed my real name so I could leave my country undetected." Daniela's eyebrows trembled. She suspected the documents were forgeries. She knew the people Vivian met in Cartagena worked underground.

The chief tapped the pen on the pad of paper as understanding dawned. If Vivian didn't use proper channels to bring Daniela here, being saved from the kidnappers was just the beginning of her problems. "I see."

A knock on the door interrupted the chief's train of thought. "What is it?"

Maverick Dotson entered, absorbing the scene. "You might have radioed me you found the lady." Dotson's mild irritation retreated, replaced by a sneering grin. The chief knew her former partner's trademark expression meant one thing: he had a find of his own.

"Chief Smart, meet Aneka Umar. We bumped into each

other on the wooded path." He rubbed his head. "Literally."

Aneka bowed her head toward the chief with respect. Smart noticed Aneka's traditional Muslim garb, a flowing tunic over loose fitting pants and a headscarf. "Nice to meet you, Aneka. Let me guess: you're hiding here, too."

Aneka ran to Daniela and the two hugged, each speaking in rapid Spanish.

"I took Aneka's statement, Smart. I think we need to have a roundup at the station with your detectives." He jabbed his thumb at Aneka and Daniela, changed his mind about speaking aloud, and strode to the chief's side.

"What are we going to do with these two?" Dotson whispered.

The chief stood up, a concrete tower of military precision. "Let me speak with Miriam Greggs. I'll meet you at the station. Keep the detectives on ice until I get there, would you?"

Miriam strutted into her office to reclaim it, shooing the police chief out of her reclining desk chair as soon as Daniela and Aneka were allowed to return to work. Chief Smart professed an exaggerated thanks to Miriam for her cooperation, which calmed the woman for a brief hiatus.

"I empathize with the police department, but I'm trying to run a professional retreat here. Surely you must understand that my clients expect privacy and a therapeutic experience." Miriam poured water from the pitcher into the glass she kept by her desk.

The unruffled chief sat in the chair on the client side of the desk, relinquishing her post for the moment. "Perhaps it would be wise for you to compose yourself. My partner left, and people here believe I'm a state inspector. Daniela and Aneka won't say otherwise for their own well-being. Let's talk."

Chief Smart handed a statement form to Miriam. "First, I need you to complete this in full for our records. Once that's accomplished, someone from here will return me to the police station." The chief remembered that she and Dotson drove together to the resort.

Miriam began to study the statement form. "And what of Daniela and Aneka?"

"You write your statement, while I make some phone calls. Perhaps you can work in the reception area." Smart indicated the sitting room outside the office.

Miriam's ears burned and she sputtered like a hot teakettle. "You would make a poor office manager, Ms. Smart."

Miriam bristled and clomped from the room, while the chief reoccupied the territory behind the desk. She bounced a little in the comfortable chair and settled in, took a deep breath, and pulled up the contact list on her work phone. Now for the hard part. Her finger hovered over the list of FBI resources before she selected the least devil in the bunch.

When Miriam returned, she slapped the written statement on the desk hard enough to create a breeze that lifted Chief Smart's shirt collar. The chief opened one eye like an ancient bloodhound surveying its surroundings before deciding to resume its nap.

"I appreciate how thorough you must have been, Ms. Greggs," the unfazed Smart said.

"Indeed. Isn't it about time you retired?" Miriam jabbed the intruder. She was used to dealing with adversaries during her tenure at the Lange Corporation, and some of them were the uniformed variety.

"Yes, I suppose it is. Who will be driving me to the station?" The chief began to rise but remembered they had unfinished business. She sat down again.

"Daniela and Aneka will be allowed to remain on the premises for now. A plainclothes federal agent will be assigned to stay here until Vivian's case is resolved." Smart enjoyed a witty thought and twisted her lips. "Or should I say a federal agent out of plain clothes?"

Miriam raised her chin in the air. "Must we be subjected to the intrusion of a government agent?"

Chief Smart understood—she shared Miriam's sentiments about government intrusion. She heaved an exaggerated sigh. "Yes, I'm afraid we must. I hope you have somewhere suitable to house the agent, who I assure you will not be sans clothing."

Miriam ignored the chief's taunt. "Very well. We have a wing dedicated to our undecided clothed members. Daniela and Aneka have rooms in that section, too. When might I be welcoming our guest?" Her voice lingered on the word "guest" with a hiss.

"Arrangements are being made. Meanwhile, Officer Dotson will return as temporary security."

Miriam stood, hoping the chief would get the message. "Oh joy, does that mean you'll be departing now?"

The chief's practiced sedate stare etched her face and she remained planted there. "I believe I'm ready to leave. Will you be driving me?"

Miriam forgot the chief was without transportation. Lucky for Miriam, she had plenty of security on staff and could spare someone for the task.

"No. If you'll wait over there, I'll let you know when your car arrives." Miriam swung her arm toward the outer seating area like a pitcher aiming for the batter's head.

Back at the police station, semi-retired officer Dotson captivated Downing and Harris with his tale of locating not only Daniela, but also Aneka Umar. The detectives congratulated him on the undercover operation but wondered how the chief would proceed with the two refugees.

While they waited for Chief Smart's full report of the operation, Downing watched over Ruiz personally. He didn't trust the man and wouldn't allow any interference for the duration they could hold him. He was frustrated Ruiz's vehicle wasn't found, even more frustrated the Dane County cops turned up nothing regarding the van or the car the perps used.

Downing set up a table outside the cell where he searched his police laptop, flagging intel about the ELN and any known associates of Ruiz. The detective confiscated Ruiz's cell phone and asked the accused to open it. Ruiz spit at him.

"I guess that's a no. No worries. I'll get a court order." Downing bluffed. He doubted they could hold Ruiz with nothing concrete except the fact he was looking for Daniela. Yet.

In his office, Harris combed through every inch of the papers Ruiz had on him, including all his comings and goings logged electronically over the past two weeks, hoping to connect him to illegal activity of any kind and find the kidnappers. Dotson jumped aboard, too, searching computer files to find Professor Obasi's imposter and a link between the two refugees.

Two hours passed without sign of the chief and the detectives grew restless. Mandy Harris waltzed into the bank of cells and greeted Downing, who looked like a caged tiger.

"Can I have a word." Mandy presented a piercing glare at Ruiz, who bolted toward the cell bars, licking his lips.

"Downing. You and Nolan need to talk. I'm here to watch Ruiz. Don't worry. He's not going to bother me." Mandy slapped her palm against her nightstick, nostrils flared, eyes on Ruiz. The prisoner retreated to his bunk. "The chief called me in. I've got this."

Downing shot Ruiz a deadeye stare and whispered to Mandy. "I'm right down the hall if he so much as twitches."

Harris and Downing were comparing notes when Chief Smart walked in. "Let's go to my office."

Dotson was already seated when the chief opened the case file and laid out the statements from Daniela, Aneka, and Miriam, one by one.

"There's plenty here for your review, but here are the highlights. Daniela Vargas is actually Daniela Bolivar, a descendent of the famous South American hero Simón Bolívar. Her father is a member of the government and heir apparent to the presidency. Except, the ELN is reconvening to stop him. And get this: Daniela's stepmother was a former ELN who still has family in the army." The chief paused to let the dust settle.

Downing whistled and Harris held one hand over his chest in disbelief.

"Then there's Aneka, who is not from Nigeria. She's a prodigious environmental scientist from Cartagena who crossed paths in all the wrong ways with the ELN. She's completing her doctorate here thanks to Vivian's foundation.

Whomever the Obasi imposter is, well, he may be connected to the kidnappers, too."

The chief passed the women's statements across the desk to the dazed detectives. "We have their recorded interviews, too, which might be helpful for a quick study."

Downing interjected. "What else?"

The chief strived to keep her tone level. "The women will stay at Natural Habitat." She raised her hand in response to the detectives' protests. "Under federal protection."

Downing swore. "You brought in the feds. FBI? Interpol?" Downing radiated heat.

"Whoa. Settle down, Detective. You think the two women would be safer and more comfortable in our jail?"

An image of the snarling Ruiz came to Downing's mind. "I guess we don't have anything better to offer them here. But the feds." His painful expression spoke volumes.

"Who's the agent?" Harris asked.

"Madrid. He was in the area already." The chief said. "Not what I asked for, but I don't have any pull." It was time to change topics. "It's your turn. Fill me in."

Downing and Harris shared the success of using Joaquín to lure in the Colombian Ruiz, his connections to the ELN, and their ability to have his passport yanked. "We want to get into his phone. Of course, he's not cooperating."

"We have enough cause to make that happen if we find the proper judge." Smart suggested, a wily look on her face. "I know a couple."

"What about Miriam Greggs? Does she need protection?" Downing asked.

The chief snorted. "Miriam Greggs was squirming like a

mad cat in a swimming pool to have us on her turf. She's smart and capable. I offered her an extra patrol around her house, but she said she would stay at the resort until Vivian is found. And I agreed we would keep her name out of the case files."

Downing and Harris protested. "You can't do that. Her statement is part of the official record." The two spoke over each other, adding objections.

Chief Smart blew a whistle she wore on a chain underneath her shirt, an old habit from military days. "That's enough. Look you two. We had two successful operations today. Let's get cracking on finding Vivian Rossi and, as you propose, her sister. If they didn't leave Wisconsin, we narrowed down the options to familiar territory."

Downing and Harris, defeated and sheepish, rose to leave the chief's office.

"Wait a minute. Downing, call your Professor Browning. She's officially reinstated on the case." The chief smiled. "Good work today, men." ∎

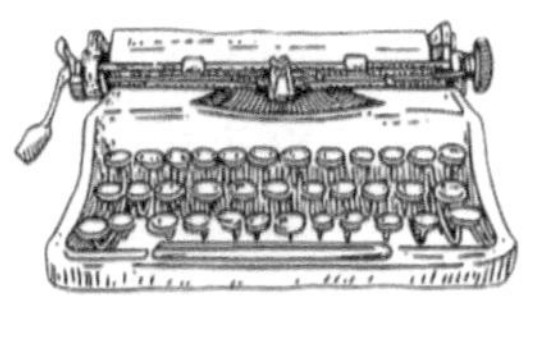

chapter 18

Romancing the Stones

Bay smarted from the abrupt dismissal by Chief Smart but convinced herself it was for the best. The police needed to concentrate on rescuing Vivian and protecting Daniela and Aneka. She couldn't fault the chief for her decision.

At least she had a clear conscience and could focus on her Friday classes, which were blessedly few. Most college students filled their schedules from Monday through Thursday, and Flourish planned accordingly, with fewer offerings on Fridays. Bay had a morning class with the afternoons free to jump start weekend grading.

She planned to ask Cass to have supper with her. Before she could make the call, a zing went through her chest when the phone vibrated in her hand. "Maybe I'm psychic after all, at least where family is concerned."

But Marva was the caller. "Professor Browning. Can you come up to the bluff?" Marva was breathless.

Bay panicked. "Yes. On my way. What's going on?"

Bay turned the Land Rover toward Bird Street.

"Best I tell you when you arrive. Just come." Marva disconnected.

Upon arrival, Bay left the SUV running and didn't bother to knock on Spirit Gardens's front door.

Marva sat in the entryway at the ready.

"You made good time," she said.

"Where's my sister?" Bay asked.

Marva climbed into the Land Rover. "Let's go. I'll talk while you drive. Take a right at the end of the lane."

Marva explained that she was cleaning upstairs when she discovered a pewter box of stones in Posey's bathroom. She shouted for Cass, who was working in the music room down the hallway.

"You see, Miss Posey used all sorts of stones for healing and energy, that kind of hocus pocus stuff. That's why I called Miss Cassandra. I know she understands magic, being she's got the touch, you know. Speaking of which, I wasn't about to touch those stones." Marva's meandering seemed to come full circle.

"Okay, got it. So, Cass took the box of stones?" Bay failed to see the urgency.

"Right. She's at Spindrift Lake on account of the stones needing cleansing, you see." Marva made it sound like a trip to the convenience store.

"And that's where we're going. Spindrift Lake?"

"You're not getting it. There's some hidden magic in cleansing them stones and your sister shouldn't be doing it alone. Them stones are harmful."

Marva's shrill tone stung Bay's ears but she increased her speed. Bay knew the kind of sensitivity that was central to

Cassandra's gifts, and she couldn't be certain how the so-called healing stones might affect her.

The women saw Cass's car parked in the wide gravel lot located at the top of Angel Bird Bluff offering a stunning view of Spindrift below jagged quartzite cliffs. Wooded trails wound down to the lake.

Bay changed from casual work shoes into sneakers while she studied the trail map posted behind the glass case on an information board. The shortest trail to the shore was also the steepest, yet speed dictated Bay's path.

Marva called after Bay that she would take the flatter trail and meet them below, but Bay didn't have confidence in Marva's agility. "Right, see you at the bottom. Be careful." Bay concentrated on the rocky path fraught with tree roots.

She rounded the end of the trail and looked at the shoreline. The late afternoon sun made golden ripples on the water thanks to a ruffling breeze. Cass knelt a few yards ahead where the shore curved around a mammoth boulder near a smooth pool.

She made out other-worldly sounds, a cross between a chant and a wail, and she hesitated to call out to her sister, instead hurrying down the shore to her side.

Cass's eyes were closed, and she clutched a golden faceted crystal, reciting a prayer of sorts, as she swished it in her palm under the water. Stinging tears flowed, and a sudden jolt lifted her to stand.

She opened her eyes, the crystal cooling in her fist, and saw Bay.

"Bay, how did you know I was here?" Cass sounded like a frail child.

"Marva called me. She said you're doing something you shouldn't do alone. I'm here. What can I do to help?" Bay reached for Cass's hand, but she snatched it from her.

"Posey used stones for healing and trauma, some of it emotional. The stones need to be cleansed each time they're used, but her time ran out before she could perform the ritual. I'm doing it in her honor." Cass gasped for breath.

"Cassandra, I can't allow you to take on this burden alone. I'm here to help." Bay claimed ignorance about healing stones but was willing to learn for her sister's sake.

Cass sat down beside Bay and dropped the golden faceted rock onto a cloth on the shore. "This is Posey's keeping box." She gestured toward the individual compartments with silk pouches that held stones, while other stones lay on top of the pouches. Bay surmised Cass had completed the ritual for the three stones lying on the shore.

"The unwrapped stones were the last ones Posey used for healing. There's an incantation to say while they are washed in fresh water. After, they can be stored again in the pouches."

"There's something else happening, though. This stone drained your energy or hurt you, didn't it?" Bay pointed at the golden crystal.

"That's citrine. It has powerful organ healing properties. Posey used it to quell her suffering from multiple sclerosis, which affected her whole body. When someone channels the power of stones and someone else touches them before the stones are cleansed, there can be negative reactions."

"Why don't you just toss them all in the lake and walk away?" Bay knew what she would do given the option.

"Because I'm honoring Posey. Because these are precious

stones. Because it might matter." Cass's lip trembled. She couldn't formulate reasons to match her feelings.

"Okay. Which stone can I cleanse?" Bay reached toward the box and felt a magnetic pull toward a multicolored polished stone. Its whorls of black, pink, and green mesmerized Bay and she touched it before Cass could stop her.

The stone froze Bay's hand in a claw-like grip while resentment and misery filled her heart. A vision of her mother, Penelope, rose in her mind's eye. Penelope rocking a baby Diana in her arms, singing her a lullaby. Bay struggled with her sense of fairness, angry with Diana for claiming her mother for herself, angry with her father for hiding the truth from Bay, angry with everyone who knew the secret and kept Bay in the dark for decades. Beyond the consuming abscess of bitterness, Cassandra's voice carved a slice of salvation.

"Lulu, move your hand through the water but don't let go of the stone."

Bay's hand was numb, but her brain moved it from instinct. Into the water Bay's hand floated, then thawed.

"Here. Open your eyes and read the incantation." Cass shouted the instruction. "Now!"

Bay read the words, which sounded like poetry, rather than a spell or wicked art. The words were English, simple, musical.

She repeated the verse twice and the hard stone grew warm and silky like lotion. The resentment and misery subsided, replaced with a peaceful resolve. "What just happened?" Bay separated from the experience, knowing she felt something she must deal with in the near future.

"Jasper. It can evoke a gazillion emotions. It's impossible to know what Posey was using it for. Perhaps to get a handle on the evil that was coming for her the night she died. I think she felt it. Are you okay?"

Bay shivered as slivers of emotion coursed through her, finding spaces to occupy. "Powerful hocus-pocus, Marva would say. I'll tell you about it sometime."

Bay observed the remaining two stones in the keeping box. "One for each of us?"

Cass smiled for the first time since Bay showed up on the lakeshore. "Lucky for us, I saved the best stones for last. At least, I hope so. Both have rejuvenating properties. Amethyst." Cass pointed at the rich purple stone covered in bright sparkling crystals.

"That one is black and white agate."

Bay admired the large polished oval stone with rivulets of lace in contrasting black and white mapping out a geometric pattern. "It's beautiful." She nodded toward the agate, careful not to reach for it.

"It's settled. The incantation is the same. Go ahead and take the agate. Let's pick up the stones on the count of three."

At first the stones sapped their strength, forcing them to their knees like puppets with their strings cut. Cass reached for Bay and forced out a whisper, "Read."

The sisters murmured the incantation, straining to speak. The second time their whispers came in unison, and the third recitation tinkled with the melody of a babbling brook. They placed the stones on the beach, exhausted.

Cass joined Bay and placed a large warm stone in her hand. Its soothing heat and smooth surface offered immediate respite while she breathed the cool lake air. Cass clasped Bay's hand with the stone radiating between them.

"It's called a sunstone. Posey gave it to me. Something she picked up in Central America. The stone absorbs the sun, and its heat is used for fatigue and sore muscles," she whispered.

Marva rounded the bend on the shore moments later, relieved to witness the serenity of the sisters sitting hand in hand, their faces lifted toward the dome of sky as the sun settled below the tree line.

She brushed her palms in quick swipes, satisfied their task was finished. "Good. Let's go have dinner, you two."

At the top of the trailhead, Marva rubbed her back and shoulders. "I'm sorry but I'm going to make a side trip to the pharmacy. In all this hubbub I forgot to pick up my prescription and arthritis cream."

Bay volunteered to go instead. "Cass, take Marva to Spirit Gardens and I'll meet you there. We can all make dinner together."

The pharmacy was a hot spot, with most people doing their shopping after work before heading home. Bay waited in line for the pharmacy tech, an efficient man who had no trouble with Bay picking up Marva's prescription. He also directed her to the aisle to locate arthritis creams.

Bay perused the options, unaware such a myriad of pain relievers existed. She read the labels, her eye on a man standing down the aisle. His hands were stuffed in his jacket pockets, and he paced around, looking over the top of the aisle toward the pharmacy counter. *He must be waiting for a prescription he dropped off.* Bay wondered if he was sick or if he had someone waiting in the car for needed medication.

She continued comparing creams and gels designed for

arthritic pain and noticed the man began picking up common items: bandages, antibiotic ointments, and aspirin. His head swiveled side to side on repeat. *Why is this guy so nervous?*

Distracted, Bay selected two different creams and made her way to the register. As she paid for the items, the pharmacy tech announced, "Prescription for Rossi. Prescription for Rossi."

Bay's heart thumped like a metronome. "Rossi," she whispered, grabbed the plastic bag from the counter, and sprinted to the pharmacy section. Peeking around the pain reliever aisle, she spotted the nervous man claiming the prescription for Rossi and paying for the first aid supplies.

Bay could barely breathe. The man could be Colombian, could be one of Vivian's captors. Her brain told her she had to follow him.

She dashed to her SUV and waited. The man climbed into a van. Bay's eyes watered. She recognized the van. It matched the one she saw men tossing Vivian into days earlier. She whispered a quick prayer for better tailing skills than when she followed Miriam Greggs, and eased the car out of the parking lot, turning right after the van did.

Bay thanked the slow city speed limits, traffic lights, and commuters that allowed her to call Cass.

"Dinner's on hold. I saw Vivian's kidnapper at the pharmacy, and I'm following the van now. Can you call Downing?"

"Are you sure about the man and van?" Cass asked.

"He picked up a prescription for Rossi. He looked nervous, and the van is a match. I've got to go, Cass. I need to focus."

"I wish I were with you. Be careful. I'll call Downing." ■

Message Received

Dear Emily,

Today is Thursday. It is Come Hell or High-Water Day. Perhaps I will see you soon. Or not. —Vivian

Vivian continued the narrative in her head. Valeria looks ill this morning. The three soldiers prowl around, making us nervous. The man named Ruiz never returned yesterday, and I wonder if he has Daniela somewhere or flew her off to Colombia. My heart is heavy, and I feel nauseous.

The skinny man named Cerdo with the shifty eyes—today his eyes dart every which way like a ping-pong ball I cannot keep up with. Raton, the big man, squeezes Valeria's shoulder as he peers at her computer screen. I see he's hurting her, and I want to kick him.

"You will finish this today," Raton growls like an animal.

Valeria removes his hand, lifting one finger at a time, until he stares in shock at her ability to do so.

"If you want this done today, I need two things." Her voice is steady and certain, and I'm amazed by her resolve, because mine is depleted.

Raton barks out some kind of Spanish curses and stomps around the table to challenge Valeria face to face. Cerdo watches bewildered. The third man, Garcia, is outside cooking venison.

"You can ask for nothing." Raton adds an insulting vulgarity meant to intimidate my sister, but today my sister is not an authentication expert for the Kent Society. Today, she's an Amazon warrior.

"Your documents can wait." Valeria turns off the screen and closes the computer lid. She stretches both arms over her head and sits beside me on the cot.

Instead of waiting for Raton and Cerdo to react, she takes charge. "My sister's wrists are injured from these zip ties. You need to cut them off. She isn't going to run." Valeria's voice holds disgust and rage at seeing me hurt. "I'm not working until you cut the ties."

Raton and Cerdo join their heads in hushed conversation, then Cerdo nods and approaches me, wielding a hunting knife. Something inside me flickers like a fire starter and instead of flinching, I meet his gaze with a fierce stare I didn't know was possible. What a marvel to me: I watch him falter. Sharp pain seizes my wrists when Cerdo jerks them and slices the plastic zips apart.

Valeria helps me move my arms because the joints forgot how, but the feeling of changing arm positions is euphoric and waylays the stinging welts on my wrists for the moment.

"Back to work," Raton says to my sister, but she keeps her

place by my side.

Valeria raises her hands and proceeds with caution to my mini handbag. She withdraws an empty brown pill bottle.

"My sister has a serious thyroid condition and is out of medication. One of you needs to take this to a pharmacy and refill it. Today." Her voice rides a steady current of fearless determination.

"No." Raton regards the pill bottle and Valeria, thinking each may bite him.

Valeria folds her hands in her lap, pill bottle enclosed. "I'm not working until she has medication. She cannot live without it, and if anything happens to her, you can kill me because I'm not going to help you." Valeria's statement is a battle cry.

What happens next is a miracle. Raton takes the bottle and tells Cerdo he will go.

Cerdo protests. "You're going to leave us here without a vehicle? You're loco. What if something happens?"

The two men speak in rapid Spanish involving hand gestures, and I can tell from their body language that neither of them looks happy, least of all Cerdo, who swears up a storm when Raton mentions Garcia, the man outside, and Ruiz, the missing kidnapper who's looking for Daniela.

Valeria and I wait and watch to see if the trap is set. Garcia brings in cooked meat, frowns at our closeness, notices my free hands, and asks for an explanation. Now all three argue at once. I see the matter is settled when Garcia and Raton stand united, glaring at Cerdo, who looks defeated.

"Guard them. Don't screw up. We will be back after we find Ruiz."

Valeria and I hold our breath and clamp our lips shut to

keep from smiling. Unexpectedly, it's two against one, and we have a plan.

Cerdo sulks and eats his fill of cooked venison while Valeria resumes her work on the computer. When my sister gives me the signal, pretending to remove something from her eye, I begin to gag; my whole body shudders in violent jolts like a seizure.

Both Cerdo and Valeria come to my side and my sister holds onto me.

"Quick. She's having a seizure. Go outside and grab a stick about this big around for her to bite onto." Valeria speaks with authority in the face of Cerdo's uncertainty.

He leaves the door open, and Valeria gathers needed objects from the outer room, which serves as a campground office. She runs in and stows a lighter and two packaged items under the cot.

Cerdo returns with a stick but can see the seizure has passed. My breathing has normalized, but I'm perspiring from the effort, and I appear to have lost control over my bodily functions thanks to Valeria wetting down my dress with tap water from our supply.

"Thank you, Cerdo. Keep this somewhere handy. She may have more seizures until she gets her medication."

The man sneers. "Don't call me that. It is a joke, a bad joke."

"I'm sorry. What is your real name?" Valeria speaks with compassion Cerdo has not earned or maybe has not received before.

"Forget it."

The arguments and events of the morning wear out the man, and with nothing else to do, he drifts off to sleep. Valeria and I are careful. I watch Cerdo and she tiptoes outside, leaving the door open a crack. When she returns, she whispers that things are in place.

Valeria watches Cerdo breathe a steady, slow cadence and prays he isn't pretending. Otherwise, things will get hairy. My sister gathered items from storage into a single box that she's sliding into the corner beside the worktable.

A loud snore wakes up Cerdo, and it takes a minute before he remembers where he is and that he fell asleep. He relaxes seeing that Valeria and I are where we should be. After a few minutes, Cerdo begins to pace. I understand his agitation. The room has one high window. Otherwise, it is a stifling cell, and he's restless to watch for Raton and Garcia.

Several more circles around the room and Cerdo opens our prison door and locks it behind him. We hear the outside door close and imagine he's gone to walk off his worries around the campground.

Valeria hands camp clothing she found in storage for me to change out of this stinky, wet dress. The pajama pants and a camp sweatshirt feel warm and are easy to move in, another important part of our plan.

"We can do this, Vivian. Summon your courage." Valeria smears some hand balm she found on a shelf around my wrist wounds and squeezes my knee. She pretends to work again.

I climb a step stool I found behind the storage shelves and watch out the window. I'm taller than average, but I have to stand on my toes to see outside. My calf muscles cramp from lack of use, so I rub and stretch them out while I stand. I may be seventy, but I still do yoga three times a week.

It feels like an eternity when I see Cerdo strolling up the

path, looking oddly carefree. I wriggle down the ladder and tell Valeria to get ready before I dash behind the shelves near the door.

When Cerdo opens the door to our room, he sees the step stool, frowns, and snarls as he notices I'm not on the cot.

"Where is she?"

Valeria turns in alarm. "Oh God. She might have fallen or had another episode." She jumps up and squats to look under the cot for me and Cerdo follows like a compliant puppy.

That's when I emerge from behind the shelves and wallop Cerdo on the back of the head with the hoe Valeria found in the toolshed by the porta potty. I get sick when I see blood running down his face from the wound. I'm not a violent person.

"Well done. Let's drag him over there." Valeria points behind the storage shelves, and my body obeys, numb to the harm I just caused to another human being.

Working in tandem, we cover his mouth with duct tape and wrap his hands and feet together. Finally, I blow out a huge breath that sounds like someone let air out of a tire.

"Should I put something on his head or prop it up with a pillow?" I ask Valeria, who stares at me like I've lost my mind.

"Why yes, we should take care of Cerdo after he and his thugs kidnapped us and plan to kill you, Vivian." Her voice was shrill. "You know that as soon as they have their documents, they will dispose of both of us."

"I suppose my mind didn't allow me to think that through," I say, but I'm processing the realization at top speed. "What now?"

"Keep watching for Raton and Garcia, while I get all the

props in place for phase two."

For the first time in years, I'm seeing my sister through new eyes. I always thought she was overly dependent on her husband, like I was in my youth. I think she's stronger than I've ever given her credit for. A storm is coming, and I'm grateful she's chasing it.

Hours pass before I hear a vehicle approaching. Valeria hears it too, and we both take our places, ready to perform the scene we've rehearsed. We're relieved to see the van by itself, which means Ruiz is still missing. That gives us a fifty-fifty chance of taking out Garcia and Raton.

Garcia opens the outside door of the cabin, and I'm ready. Like a hurdler launching from the starting blocks, I bound forward down the office aisle and plunge the truck dolly with all my might into Garcia's torso, forcing him out the door, where he lands with a thud; the wind knocked out of him.

Raton, confused about what's happening to Garcia, lets his guard down, which is what Valeria hoped for. When Raton stares at Garcia on the ground and sees me in the doorway, Valeria confronts him with bug spray and a butane lighter, her finger on the trigger. The thug staggers backward with a yelp when Valeria lights the spray, creating wild flames and noxious fumes.

Raton coughs and starts to flee but falls to his knees, retching. Valeria drops the lighter and pulls off the leather work gloves, another find in the shed, while I pin down Garcia by sitting on the dolly so he can't move his arms or the tops of his legs.

Valeria rushes to the water spigot and turns on the hose. A full stream of water through the attached power nozzle greets

Raton's body. He turns over face down on the ground and a relentless Valeria keeps the pressure on him. No matter where he moves, water follows, and she hopes it's enough to wear him out.

With renewed vigor, Garcia tries to pull his arms free and kicks the ground with his feet, trying to dig in his heels for leverage. Garcia's bigger than I am by fifty pounds or so, and I know I'm going to lose the battle soon. I pull out opened powder packets concealed under my sweatshirt and spill them over Garcia's head while he cringes and whimpers, tears streaming. Like I said, I'm not a violent person and I feel the pain of others. There's no joy in burning the daylights out of this man. I keep reminding myself that this is the only way for us to survive and save our students.

―――――――――――――

Downing and Harris followed a hunch and sped down the country road leading to Cliff Marsden's house.

"I hope Marsden's there. We need to pressure this guy. He's the key. Hell, we might stumble into the kidnappers' lair." Downing, feeling an adrenaline rush, rambled. The detective urged the unmarked car onward around curves through a thick wooded landscape.

"At least we have a search warrant. If he's not there, maybe something we find will lead us to the kidnappers." Harris crossed his fingers and held onto the armrest while Downing sped up.

Marden's property began with a long dirt driveway that forked off into a fire lane along a cornfield. The unmarked car veered left at the last minute to take the fire lane where the detectives could hide by the tall cornstalks. Downing jammed the car into park and left it running when Harris pointed out the old farmhouse about forty yards uphill.

"Let's walk from here and keep the car hidden."

"Looks like someone's home." Harris pointed to a pickup truck and a sedan by the garage.

When the detectives drew near, they smelled a charcoal grill and meat cooking behind the house. They signed to each other to split right and left, hoping to surprise Marsden.

Downing came into Marsden's view as the man was flipping burgers, unaware Harris stood behind him around the house's corner.

"Cliff Marsden. You're a hard man to find." Downing's weapon was trained on the man.

Marsden startled, slammed the lid shut on the grill, and sprinted the opposite way, head-on into the barrel chest of Officer Harris.

"Going somewhere? We don't want to ruin your dinner, Marsden." Harris chuckled. He put Marsden in cuffs.

"What am I being arrested for?" Marsden complained.

"Nothing yet. We need you to stay put until you answer some questions."

Downing holstered his gun. "Let's go inside, shall we?"

Marsden dragged his feet. "Can we talk outside? I'm entertaining a guest."

Downing pulled his weapon out again, while Harris strong-armed Marsden into a lawn chair by the grill and told him to sit still.

Downing found a brooding redhead lying on top of what was presumably Marsden's bed, clad in a flimsy robe. A bath towel lay on the bedroom floor and steam curled outward from the bathroom.

Downing cleared his throat, and the woman jumped off the bed and dove for her clothes nearby.

He showed the woman his badge. "Shh. It's okay. I'm not going to hurt you. I have to secure this house, so stay here until I tell you otherwise. Understand?"

The woman nodded, holding her breath.

"I'm sending an officer in to secure the house. His name is Harris. He will have questions for you after he's finished. He has a search warrant. Please don't touch anything in the house or in this room."

"Can I get dressed?" Her wispy voice trembled.

"Why don't you wrap up in the bedspread, Ma'am? Once the officer sweeps the room, he'll clear you to get dressed."

Downing searched for others according to routine, returned outside, and talked to Harris out of Marsden's earshot. Harris produced the warrant, waved it in the pilot's face, and entered the house.

"Let's get this over with, Marsden. We know you helped some Colombians with kidnapping two women. Why don't you tell us where they are." Downing stood over the man.

"Where who are, detective? The women or the kidnappers?"

"Cute. I don't have time to play games here. We both know it. So, you can cooperate which will go on record, or you can go straight to jail. There's an empty cell next to Ruiz, unless you'd rather be together."

Marsden shrunk into his chair and hung his head, desperate to think of an advantage. "I didn't help them kidnap those women. I flew the plane, that's it. They hired me to fly them to Massachusetts and back to Wisconsin. That's my part."

"Shut up, Cliff. I know how you operate. Where are they now? These thugs know diddly about Wisconsin, but you do. You must have told them where to hole up." Downing's seething words spewed into Marsden's ear from behind him.

"You won't find them on my property." Marsden's cool act wasn't convincing, but his antagonism was.

Harris returned, holding a beer can koozie and coaster. "I got something. Let's go."

Downing bolted to the car while Harris covered Marsden. At the top of the driveway, the two shoved Marsden into the back seat and restrained him.

"Last chance, Marsden. Peaceful Pines Campground?" Downing asked.

Marsden grunted.

Peaceful Pines Campground occupied fifty acres with sites among towering pines and old growth oaks, hickory, and birches. Bordered on one end by the private Peace Lake, most of the rural area surrounding the camp included summer cabins and cottages, making up miles of refuge for people looking for an escape.

When Bay noticed fewer cars driving on the road, she decided to pull off on the shoulder near a bend in the road and give the van some space before crawling out to follow again. Her cell coverage was dismal between the woods and rolling hills, so she didn't know if Cass reached Downing and couldn't call him herself either.

She couldn't know that Downing plotted a course on the county map and handed the map to his partner to help navigate.

Coming the opposite direction from the detectives, Bay slowed her speed to watch for any place where the van pulled off, since she couldn't see it any longer. Around a wooded curve, she noticed a sign for Peaceful Pines Campground and saw a tall plume of smoke rising through the trees ahead.

Bay pulled into the entrance to Peaceful Pines and followed the sign that led to the office. She stopped short when she saw the van parked a few yards down the dirt roadway. She crawled to the back of the Land Rover to retrieve binoculars, rolled down the window, and surveyed the van and office area. The van prevented her view of the office, but her heart told her this was the place, and she had to help.

Bay eased the SUV toward the office, blocking one exit the van could take. Should she leave her vehicle running for a quick escape? She decided to turn it off and pocketed the keys, closing the door with a dull thud. When she heard a ruckus coming from the other side of the building, she realized she was parked behind the office. Crouching, she crawled on her knees toward the fray, looking for any useful weapon.

Further down the road, Downing and Harris noticed the smoke signal, too, and raced toward it, coming to the campground's rear entrance. The long dirt road bumped along for half a mile before it opened into a community clearing space for campers. The fire burned merrily, contained within a metal ring.

The detectives proceeded down the road again and collided into a scene that might be part of a comic book. Downing activated the car's siren, drawing the attention of the two women who appeared to be in charge.

He and Harris leaped from the car and scrambled in two directions, Harris pinning down the man called Raton while Downing pulled Vivian off the truck dolly so he could roll Garcia onto his stomach and cuff him.

The detective reached for his service gun when he saw movement at the corner of the building. *Must be the third kidnapper.* When Bay stood up with her hands in the air, he almost dropped his revolver but recovered and motioned her to get down.

Valeria and Vivian clung in a tight embrace under the porch overhang, wet with water and sweat, cold and shivering. Valeria found her voice.

"Cerdo is inside. We wrapped him in duct tape." The wiry-haired woman pointed to the front entrance.

"Downing, can I help these women?" Bay asked. She pointed behind her. "My car's over there."

"Take them and sit inside until we come for you." Downing spoke as he moved toward the office. "Lock the doors and stay low."

Harris loaded Raton beside Marsden in the unmarked squad, leaving Garcia crying and hacking from the powder Vivian poured on him. Harris radioed for an ambulance and stood between Garcia and the unmarked squad while Downing stole into the office.

The man called Cerdo lay on the floor unconscious, a small pool of blood under his head. Downing pushed his feet, but Cerdo failed to respond, so Downing radioed Harris to call for a second ambulance. Downing removed the duct tape from Cerdo's mouth with care. It was tempting to cause pain for the criminal, but Downing didn't believe in torture.

He emerged from the office, leaving the door ajar. "Number three is out cold with a head injury. I bet someone hit him with that hoe leaning against the wall there. Back up coming?"

Harris nodded, keeping his eyes on the two culprits in the squad. "Back up is ten to twelve minutes out and the ambulance about the same. Gotta sit tight. What in hellfire is Bay Browning doing here?"

Downing shrugged. "Maybe she's psychic? God forbid."

Chief Smart rolled up behind the Land Rover and maneuvered around it, hitting tree roots and low spots before pulling up against the nose of the detective's squad. She and the deputized Dotson swung open the doors and climbed out with weapons drawn.

"What's the four one one? The chief eyeballed the two in the unmarked car and the whimpering man on the ground.

"The two kidnapped victims are sitting in Professor Browning's vehicle. Expecting an ambulance anytime to transport them. Another ambulance will take this guy and the perp inside who can't be moved. He's unconscious." Downing tried to resist a smile from forming.

"Why's that one whining?" The chief nodded toward Garcia.

"He took a few hits of color-changing campfire powder. Nasty stuff, like tear gas." Harris explained.

"And the man inside?" The chief started walking to the office.

"Hit in the back of the head with that hoe," Downing said, indicating the blood-streaked implement still in the place where Vivian left it.

"Unorthodox, but well done I suppose, detectives."

Harris and Downing answered in sync. "Not us, Chief. This

is how we found the bad guys."

Chief Smart spun around, eagle-eyed. "The victims attacked the perps?" After the detectives nodded, Smart's lips curled upward at the corners. "Looks like another long night. And Professor Browning, is she okay, or did she take down the lug that's hooked in your back seat?" The chief pointed at Marsden, whose face was blotched with dirt.

"No Ma'am. That one's on us. Cliff Marsden, pilot and accessory to kidnapping." ∎

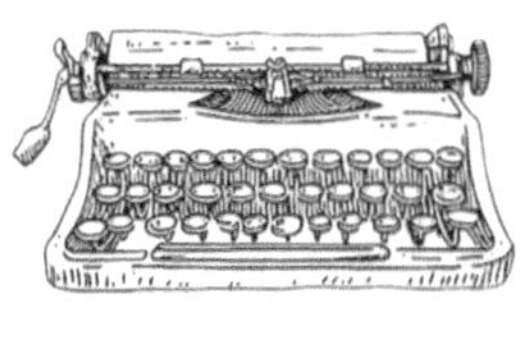

Dinner and a Recap

Friday was a slog. Bay gave her statement to Detective Harris last night, explaining that it was dumb luck she'd stumbled on the kidnapper picking up a prescription for Vivian at the pharmacy. She didn't think she was acting rashly. She recognized the van, called her sister to let the detectives know about it, and pursued it like any law-abiding citizen would do. That was her position, and she stuck to it.

But that wasn't the end of her night. She trekked to the hospital to check in on Vivian and Valeria, finding them in separate rooms under tight security. Luckily, Vivian's guard was officer Mandy Harris, who allowed Bay a minute to see Vivian and wish her a quick recovery.

"I knew I chose the right woman to help me out of a bind." Vivian clasped Bay's hand and pressed it against her chest.

"You're the brave one, Vivian Rossi. We have much to talk about. For now, rest well, and I'll be by to check on you." Bay gave the petite woman a gentle embrace.

But Vivian tugged on Bay's hand. "I need to tell you something. The 'Master' letter—the one I read at the poetry slam. It's a fake."

"How do you know that?"

"Valeria told me while we were being held captive. She knew how meaningful it was for me to sponsor Daniela and Aneka. Selling the Emily poem at auction made that possible. I had to buy their escape from Colombia."

Bay wanted to cry. "What a selfless act, Vivian." She wondered how many people would spend that amount of money to save a stranger. "But if the 'Master' letter is a fake, who wrote it?"

"Valeria did. She hoped to authenticate it and sell it, so I could sponsor more refugees." Vivian's confession spent her strength.

Bay dropped her hand and stood. "I'll go now. You rest. We'll talk again."

At least Bay's Friday teaching load was light, and Stasia, the assistant dean, told her to skip office hours and get some rest. The police briefed Stasia about finding Vivian and her subsequent hospitalization. Chief Smart gave credit for Bay's involvement.

Bay's mind didn't allow rest, however. Instead, she called on Cassandra at Spirit Gardens and enjoyed the change of scenery, helping Cass with herb and blossom drying in the Firehouse. While they worked, the two wove stories about the kidnapping, Valeria's involvement, Miriam Greggs, Daniela, Aneka, and the Colombians.

"Okay, that's enough speculation for one day. Why don't you

invite Downing to dinner tonight and we can pump him for all the gory details?" Cass rubbed her palms, savoring the idea.

Bay agreed but returned to the patio moments later, shaking her head. "Downing is buried in paperwork and evidence, or as he calls it, 'pouring the facts into concrete', so he can't leave, but he promised to fill me in over the weekend." Bay sighed. "Guess we have to keep spinning theories."

"I'm relieved you didn't get hurt, Lulu. When I couldn't reach Downing directly, I almost went after you myself." Cass relayed her phone call with dispatch.

"Downing had his hands full with Marsden, but he showed up exactly where and when we needed him." Bay was anxious to express her thanks to the detective personally.

Marva announced an early dinner in the solarium where flowering plants and ornamental trees brought the rainforest indoors. Marva insisted on serving them herself after Bay's ordeal.

"I feel personally responsible, Miss Bay. You wouldn't have been in danger if you hadn't gone to fetch my prescription." Marva squawked.

The sisters enjoyed plates of acorn squash stuffed with savory ground turkey, mushrooms, zucchini, carrots, onions, and pine nuts, which rejuvenated their spirits.

Marva promised cinnamon roll bread pudding, warm from the oven, for dessert topped with crème fraîche for contrast.

Dinner ushered in a return to normalcy for the sisters and Cass determined to tap Bay about the experience at Spindrift Lake with the healing stones.

"Can you talk about what happened to you at the lake, Lulu?"

Bay closed her eyes as she pushed aside her plate. "I felt

like everyone I loved was set against me, and I was overcome with resentment because of it. I guess I haven't really accepted Diana and I feel like a troll because of it."

Cass reached for Bay's hand in support. "You and Diana are getting on well, though."

"True. Yet, I can't shake off how betrayed I feel at times when I think that everyone, all of you, kept Penelope's secret for years. You allowed me to believe she was perfect. Damn, Cassandra, I've kept our mother on a marble pedestal that reaches to Heaven." Bay wriggled away from Cass's grasp.

"But I thought…" Cass began. All the progress they'd made seemed to pop like soap bubbles.

Bay stiffened in her chair, a rigid tree unwilling to bend, ready to face a storm. "Cass," she said softly. "It's true about Diana and me. We are getting on. And you and me: we're good. And dad, too. Cleansing the stone taught me two lessons. One is that I need to get over the loss I feel about our mother, because you, Diana, and Dad lost her, too. And two, I can't move forward until I confront all the conspirators."

Cass shot Bay a look of approval. "You're going to call Aunt Venus."

Bay nodded, and Cass's face issued a challenge. "What about Penelope Browning?"

"Oh, I hadn't thought of that." Suddenly moving forward felt daunting. How was she supposed to confront her dead mother?

Bay fell out of tree pose during her yoga practice, the third pose she couldn't manage that Saturday morning, despite her typical mastery of the positions. She knew she was reeling from days of anxiety over Vivian, besides trying out her own detective skills, for what they were worth.

When her phone jangled, she didn't hesitate to skip the end of her session and swipe the green dancing icon.

"Detective Downing, my rescuer." Bay giggled, mostly from lack of sleep.

"What's that, Professor? I doubt it. You're not the damsel in distress type." Downing's voice had a strained edge from plenty of sleepless nights.

"Breakfast?" Bay hoped his call meant a recap of the kidnapping case.

"Naw, I can't. I'm at the office, trying to wrap up some loose ends this morning."

To his credit, he sounded disappointed in delivering the news, but Bay figured his call meant she was on the hook to review her statement, exactly what she didn't need on a Saturday.

"I called to see if you'd mind helping me clean out *My Piggy Bank*. This afternoon?"

Bay giggled at the double meaning. *My Piggy Bank* was the name of Downing's boat, a cabin cruiser he'd spiffed up himself. Bay enjoyed excursions on it over the summer, complete with private dinner picnics and sunsets aboard.

"I'd be happy to." Cleaning out a boat could be the perfect remedy for her busy mind, she thought.

"Pick you up at one."

Skipper Sam's marina on Three Witches Lake buzzed with activity from boaters who either took their babies out for the final spin of the season or moved them to dry dock for the winter.

Instead of burning off, the morning fog settled over the lake, forecasting a possible storm. Bay shivered in her jeans and plaid flannel shirt and would be happy to warm up by cleaning.

Downing showed up at Bay's with takeout from The Dragon's Den, a quick Chinese diner, and the two downed spring rolls and spicy Kung Pao chicken over fried rice before making the half-hour drive to the marina.

Downing looked around the lake with longing. He hated to surrender to the season of frozen waters and short gray days. He gazed at the boaters fighting the wind. "I'd rather remember the best day on the lake then take the boat out in this."

"I agree. It's cold and might storm any minute." Bay steadied a bucket of cleaning supplies onto the boat before pulling herself aboard. A step behind her, Downing juggled a broom, mop, and lightweight vacuum and handed them to Bay.

"I'll get the empty bins from the trunk," Downing said.

Bay volunteered to strip the bedding and clear the linens out to be laundered and stored until spring, while Downing sorted food items in the galley. It wasn't long before the rhythm of sorting and cleaning hummed along with enough familiarity for them to relax and talk.

Bay stood in the galley, washing down the insides of cupboards while Downing packed cereal, crackers, and other staples into bins.

"I wanted to tell you about the fake Doctor Obasi." Downing finally cracked open the lid on the topic of Vivian's case. "The feds came through on that one. They detained him at the airport in Chicago. Turns out, he's part of the same Colombian faction."

Bay stopped scrubbing in surprise. "Really. So, he wasn't

from Africa? I mean, I know Aneka was from Cartagena, but the real Doctor Obasi, her uncle, is from Nigeria."

Downing looked for the expiration date on a box of crumb breading. "Right. We found the connection between Daniela and Aneka. The Colombian faction isn't the regular ELN rebel group from the nineties. These guys are extremists who want to kill everyone left who is descended from the hero Simon Bolivar. It was logical for them to start with women, especially younger ones who might have children."

Bay wrung out the cleaning rag in some pine-scented solution. "Are you saying Aneka and Daniela are both related to Simon Bolivar?"

Downing nodded. "But they're safe now, we think. Vivian's kidnappers weren't the brightest of the bunch. One or more of them is certain to rat out others in exchange for leniency. Besides, the women have a security detail."

Bay saw Downing place a wooden box of tea bags into the bin, and she pulled it out again. "I'm cold, aren't you? Why don't I put on the kettle?"

Downing frowned. He wasn't a huge tea fan. "Sure. I think there's instant coffee in that corner cupboard for me, if you don't mind."

"Of course." She nibbled on the corner of her pointer finger, thinking about her question. "What about Valeria? I know I'll be able to talk to Vivian soon, but I don't know how to broach the topic of her sister. Why did the kidnappers want her?"

Downing kept working, snapped the lid on one tub, and started filling another one. "You knew Valeria worked in authentication of historical documents. She also forged travel documents for Aneka and Daniela. She did it, she says, to fast track them to safety in the U.S."

Bay sucked in her breath. "Oh my. Did the kidnappers want her to forge documents for them, too?"

"They got wind of her abilities. They figured by taking Vivian, Valeria would forge papers for them to travel freely around the globe, and that Vivian would disclose the locations of Daniela and Aneka."

"Is Valeria under arrest?" Bay lowered two coffee mugs from the shelf above the sink and spooned instant coffee into one.

"When she's out of the hospital, she goes into federal custody. She retained an Irish lawyer from South Boston. I think her chances are good she won't do prison time. Falsifying government documents, even for a righteous cause, won't sit well with most judges. Things might get knotty for her."

Bay stopped browsing the tea choices, the weight of Vivian's fate dawning on her. "Did Vivian know about the forged documents?"

"Valeria protested ten different ways that her sister is innocent, too naive to understand that the papers were anything but the real deal. I don't buy it, though. Vivian knew the documents gave the women aliases for their protection. She had to put two and two together." Downing stopped, remembering the long interviews with the two women.

Bay protested. "Knowing Vivian's idealism, I'd bet she didn't understand what her sister was up to. I think Vivian supposed the government would approve of legal aliases for the women and sanction the documents."

"You do, huh?" Downing scratched the stubble on his chin. "So that innocent act of Vivian's is the real deal?"

Bay nodded. "I could be a character witness for her. I can't see Vivian knowingly being part of anything dishonest."

Bay poured water from the kettle into the coffee mug and over the English breakfast tea in the other mug, lingering over the hot steam. "What about the private pilot?"

Downing snorted at that. "Cliff Marsden," he said with contempt. "He's sitting in jail now, but he'll make bail Monday. I think he's going down as an accessory to kidnapping. He's going to lose his wings." Downing laughed, enjoying the justice of it all.

Bay passed him the coffee and played with dunking the tea bag to hurry along the brew. "Did you finish your paperwork this morning? You seem to have everything wrapped up."

"Yep. I never saw a case wrap up so fast, like the perfect storm lassoed all the culprits at once." Downing took a sip. "I admit, the feds helped us out and didn't get in the way."

Bay laughed. "That says a lot coming from you. I'll add that your interim Chief Smart is a force to be reckoned with."

Downing agreed. "She's a by the book officer. Heck, she probably wrote the user manual. But she can still surprise us. I don't think we'll have her long. She wants to head for warmer territory before winter."

"Speaking of warmer territory, what do you say we wrap up this project, Bay, and find some heat." Downing's gaze held fire.

Bay blushed. "I think it's getting warmer in here already." ∎

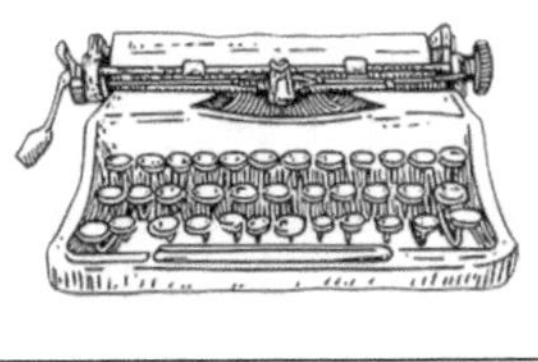

chapter 21

And Then There Was Nun

Now that Vivian's kidnapping ordeal was over and it seemed the refugees were secure, Cassandra turned her rightful attention to solving the mystery of Posey's past. She started by doing her homework on the convent located in Saint Francis, a bedroom community south of Milwaukee. The Saint Francis Sisters formed in eighteen forty-nine and originally cared for orphans and assisted German immigrants. Now, the sisters focus on pastoral ministry, special education services, health care advocacy, and environmental stewardship.

Cass wondered how old Sister Philomena must be if she knew Ramona Hollingsworth, who had been dead for more than twenty years. To Cass's surprise, she learned Saint Francis housed residents celebrating sixty years or longer of sisterhood. That made her hopeful she would find the nun, if not at the convent, at least walking among the living.

A recent encounter with her parole officer, Kelly Weber, still echoed through Cass's conscience. The officer, dressed in her smart military green uniform, appeared out of the blue as was her custom and stood in the Firehouse kitchen days earlier.

Two things about that visit bothered Cass. First, Kelly Weber complained of aching feet and asked Cass if she had any concoctions to relieve the pain. Cass imagined the no-nonsense parole officer was too robust to suffer from any ailments, much less ask for a natural remedy to help her. And from Cassandra besides? A convicted felon? Cass complied and days later, Kelly Weber called to say the remedy was helpful.

Second, Kelly Weber congratulated Cass on her stability and excellent record since her release from prison. Cass knew the professional officer was not the type to veer into anything personal or complimentary. Making matters worse, Cass didn't deserve the compliment. She was conning people again—Monica Frazer, for one. And she was a bad influence on her sister, Bay, asking her to tail Miriam Greggs. Cass told herself she acted on Posey's behalf to find out the truth, but a con is a con.

With that weighing on her mind, how should she visit and interrogate a nun?

Cass toyed with that question as she pulled into a wide parking area at the expansive religious campus, its church steeple reaching upward to the glittering sun. The convent sat by the shore of Lake Michigan, which occupied the entire eastern view along the street.

Cass slung a large purse over her shoulder that carried a notebook, pen, and water bottle among the normal contents. She paused at the impressive sculpture of Saint Francis of Assisi, the patron saint of animals, his arms reaching out to the woodland creatures and birds surrounding him in a natural setting.

Something struck her senses when she entered the main building, prodding her to stop pretending. Play it straight, an inner voice instructed; be honest. Ask and you shall receive.

The soundtrack followed her into the reception office where Sister Ann, in casual dress like a typical office worker, greeted her and offered help.

"I'm sorry. I guess I expected you would be in a black and white gown, wearing a habit, Sister Ann," Cass confessed. "I hope you can help me. I'm here to speak to a Sister Philomena. I suspect she's quite elderly. She used to live in Prairie Ridge, which is where I'm from."

Sister Ann rose and went to a filing cabinet. "I could locate her on the computer, but it's faster for this lady to do it the old-fashioned way." Her smile was warm and authentic, but she spent time reading Cassandra, from top to bottom.

"You're certainly not the first to expect us to wear traditional dress. Some do. Most will for solemn or ceremonial occasions. Otherwise, we like to look like regular people. It's the best way to help others, you know. What you see is what you get." She sealed her plain speech with a firm nod.

Cassandra wouldn't underestimate this woman. She intended to walk the straight path, unless warranted.

"Ah, Sister Philomena. Yes, we have two. The one you seek was from Prairie Ridge and she is Sister Philomena Berta. She resides in the Clare Building. Let me call over for Sister Augusta, and she can escort you."

Sister Augusta, a buxom woman with razor cut jet hair and deep crevices where her brows often pinched inward, gave

Cassandra a thorough going over, or at least it seemed that way to Cass.

When the nun spoke, her voice matched her haircut, sharp and to the point. "Miss Browning, how are you acquainted with Sister Philomena?"

"I'm not," Cass answered bluntly. "I want to ask her some questions about a family I worked for in Prairie Ridge. Someone told me to reach out to the sister for information."

"I see. Walk with me." Sister Augusta exited the building and proceeded down a stone walkway leading to Clare House, which appeared to be a one-story sprawling apartment building that resembled a convalescent home.

"Sister Philomena no longer performs duties in our chapter, but remains here in retirement and attends some activities and Mass. She can be difficult to communicate with at times, so I cannot say how you will be received. She's quite stubborn and suffers from dark moods." The nun stopped on the walkway to gauge her reaction.

Cass remained impassive although her insides sent off warning signals. "All I can do is try to speak with her. I truly need her help in solving a family mystery. It may help her to talk about it."

"Humph. That, I doubt."

The two continued in silence until Sister Augusta opened the entrance door and held it for Cass.

"Sister Philomena is in room twelve. Just knock and announce yourself."

Cass was astonished. "You're not coming with me?"

"I will be in the office, just steps away, if you need anything. Press the wall button by Sister's bed. God speed to you, dear."

The nun crossed the threshold to the sanctuary of the office and closed the door.

As Cass traversed the hallway, she noticed about half the doors were open, ready to welcome visitors. Her senses, prepared for the typical elderly facility smells, enjoyed the scent of fresh lake air combined with assorted fragrances, some citrusy, some floral, but not unpleasant. The door bearing the number twelve was closed and Cass felt a sudden urge to run, abandoning her mission. She collected herself and conjured a picture of Posey in her mind, then knocked on the door.

"Sister Philomena, you have a visitor," Cass said, thinking that sounded silly, but what exactly should she say?

"Who is it?" The sharp retort shot through the wooden door.

"My name is Cassandra Browning. I'm from Prairie Ridge. I used to work for the Hollingsworth family."

"Who did you work for in the family?" Sister's voice rang out like the vibrato of a cello played with steel wool.

"I worked there as a personal assistant." Using the past tense always sent Cass's feelings swaying like an untethered boat.

"What do you mean by that—you worked there? You no longer work there?"

Cass understood. Sister Philomena was skeptical.

"Right. I work for the estate, Sister." Cass tapped her foot against the wall, impatient with the woman. Was she supposed to speak through the door the entire time?

"Come in and close the door behind you."

The young woman and the elderly nun took stock of one another. Cass decided the sister was perhaps in her late seventies. She wore a plain gray house dress and pulled a pine green cardigan around herself as she sat forward in the brown recliner that nearly swallowed her whole. The bedside table was a confessional, sharing the sister's condition. A wide basket contained numerous brown pill bottles, while an IV pole stood guard at the head of the single bed.

"Here. Pull this chair around and sit across from me where we can see each other." The nun instructed Cass, pointing, although the room only had one chair besides the recliner.

Cass set down her purse and lifted the cushioned chair to carry it over.

"Hello, Sister Philomena. Thank you for seeing me."

The nun took a round watch out of her cardigan pocket, opened it and snapped it closed again with expertise. Cass surmised she was on the clock and better make this visit count.

"Could you tell me if you're related to Ramona Hollingsworth?" Cassandra speculated about the connection between the nun and the family, and her question was standard coming from the point of view of finalizing an estate.

Sister bristled and picked up a cup from the service table by the recliner. Her hands worked to steady the cup.

"What business is it of yours?" The nun swallowed a hefty draught and settled the cup onto the table again. "Did you say you worked for the estate? Has Ramona died?"

Cass noted the nun's interest sounded personal. "I'm sorry, Sister. Ramona has been gone for over twenty years. I was Posey's personal assistant and I'm afraid she too, recently passed away."

"Why are you here? Why bring that name into my sanctuary?"

The nun's gaze pierced the air, and Cass could feel the woman's heat. She'd hit a vein.

"I'm trying to find answers to a mystery. Posey Hollingsworth spoke of a strong memory involving a nun and her mother arguing in the salon at Spirit Gardens House. I think you are that nun."

"I see. You say Ramona is dead? And Posey? What of Lionel?"

"Lionel died before Ramona."

"No family left to speak of?" Sister Philomena nestled into the chair cushions looking like a child who polished off someone else's dessert.

Cass ignored the nun's obvious pleasure. "I think you know better."

Sister Philomena looked through Cass with eyes that transformed from blue to black. She sprang forward with catlike precision and grasped Cassandra's hand with her bony claw. "What kind of sorceress are you?" Her voice was dry paper.

The momentary contact was enough for Cass to receive one revelation. "You're Ramona's cousin and… there's someone else in the family picture."

The nun yanked her hand away hard enough to leave a gouge in Cass's palm from her nails. Cass stared at the gouge as if it might have more to say, then changed tactics.

"Sister, please, it's clear you're not well. Wouldn't it be good to clear your conscience before you encounter God at Heaven's gates?" Torn between closing her eyes like a demure novitiate or challenging the nun, she chose the latter.

Cass didn't expect the sister to hang her head and whimper.

"Ramona and I were second cousins. When I was fifteen, I got into trouble. The worse kind for a teenage girl in the early sixties." Her voice faded to a papery rasp, and she turned her head to peer out the window that overlooked a grotto.

Cass knew the kind of trouble Sister Philomena must mean. "What about the father? Was he helpful at all?"

The nun's eyes darkened to chisel points, glinting like flint. "None at all. I embarrassed my parents. They disowned me. I went to work in a factory, but trying to work and take care of a child had its difficulties. The factory didn't understand that. When she was four, I found myself without a job."

Cass knew women like Sister Philomena, desperate and poor. Many of them turned to crime. "I cannot imagine how hard that was."

Sister continued to stare out the window, her eyes fixed on the statue of Mary in the grotto. "Ramona and Lionel had been unlucky, unable to have children. I begged them to take mine, and they did. After I made sure she was living in a secure home with relatives, I joined the sisterhood."

"But the Hollingsworths didn't keep your daughter, did they?"

The nun swiveled to face Cass, wearing a bitter mask. "No. They cast her aside shortly after Posey was born. Sent my Joanna to an orphanage where I lost contact with her forever." Her strangled voice reached into Cassandra's soul.

Cass tossed the information around her mind. *Joanna? Could Sister Philomena be the mother of Posey's killer, Joanna Stengel?* Is this why Joanna blackmailed Posey? Joanna called herself the rightful heir to Spirit Gardens.

Cass drove straight through the yellow traffic light. "Do you know what became of Joanna? How old she is now?"

"She must be sixty, but she is lost to me. Ramona never

answered my letters. I hope a suitable family adopted her. That has been my prayer all these years, and my suffering. I abandoned her."

The nun rose with effort, weighed down by grief harsher than her ill health. "Now please, go. I must lie down and rest before Mass."

Cass watched Sister Philomena sit on the edge of her bed, take off her slippers, and lie down underneath a knitted afghan. She began to finger her rosary beads, moving her lips in a whispered prayer.

Cass dared to drift to the nun's side and place her hand over the hand that grasped the cross at the bottom of the rosary. Sister Philomena's eyes flew open in outrage. She dropped the rosary as if it caught fire and clawed at Cass's hand to tug free.

"What else do you want from me, Devil? I have spent years atoning for my sins."

Cass faltered, dropping her hands to her sides as she knelt beside the nun. The woman possessed her brand of spirituality and Cass would not interfere with it, despite the nun's opinion of Cass's abilities.

Cass ventured forth in a firm, soft voice. "I know the pain of keeping a secret, Sister Philomena. No amount of atonement can erase it. No whispered prayers can heal the wound in full."

Sister closed her eyes and gasped for breath. Her lips moved in silence and finally a single word gurgled forth, a plop of water sizzling with heat: "McGann."

Cass gasped in disbelief. "Did you say McGann?"

Sister's voice, raspy and weak replied. "The judge. Now be gone." She clutched the rosary once more and turned her back on Cass. ■

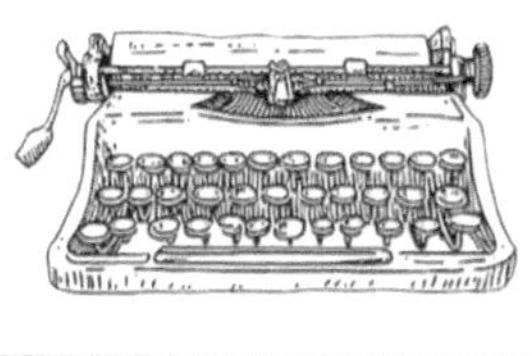

chapter 22

The Literary Society Awakening

The Prairie Ridge Literary Society President, Joyce Strost, wanted to reconvene regular meetings, as planned before Posey's death, so Bay, the new secretary, asked Cassandra if the fall meeting could be held at Spirit Gardens. Posey and Joyce co-hosted the monthly book club there, since the Bluff Bird members were likely to attend rather than lower their standards by going into town.

"Gretchen Lange said to continue following Posey's schedule. And the meeting will be a warm-up prior to Abigail Adams's one-hundredth birthday party in two weeks." Cassandra made a note in her work journal with the date and time. "You and I can talk to Marva. She's done dozens of these, and she'll know what to serve."

Bay invited newly hired Flourish professor, Angelica Trevino and her mother, Linda. The efficient idea killed two birds with one stone, since Linda was a member when she lived in Prairie Ridge years ago, and because Bay wanted to introduce Angelica to the locals in small servings. Bay hoped Angelica would feel at home quicker than Bay did when she began teaching at the college.

Joyce invited Cassandra to join the society. She was Posey's protégé, after all, so it seemed fitting. After a three-month hiatus, full attendance was expected, making the number twenty-four plus three with Cass and the Trevinos.

Marva and Cass surrendered the usual meeting space in the cozy front salon because of the numbers, and capitulated to using the black and white salon, an expansive living room seldom used in Posey's time as mistress of the estate.

Ramona Hollingsworth admired the stark attitude of the spacious salon, which she decorated from scratch, cleverly adding a baby grand piano, a main feature. The salon evoked masculinity and control. Each furnishing and decoration in white had a corresponding black twin.

Posey rejected the room after Ramona died. In defiance, she covered the furnishings with red satin coverlets and moved the piano upstairs to the music room, a guest bedroom featuring musical décor. Its location adjacent to the ballroom made maneuvering the piano back and forth a simple task.

Cassandra and Marva donned imaginary cloaks of betrayal when they thought of their mistress, each woman casting off the red silks to air out the furniture.

"What choice have we got? Those decrepit folks can't be expected to go upstairs to meet," Marva said.

"I know. And the solarium would echo with twenty some people in it." Cass recalled a luncheon of six created a buzzy cacophony when the voices bounced around the glass walls and ceiling.

So, it must be the black and white, but Cass showed her allegiance to Posey by adding vases of autumn mums from the florist in red, orange, yellow, and lime to brighten the room. As she pranced past Ramona's portrait hanging over the mantle, she thumbed her nose at the matron. Ramona, decked out in a dazzling white silk gown with a long glossy mink stole draped over her left shoulder, peered down with disapproval.

Linda Trevino rushed into the house ahead of her daughter with a gaiety that infected Joyce Strost. Besides Posey, Joyce didn't know any members who embraced the society with such joyous enthusiasm. She linked her arm through Linda's and made introductions around the salon.

"This room hasn't changed a bit except the flowers." Linda remarked to the members. "When my husband and I lived in Prairie Ridge, I was a member of the society and we met here. Ramona used to say this room most closely resembled her mind. She believed everything could be contained in either a black or white compartment."

Another bubble popped into Cassandra's head. Did Cass share Ramona's philosophy? Between conning Monica Frazer and Kelly Weber by proxy, and the encounter with Sister Philomena, Cass felt uncertain about gray areas. Was Ramona good or evil? A loud inner voice challenged her. *And what about you, Cassandra?*

Bay nudged her sister, bringing her out of her reverie. "We're the only people here Angelica's age, so let's make her feel welcome, okay?"

It was clear Angelica would stick close to her mother's elbow. Linda's gregarious chatter drew the curious members into her circle.

"When did you live in Prairie Ridge? I'm trying to recall if we've met before." Helena Davies, an angular woman around sixty, inquired.

Linda moved closer, ignoring social distancing, and scrutinized Helena's features. "My husband Fred taught history at the college in the nineteen eighties. We lived in town on Woodland Avenue, near the library."

Helena considered the location and time period. "I see. No, we've never met before. My husband and I purchased the Colonel Angell estate in the nineties. Roger is a plastic surgeon in Madison."

Helena studied Linda's tiny figure and defined Italian features, thinking the woman might welcome a nose alteration. She admired her high cheekbones though, judging them perfect.

As the members dispersed into their usual clusters, many remarked about Linda Trevino's petite figure compared to the curvy Angelica, a head taller than her mother.

Joyce ushered Linda and Angelica to a charcoal damask love seat before the members began flitting to their territories.

Linda was exuberant. "Mrs. Strost, I can't tell you how thrilling it is to be on Angel Bird Bluff again." She sighed in contentment.

Joyce retorted using a stage whisper. "Really? I wouldn't call the bluff experience thrilling unless you're referring to the necessity to hold on to your dignity for dear life."

Joyce did not live on the bluff. She was considered a lowlander, although her success and wealth were on par with the bluff dwellers. Joyce attended most of the same functions, navigating through the birds like a second-class citizen.

Helena Davies and Rue Lawson sat side by side in two vacant curve-backed chairs next to Linda and Angelica, through the process of exclusion. While the birds flocked in and nestled into their usual spots, Helena and Rue were leftovers. Rue, an accomplished pianist, lived below the bluff in the same vintage neighborhood as Joyce, while Helena often found herself outside the inner sanctum due to her manner of sizing up the birds for plastic surgery.

By default, the two men present, Joe Bryant and Professor McNelly, took the last available seats. McNelly sat across the room from Bay, his colleague at Flourish. Their difficult history continued to puzzle Bay. McNelly, a former priest, was a vault of town secrets, and Bay, though she lacked evidence, didn't trust the man. Her mind noted he sat in the exact middle of the members, an appropriate spot for a man who lived between worlds—the bluff and town.

The din of excited chitchat continued among the hives of women, who were catching up on vacations and summer activities. Linda turned toward Helena and Rue to become better acquainted while Angelica seemed unable to focus, taking in bits of conversation from every direction.

Helena gazed at Linda, a specimen under a microscope. "You know, you and your daughter have unique features. I know faces, and yours are very distinctive. She must resemble your husband." Helena's crisp delivery was met with Rue's disapproving expression.

The unfazed Linda blurted the explanation. "My late husband and I adopted Angelica when she was a baby." Linda's brash announcement changed the temperature in the salon. Those within earshot gasped and passed along the information.

Linda reached for her daughter's hand in a show of unity, and Angelica smiled and waved, as if she'd just won something. Reactions ranged from shock to embarrassment to pretended delight. Bay and Cass whispered that the scene felt like something from a Jane Austen novel.

Cass elbowed Joyce to get the meeting rolling, and the ever-smooth president wasted no time in welcoming everyone and reading a short verse in Posey's memory. Leave it to Joyce to shift from the picking session to a Literary Society meeting with an agenda and reading list.

"You can see the calendar for the meeting dates and times through May, along with which book will be discussed each month. Today, I asked everyone to bring a poem to share—a little ritual to embrace literature anew, in the ashes of autumn. What a perfect time to dig into books."

Linda, Angelica, and Cassandra were recognized as new members, and Joyce reminded the group of Bay's membership that began at the June meeting when only a few members attended.

Time dragged on while people read poems, some long-winded and others, pleasantly short. Several members pretended they'd forgotten their poems, ending the recitation in less than two hours.

Cass fought off sleep and excused herself early to help Marva with refreshments, which the housekeeper wheeled in on a large serving cart. A side table bearing a zebra design of inlaid wood, was laden with salad plates, cups, napkins, and silverware.

Members broke off into new groups, stretching their legs, and walking about the room to admire the furnishings.

Winnie Harper, a sharp-tongued woman with wild hair, made a beeline for Linda, who was talking with some of the lowlanders.

Winnie and her entourage butted into the group with urgency.

"So, you knew Ramona. Tell us what she was like. Most of us didn't know her personally."

Linda suddenly realized the motive of some of the members, and she curbed her tongue, choosing her words with care.

"I've only been here a couple of times. The society most often met in the library when I lived here. I knew Mrs. Hollingsworth through her charity work. We sometimes volunteered at the same events."

As the women leaned in and more joined their enclave, Linda forgot her discretion in favor of their interest. "Mrs. Hollingsworth was helpful to me. She encouraged Fred and I to adopt. We'd given up hoping for a child. I was ten years older than Fred and almost fifty by then. Ramona confided she'd had a change of life child when she was nearly fifty."

"And did you know Posey Hollingsworth?" Winnie prodded, hoping for more unvarnished tittle.

"No. I can't recall meeting Posey." Linda flushed, suddenly remembering that Ramona never spoke about her daughter the way most parents do, telling anecdotes, bragging about their accomplishments, or sharing photographs. She wished she could escape the collective and sit down again.

Rue Lawson spoke from the edge of the group. "It's nice to have you with us, Linda. I'm sorry to hear about your husband's passing."

"Fred's been gone nearly three years, and I was happy to return to Madison where I grew up. Of course, the neighborhood has changed. Most of the Italians dispersed, and the oldest are dead and gone." Linda laughed, recalling memories of her nana, which she did not share.

"I was hopeful when Sunny decided to apply for the theater position at Flourish, and thrilled when she told me she was hired. I'm seventy-seven now and can do with some company." The exuberant Linda wilted before them, and Angelica witnessed it from the corner where she conversed with two of the college staff along with Bay and Cass.

The sisters turned toward Angelica. "I think you should rescue your mother from that herd of cats." Bay suggested.

"Excuse me." She stepped to Linda's side. "Mother, we should be going. I need to stop at my office and gather some things." Angelica took her mother's arm.

"Yes, thank you, Sunny." Linda nodded to the members. "This has been quite lovely." Linda smiled and Joyce escorted the pair to the main entrance.

Joyce was the last to depart Spirit Gardens, leaving Bay, Cass, and Marva heaving sighs of relief.

"Let me finish up in here. You two can find somewhere else to be." Marva shooed Cass and Bay out of the black and white salon.

"What's bothering you?" Cass asked as the sisters beat a path to the Firehouse, which seemed to be a favorite location of late.

"Oh, something Linda Trevino said about Ramona Hollingsworth categorizing things as either black or white." Bay picked up jars of dried herbs, reading the labels while she cruised the pantry shelves.

"And you're relating that comment to what?" Cassandra considered the comment too, rattled from her visit to the convent.

"I spoke with Aunt Venus," Bay said. She stood erect in the pantry and stared at the jars. "I'm embarrassed about it. I accused her of lying, deceiving me on purpose. It wasn't pretty, Cassandra."

Cass understood well how impulsive words and deeds produced regrets. "For your own sake, you needed to confront her to move forward. She will get past it." Cass filled more jars with herbs and dried flowers, writing out labels in her flowing script.

"Remember how I was drawn to the black and white agate that day at the lake?" Bay turned toward Cass. "I wanted Aunt Venus to understand why I called out of the blue, so I explained about cleansing the stones and how consumed with bitterness I was."

Aunt Venus's words, engraved in Bay's memory, rushed in to challenge her again as she stared into space:

"The trouble with you is that you think in a straight line that starts with your image of Penelope and ends with your hurt feelings. You weren't alone in feeling betrayed. Life is like that lace agate, filled with curves and rivulets. Nothing is a straight path, Bay Browning. It's complicated and messy, and when you think you figure out the pattern, it shifts. Grow up Bay. And forgive those who were trying to protect you."

"Lulu, Lulu, snap out of it." Cass stood beside her sister and led her by the hand from the pantry. "Come sit down over here." Cass's contact with Bay gave her insights into Aunt Venus's words.

"No, I sat all afternoon listening to some poor poetry recitations. The point is, Aunt Venus was right. We all lost something because of Penelope's decisions. It's past time for me to get on with it." Bay took over filling jars while Cass wrote labels.

"Easier said than done, but knowledge is power, right? You know what you want to do, and you will do it. I have my own confession to make." Cass relayed the story of her visit to Sister Philomena.

Bay paused, stunned, her basil-filled hands hovering over the mouth of a jar. "Posey's killer is also her cousin. Revenge is a powerful motivator."

"I don't know where to file this information. It doesn't help me find Posey's treasure." Cass trembled. "Worse, I doubt I can trust Anthony."

"Wait a minute. What are you talking about?" Bay cocked her head and frowned, hoping her sister wasn't jumping to conclusions. She knew Anthony acted as the intermediary between Posey and Joanna, because he was Posey's personal attorney.

Cass looked glum. "Sister Philomena said Judge McGann is Joanna's father. Anthony's been covering up for his grandfather this whole time. That's why Joanna was blackmailing him."

Bay hugged her sister and let her tears spill on her shoulder. Weren't they just talking about betrayal. Here was Cass, feeling another betrayal from someone she trusted.

"You need to talk to Anthony about this."

"I know," Cass whispered between sniffles. "I'm dreading it." She held her head high and wiped her eyes to shake off the impending clash.

"I want to give you something, Lulu." Cass reached for Posey's keeping box she'd placed on the shelf above the Firehouse cooktop. A recipe card fluttered to the tiles when she slid out the pewter box.

Bay bent down to retrieve the card and began reading the odd verse written on it.

"Persuade Emma to ride the gray ghost on the wind to the Abbey. Meet her under the giving tree where the mangoes grew before cholera. The Three Sisters follow the owls where the moon wanes to find the victor of pain and valor." Bay read the script aloud, drawing Cass's attention.

"Where did that come from? I put it in my apron pocket days ago, but when I went to look for it, it was gone." Cass suspected the card had a mind of its own.

Bay read the card over several times. "What does it mean?"

"Don't call me crazy, but I think I was meant to find it. It's a companion to Posey's letter. Another piece of the treasure hunt." Cass confided.

Bay had a copy of Posey's letter but confessed she hadn't reviewed it in weeks, nor thought about it in the aftermath of Vivian's kidnapping. "May I take this home with me? I do my best thinking at night. Alone. In the dark." Bay's delivery imitated Dracula.

Cass hesitated, then relinquished. "Promise me you won't lose it." She picked up her cell phone from a nearby table and snapped a picture of the note card. Cass believed the enchanted card might lead her to Posey's secrets.

"Here, I want you to have this." Cass opened the pewter box of stones and handed the black and white agate to Bay.

Bay gave the stone a penetrating glare, suspicious to touch

it again.

"Don't be afraid of it. It's currently inactive. You don't have to use it for anything. I want you to keep it as a reminder." Cass placed the stone in Bay's palm and closed her fingers around it.

Bay relaxed. "Thank you. It feels normal, like a rock." Bay pocketed the agate.

"By the way, how is Vivian doing?" Last Cassandra heard, the woman left the hospital days ago, and she thought Vivian might attend the Literary Society meeting.

"I stopped by her house yesterday to bring her flowers and an apple pie I bought at the orchard." Bay worried about Vivian but found her sturdier than ever.

"She told me she's seeing a therapist to deal with the ordeal and some past clutter she needs to surrender." Bay thought about Vivian's tote bags, which she returned to the woman per police request a few days earlier. Bay didn't see the tote bags anywhere near Vivian during their visit, possibly a sign of progress.

"Don't we all," Cass said, but was met with Bay's distracted stare. "Have clutter to surrender." Cass added.

Bay gave an absent nod. "Vivian's also happy the college hired temporary teachers. She intends to spend the winter term at Amherst teaching a Dickinson course. Funny, she confided to me that the poet helped her through the kidnapping." Bay had expected her to credit her sister Valeria.

Cass laughed. "From what you've told me about Vivian, that rings true. Will the U.S. send the refugees back to their home countries?"

"No. They're under federal protection until further notice. I suppose we won't hear any more about them, unless you talk to Marcel and Lisa Domingas, that is." Bay considered the case closed, but the complicated ordeal still rattled her mind.

Marva interrupted the sisters' discussion. "You have a visitor. It's that new professor. The one with the whacky mother." Marva, hands on hips, appeared perturbed at the intrusion.

Bay and Cass giggled at Marva's usual flippant delivery. "Angelica Trevino? You can bring her to us, if it's not too much trouble," Cass said.

A sheepish Angelica found her way and sat in a cushioned rattan chair, surveying the Firehouse in wonder. "What a cool summer kitchen. What do you do in here?"

Bay jumped in. "Cassandra is an apothecary. So was Posey Hollingsworth. Cass is drying herbs and flowers for teas and tinctures. She's working on a skin cream at the moment." Bay bragged.

Angelica was impressed. "I might ask you for something to help my mother. Which brings me to why I'm here. I had to return to apologize for her strange behavior. She hasn't been herself since my father died. That's another reason I applied for the Flourish position. I want to keep tabs on her."

"Perfectly all right. We've seen a lot weirder folks than your mother." Cass eyed Bay, nodding.

Bay gauged Angelica's reaction, thinking Cass's statement was a bit harsh, but Angelica laughed in relief.

"I want to make a respectable impression, and I think these high-class people are probably calling us fools. I saw how they goaded her, hoping she'd drop a bombshell about Ramona Hollingsworth." Angelica was torn between embarrassment and indignation.

"The Bluff Birds are an acquired taste. Mostly entertaining.

Sometimes enlightening," Bay said.

Cass rose to their defense. "They're not all bad. Many of the Bluff Birds are intelligent and charitable. Posey Hollingsworth was the best of the nest." Cass became misty-eyed.

"Well, I don't want to tarnish the reputation of my father, the late great historian, Frederick Gunderstadt." Angelica twirled her hand with a flourish.

"Gunderstadt? I take it, you don't use that name." Bay pondered.

Angelica leaned forward to share personal details. "There's another story. My mother's nana, my Nana Bea, said she would disown my mother if she changed her name to something god-awful sounding. My mother kept the Trevino name and promised her all the female offspring would follow suit."

Cassandra warmed to the idea, thinking her mother and aunt, the Charming sisters, might have been tempted to embrace that tradition. "I heard your mother call you 'Sunny.' Where did that come from?"

"My parents called me that from my earliest memory. There may be nothing to it, but now I'm curious. Guess I'll ask mother when I see her," Angelica offered.

Before Angelica left, Cassandra handed her two packets of herbal teas for her mother to try. "This one promotes balance. This one helps with anxiety. I put cards in each bag describing the ingredients and how often to use them. I have options, too, if she wants to experiment."

Angelica thanked her. "My mother drinks tea, so this is a good start. Baby steps." ∎

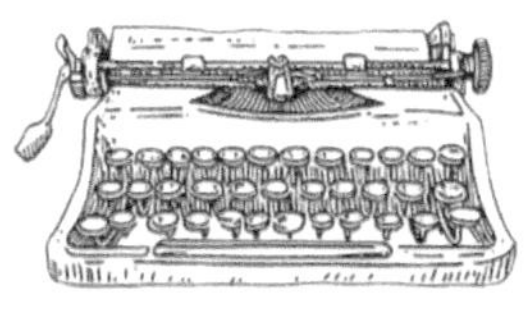

chapter 23

Hide Your Lying Eyes

The last time Cassandra and Anthony spoke was the day following Vivian Rossi's kidnapping, after Cass told him she successfully opened Vivian's safe. Cass considered her story a pilot test, hoping the man she loved would applaud her daring, or at least not reprimand her for it.

She was wrong.

"Cassandra, you cannot break into a private citizen's safe, especially in the deceptive way you went about it. Conning a police officer." Anthony scolded Cass. "Wait a minute. You're not serious, are you?"

Cass glared in reply and stalked out Anthony's door. He called her after cooling his heels for a week, suggesting a dinner date and sounding like an amnesia patient. Cass declined, saying she needed some time alone.

Before Cass's session with Sister Philomena, she planned to invite Anthony to Spirit Gardens for a heartfelt exposé, from her teenage exploits to becoming a professional grifter, and her downfall of capture and conviction.

After speaking with the sister though, and learning Judge McGann fathered her child, her outrage claimed top billing in her mind.

She called Anthony, kept her temperament on simmer, and suggested he come to Spirit Gardens for evening drinks. Cass knew she couldn't sit across from him and pretend to enjoy a dinner date.

Cass bid goodnight to Marva without letting her know of her evening plans. The housekeeper teetered between nosy and caring, and struggled to mind her own business. She told security to expect a visitor and gave the officer his name.

Anthony, buoyant and charming, practically danced through the doorway on the moonless October night. When he saw Cassandra, he grew shy, kissed her cheek, and handed her a bouquet of fiesta daisies, her favorite.

"Thank you. These are beautiful. I'll put them in the kitchen. You know where Posey's library is. Meet me there." Cass had practiced tranquility for hours before Anthony's arrival. Meditation and yoga followed by calming tea were part of the preparation.

She found Anthony sitting in the library in Posey's favorite leather chair beside her father's antique globe. That alone notched up Cass's pulse. *How dare he sit in Posey's chair.* Anthony and Posey always met in the library, so he must know Posey's claim to her father's chair. She needed to get a grip.

"What about drinks, Cassandra?" Anthony asked.

Cass forgot she'd included drinks in the invitation—she was caught up in the speech she intended to deliver. "Oh, let me grab something from the bar. Do you have a preference?"

"A whiskey sour would be nice." Anthony decided the cocktail would take off the edge he suddenly felt under Cass's scrutiny.

Cass made two cocktails, extra weak. She wanted both of them to have their wits for this conversation.

Anthony stood and proposed a toast, to which Cass said without hesitation, "To honesty." She clinked her glass to his before he had a chance to react.

"Okay Cassandra, what's going on?"

"Sit down, Anthony, over there." She pointed to a burgundy leather wing chair, and she followed to stand before him, blocking the door.

"Anthony, it's time for the truth. We've both been keeping secrets from each other, and I can't be in a relationship without honesty." Cass began.

"Does this have something to do with you breaking into Vivian Rossi's safe? Look Cass, I don't want that to become a habit, but…"

Cass cut him off. "I need you to listen. The reason I could break into that safe is because I've had a lot of practice. I used to be a professional con artist and thief, Anthony. I served time." In her heart of hearts Cass wanted to add that all of it was in the past, but the memory of conning Monica Frazer, the Holllingsworths' former housekeeper, stood in her way. She clammed up.

Anthony laughed and tossed her a flirtatious look. "Right. So, tonight is all about role play? You should have told me, and I would have thought about my part." Anthony wore a dreamy look and was halfway out of the chair before Cass pushed him backwards.

"This isn't role play. I'm serious. I'm on parole. I've been out of prison for a year, spent three months in a halfway house, then came to live with Bay. Ever since, I've been changing, reinventing myself. Posey and Bay are angels, giving me more grace than I deserve." Cass quieted. "And so are you. That's why you need to know the truth."

Anthony stared into his cocktail tumbler and drained the glass before setting it down with a thump on the table. "You've been lying to me all this time." His voice sizzled with ire.

Cassandra's feet were rooted to the spot like a sparrow making itself invisible to a hawk. Inside, she fought off the vulnerability consuming her in favor of her former fierceness. Yes, Anthony had reason to be hurt, but so did she. In her grief, he might have provided clarity about Joanna's motive for murder. Instead, he was mute.

Anthony stood and sideswiped her to escape.

"Wait." Cass found her voice and turned to stop him. "Anthony, stop. I know the truth about your grandfather. Judge McGann." Cass seethed when she said his name.

Anthony spun around to face her. "That damn Gretchen."

Cass didn't comprehend. "Gretchen Lange?"

Anthony, red-faced, broke into a rant. "I suppose since she's the estate attorney, she thought it was her duty to tell you about the judge's indiscretions. Illegitimate children popping up all over the state. I've been paying for the judge's sins since I took over the law firm. First my father, now me." Anthony kicked the chair leg and it almost toppled.

Cass was dumbstruck for a beat. "How did Joanna know she was related to you and to Posey?" She neglected to discuss her visit with Sister Philomena for now.

Anthony scrunched his face into a twisted scowl. "Ramona knew, of course. When she found a farm family who would take Joanna, it came with a price. They knew Ramona had money, so they bargained for payments. Sort of like child support. Joanna remembered living at the estate. She snooped around the farmhouse and discovered the paper trail of adoption and payments from Ramona, then took matters into her own hands. I think Ramona was tired of being the cash cow, so she told Joanna who her famous father was." Anthony's anger reached a boiling point during the revelation.

There were two snarling creatures in the library. Cassandra tried to tamp down her fury and process Anthony's disclosure. "Back up. You mean there are more children like Joanna Stengel? Why would you cover up the disgusting actions of a man who's no longer living?"

Anthony's shock at unleashing the truth overwhelmed him. He'd carried the burden for so long, he couldn't manage his feelings. "Cassandra. You know my family name means everything to me. In a community this size. My law firm. Who would trust the McGann name if they knew the truth about my grandfather? He was a damn judge, for God's sakes."

Cass wanted to slap his face or stomp on his foot, something to make him comprehend the weight of this secret. "You're not to blame for what the judge did. You can't carry his guilt. And you shouldn't protect him. It's wrong, Anthony."

"Don't stand here and lecture me about ethics, Cassandra. You're in no position."

"But I am. I'm an expert in carrying around guilt. In knowing right from wrong and doing the wrong thing anyway." Suddenly, Cass felt a surge of strength course through her.

"And you know what? It's not too late to do the right thing."

Anthony drooped. His legs lost the ability to hold him up. He leaned against the table, eyes gazing at the floor. "I can't. I won't."

Cassandra's heart snapped shut like a Venus flytrap. Anthony realized that he was the fly. The problem was, Cassandra wasn't prepared for that. Her plan of confessing first, hoping Anthony would reciprocate, rushed out of reach like dandelion fluff in a violent storm.

"You can leave now, Anthony, with my sympathy." For Cass, the storm had passed, leaving her with detritus. ∎

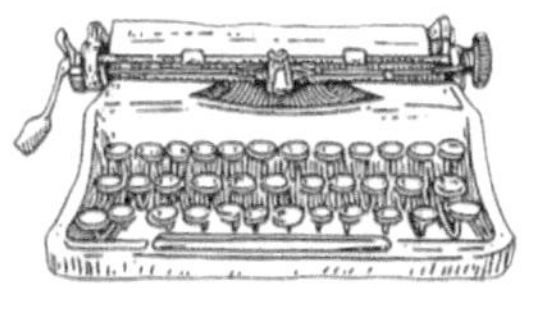

chapter 24

Where Rabbits and Owls Live

The next day, Cassandra consoled herself with two of Marva's morning glory muffins with extra butter. Marva noticed Cassandra's sulky mood, but the two planned to design a menu for Abigail Adams's milestone birthday, so she waited Cass out.

Between Marva's keen memory and Cassandra's visits with the grande dame, the pair concocted a menu featuring an array of finger foods, most with autumn flavors. Marva gushed over the crowning centerpiece, a three-tiered cranberry layer cake with caramel icing and a cinnamon-apple curd filling. She continued to draw the outer decorative elements while Cass completed the guest list.

"Yikes, I keep adding to the list. You know we can't afford to snub anyone. I have to invite everyone who currently lives on the bluff, plus the people Mrs. Adams gave me, plus the literary society folks." Cass moaned.

"No worries. You know they won't all show up anyway. The ballroom holds fifty and then some. Do you have more than that?"

"No, but we can't expect Mrs. Adams to go upstairs, Marva, so it's either the Zebra room or where?" Cass complained.

Marva snorted. "So that's what we're calling Ramona's salon, eh? We can use the Zebra room. We'll add colorful decorations and…I have an idea." She twirled her purple hair tendril around her finger, pleased with herself. "We can swap out some furniture. We can get rid of all the black and white chairs and replace them with the ones we use upstairs."

"Perfect." Cass clapped. "I'll get some muscle in here to help. Meanwhile, the party is two weeks away. First things first: I need to crank out these invitations today."

Marva clicked her tongue. "Are you going to deliver them by horse and carriage?" Her smirk was a jab at the Shakespeare-themed costume party where Cass insisted on donning vintage servant garb to hand deliver the invitations.

Cass sighed, remembering Posey's final party and everything that had changed since June. "No, they will go by courier. And by that, I mean FedEx."

Cass checked the time. "Bay's coming to help. I'll go wait by the entrance for her."

When Bay arrived, Cass ushered her to Posey's study where paper, stamps, ink, and fancy punch cutters awaited.

"Here's the design. I think it's perfect for Abigail Adams." Cass showed her sister the mock-up card adorned with bluebirds holding a birthday banner with "one hundred" in gold lettering. "We'll stamp the birds on white, framed in deep cherry, and back them in this goldenrod color."

"I love it. Let's get it knocked out, so you can call FedEx." Using the piecework method, making all the banners at once, all the bluebirds at once, and so on, assembly still lasted hours into the afternoon.

Cass stretched her arms and rolled her neck around. "Geesh, I'm sorry this took so long."

Bay imitated her sister, stretching and shaking the cobwebs from her brain. "It's fun to do something with my hands other than grading essays. But in the future, let's invite Diana to come over to help."

Marva knocked on the study door and entered like a whirlwind. "You two have been at it a long while. Let's see." She fussed over the design and colors and settled two bags onto the coffee table near the sofa. "I lost track of time, so I ordered from that Indian place you like."

Bay held up one hand, palm outward. "If you don't mind, I could use a walk. I've been sitting for hours and need to limber up. Marva, do you think we could reheat the food afterwards?"

Marva grinned and scooped up the two bags. "No need for that. I'll set them in the warmer and you two can retrieve them when you wish. I'm heading home."

After Cass and Bay walked the gardens around Posey's estate and took a jaunt along the wooded paths where people rode horses, they returned to eat their fill of chicken biryani and vegetable korma with a side of samosas in the kitchen.

Bay launched herself from the breakfast nook seat, switching from contentment to expectation. "I can't wait any longer." Bay pulled the note card with the cryptic message on it from her purse and waved it around.

"I think I might know the meaning of some of this. Book titles for starters." Bay announced.

"I've been through Posey's library fifty times at least, poking around with her letter."

"But you said you didn't have the note card until yesterday." Bay argued.

"I didn't, but I used the photo I took of the card to look in the library last night. It's a mishmash that doesn't gel." Cass slouched in the chair with a huff.

Bay wouldn't surrender. "Get the letter out. Come on. We're going to compare the letter and the note card, side by side." She placed the card on the countertop, while Cass fetched the letter. The women studied both notes.

Persuade Emma to ride the gray ghost on the wind to the Abbey. Meet her under the giving tree where the mangoes grew before cholera. The Three Sisters follow the owls where the moon wanes to find the victor of pain and valor.

You and I are sisters of the sacred earth, daughters of the midday sun and the full moon, and I am grateful for the time we were planted together in the same soil. Please take my book of remedies from the summer kitchen and keep my spirit alive by remembering me when you craft them. This will be justice. As a witness to my indiscretions, I beg you not to judge me too harshly. None of us want to be in calm waters all our lives. Your friendship is assuredly the finest balm for the pangs of disappointed love. But do not miss your chance at happiness. You are the bravest person I know—not since my father have I known someone so brave. You asked me often about the past. The answers are here, in the treasure I left for you. The key will unlock it. Seldom, very seldom, does complete truth belong to any human disclosure; seldom can it happen that something is not a little disguised or a little mistaken. —Posey

Bay pointed out quotes from Posey's letter that matched clues in the note card.

"Look here, where Posey says 'none of us want to be in calm waters all our lives.' That's a line from Jane Austen's *Persuasion*. The first word on the note card is 'persuade.'"

Cass began to protest that the words were not an exact match, but Bay cut her off.

"And here. See Posey's long sentence here: 'seldom does complete truth belong to any human disclosure' and so on. That's from *Emma,* a second Austen reference. Don't you see: 'Persuade Emma' on the note card. What else could it mean?" Bay drummed a fanfare on the table.

"Bay, I told you I looked in the Austen section. Exhaustively." Cass blew a puff of air in disgust. She spent most of the night in the library after Anthony left, and lack of sleep was taking a toll.

"Now look at this." Bay continued, ignoring her sister. "Posey's letter says, 'your friendship is the finest balm for the pangs of disappointed love.' And on the note card…"

Cass broke in. "Yes, disappointed love has to mean her relationship with Malcolm. They loved each other all the way to the end, but something drastic happened that summer before Posey's last year of high school."

Bay redirected their course to the note card. "The first sentence on the note card uses the word abbey and it's capitalized. The disappointed love is a part of *Northanger Abbey*, another Austen novel."

Cass shrugged. "So what?"

Bay shifted into an animated presentation. "If we follow the book theme, *The Giving Tree* is a story poem by Shel Silverstein, mangoes would be from *The House on Mango Street*, and cholera refers to *Love in the Time of Cholera*. With Posey's interest in Latino culture, she probably read both novels."

Cassandra rubbed her temples, concentrating, and Bay kept silent so she could think.

"The library doesn't have any children's books, and I don't recall a culture section. Lionel Hollingsworth's collection is classical, traditional. Lots of dead Americans and Brits." Cass rose from her chair and began pacing, muttering to herself. Something was niggling at her mind. She picked up the letter in one hand, the note card in the other, and called on her gift to lend guidance.

When she opened her eyes again and set the writings down, she pouted. "I don't understand. A large rabbit. That's what I saw, Bay." Cass's head hurt.

Bay riffed through the possibilities. "*Alice in Wonderland, The Tale of Peter Rabbit, Winnie the Pooh, Watership Down.*" Bay paused when Cass ran over to hug her.

"The Rabbit and Owl Room," she said, bouncing on her toes like a child.

"Do enlighten me."

"Come with me. I'll explain on the way." Cass snatched the letter and card off the table and scampered up the grand staircase to the second floor, onward to the end of the hall, and up a smaller stairway leading to the third floor.

"Nobody really uses the third-floor turret room. Posey was in too much pain and there's only one room and bathroom up there. When I came to work for Posey, she told me to explore the house freely, so the tower was the first place I went. I mean, every kid wishes they had a house with a princess tower, right?" Cass spoke as fast as an antique ticker tape machine. She stopped outside the door of the tower room to catch her breath.

"I give you—the Rabbit and Owl Room. At least, that's what I named it when I saw it. It's the old nursery, one of the few rooms that never underwent a remodel." Cass opened the grainy walnut door and ushered Bay inside.

The round room's wide plank floor was mostly covered by a round wool rug depicting the three bears walking through the woodland to their cottage. A humpbacked trunk occupied space under the dormer windows, probably filled with toys. A child's table and chairs, a bouncing pony on springs, a Victorian doll house, and a single bed filled most of the circular space, bordered by curved bookshelves extending floor to ceiling. When Bay examined the wallpaper, she understood Cassandra's assigned title. Colored in nighttime blue and forest green, the paper depicted a woodland scene occupied mostly by owls and rabbits, with a stray fox and squirrel tossed in.

"The bookshelves. This is where the children's books are, but I see some of Posey's favorite books are here, too." Cass rode a wave of excitement.

"Okay, let's take it from the top. Find the Austen section." Bay held the card, while Cass searched.

"Got them. *Persuasion, Emma, Northanger Abbey*. I'll pull them out."

"Wait," Bay said. "This house was built in eighteen eighty-five, you said. I'm betting you're going to find a secret room connected to this room. Pull the books forward, but don't remove them. There must be a sequence that opens the way."

"Right, Doctor Watson." Cass pulled the Austen novels

forward, then located *The Giving Tree* on the second shelf from the bottom and pulled it forward. "Where to next?"

"Find *The House on Mango Street* and *Love in the Time of Cholera.*"

Cass searched along the shelves and finally found a cluster of books that Posey likely read as a teen. Most of them were modern and many featured multicultural stories. Cholera was first with several books in between before Cass reached Mango Street. "Posey alphabetized this section," she said, pulling each book forward while Bay listened for creaking of any kind or the sound of a springing latch.

The two reached the end of what they knew, so Bay joined her sister in the hunt, studying the shelves with laser focus. Cass followed her intuition and began viewing the whole room.

"Look at this." Cass pointed to a framed photograph sitting on a decorative shelf with knickknacks. "This is Posey's father taken from one of his trips to Guatemala. Posey said it was her favorite picture of him. Those volcanoes in the background: They're called the Three Sisters."

Bay's heart skipped a beat. "That must be it. So, we follow the owls. The wallpaper is covered with owls but…"

"But we're looking for the waning moon. See the top part of the design. It shows different phases of the moon. The waning moon is over there." Cass pointed.

"Great, now if we can determine what the victor of pain and valor means…" Bay squinted in the fading light. "I'll turn on the floor lamp over there. You stay standing under the waning moon."

The extra light helped, and Bay began reading book titles in a straight line under the wallpaper moon. "*Les Miserables* by Victor Hugo. It certainly is an epic novel of pain and valor."

Cass left her post. "How did you figure that out?" She pulled out the fat novel to match the others.

"Process of elimination. It's my best guess."

"I don't see anything. Nothing moved. I didn't hear anything either." Cass deflated, huddled on the rug.

Bay knelt next to her, card in hand. "This border must be part of the code. A pictogram. We're not finished yet."

The linear artwork showed hand drawn evergreen boughs, pinecones, and a raven with a coin in its beak, holding an arrow in its claws.

"Time to study the wallpaper again." Cass stood up and turned on her cell phone flashlight to see better. Bay followed suit.

"This reminds me of the hidden pictures we used to get in those monthly magazines when we were kids." Bay started on the opposite side of the room.

"There are plenty of pine trees and boughs on this wallpaper, but I'm not finding a raven." Cass grumbled.

"It's here." Bay shined a light on the top end of the curved bookshelf. Carved into the woodwork, a raven perched on a pine bough. His beak held a coin, and his claws clutched a downward pointing arrow. The raven's gleaming eye might be mocking them or congratulating them: time would tell.

Bay felt all around the woodwork that was the raven's home, prodding for a switch or hidden spring, without success.

"The arrow points downward, so the latch must be somewhere below, on the baseboard maybe?" Cass ventured.

The sisters continued the search, their fingers looking for

any hold, nub, or niche that would trigger a door. Stiff fingers and cramped hands were their reward.

The two collapsed sideways on the single bed. "We're missing something," they said, almost in unison.

"Another book perhaps?" Bay suggested. "Come on, let's look on the shelves below the arrow."

When they reached the bottom shelf, a noticeable bulge appeared, seeming to push the whole set of books askew. Bay began removing them one by one and handed them to Cass, so they could get a better look.

Cass noticed the cover of *Treasure Island* and began to point. "There are coins on the cover, like in the raven's beak."

Bay pulled the adventure story forward and they heard the woodwork groan. "Should we put the other books back?"

Cass pushed her sister aside and reached behind *Treasure Island* where she found a latch. She pressed against it and with a snap, the wall at the foot of the single bed popped open, revealing a narrow entrance about four feet tall.

Cass grabbed Bay and twirled her around. "Well, that was easy." She laughed.

Bay excused herself. "I'll be downstairs if you need anything."

Cass expected the rectangular room to smell like a musty attic because the hidden enclave was enclosed on all sides, instead she was kissed by Posey's scent, the smell of lavender, lemon, and frankincense. A sleigh bed sat against one wall near a large floor lamp that offered light for reading, light shared with the mission rocker in the corner.

Cass brushed her hand over the rocker's embroidered cushion, a sun motif that could be mistaken for a blooming sunflower. Inside the burnt orange sun, a smaller blossom showed off in earth tones of terracotta, gold, and cream. Sharp jet-black spears radiated from the large sun. The sleigh bed paired with the walnut rocking chair, its bedspread a copy of the rocker cushion.

Nearby, a wooden claw-foot table reported Posey's presence: an empty floral teacup with a brown ring on the bottom sat next to an old typewriter, along with a pair of Posey's reading glasses. Cass gazed upon the specs with reverence despite their everyday use.

A large armoire occupied most of the opposite wall, except for a writing desk nestled into the corner next to a floor lamp matching the one by the rocking chair. Cass ran over to the desk, discovered it faced inward and maneuvered herself into the space where an antique Victorian corner chair offered the writer a place to perch. The desktop appeared to open upward but was locked.

Finally, she hoped, here was a place to use the ornate key Posey left for her, the key Cass wore around her neck since the day it was passed on to her. She turned on the floor lamp to brighten the dark corner and tilted its shade so she could see the lock. The ornate key slid in, and the desktop gave way.

Cass lifted the lid and found what she expected. After months of speculation, she anticipated finding a diary. In this case, there were two, side by side with mismatched designs.

She opened the floral tapestry cover and sniffed the ink and paper, recognizing Posey's script. The initial entry was dated nineteen eighty-five. The writer says she is eleven and will be continuing the journal begun by Emilia, "the woman who is my real mother." Cass gasped and decided to open the other book, bound in soft caramel-colored leather stamped with birds and trees. The pages exuded an earthy scent, and the ink smelled like metal. The writer's name was Emilia Sosa from Antigua, Guatemala.

Emilia's story of meeting Lionel Hollingsworth captivated Cass, urging her onward. Her father was a medical practitioner who worked with Lionel during his outreach missions in the remote Guatemalan villages. Eventually, Emilia joined to assist them, although she was a botanist by profession.

Cass whispered, "Of course! That's where Posey's green thumb came from."

The two fell in love, as Emilia described it: "love cascaded over us like a waterfall every time we were near." When she called Lionel to tell him about the baby, he wept and returned to Antigua to retrieve the woman he loved.

The foolish Lionel believed he could leave with his beloved, trading Spirit Gardens and a tidy sum of cash for his freedom. He should have known better. Ramona agreed that Emilia would live with them in the capacity of housemaid, whom they would hide from public view, then they would adopt the child as their own. Ramona played the part of an expecting mother, wearing maternity clothing and faking typical symptoms.

"Lionel tells me not to worry. He will play along, and we will leave when our baby can travel. Lionel purchased a beautiful home in Antigua near my family. We will make our own family. For now, I will try to avoid Ramona. As I grow rounder, the sight of me makes her spit and fume, so she begins to avoid me, too."

Emilia's words matched Posey's description of her mother, and Abigail Adams painted Ramona with a similar brush. Yet,

Cass could understand the betrayal Ramona must have felt.

Cass paused to stretch and extricate herself from the corner chair, pacing the room, book in hand. She began to skim the pages, looking for words of interest, something to reveal what became of Emilia. She stopped on a page where Emilia described her bedroom.

"I could hear Lionel and Ramona snarling at each other downstairs. Ramona wishes to relegate me to the third story where the live-in housekeeper resided when Lionel's father was a child. I don't care about that, except Lionel says the room is unfinished, gloomy, and he doesn't trust the dingy staircase leading to it. Lionel, in his stoutest voice, says I will have any room in the house I choose, and she surrenders. When I move my things into the second story room across from Lionel's, Ramona's face could melt concrete. The room suits my botanical mind, papered with honeybees dancing from violets to daisies, and the mission furnishings remind me of home."

Cass stopped to gaze upon the armoire, sleigh bed, writing desk, and rocker—pieces crafted with simplicity and Latin American style. "This wasn't Emilia's bedroom. Posey took over Emilia's bedroom. I wonder how this room came to be."

Cass strolled around the secret room, then returned to the nursery for a breath of fresh air, still turning the pages of Emilia Sosa's diary. She wondered where Bay was, wondered what time it was, and needed to use the bathroom, but she kept reading.

She skipped the pages where Emilia wrote details about her daydreams of sharing a life with Lionel. She skimmed the descriptions of heirloom jewelry and keepsakes she brought from Guatemala along with lengthy accounts of her family tree and childhood stories. She will read these in the future. Finding the climax of Posey's history was front and center.

Cass became impatient and began thumbing ahead, reading the dates on the entries. When she reached the final date, she observed Emilia kept the diary for seven months, the time spanning her pregnancy as she knew it. She backtracked a few entries to locate Posey's birthday.

"Our May baby is here, and we will call her our little butterfly, Mariposa. My eyes are heavy, and I am weak. I must rest so I can take care of her."

The next entry is dated three days later. "Lionel says I lost a lot of blood and need to rest to get stronger. I barely see our baby who comes and goes in the shadows, in and out of the cradle beside me."

A week later: "Lionel looks haunted. When he visits, he carries the baby for me to see her. He handles both of us like we're spun glass. I love this man. Olga, the angelic housekeeper, brings me broth and tea and will not leave until I've finished it all. She stays with me until I fall asleep again. Once, Ramona visited and Olga stood to leave. I begged her not to go. Ramona stared at me as if I were made of smoke and air. I see the horror on her face and in that moment, I know I'm dying. She tells me she will call my daughter Mary Ellen and expects me to understand."

Cass pictured the scene, rolling past her like film. She sees how vulnerable Emilia is, but the picture of Ramona lacks clarity. First, she is haughty, arrogant, powerful. The scene fades to shadow and Ramona emerges almost saintly in her compassion for Emilia. That image fades, too, and finally she is the woman Posey described—pragmatic, realistic, and distant.

Hot tears slid down Cassandra's cheeks.

Journal closed, Cass slipped into the attic room and returned Emilia's diary to the writing desk. She hesitated over Posey's diary even as she reached for it. It was late, and she was tired. The drama of the discovery was enough to digest for one night.

Bay poked her head around the door and held out a plate. "It's getting late, and I thought you might be hungry."

When Cass saw the open-faced peanut butter and banana toast, fresh tears spilled. Every time Cassandra ran away and returned home again, Bay made this very dish, all she could manage at her age.

"Come on in, Lulu." Cass patted the sleigh bed as she took the plate over to the rocking chair and began to nibble.

Instead of sitting, Bay perused the cozy room, picked up the songbird figurine that chirped a musical ditty and opened a carved trinket box containing a beautiful rose gold pendant. When Bay walked over to examine the pendant in the lamplight, the jewel caught Cass's attention.

"May I see that?" Cass took the pendant, amazed to see that it was the one Posey wore every day, except for formal occasions. The piece featured the Mayan sun, inlaid with lapis and carnelian in the rosy hued setting. "I wondered what happened to this. I suspected Malcolm Hunt claimed it for himself."

"Explain it to me," Bay said.

"Posey told me it's a depiction of the Mayan sun, a gift from Guatemala. I always assumed her father brought it for her from one of his missions there. I'm guessing this belonged to Posey's mother."

"Ramona? From what I've heard that hardly seems to be her style." Bay retorted, turning around. A thread of light on the wall by the armoire drew her attention. She opened the double doors wide and gasped.

"Cassandra, did you see this? It's a window overlooking the patio." Light streamed in from the security lights through the square space where part of the armoire's back panel was missing.

One side of the armoire served as a hanging closet with two low drawers, while a dresser with a mirror above it stood on the opposite side. Except the mirror was gone. Hanging in its place, an oval-framed portrait of a woman smiled at Bay and Cass.

"This must be Posey in her twenties. I wonder who painted it." Bay admired the artist's technique, capturing the perfect contentment of the blossoming woman wearing the canary yellow blouse embroidered with colorful flowers and birds over a bright green skirt.

"Come sit with me and I'll catch you up." Cass remembered she needed a bathroom break. "On second thought, give me a minute."

———

During Cass's break, Bay made a pot of chamomile vanilla tea and brought it up on a tray to the nursery. She tossed some fresh blueberries and raspberries into a dish to nibble on, too.

As they sipped and snacked, Cass regaled Bay with the dramatic tale of Emilia's and Lionel's love affair. Both shed tears at the unhappy finale where it seemed nobody got what they wanted.

"Except Ramona. She wanted a child. How convenient that

Emilia would be out of the way forever." Cass tossed out the bitter barbs of someone grieving.

Bay patted her on the shoulder. "Maybe not. Every time we hear about Ramona, she seemed unhappy. I'm not saying I feel sorry for her, but she raised a child who would never be hers with a man who did not love her."

Cass shrugged, noncommittal. She wouldn't forgive Ramona that easily. "I believe Posey's diary will shed light on that subject."

"I guess I know what you're planning: an all-nighter?" Bay asked.

Cass eyed her sister. "I won't be able to sleep anyway. Can I ask a favor? Will you spend the night? I'd feel better if you were here, Lulu."

"Of course. Just try kicking me out," Bay laughed and hugged Cass. "If you need me, I'll be sleeping in the rose room." Bay knew her way around the bedroom that housed the costumes for Posey's famous parties. She imagined her mind might not settle into sleep either. ▪

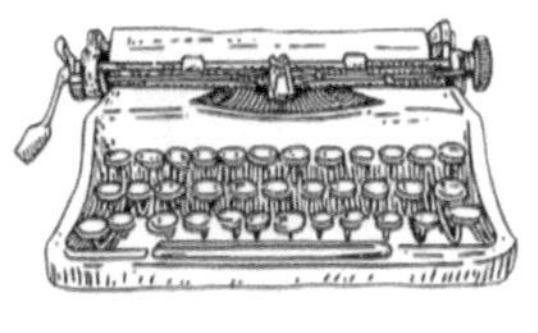

chapter 25

Pieces of Posey

Bay yawned, feeling the midday residual sludge of staying up too late. Grateful Monday classes were over, she packed her tote bag with a light load of papers to critique and contemplated an early bedtime.

Besides being a Monday, Bay spent most of the day fighting off the distraction of her early morning conversation with Cassandra. At five a.m., Cass poked her in the ribs until she sat up, bleary-eyed, and took the coffee her sister offered.

She'd read Posey's diary most of the night, nodded off to sleep on the sleigh bed for about an hour, then clambered down the stairs to wake Bay, chomping at the bit to tell her the highlights.

Posey discovered she was pregnant during her junior year and expected the child's arrival in September. She'd been able to hide the evidence during the winter months into early April, but finally her mother figured out the truth and hired a tutor for the remainder of the school year. To the public, Ramona said Posey had a rare disorder.

Posey told Malcolm about the baby in February and told Lionel in March, but she refused to share the news with Ramona, whom she did not trust. Malcolm promised to marry Posey after they graduated, but that was another year yet.

By summer, everything shifted. Malcolm's parents sent him to Europe to study French and international business. He and Posey were separated, certainly contrived by Ramona and Malcolm's parents. Lionel was powerless to help his daughter. In August, Lionel went on a three-week medical mission to Panama and promised Posey he would help her sort things out when he returned.

But the baby had other plans. When Posey went into labor early, Ramona hired a midwife who administered some powerful drugs and delivered Posey's baby by C-section. The mixture muddled Posey's mind and after she delivered the child, a boy, Posey slept for three days. When she awoke, confused and groggy, Ramona gave her the baby to hold. Posey pinned the Mayan sun brooch inside the baby's undershirt and thought about what his name should be. The jeweled pin was Posey's gift to share, a gift her real mother passed on to her from her mother. Posey kept the pin a secret from Ramona.

That was the last time she held her son. When Posey woke after two more days, a distraught Ramona told her the child died during the night from a lung infection. The midwife was at Posey's bedside too, administering drugs that kept her in a fog. When Lionel returned, Ramona shared the ordeal. Posey was unable to add much to Ramona's account.

Ramona insisted Posey finish her senior year with a tutor and not show her face in any social circles. After living the life of a shut-in for the entire year, Posey left for Amherst after her eighteenth birthday and didn't return to Prairie Ridge for four years.

"What about Posey's father?" Bay thought the two were close.

"Lionel visited her in Massachusetts, without Ramona."

Bay didn't know how to react or where to begin to ask questions. Both sisters needed to process the story before they could talk about it. Bay needed a shower and breakfast before her teaching schedule began, and Cass was desperate for sleep.

At Flourish, Angelica Trevino tapped on Bay's open door and Bay beckoned her inside with a wave.

"You've survived your second Monday at Flourish, so you're officially a veteran." Bay remembered her own insecurity after discovering she was the youngest professor on staff at the college and wanted to spare the newbie from that feeling.

Angelica looked doubtful. "I haven't even started teaching yet. It's too early to call me a veteran."

Bay understood but hoped to lighten her mood. "You're right. How is job shadowing?"

Angelica plopped onto an office chair. "I've taken pages of notes and there's a lot to learn. I'm lucky I have six weeks to get my feet wet. I doubt Clarice Yardley's ready to give me a five-star review."

"I wouldn't worry about that. You have plenty of time to dazzle Clarice. She's a perfectionist. She's probably training you to be the same." Bay reassured.

"I wish you could be my mentor instead," Angelica said.

"I would have volunteered but I'm busy mentoring Vivian

Rossi's temporary replacements. If it helps, I know how you feel. I was in your shoes not too long ago." Bay giggled, remembering her mentorship with the bored and nonchalant Jen Yoo. "My mentor and I got off on the wrong foot and now she's one of my best friends. So, there's hope."

Angelica wrinkled her nose at the notion of being friends with the high maintenance Clarice. She absent-mindedly rubbed the brooch pinned to her pumpkin-hued sweater, a habit she repeated when she felt stressed.

Memory kicked in and Angelica jumped from her seat. "I came by to tell you I asked my mother about my nickname. I should have guessed, really. When my parents adopted me, they said I was wearing a sleeper and a double-breasted undershirt. This brooch was pinned where the folded cloth of the undershirt overlapped." Angelica fingered the brooch on her sweater, a silver sun with inlaid turquoise and opal.

Bay gulped and swallowed her initial response. "That's very pretty. You've had that your whole life?"

"I have. I thought my parents gave it to me when I was too young to remember. It turns out, I arrived wearing this pin, and my mother began calling me Sunny from that moment on."

Bay treaded with care. "Aren't you curious about the pin's origins? Or your own, for that matter?" Bay and Angelica were about the same age, so Bay figured the woman would let her know if she overstepped.

"Sure. Especially after my father passed. I asked my mother questions, but she said I was born in New York City, and it would be hard to track down my biological parents." Angelica looked bothered.

"What is it?" Bay prodded.

"Last week I was looking through the Flourish history publications during my father's time, hoping to find some photos. My mother tells people they lived here in the nineteen eighties, but my father didn't leave until nineteen ninety-one."

Bay shrugged. "When people get older, they often generalize or estimate time."

"That's the year I was born, though. I found a photo from my father's farewell party in August of that year. I was born in August. My parents didn't move to New York until Labor Day weekend."

"Hmm. I suppose that's a little odd. But adoptive parents often have to wait a while for newborns. You know, processing documents and the like."

She changed the subject. "Tomorrow night, I'm going out for a cocktail with Jen Yoo. I think you two would hit it off. Can you join us?"

Angelica's face brightened. "Yes. Thank you for asking. I hardly know anyone besides you and your sister, Diana. She's unearthed several theater resources for me."

Bay buzzed Cassandra from the Land Rover as soon as she left Flourish. "Cass, I've got news. Angelica Trevino stopped by this afternoon to tell me about her mother's nickname for her. Turns out, when the adoption agency delivered her, she wore a sun brooch pinned to her undershirt. Maybe it's nothing."

"Doesn't sound like much of a mystery, Bay." Cass was mixing dandelion, nettles, and chickweed for a calming tincture.

"Think about it, Cass. I saw the brooch. You told me Posey pinned a Mayan sun brooch inside her baby's undershirt." Bay couldn't contain her excitement.

"Except Posey had a son and her baby died." Cass faltered. Was it possible Posey didn't have a son and her baby didn't die? "You saw the pin. It matched Posey's pendant?"

Bay wavered. "Not exactly. The sun motif matched, but the piece was silver with inlaid turquoise and opal." She soldiered onward. "Wait, there's more. Angelica was born in August, nineteen ninety-one. The time frame matches. And her mom acts sketchy when Angelica asks questions."

"Gracious, do you know what this could mean, Lulu? I need to think about whether I can be involved in this." On top of the discovered diaries, the new information made Cass twitchy.

Bay sipped tea in her reading chair at home as the sentences on the essays swam before her eyes. It was impossible to concentrate with Posey's diary entries repeating themselves in her head. She surrendered, shoved the essays into the file folder she brought home, and laid her head against the chair cushion.

When her phone jangled with Cass's photo in view, she nearly dropped it in her rush to answer.

"Bay, I convinced Linda Trevino to come for tea on Wednesday. No false pretenses. I said I had something serious to discuss with her. She's a strange woman, wasn't at all curious about what I wanted. She acted pleased to be invited."

"You're going to share the diary information and ask about Angelica's adoption?" The flood of relief surged over Bay, telling her Cass was doing the honorable thing.

"Yes. Unlike Miriam Greggs, I don't want to hold on to a secret like this, if it turns out to be true. It shreds my spirit, Lulu." Cass thought about Anthony McGann and Sister

Philomena. Deep inside, she herself carried the pain of her own mother's past.

"I understand, Cass. What about Malcolm Hunt?"

"We're going for a sunrise horseback ride on Wednesday. Wish me luck." ▪

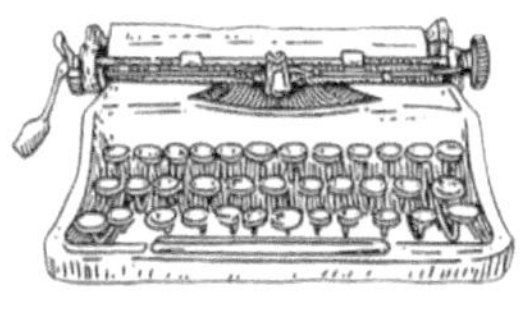

Straight from the Horse's Mouth

The sunrise was barely a promise in the sky when Cassandra met Malcolm at the Fox Hollow stables. Despite the early hour, Malcolm stood chatting with the horses as if it were the most normal thing in the world to do. He looked comfortable in blue jeans rather than formal riding clothes, and when he glanced at Cass, he burst into a boyish grin.

"Hey, great minds think alike, Ms. Browning." Malcolm noticed Cass, too, wore jeans topped with a chamois shirt.

"Good almost morning, Mr. Hunt. I felt the chill in the air and decided riding clothes might not do. How kind of you to get Fauna saddled for me." She hesitated. "Please call me Cassandra. I think it's time."

Sorrow clung to Malcolm's handsome profile after the terrible losses he suffered that summer. "All right, Cassandra. I was happy to prepare Fauna. The stable is my happy place. You walked in on my conversation with the horses. Let's just say, I can confide in them without suspicion."

Cass couldn't help but wonder if Posey might be alive if she and Malcolm had married, rewriting history. She mounted the cream-colored mare and followed Malcolm down the trail until it opened up, and they could ride side by side.

A cool mist hung low over the woods, making for a spooky atmosphere reminiscent of Halloween ghost stories. The two rode in silence for the most part with Malcolm pointing out animal tracks and migrating birds from time to time. For her part, Cass was wound tight like a jack-in-the-box, ready to pop.

When the horses reached a fork in the road, she pulled up and Malcolm stopped.

"Let's turn toward Spirit Gardens. Marva made breakfast." Cass intended to have a clever reason for Malcolm to visit but came up empty.

Malcom's curious expression met Cassandra head-on. "Why do I get the feeling I'm walking into a hornet's nest?" He teased.

Cass relaxed. "Marva made your favorites. You can't say no."

Instead of making a grand formal affair of breakfast, Cass asked Marva to set the table in the breakfast nook area of the spacious kitchen. Malcolm folded Marva into his arms, like one would a child since the housekeeper barely reached the man's chest. When Marva broke away, Cass noticed her wet face. Everyone who loved Posey continued to feel her absence.

Malcolm rubbed his hands together, anticipating his favorite breakfast: Monte Cristo sandwiches with cranberry jam, home fries, and chunky applesauce. Marva celebrated Malcolm's joy of eating by dancing a little jig to the kitchen sink, calling over her shoulder. "Mr. Malcolm, you'll need to take a few jars of applesauce with you. I canned them yesterday."

Cass ate as heartily as Malcolm, but in lesser quantities. When Malcolm continued into a third helping, she sipped coffee, distracted by her thoughts.

He finally leaned back, patted his full stomach, and groaned. "Corrine doesn't allow me to indulge like this. That's why Marva's cooking is such a treat. But don't tell Fanta that."

Malcolm was a deft man, one of the reasons he was a successful businessman, so Cass expected he knew there was more to the visit than Marva's cooking.

"I guess it's time to level with you, Mr. Hunt." Cass began. "Come with me. I want to show you something."

When the two arrived on the third floor of the tower, Cass led him into the Rabbit and Owl nursery and popped open the secret door by pushing the switch with her foot.

"Is this Posey's treasure? The secret she wanted you to find in her letter?" Malcolm peered around the snug room while his eyes adjusted to the dim lighting. Cass watched for any revelation on his face, but he remained stoic.

"I found Posey's diary, along with some letters she pilfered from Ramona's desk when she snooped around over the years. There's a lot in here, but I think you should read it." Cass handed Malcolm the tapestry-covered book. "You're welcome to make yourself comfortable in the library."

Malcolm held Posey's book like a delicate blossom. "It smells like her." He peered around the room once more. "What is this secret room?"

"It's all in there," Cass said.

Much later, Malcolm found Cassandra standing in the grove of maples that enclosed Spirit Gardens' burial plot where Lionel and Ramona Hollingsworth lay beside each other, with Posey adjacent to her father. Cass transplanted three blue hydrangea bushes in an arc around Posey's grave from the Firehouse garden.

Malcolm aged since breakfast, and Cass noticed his red-rimmed eyes and swollen face.

"I knew Posey was having our baby, but to read her account is awful. I should have been with her." Malcolm sat on the garden bench on the graveyard's perimeter, covering his face with one hand.

Cass teetered between wanting to offer comfort or resolution. "Why weren't you with her?"

Malcolm disappeared into the past, stone-faced. "When Posey and I told our parents we planned to marry, Mr. Hollingsworth was in our corner, saying he would help us sort things out. Our parents dismissed us, though. Certainly, with the intent to plot our demise."

Malcolm kicked at the ground by the bench, anger rising. "Ramona told my parents something, and now it's clear what that was, because they declared Posey an unsuitable match, shipped me off for the summer, and sent me to a boarding school for my senior year."

Cass softened. "To be fair, you and Posey were only seventeen, Mr. Hunt. I'm not defending your parents or Ramona, but you can't blame yourself."

"Right," he said with sarcasm. "The thought of Posey going through everything alone. I mean, I thought her mother would take care of her. But after reading this... Ramona must have resented Posey her whole life."

Cass interpreted Posey's entries as Malcolm did, but she didn't know Ramona personally. Of all people, Cass knew how it felt to be a bitter teenager, angry at their mother. After reading Emilia's diary and Sister Philomena's unanswered letters to Ramona, Cass accepted Posey's version of the truth.

Malcolm picked up a fallen red maple leaf and began breaking it into tiny pieces along its veins. "Lionel was a decent man. I'm happy Posey had her father and that he had her. At least that was something."

"Yes." Cass agreed, thinking of the passages about the secret room. "I don't know how they managed to do it, but I'm happy they kept the room a secret from Ramona. Lionel moved all of Emilia's keepsakes and furnishings upstairs and it became his refuge." Cass thought of the old typewriter, curious if she would find other personal documents, perhaps typed by Lionel.

Malcolm rubbed his neck, elbows propped on his legs. "I don't understand why Posey never told me about Emilia, about the secret room, about her mother. I mean, Ramona. We never kept secrets from each other."

Cassandra thought about the family secrets she kept for years from Bay, the person she loved most in life. "Don't doubt Posey's loyalty, Mr. Hunt. I'm sure she was waiting for the best time. Sometimes, there isn't one."

Malcolm stood up and walked around the grove to shake off his uncertainty. "You may be right. When we were growing up, Posey and I thrilled in every adventure and the simple joy of spending time together. We were best friends, then lovers caught up in a romance. We missed our chance, though. After that summer, we didn't see each other for four years. Posey went out east to college and didn't come home."

Cass kicked at some fallen leaves and gazed at the autumn colors of the maples. "And when she came home, you and Corrine were married."

Malcolm spun toward Cass, another painful memory resurfacing. He took a deep breath, hesitated, and plodded on. "Corrine was pregnant. I had to do the honorable thing."

Cassandra wanted to cry, cry for Posey, for Malcolm, and for Corrine. "Oh my. How did your parents handle that?" Cass doubted the Hunts were any happier about Corrine than they had been about Posey, except that Malcolm was an adult.

Malcolm fumed. "Handle it? I'll tell you how they handled it. They bargained with me to marry Corrine to avoid a scandal. My brother Mitchell was launching his political career. If he married his pregnant fiancée, he could kiss his political ambitions goodbye. So, I married her and raised his son as my own."

"Edison is..." Cass whispered.

"My nephew by biology. But he's my son." Tears trickled down Malcolm's face. "My parents knew Corrine would rein me in. She's ten years older than I am. They considered it a favorable business deal for everyone. When you're rich, the one thing you can't afford to have is emotion, Cassandra."

Cass ran to Malcolm and gave him a tight hug. "I'm sorry for everyone involved." Malcolm accepted Cass's consolation until the pain subsided.

"Did you see Emilia's footstone?" Cass took Malcolm's hand and led him to the plot. "A receipt fell out of Posey's diary. She'd hired an engraver to finish her mother's stone."

The polished granite stone was etched with butterflies on flowering vines surrounding the name Emilia Sosa, her birth and death dates, and home of Antigua, Guatemala.

"I called the engraver yesterday, and he said he could deliver it in the afternoon. He's had it finished since July. Well, Posey was tired of the anonymity. She wanted to claim her mother by name," Cass said.

"May I come over another day and finish reading Posey's diary? I read some of it too fast. And Emilia's diary, too?"

"Of course you may. You're part of her story. You should read both."

"Thank you, you're a kindred spirit, Cassandra Browning. And I think it's time you called me Malcolm." ■

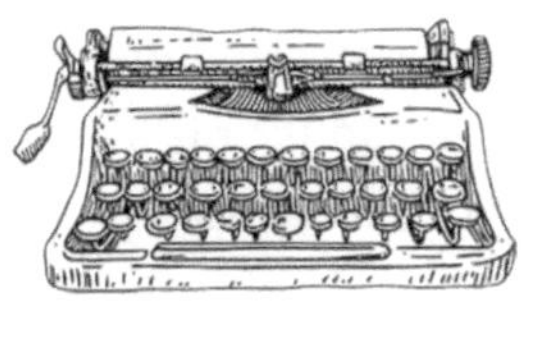

chapter 27

We Read It in the Tea Leaves

"I have to say, I'm glad that's over." Marva gave the scone dough an extra slap. She and Cass partnered to prepare the tea service for Linda Trevino.

"What's over?" Cass prepared miniature sandwiches with cucumber, hard-boiled egg slices, watercress, and fresh herbs. Marva insisted on fussing even though Cass thought tea with packaged cookies would suffice.

"Your treasure hunt. The hidden room. The diaries." She smacked the dough ball a few times on the counter. "And the secrets of course." Marva pulled a sour face.

Cass winced. "I told you when Malcolm Hunt finishes reading the diaries, you're welcome to read them, too. But promise me you're not going to blab to your sisters. It's none of their business." A wayward cucumber slice skidded across the counter.

Marva wasn't convinced. "I don't see why I should read them at all." She made the rolling pin dance across the floured dough ball in multiple directions.

"Because you're family, Marva." Cass made it simple.

Marva stopped rolling to cross her arms. "Is that so? Explain to me how come I didn't know about a secret room on the third floor? I guess Miss Posey didn't trust me after all."

"Don't be silly. You know that's not true. I think Posey wanted to keep the room and everything in it for herself. It was the one piece of her real mother she could treasure."

Marva cut the scones into rounds and slid them into the cooler. "You're right. I s'pose I would feel that way, too. Now let's talk about this tea party, Miss Cassandra. There's more to it than meets the eye. You're hiding something."

Cass continued to practice being honest, a habit in progress. "I suppose, but I will enlighten you when I can."

Linda Trevino rang the front bell minutes before four o'clock and Cass ushered her into the solarium.

"I thought you'd enjoy the solarium. Posey often served tea or breakfast in here."

"It's beautiful to be surrounded by plants and flowers, especially with winter coming soon." Linda eyed Cassandra's informal jeans and Henley.

"I didn't know how to dress for tea, I'm afraid." The thin woman looked charming in a fall-print sweater set and tan slacks.

"You look lovely, Linda. Is it okay to call you by your first name?"

She dipped her head in ascent. "I heard Posey was an accomplished gardener and made her own tea blends," she remarked.

"Yes. Her father encouraged her talents. He added a

greenhouse to the south side of the estate and a summer kitchen." Cass thought about Emilia, a botanist by profession, and couldn't resist adding, "I imagine she took after her mother."

Linda frowned. "I don't recall Ramona being interested in gardening. Ah well. I remember how Angelica loved flowers as a child. She begged to plant seeds every spring for her own garden. When I was a child, my mother and nana insisted that me and my sisters weed and water their huge vegetable garden all summer long. Maybe that's why gardening doesn't appeal to me."

Cass cleared her throat. "Speaking of Angelica. She mentioned some interesting things the other day. Her nickname, for instance. Sunny. She said it came about because of a jeweled sun pinned to her baby undershirt." Cass refilled their cups, careful not to appear too eager.

"Yes, that's right. My husband and I adopted her when she was a newborn. I saved the pin because it was the only connection to her past. I couldn't bear to toss it out." Linda suddenly seemed lost in thought.

"That is a unique clue to Angelica's birth, but she said she didn't pursue searching for her birth parents." Cass tread with care.

"She mentioned it at times during her teens and college years, but the adoption was private. Fred handled the legal parts, and I signed on the dotted line without giving any of it a thought. I was too excited to become a mother." Linda nibbled on purple grapes and plated another watercress square.

"It's just that Angelica seemed confused about where she was born. She found some photos at the college that showed her father's farewell party in the summer of nineteen ninety-one, the same year she was born." Cass took a serene sip of tea.

A flustered Linda began to sputter as her head calculated the math. "Why I believe that's right. We moved to New York soon after the party. Fred's new term began shortly after Labor Day." Her firm nod indicated the matter was settled.

Cass unraveled another thread. "Angelica wasn't born in New York, was she? She was born here in Prairie Ridge."

Linda shifted in her seat and set her plate down onto the glass table. "Why would you say that?" Before Cass could select her response, Linda began arguing with herself in an agitated mutter and Cass decided to wait.

"Of course this is the reason you asked me to tea. The question is: are you trying to blackmail me or what is it you want?" Linda was becoming paranoid, something Cass didn't intend.

"I don't want to blackmail you, and I'm sorry to worry you. I've been looking into Posey Hollingsworth's death, and I found her diary, Linda. I'm wondering if Ramona helped you and your husband with the adoption." The toothpaste was out of the tube, and Cass didn't regret it.

Linda wrung her hands and took a shaky slurp of tea. "I didn't find out until Fred got sick. I mean, how stupid could I be? I should have known getting a baby that fast in such a secretive way might not be aboveboard. I never asked any questions." Linda's agitation surfaced in disconnected sentences.

"It's okay, Linda. Let's back up and start at the beginning. Ramona suggested you and Fred should consider adoption. Do you remember when that was?"

"It was the last summer we lived in Prairie Ridge. Right after graduation in May, Fred was offered the New York position. I volunteered at community events and saw Ramona several times that summer."

"And when did your husband bring Angelica home?"

Linda's thoughts jelled and she felt calmer. "Angelica was born August tenth. A woman from the adoption agency delivered her to our home at the end of the month just before we left town." Linda's sweet memory vanished, replaced by the news she learned years later.

"When Fred was diagnosed with heart failure, he saw me sorting through personal papers. Before I could find it, he told me about a contract between Ramona Hollingsworth, Claudia Hunt, and Fred. An attorney named Jefferson Lange assisted with Angelica's adoption."

Cass leaned forward, certain the truth was a breath away. "Did you ask why Ramona and Mrs. Hunt would be involved personally?"

Linda began to cry. "I guessed it, but it was too awful to consider. Why would anyone want to offer up their grandchild? Posey, or as Ramona called her—Mary Ellen—was so young. Ramona told Fred she nearly lost her life having the child, and she wanted it all to disappear. Ramona said we would be doing the families an extraordinary favor by adopting the baby. A win-win, Fred said."

Cass seethed on the inside; little needles poked at her rib cage. "How lucky for the Hollingsworths and Hunts that you would provide a solution by carting off the evidence. It must have eased their guilty consciences not to have to think about Angelica. I'm here to tell you that Posey's diary tells a different story."

After Cass shared some of the details about Posey's pregnancy and the alleged death of the infant, Linda cried fresh tears at the deceit.

"I tried to tell Angelica a couple of times after Fred passed, but I couldn't do it. I didn't see how it would matter anymore." The rest of Linda's words dribbled away.

Cass would not, could not, chastise the woman. She imagined Angelica lived a good life with Fred and Linda. At least they'd saved her from Bluff Bird drama.

"What will you do now, Linda?" Cass asked.

"Now I must prepare for the oncoming storm when I tell my daughter the truth. Like the name of this house, Angelica is a spirited woman. Perhaps like her birth mother?"

Cass mustered an encouraging smile. "Indeed." ∎

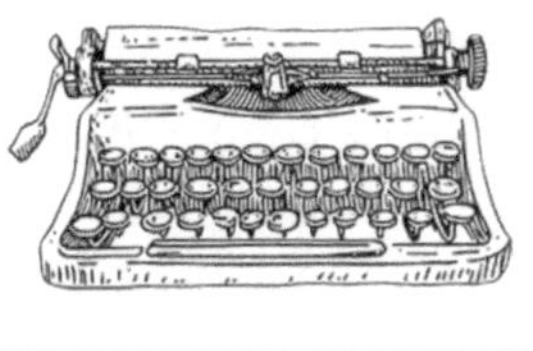

chapter 28

The Sunny Side of Life

The morning rain surrendered, replaced by a pale sun that grew stronger with the afternoon's arrival. The entire landscape presented Abigail Adams with a vibrant birthday gift. The sun showed off autumn's glory, trimmed by the evergreens, a reminder of life.

After Cassandra's fateful high tea with Linda Trevino, events of a lifetime tumbled about like a snowball running down a hillside. Angelica learned the truth, and she asked to read Posey's diaries, hoping to know her birth mother personally.

Of course, Malcolm Hunt was another player in the unfolding drama. Someone must tell him he has a living daughter, and that task fell to Cass by default. Malcolm refused to believe it at first, and since Cass supposed that could happen, she said the daughter would offer to take a genetic test.

Once Cass shared the whole story as she knew it and gave Malcolm time to process it, he agreed that Angelica should read the diaries.

"But I'm not ready to meet her, Cassandra," Malcolm said during their conversation.

Cass laughed. "She's not ready to meet you either. That's in your capable hands. The two of you have to steer the course now."

"First, I owe it to Corrine to tell her the whole story." Malcolm didn't appear worried, but Cass did.

"Good luck."

"Corrine will understand. She always knew I loved Posey, just as she loved my brother, Mitchell. I don't think she will deny me the chance to be some kind of father to my daughter, not after all we've gone through."

What surprised Cass most was that both Angelica and Malcolm accepted invitations to Abigail Adams's one-hundredth birthday party, each knowing the other would be in attendance—less than two weeks after finding the truth about their relationship.

Besides working with Marva on the birthday party details, Cass hoofed it around Spirit Gardens, Marva by her side, to continue the inventory of Posey's estate, which was becoming complicated. Cass contacted Gretchen Lange to inform her of an heir, setting legal dealings into motion and delaying probate for several more months.

On the day of the party, Abigail arrived two hours early, fussed about the estate, poked around Posey's greenhouses to admire the exotic shrubs and tropical trees, and basked in the change of scenery.

"It smells darn lovely in here, Cassandra. May I take some of this scent home with me?" Abigail looked over her glasses at

Cass, a twinkle in her eyes.

Once the birthday greetings and gifts were bestowed upon Abigail, singing commenced thanks to Sharon Barnes, a talented piano player and retired Flourish College Dean. Sharon was thrilled to entertain an audience with a barrage of requests.

Marva offered second helpings of birthday cake accompanied by affogatos or port, if desired. Gretchen Lange congratulated Cass on the party's success.

"A true Posey party, Cassandra. She couldn't have made it better." Gretchen slipped off to chat with some of the Bluff Birds.

Cass found Bay standing with Vivian Rossi, a woman making a stunning comeback. Vivian's cheeks were rosy, and she had gained a little weight, giving her skin a healthy glow. Cass greeted Vivian by gently placing her hand on her arm. "You're looking well. I'm glad you decided to come."

Vivian's smile was a bit strained. "One cannot remain in seclusion forever, Ms. Browning."

Bay looped her arm through Vivian's. "It's like your Emily Dickinson poem, the wind blowing in 'like a bugle' and bringing a wild storm, and yet the world 'abides' it. Just like you. You've endured a tempest, Vivian. And you're still standing." Vivian squeezed Bay's hand.

From the refreshment side of the room, a debonair Malcolm Hunt, two apple ciders in hand, approached a young woman with caution. The closer he came, the more at ease he felt. He'd recognize the brunette woman with Posey's circular face and sculpted cheek bones anywhere.

"Hello. I'm Malcolm Hunt." He passed a glass of cider to the woman.

The woman smiled into the face of the man whose gray stormy eyes matched her own. "Angelica Trevino. It's good to meet you."

She held out her hand and Malcolm kissed the top of her slender fingers.

"No, Miss Angelica, the honor is all mine."

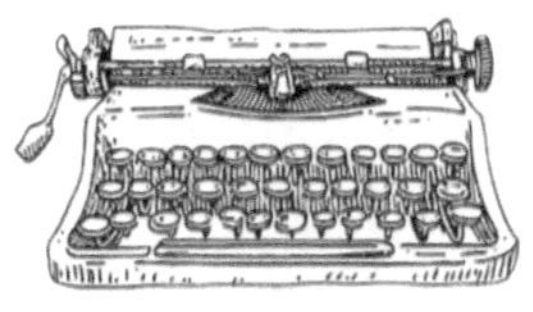

Afterwords

When I began conceiving *Poetry Slammed*, I knew the story would include a "newly discovered" poem by a famous deceased poet— but which one? I thought about Keats, an English poet who died of tuberculosis at twenty-five just as he was coming into his own. I thrilled that he was a Romantic poet, writing about Greek classical themes and love. In the end, Keats's story, filled with tragedies, would overshadow the plot of this mystery, so I moved on. After consideration, I returned to the poet who first came to mind: Emily Dickinson. Female, American, an enigma in perpetuity: Dickinson's poems still perplex the mind even as they resonate in their exploration of universal questions.

Dickinson, respectfully known as *The Poet* or the *Belle of Amherst*, wrote eighteen-hundred poems, of which ten were published in her lifetime. Originally, I planned to write the plot's discovered poem in Dickinson's style, then changed my mind. If nothing else, I wanted readers to have something authentic from her. I enjoyed revisiting some of the Belle's classics and reading poems new to me. When I encountered a few poems about storms, I knew I found verses that complemented one of the prominent themes in I—navigating life's storms. I made certain *There Came a Wind Like a Bugle* was in the public domain in order to comply with copyright law.

As my research into Dickinson deepened and the mystery plot

developed, I realized adding a "Master Letter" would provide intrigue and increase Vivian's coffers in her endeavor to sponsor and protect refugees. Since there are only three "Master" letters, I didn't feel right reprinting any portion of them, so I decided to write one myself; a fourth letter. I won't pretend my version is written to Dickinson's standards because my mother didn't raise a fool. Still, I enjoyed my attempt at capturing The Poet's spirit and desire, and I beg your forgiveness if you find it superficial.

I talked with the expert guides during my visit to Emily Dickinson's home and museum, confiding my plans for *Poetry Slammed*. I found out from one guide that a letter between two Dickinson neighbors was discovered about four years ago. In the letter, one neighbor says they received a poem from E.D., copied the poem into the letter, and asked if the second neighbor could shed any light on its meaning. The guide said the letter and second-hand poem are still being authenticated to date, demonstrating the meticulous act of true authentication. I shortened the time frame of poem verification in *Poetry Slammed* to a few months for the sake of pacing, but I think it's appropriate to mention the real process.

Thank you for reading *Poetry Slammed*, and hanging in there after Shake-speared in the Park left many of you reeling over Posey and wondering about her past. I hope you will agree it was worth the wait.

Thank you to my editor and key advisor, Kay Rettenmund, to my cover and interior designer, Terry Rydberg of Fine Print Design, to Victoria Nania for her help with the ebook version, to my ARC readers/reviewers for their time and thoughtfulness, and to my husband for a million little reasons.

Oh, the places I want to go next up in my writing world! Frankie Champagne of the Deep Lakes Mysteries is not finished with me yet, so we've been having conversations about her next ventures. Meanwhile, the first books in the series are being recorded for release in audio versions. The Bay Browning series has more literary mystique to explore. I'm currently plotting a mini-series of Christmas Market Mysteries that I plan to publish in four two-hour novellas in 2026–27. Follow my newsletter on Substack under Joy Ann Ribar for more details (and catch me on Facebook and Instagram for announcements).

A final nod to Emily Dickinson. In her time, people described her as eccentric, an outcast, strange, rebellious, abnormal, and more. Her response to those charges, recorded by her niece, Martha Dickinson Bianchi, in *Emily Dickinson Face To Face*, was to say that Emily was just being herself and couldn't understand why that caused social upset. For everyone who has ever been labeled weird, know that "you are fearfully and wonderfully made."

JAR

About the Author

Joy Ann Ribar is an RV author, writing on the road with her author husband, LJ, roaming around in their Winnebago View. Joy's cocktail of careers includes news reporter, paralegal, English educator, and aquaponics greenhouse technician, all of which prove useful in penning mysteries.

If you want pastries without calories, wine without the hangover, and drama with a dose of laughter, come home to Wisconsin and the **Deep Lakes Mysteries**. Frankie Champagne and her business partner, Carmen, serve up pastries (recipes included), fruity wines, and witty conversations at Bubble & Bake, while they investigate crimes on the side.

Joy's Bay Browning Mysteries blend edgy, traditional, and paranormal elements twisted around classical literary themes that readers will recognize. Join Bay and Cass, a pair of polar opposite sisters in a mid-size Wisconsin town, trying to avoid trouble, even as trouble finds them. *The Medusa Murders* is a triple award-winner (Book Fest, Readers Favorite, PenCraft). *Shake-speared in the Park*, at the time of publication, is currently short listed for the Mystery and Mayhem 2025 award from Chanticleer International Book Awards.

See more at *https://joyribar.substack.com*

Also by Joy Ann Ribar

DEEP LAKES MYSTERIES

Deep Dark Secrets, BOOK 1

Deep Bitter Roots, BOOK 2

Deep Green Envy, BOOK 3

Deep Dire Harvest, BOOK 4

Deep Wedded Blues, BOOK 5

*Deep Flakes Christmas–
A Nisse Visit*, PREQUEL

BAY BROWNING MYSTERIES

The Medusa Murders, BOOK 1

Shake-speared in the Park, BOOK 2

Poetry Slammed, BOOK 3